Sour Grapes & Sweet Tea

Sour Grapes and Sweet Tea

Jane W. Rankin

Winfree Oaks

Denver, North Carolina

ISBN: 978-1-7329958-4-0

Book design: Diana Wade

Winfree Oaks Publishing
Denver, North Carolina

To the sisterhood of women everywhere.
Hold tightly to your friendships and when life
hands you lemons, make lemon meringue pie!
(Lemonade is over-rated.)

CHAPTER 1

*A*merican Airlines flight 962 from Raleigh to Charlotte was packed as tight as a Thanksgiving turkey, but compliments of my dearest friend, Betsy, we were sitting in the rarified air of first class on this, and the connecting leg, to Palm Beach. I was riding shotgun, so to speak, for a two-night trip to Wellington, Florida, to help Betsy look at some horses and hopefully find "the one." My duties as a high school art teacher were on hold during winter break, which allowed me the freedom to come along and add my two cents. Seldom was I at a loss for an opinion, and when trying out horses, an additional rider and another set of eyes and ears was always a plus.

Betsy fell asleep as I watched the midday December sun slip in and out of the fast moving clouds. This was our third excursion to Wellington, seventeen years after I'd made my maiden voyage with her to look for a new mount. Finding just the right fit of horse and rider is more difficult than one might think, and you have to sift through a great deal of sand to find the true gem. Betsy had been very fortunate over the years, and we hoped this trip would prove just as rewarding.

Being along for the ride offered me several luxuries: not

caring about the price tag, getting to ride some wonderful horses, and staying in an amazing home in Palm Beach. Ellen, Betsy's cousin, had a winter house there and allowed us full rein of her property when we were in town.

The first time I'd visited, I hadn't changed from my school clothes and arrived sporting a faded pair of slacks, tennis shoes, and an oversized sweater. Clearly, I didn't quite understand the definition of knock-around clothes among the rich and richer, and I knew the second I disembarked that I was terribly underdressed. The next day was slightly better, wearing breeches and tall boots, even though they were last year's design, and I promised myself to never repeat that mistake. It wasn't that I didn't own suitable clothes, just that I hadn't brought them.

Returning my seat to the upright position as we prepared for landing, I smiled, thinking, *Your arrival outfit has come a long way, Sarah Sams: from faded cargo pants and Keds to Ralph Lauren and Ferragamo.*

Ellen's property overlooked the Atlantic, and we were offered the use of not only her home, but everything that came with it: a housekeeping staff, a car and driver, even a personal chef. Holy cats, this was top-drawer living at its best and a complete one-eighty from my working-mother, ham-sandwich-for-lunch way of life.

The driver was waiting for us at baggage claim, and securing our luggage, we were on our way. Crossing over Royal Park Bridge, I knew we were getting close—Ellen's home oozed good taste and gentility. After a late dinner on the patio and a drink overlooking the ocean, we were off to bed. The guest rooms were amazing and decorated no doubt by a professional granted an eye-popping budget.

The next morning, we headed to Wellington—one beautiful horse farm after another—home of the Winter Equestrian Festival, or WEF—and a cornucopia for horse hunting. Henry Black was Betsy's go–to-guy and owned a farm outside of the village. We rode five horses that day, and she fell in love with one in particular. Henry agreed to ship the big Thoroughbred to Betsy's farm in Hadley Falls for a two-week trial. After signing all the necessary paperwork, we were invited to join Henry and his wife for dinner at their club. It was a wonderful old place, and we enjoyed a relaxing meal in our come-as-you-are riding clothes. We talked horses and horse showing for hours.

On the return flight to Raleigh, Betsy practiced the "I found an amazing horse and he'll be here in three days" speech she'd use on her husband.

"This is ridiculous," I said stopping her mid-sentence. "We've come here three times in seventeen years, and have found a horse each time. Frank knows you're not coming home empty-handed."

"Yes, but this one is way over budget," Betsy said.

"They're all over budget," I laughed. "Frank will grumble over the cost, but in the end he doesn't care. That horse is the perfect adult hunter, never refuses a jump, and you'll be in the ribbons every time. All your husband really cares about is that you're happy."

"Will you tell him for me?" she squeaked, closing her eyes.

"I absolutely will not," I said. "Now eat your first-class mixed nuts, and stop worrying."

My husband, Parker, met us outside baggage claim, and we

chattered on and on about our three days in "tall cotton" while making the hour drive to Hadley Falls. Dropping Betsy off at her farm, and with a chuckle, I wished my friend all the luck in delivering her "guess what I found" soliloquy.

The rest of the evening was spent with Parker watching a bowl game, me unpacking my carry-on suitcase, and Annie, our golden retriever, sniffing my bag in an effort to determine where I had been.

"Remember, we're going to Bill and Margaret's tomorrow night to ring in 2008," I said, on my way to the laundry room.

"Ugh, that thing is so boring," he moaned. "It's the same every year."

"Of course it's the same every year," I said. "So are Christmas morning, Valentine's Day, and Thanksgiving, just to name a few."

"Well, we're leaving right after the ball drops," Parker insisted.

"Okay, but why don't you want to go all of a sudden?" I asked. "You've always had such a good time."

"I'm just tired of it," Parker said.

How strange, I thought. Parker loved parties—especially this one. I decided not to press the issue. I'd spent the past three days in the lap of luxury having a great time, and maybe he was envious. It would pass, I was sure of it.

CHAPTER 2

$\mathcal{W}$ednesday morning, I was at my desk, trying to get back into the educational groove after two weeks off. As the morning worked its way to noon, things returned to life as I knew it in high school: whispery girl gossip about who broke up over the holidays, boy talk about who got the better-than-ever sneakers and who scored a new phone. January was such a long month, and such an enormous let-down after Christmas, so I put my pottery and weaving units in the post-holiday dead zone. Those hands-on projects were always a huge success.

Parker was hard at work with his lawn and landscape business, which struck me as a little strange for that time of year. In the past, he had used January to overhaul all the equipment, replenish his inventory of seed and fertilizer, and drum up new accounts, but usually that didn't take up so much of his time.

"I made a reservation for us tomorrow night at the Tinker Inn," Parker said as he walked in the door after work.

"Fun—a Saturday night out! And the Tinker Inn—what's the occasion? Are we celebrating that dreary January is finally over?" I asked. Yesterday was the end-of-the-month payday for his employees, which could prove a financial pinch considering the lack of revenue for landscapers in the winter.

"No occasion. I just thought you would enjoy a night out," Parker said.

"Good evening. Do you have a reservation?" asked the hostess as we walked in.

"Yes, Sams for two," Parker said.

Janice, as her name tag announced, took two menus and a wine list and showed us to our table. The surroundings were lovely, and the food was amazing, but the entire evening had a quiet overtone of the Last Supper. I couldn't put my finger on it, but something was definitely different. Parker and I exchanged "remember when" stories and we talked a lot about our two daughters. He was especially chatty about their both being out of college now, settled in their jobs, on their own, and how proud he was of them.

At home, Parker crashed into bed as soon as he changed out of his clothes, and blamed the wine for his lack of interest in anything else that evening.

The following Tuesday it all became clear. Parker came home early and said he needed to talk to me. I took a seat in my favorite chair in our den and listened as my husband of nearly three decades explained that he was leaving me for his chiropractor. "Sarah, there's no other way of saying this: I'm in love with Pam, and we're planning a life together."

Pam? About a year ago, Parker had taken a terrible fall while topping a tree and, on the advice of his doctor, began seeing a chiropractor—Pam. Obviously this thirty-something

Dr. Feel-Good had become more to him than the every-other-Wednesday spinal adjustment on his monthly agenda.

I sat as starched as the frozen landscape of that early February afternoon as Parker announced his plans to deplete our savings and checking accounts by half. The wheels were already in motion for him and his new love to move to New Bern, two hours away. For years, he and I had been considering retiring to that charming city nestled at the confluence of the Trent and Neuse rivers, and now he'd be going there with someone else.

"Sarah, I never meant to hurt you. Sometimes things just happen," Parker said, standing in the doorway of the den. "For now, I'm just going to get some of my clothes and bathroom stuff. I'll give you a call in a few days and we can figure out when I can get the rest of my things. I'm staying at the Hampton Inn until I get situated. I'll let you tell the girls."

As Parker turned to walk away, I said, "If you honestly think I have any intention of swallowing so much as an ounce of what you are shoveling up, then you don't know me at all! You knew exactly what you were doing with Pam the chiropractor and also the end result. So, yes, Parker, you did mean to hurt me, and your children too. Was that what the dinner at the Tinker Inn was all about?"

"Well, yes, I was going to tell you over dessert but lost my nerve," Parker said. "I was scared that you'd go ballistic in the restaurant."

"Really," I said, while trying to catch my breath. "Why on Earth would you think that? We've been married for twenty-seven years, never really had any kind of trouble, always cared for and about each other—why would you think this news would shock me?"

"Just let me get some of my things and we can talk some more later," he said.

"No," I snapped. "We'll talk now. Why are you doing this?"

"I just don't love you anymore, Sarah," Parker said stepping back and lowering his head. "I don't know when it happened, how, or why, but I just don't love you."

Parker disappeared down the hall and into our bedroom while I remained glued to the chair with Annie at my side. As I listened to him open and close closet doors and dresser drawers, tears streamed down my cheeks, and my emotions jockeyed between fury and disbelief. Getting a grip on myself, I walked into the kitchen and started to work on dinner. I didn't really know what else to do, but I couldn't just sit in that chair. I offered a quick prayer that the paring knife I was holding would be used only on the thawed pieces of chicken.

At the squeak from the hardwood hall floor, I looked up to see Parker in the doorway with his suitcase in one hand and a duffel bag over his other shoulder. The visual was absolutely crippling and one I wasn't sure I would ever forget. "Well, Sarah, I guess this is goodbye," he said searching for his next sentence.

"Apparently it is, Parker," I replied. "I think you should just go." And with that . . . he was gone.

CHAPTER 3

Within the week after a local funeral home lowers your loved one into the ground, it is not unusual for one of their representatives to drop by your house, express their genuine condolences, and hand you the bill. In the South, the family-owned mortuary may possibly bring you a warm chicken pie and a container of green beans, but rest assured, they'll also have the required invoices in hand. Rather than mailing the paperwork, this personal touch is a much softer approach to a heartbreaking situation, but regardless, business is business.

My set of circumstances was similar to a death in the family: it was the death *of* our family. So I knew that with this situation, there was going to be business to take care of.

Hadley Falls, a city of sixty thousand, give or take a few, located in northeastern North Carolina, was no different from any other town: news of this break-up would travel faster than kudzu. My first concern was to tell my children before they heard it from some other source. I could work on my own feelings later.

After dinner I put Annie out in the fenced-in backyard and decided to call Emma first. As my oldest daughter, she had accrued more life miles and would perhaps have a better understanding of the reality that was now our lives.

"Hi, my sweet girl," I said. "I hope you're well?" I waited to hear the affirmative. "Good. And how are Scott and that cutie pie dog of yours?"

"We're all fine, Mama," Emma replied. "What's wrong? You sound strange."

"I won't beat around the bush. I have some difficult news, and I'm truly not sure how to say this, so here goes," I answered. "When your dad came home from work this afternoon, he said we needed to talk. He actually did most of the talking, and the topic of his conversation was that he is ending our marriage."

After a very pregnant pause, Emma said, "What? What the hell? Mama, who is she? Do we know her?"

I nearly fell off the kitchen stool. "How'd you know there was another woman?"

"Oh, Mother, please." Emma sighed. "You've spent too much of your life either teaching, being our mother, or at the barn. There is *always* another woman. Wait—it's not a man, is it?"

"No it's not a man," I said, and cleared my throat. I delivered a brief review of what I knew. "Emma, I've become one of those women who swore she never knew what was going on with her husband, but seriously—I didn't. I've been truly duped and outwitted. The other woman is his chiropractor, so I do now know how he managed his trysts, most probably how often, and a pretty good idea for how long. I feel so stupid, and I'm mad as hell!"

I kept it to myself that Emma's daddy planned to take his half of our savings and checking accounts. By law he had every right to do so, but for some reason that announcement had stung almost as much as him saying he didn't love me anymore. Perhaps it was his dictatorial tone. "Apparently they've already got plans for the two of them to move to New Bern."

"You are not stupid, and I never want to hear you say that again." Emma said. "From now on, my father will be referred to by me as 'a total piece of crap.' I'm not fucking believing this."

Ordinarily I would have taken strong exception to her language, but this time I agreed with both her tone and her choice of words. We finished our conversation with the possibility of me selling the house. I couldn't really explain why that had popped into my head so soon after Parker's news, but it had. Maybe I felt like I needed a fresh start. After a few rounds of *I love you* and *take care*, we said good night.

Inhaling to the cellar of my lungs, I dialed Sidney's number. She would be devastated. She and her father were very close, and she would take this as personally as I did. After our usual hellos, I broke the news as gently as possible. Sidney could hardly find her voice. I told her things would be fine and she didn't need to talk to me right now. She was the quiet one and would mull this over in her mind before talking to me or anyone else, except perhaps her sister.

"I'm going to say goodbye for now, and I'll call you maybe tomorrow," Sidney said with an uneven tone. "Mama, tell me the truth: Is there another woman? Is Dad having an affair?"

"Yes, baby, he is," I answered. "I know this is a cliché, but it doesn't mean he loves you any less."

Sidney spoke right up. "Oh, yes, it does. It very much does. Dad hasn't left just you—he's left us all. Our family, our memories, and our traditions are over, and my father destroyed it all. I have to go. I love you. I'll talk to you later." And she hung up.

I knew it was best to leave her alone for a while. She would call back in a few days and we would continue our conversation. My youngest daughter required some time to factor the information and wrestle with her emotions. I, on the other hand, needed an immediate set of ears that would listen without judgment and for as long as I required. That comfort could only come from Betsy, who possessed the gift of listening without judging.

Betsy knew something was going on the minute I said hello. "What's wrong? What's the matter with you?"

"Could be the fact that Parker announced this afternoon he was leaving me, and on the arm of his new love interest, Pam the chiropractor," I said taking a breath.

"You're kidding!" Betsy shrieked.

"If only I was, but it's true, and hold on, there's more. They're moving to New Bern, if you can believe that. How many times have Parker and I talked about retiring there? Seriously, I am so mad I could spit nails! I feel dumb as dirt that I didn't catch on. I'll tell this to you and only you, and you're sworn to absolute secrecy, but Parker and I were still having sex, so I guess he was dipping his wick in two wells. I think I might just throw up."

Catching my breath, I continued, "I know this is crazy, but I keep thinking that I want to move—not out of Hadley Falls, just to a new house. I feel like this space, this house, is full of lies. I don't even want to sleep in my own bed. Talk about the biggest lie of all!"

"I understand why you would think about moving," Betsy said. "Let's revisit that thought over the next few days. Have you told Emma and Sidney?"

"Yes, and those were two of the hardest phone calls I've ever made," I said. "Emma is livid, and Sidney is devastated. If this situation just involved Parker and me that would be one thing, but it doesn't—it includes my babies! Betsy, I'm so mad I can hardly see straight! You know me, right now, I'm as angry with myself for being clueless as I am with Parker.

"Sarah. That's ridiculous."

"Well maybe that's not quite true, but there are just no words to explain how I feel."

After a bit more conversation I thanked my treasured confidante for her time and wisdom. I added that I was sorry, but I just couldn't call Margaret. She was almost as dear a friend to me as Betsy, but that story was something I could not tell again. I was mentally exhausted. Betsy said she would give her a quick call and assured me that all would be well.

Walking into my bedroom, I realized I could not possibly sleep in *that* bed. The guest bedroom just down the hall would be my resting place for as long as I remained in my house on Washington Street.

Settled under the covers, I wrestled with the events of the day. I realized my day-to-day existence was going to be greatly refashioned, and some serious changes to my life would be essential for me to keep my sanity and my head above water. I felt an anger rising in me that I wouldn't have thought myself capable of.

Reaching to turn out the light, I buried my head in the pillow, and bellowed: *"Son of a bitch! That lyin', cheatin', son of a bitch!"*

CHAPTER 4

$\mathcal{I}$ phoned Betsy on my way to school the next morning. Assuring her that I was okay, I tossed out the idea of "the horse women" getting together on Friday night at my house for an evening meal. It was short notice, but we could pull it off. The six of us had spent many evenings of our adult lives sitting around someone's dining room table. We often enjoyed a meal that lasted for hours in celebration of anything we could think of, or helping each other work through a serious issue.

Close friends are priceless. I was lucky enough to be blessed with the companionship of five extraordinary women. Our sisterhood was an eclectic group of intensely individual women, which perhaps offered the strongest threads in our woven tapestry of friendship. Since we'd ridden horses together for at least fifteen years, our sport took the top spot of shared interests; cooking followed closely on the list, gardening was a year-round project, as was antiquing, and a strong commitment to a natural way of living tied up our top-five favorite things. As is true of most horse people, we had "gone green" decades before the idea had gained global awareness.

The six of us came from different parts of the world, but

our blend of common interests and the appreciation of our intrinsic differences had kept our merry band together for years. We had stumbled across each other one crisp November Sunday morning at a hunter pace competition. Standing in line at the sign-in table for our group paperwork, I listened as the lady in charge of team credentials welcomed the rider with the curly hair to the competition, handed her a packet, and asked how far a drive it was from Hadley Falls.

"Not too far. It's about a two hour drive," the woman answered.

"Hi," I said as she turned to walk away. "I'm Sarah Sams— we're also from Hadley Falls. And if I'm not mistaken, I think we've actually met once before, at an equine wellness class last year at the community college?

"Yes, I do remember you. Hello again," Margaret said, reintroducing herself.

As we walked across the field, I mentioned how interesting it was that our paths had not crossed until now. She said that she and her friends Elizabeth and Jennifer usually participated in the March competition. I added that Betsy, Rose, and I almost always chose this one, but how fun it was to find three more riders from Hadley Falls and just five trailers down from ours. Before leaving for the start gate, Margaret and her friends came over to our trailer, we all talked, and made plans to meet up again after our ride at the lunch tent.

We had a wonderful time that day, cantering the course of high and low jumps, trotting the winding paths through the tall pines, and flying through the deep sand. Both teams were also lucky enough to ribbon by finishing in the top six. That alliance of happenstance grew into a sisterhood of forever. Several weeks after the competition, Margaret moved her horse to where I kept mine, and we were as thick as thieves from that day forward.

Margaret and I were the two native North Carolinians and the only true southerners. I grew up in Iron Springs, a small, two hundred year old town in northeastern North Carolina whose roots were courtesy of the longleaf pine and the naval stores industry. Margaret hailed from a postcard-worthy village, deep in the Smoky Mountains. From the still functioning, barber pole, to a bench in front of each shop window, her hometown could have easily posed for Norman Rockwell and possibly have made the cover of *The Saturday Evening Post*. She was a wild child, and the most independent woman in the group.

Margaret owned the most wonderfully quaint bookstore that just begged for you to come inside. It came complete with iron gates, a tiny courtyard with moss-covered brick walls, and her Westie, Winston. As the official greeter of Maggie's Alley Bookstore, Winston had gone to work daily since he was a puppy. Margaret had one employee, and they staggered their lunch hours so the store would always be open. Each day at eleven thirty, Margaret would remove her apron, gather her purse, and leash the dog. Then she and Winston would make their way down the alley paved with bricks worn smooth by time.

Betsy, a New Englander to the bone, held fast to sounding totally out of place with her pronunciation of tomato and had a very interesting family history dating back to the earliest settlers. Her generational stories were fascinating and her gardening skills were amazing. Our youngest daughters had ridden at the same show barn from the time they were four, which was how we'd met over seventeen years ago.

Rose grew up in London's East End, not quite within the sound of the Bow Bells of St. Mary-le-Bow. She was a brilliant scholar, an amazing cook, and had never been married. She'd come to "the colonies" twenty-two years earlier and decided to stay. Rose was the free spirit of the group, and I admired her self-confidence.

Jennifer ventured south from Toronto, Ontario, as a result of her husband's job. She started a catering business shortly after they moved to town, and in less than two years, she'd grown it into a very successful restaurant, River's Bend, just around the corner from Margaret's bookstore. Margaret had a standing order for lunch each day of the week, which she collected during Winston's noonday constitution. Jennifer was always late, and the quiet one, but when she spoke, you listened.

Elizabeth, the petite and rather glamorous, perfectionist, had migrated across the country from California. She was highly competitive, and as a result of having been in television commercials throughout her early childhood—was very wealthy. We loved to hear her stories about that part of her life, but she would add —"all that glitters is not gold." That statement provoked a touch of mystery, but Elizabeth insisted she only meant that acting was hard work for a child.

At any gathering, the hostess for our evening meal had the responsibility of the entrée—except for Margaret, our vegetarian. After the ill-fated nearly raw turkey dinner, we all agreed that she should stick with just bringing a vegetable. Everyone had her specialty, and our dinners were not only delicious, they were also hysterical. Something would always trigger one of us to go off on a tangent of some sort and, conversationally speaking, it was game on.

For our first post-Parker dinner, I decided to do it up right and prepare a rack of lamb for the five meat eaters and vegetarian lasagna for Margaret. I pulled out all the stops and dressed my dining room table in my finest linens, china, crystal, and silver. Realizing the main topic of conversation would be my current situation, this was a very important meal to me, and it needed to look the part. Using my grandmother's phrase, "puttin' on the dog" was never work for me; it was absolute joy, something I dearly loved to do, even when highly stressed. Maybe especially when highly stressed—it gave my mind a good place to go. To me, a beautifully set table created a still-life worth painting. My mother always said, "Why have lovely things if you never intend to use them?" I agreed wholeheartedly with her philosophy.

Betsy was the first to arrive, and as usual was dressed in a very colorful outfit and matching shoes. I always laughed that she must have owned at least fifty pairs of shoes. With her funky designer reading glasses positioned on the top of her head, she handed me a brown paper bag as she walked into my kitchen.

"What is it?" I asked, peeking in the bag.

"It's what you need to help you over this bump in the road," Betsy said.

"Bump?" I chuckled. "A bump would be an upgrade."

"It would not, and I won't let you think that way," Betsy said sharply.

Opening the bag, I reached in and pulled out a CD. The cover displayed the likeness of a famous inspirational speaker who vowed to divert my thoughts, alleviate my fears, and push me in a positive direction.

"Now, before you make a face, I want you to promise you

will listen to this man with an open mind," Betsy said.

"You do realize that listening to a man for any reason is not exactly where I am these days," I said emphatically. "But I promise I will be open to all suggestions, and I thank you for the thought and the love behind the gift. And what do you mean, before you make a face? I don't make faces!"

"Oh my God," Betsy laughed. "You make a face over everything. I always know what you're thinking by the look on your face. That is why I know you will discount this man's wisdom before even giving him a chance."

"I will not," I said, laying the CD on the counter. "Hey, I wonder how late Jennifer will be tonight? I might need to turn down the heat on the oven if she's more than thirty minutes behind the others."

"Ordinarily, that would be a good idea, but Elizabeth is in charge of getting Jennifer here on time tonight. We all talked behind your back about the importance of this evening, and it was clear that we all needed to be on time for once," Betsy said, patting me on the shoulder.

With that, the doorbell sounded, and Margaret said hello from the foyer. As she walked into my kitchen, I could smell the spinach casserole before she'd even removed the foil. It was without question my favorite dish in her recipe box, and she'd probably made it especially for me. With a strong and deliberate hug, Margaret handed me a small gift bag with multicolored ribbon tied through the handles.

I knew it had to be a book, and could only guess that it too was some sort of self-healing wisdom nonsense from an alleged authority on the subject who'd probably never been abandoned like me. Remembering Betsy's mention of my making faces, I tried to hide my cynicism.

"Thanks," I said giving the tail of the ribbon a tug. "Now what do we have here? Oh, how beautiful!" I said, as I opened the bag. It wasn't a book, but a beautiful pair of silver pendant earrings that resembled the shape of dripping asymmetrical hearts. "Margaret—these are fabulous. Thank you. I'm going to wear them right now."

Margaret was a very straightforward person, and I knew the dripping-heart motif carried its own symbolism of perhaps the condition of my actual heart. She must have known the artist in me would pick up on the implication. Replacing my old earrings with the new ones, I turned and asked how they looked. My friends agreed that my new adornments were perfect, and I gave Margaret a thank-you hug.

We began to fuss around in the kitchen and were startled when Rose said, "Hello all! Something smells incredible. I let myself in."

"Sorry," I responded. "I guess we were talking so loud we didn't hear the bell . . . imagine that!"

"Yes . . . imagine that indeed," Rose said with a chuckle. She was very funny but rarely intended to be. With my strong southern accent and down-home colloquialisms, I always thought she saw me as a country bumpkin of sorts, if a surprisingly witty and intelligent one. I once mentioned this to her, and she said it could not have been further from the truth. Adding that she admired my internal strength and creative abilities. Her comments had left me surprised, delighted, and a bit more relaxed around her—though it was always a little stressful to cook for her.

Rose was a gourmet cook who had penned two very successful cookbooks. She was also the author of Tea & Crumpets, a monthly syndicated column that appeared in most major newspapers in the country. Her byline was still Boston, but the reality was she lived in Hadley Falls, whether she admitted it or not. When pressed, she'd say, "I hang my hat on a good many racks."

When we asked for a recipe, Rose would list the ingredients as a bit of this or a pinch of that, continuing with, "Just mush it round and pop it in the oven." Naturally her cookbooks were spot-on, with exact measurements and all the rest. She was positive the consumption of good wine was essential in the digestive process of any solid food. As we tipped our glasses, she would say, "The French have it right, girls, and your arteries will thank you. Except for you, Sarah—that diet cola may kill you one day."

"Hello?" a voice shouted from the dining room. It was Elizabeth, but she was alone.

"Where's Jennifer?" Betsy asked.

"Oh, I don't know. Am I supposed to know where she is?"

Rose jumped in. "Yes. I thought the two of you were coming together."

"She's parking the car," Elizabeth said. "I love you, Daisy Mae," she continued, giving me a tender hug. "Margaret told me that the son of a bitch, as I understand we're calling him now, has moved out and left you to tend to things on Washington Street." It was just the relief we needed to break the ice.

"What's going on?" Jennifer asked as she came in, putting her offering on the counter. "I always miss the best stuff, and it's never as funny in the retelling. I had a transport disaster with my salad, thanks to one of my employees not using the correct box. The bowl was so slick it fell on the ground. So here I stand with grass on my salad bowl, pine nuts everywhere, and—what? What is so damn funny?" Jennifer demanded.

"You are!" we said. And with that, our group of six launched into hours of conversation and good food. Over the course of the evening, it was decided that moving might be the best thing for me to do: truly a fresh start to the second half of my life, a project to keep me busy doing something I loved, or simply opening a door to new possibilities. I said that I wanted to stay in the historic part of town, was thinking of a smaller house, and that after taking different routes to the barn and the market, I had seen several homes that appealed to me.

One in particular, a ramshackle cottage on Brook Street, had caught my fancy, and they all knew which one it was. As we all but licked the plates clean of Elizabeth's incredible German chocolate cake—my favorite—I asked if anyone had time in the morning to ride over to the wreck of a house and have a look around. Everyone raised their hands, and Betsy offered to collect us all in her Suburban so we could ride together. I smiled at my friends, all so eager to help, and said I would call the realtor and get the key.

As always, Margaret rinsed the dishes and put them in the dishwasher. While Rose and Betsy worked on organizing the leftovers, they made fun of me for having all my plasticware and matching tops so organized. Jennifer mumbled nonstop about her employee's shortsightedness as she picked dried grass from the counter, her bowl, and the floor. Elizabeth cut everyone an extra piece of cake to take home with them, and I beamed with delight as I placed a section of foil over each slice.

That night confirmed I was not alone on Washington Street. Far from it, I had five dear friends who would not allow me to drown in my valley of uncertainty. With all the dishes taken care of, everyone said good night and that they would see me tomorrow morning around nine o'clock.

The next morning we all piled in Betsy's oversized SUV and made our way to Brook Street. As we stood shoulder to shoulder staring at a house that was obviously struggling to survive, no one spoke a word at first.

Stepping forward and turning toward my friends, I said, "Now keep an open mind, and imagine how wonderful this house once was," I said. "I've been all though it, and it seems fairly sound; it's been empty for years and is a cosmetic wreck. Naturally, I'll have it inspected by a professional, but one look under the house will tell you that the furnace and the duct work are not in good shape. You'll see when we go inside it's kind of messy. The windows will need to be replaced, the bathrooms need help, but the foundation appears to be solid. Oh, and this is funny: it's not air-conditioned, and there are no electrical outlets in the bathrooms, but that's easy to fix. I love the wraparound porch, but I'll need to replace a few rotten boards on the corner."

My five best friends swarmed around that house like gnats circling a dirty dog. Each woman, excluding Rose, who was being suspiciously quiet, had her own ideas on what to do, where to start, and how to maintain the original 1920s look of the structure. We all agreed that the back room, which was an obvious do-it-yourself addition, would need to be torn down and rebuilt.

After our self-guided tour, we lined up along the front sidewalk. Rose, who had reserved her thoughts for the last, said, "I think this is an excellent choice for you, Sarah. You know how to fix and build almost anything. We can all pitch in one weekend and clean up the property. As you said earlier, I would insist you have the house inspected before making an offer, but don't give the owner a dime over eighty-five thousand. After some money invested in repairs and other parts simply torn down and rebuilt, I think you could see a huge return on your initial investment."

"Thanks, Rose," I said, thrilled to have her support. "There is something about being here that calls to me. I know it sounds weird, but I think I'm supposed to live at 528 Brook Street."

Walking back to Betsy's car, I looked over my shoulder and back at the house. *I can see it,* I thought. *I can see myself sitting in my wicker furniture on that wraparound porch . . . heavenly*

CHAPTER 5

The following weekend, Emma flew in from Rhode Island, and since Sidney lived in Raleigh, she picked her sister up from the airport and they rode together to Hadley Falls. Having them both home was wonderful, and we stayed up too late Friday night watching an old movie and eating popcorn. They both slept until around ten o'clock the next morning, and our trio spent most of Saturday talking about every aspect of listing the old house, purchasing a new one, and what things they wanted to keep for their own homes.

Before they left that Sunday afternoon, I drove them by a few of the properties under consideration. They were all in our current neighborhood, an area full of character, and a few characters. I loved the canopy created by tree-lined streets, chimneys covered with ivy, and the eclectic assortment of architecture. My girls shrieked with alarm that I might actually consider the purchase of any of the properties we saw, as all were in varying degrees of disrepair. I saved my favorite house for last—the one on Brook Street.

Both of them sat speechless as they stared at the dilapidated old house. But I knew I needed a fresh start. Moving wasn't a knee-jerk reaction to Parker's leaving; it was the realization of my internal need to heal in a new place and make it my own.

"Mother—you can't be serious," Emma exclaimed, breaking the silence.

Sidney's huge brown eyes welled with tears as she glared at the front of the house. "Can you fix it?" her voice quivered. "Oh my God, Mama, you aren't really thinking about buying that house?"

"It's wonderful! You need to look at the bigger picture," I said. "It just needs a bit of sprucing up."

"Sprucing up—are you kidding? It needs to be demolished!" Emma shrieked.

"Let's get out of the car and take a closer look. You'll see how fabulous it truly is when you feel her energy," I said, feeling confident.

"Oh my good Lord. Is this some sort of woo-woo connection with Mother Earth and your inner self?" Emma asked.

"Perhaps," I said, trying to wiggle the front gate free from the overgrowth. "You shouldn't be so quick to discount our connection with the universe. We're all one small piece of the bigger puzzle called life."

"I totally agree." Sidney giggled, wiping the tears from her cheeks. "And clearly the spiritual gate is fighting our coming in. So let's listen to the house and just leave."

"No," I said as we stepped through a maze of vines growing in every direction and variety, finally reaching the porch. Standing at the front door, I began to explain my plans of resurrection. The girls stood, each with folded arms, united in their disbelief. I reached into my pocket and pulled out a key, opened the door, and we stepped inside.

Clearing her throat, Emma said, "I'm sure you can fix this house, and it will be wonderful, but what I don't understand is why you don't just buy a house that is, uh . . ."

"Not condemned?" Sidney deadpanned. "Mom. Look at this place. There are vines coming in from the windows, pieces of the ceiling are on the floor, and check this out," she said, standing beside the fireplace.

Emma scurried over to see what Sidney had discovered. "Holy crap," Emma exclaimed. "Mother, this place is a crack shack!"

"Oh, it is not," I said realizing I had not actually looked past the stack of logs in the fireplace.

"Yes it is," said Sidney, pointing to a discarded syringe, a misshaped spoon, and a few other small things resting in the absolute darkest corner of the fireplace. "That's why there are burn marks all over the place. Come on Emma, let's check out the rest of this charming drug den."

Walking behind my two children, I continued to defend the house, mentioning that she needed me to return her to her glory days. Emma could not let that comment go. "Glory days? Are you kidding me? Oh look, that's sort of cute. You can go on the wraparound porch from the kitchen. Come on Sidney, you go first," Emma said, putting her hand on the small of her younger sister's back.

Sidney opened the wooden door, took hold of the screen door handle, and as she pushed it open, the whole thing fell from the hinges. Standing on the porch with a door in her hands, Sidney turned and, speaking through the rust-encrusted screen, said, "I can only hope you are getting a good deal on the

27

purchase of this treasure. I also trust you will understand why neither of your children plans to return to this Shangri-La until it is fixed. Where do you propose to sleep while this structural nightmare is being worked on?"

"Well, I do have a plan, and here it is," I said. "I ran into Nate Tuttle from the bank the other day at the grocery store and asked about a bridge loan and what that involved. He said it wouldn't be a problem and to come see him when I was ready to buy. If the owner of this house and I can agree on a price, I'll buy this one and put the For Sale sign in the yard on Washington Street. I'll stay in the old house until a few things are done here."

"Such as?" Emma asked.

"You know, after the floors are sanded and refinished, the bathrooms retiled, the kitchen floor reworked, and all the painting is complete, I'll move in. There'll be lots more to do I'm sure, but I had rather be living here to keep an eye on things."

"Do you really have to sell our house, Mom?" Sidney asked.

Emma rolled her eyes. "Don't be stupid, Sid. Of course she does. Go ahead, Mom."

"I do, but I also want to. Just trust me on this, honey. Anyway, I think it will go fast, so I should be able to make the transition fairly smoothly, I hope. Fingers crossed. Now, before we run out of time, let's continue the tour. This house is really not that bad. You two are just not visionaries like your mother. This is an adventure!"

"Mother, are you telling us the truth?" Emma questioned. "Do you really have enough money to live on? Does Sibby know about this?"

"Yes," I said, smiling and hoping I was correct. "I have plenty of money to do this. Our old house will more than pay for this one, and yes, your grandmother is fine with my decision. This house and I need each other. You'll see: she will be perfect by Christmas, and your stockings will hang from the mantel, just like at the old house."

"Before you light a fire in that death trap of a fireplace," Sidney said, propping the dislodged door against the porch wall and dusting her hands, "make sure you have it checked out. You might also take the time to have the chimney swept for bags of pot. I can see it now—you light a fire, and every bird and bat within three blocks is flying high—then drops dead to the ground."

Emma said, "I would get the police in here to check it out before you move in. That way if something were to happen, you would be in the clear."

"Happen? What could happen?" I asked, alarmed.

Sidney, the calming child, answered, "Mom, it will be fine. But since it really is a place where people have done drugs—it would be a good idea to have the whole house checked out."

Moving into the front bedroom, both my children commented on the size, or lack thereof, of the closets. The bathroom off the master bedroom had been a conversion of a smaller room that was perhaps a nursery. I loved the ball-and-claw tub, but I would have to do something about the rust stains. Floor-to-ceiling cabinets had glass front doors with a few missing panes. The tile floor was a mess, with broken pieces lying around, and the wallpaper hung from the corners like wilting lilies.

Emma asked, "Is there an attic? I'll bet there's some scary stuff up there for sure."

"Yes, actually, there is an attic," I said. "The back bedroom appears to have two closets, but one is actually the door to the attic stairs. I haven't taken the time to check it out. Feel free to take a look, but be careful—the floor boards might give way, or you might stumble over a body."

"She doesn't realize that to be a completely real possibility," Sidney said laughing with her sister. "Come on, Emma—let's go see what lies above."

I walked down the hall, pointed to the middle bedroom as we went by, and into the back bedroom. Opening a small six-paneled wooden door, I flipped on the light, and said, "There you go! Isn't this a quaint little set of stairs? Imagine how much fun the original owner's children had playing up there."

Both girls stood motionless, staring up the distance of fourteen steps to the unknown. I had never considered that anything out of the ordinary could be in that space, but was now a bit unraveled at the thought. "Oh for pity's sake, come on," I said, and up I went. Sidney grabbed my coat-tail, and I was unable to see if Emma was even taking the stairs with us.

Reaching the top, we found a huge open space with tons of boxes piled all around. Old clothes hung from makeshift lead-pipe rods, and stacks of canning jars occupied the closest corner. "Oh my gosh, would you just look at this?" I said with amazement. "These blue Ball canning jars with zinc lids—they're actually worth something."

The girls began to carefully poke through the piles. Emma found a complete collection of Nancy Drew and Hardy Boys books and declared them hers. Sidney discovered a set of salad plates, and by opening several more cartons discovered an entire service for twelve of a lovely old rose china pattern. Without missing a beat, she laid claim to the dishes. I reminded them both that I had not yet bought the house, and the contents of the attic were not mine to dispense.

"If you buy this charming dump, do you get to keep what's in it?" Sidney asked.

"Hmm," I said. "I really don't know, but I'll ask my realtor. Oh, I hired Helen Dunn at Maple Real Estate. Emma, do you remember her son Billy from school?"

"Yes, and yuck," Emma replied, still insisting that Sidney be given the bedroom with the stairway to the scary attic. Sidney laughed and said she would be happy to have that room, adding that she had no intention of coming back until the house was up to code in every way. Emma avowed that she would return only when her husband, Scott, could accompany her.

They had accepted my decision to buy the house. They couldn't understand why I wanted it so badly, but were resigned to the apparent fact that 528 Brook Street was going to be their mother's new address. I closed the front door and gave the house a smile. Sidney was the last one through the gate and left it standing open.

"Sidney, you forgot to shut the gate," I said.

"The spiritual energy will get it." She laughed.

"Just in case it's not strong enough—go close it please," I replied.

With an aggravated posture, Sidney returned to the end of the sidewalk and gave the gate a tug. The gate, along with one complete section of picket fencing, fell flat into the front yard. Both girls dropped to the sidewalk with uncontrolled laughter, and Emma said while catching her breath, "Sometimes, Mother, you just don't know when to leave well enough alone, but we love you very much."

"I love you too. I'll call Helen later and explain what happened. Now we really to need to get a move on, or you're going to miss your plane."

We piled into my car and drove the eight blocks back to the wonderful old Victorian that had kept them sheltered for so many years. I had a flashback as we walked up the sidewalk—this was where each child learned to ride their bicycles, to roller skate; it was their palette for buckets upon buckets of sidewalk chalk creations; the cause of many a skinned knee.

The front porch had held witness to each girl's first kiss and prom-night pictures. I had logged a million miles rocking both of them in the upholstered porch swing. But it was time to move on, and I knew that as well as I knew my own name. Everything in life runs its course, and this wonderful old house had finished a job well done.

CHAPTER 6

$\mathcal{I}$t's widely known that a pale-blue porch ceiling keeps "haints" away. Some folks believe that ghosts are afraid of water, and thinking the blue is liquid, will not cross over into your house. Others consider that soft color to represent the sky, and wasps and hornets will not nest in the corners of their ceilings. Either way the velvet-soft hue was a lovely accent to the pale yellow Hardie board siding, and an excellent deterrent from cohabitating with the supernatural or the onslaught of insects.

Over spring break, Betsy and I had painted the porch ceiling the softest blue, so I was safe on the insect issue. But there was still one ghost I could not keep away: Parker. While I had been quick to move to my new house and get away from all the reminders of the life we'd shared, I'd been slow to pull the trigger on the divorce. Almost four months had passed since that cold February day and Parker's announcement and I still hadn't secured legal counsel.

It was late May when the pressure cooker of uncertainty exploded into night sweats and panic attacks. That Saturday morning found me in a stew. I called my two best friends and explained the situation; they dropped whatever they were doing, and twenty minutes later, they were standing on my front porch. Pouring three cups of tea, I passed the coffee cake, and asked their thoughts on a good divorce attorney. I felt the need to get things in writing.

Due to my father's insistence, some things had been set in stone since before Parker and I were married. I'd inherited the house on Washington Street from my Aunt Lucy, and thanks to our prenuptial agreement it, and a few other things, belonged to me. Parker had already taken his personal items, but I felt I could never truly move forward without paperwork.

"Never mind how we know," Betsy said, sipping her tea, "but Parker has hired Blake Mitchel, and we strongly suggest you retain Kathy Upchurch. She's one of the most prominent divorce attorneys in the city and only represents women. You know she has the reputation of, 'well, if she's hired Upchurch, you're up'— pardon my French—'shit's creek.'"

Margaret pointed her thumbs toward her chest. "This 'we' wants you to rethink buying the gun I suggested and shoot the bastard. Not actually kill him, but a good grazing, or a near miss should do the trick and scare the life out of him."

I laughed. "I can't say I haven't considered it, but I think I should let the courts do their job." I promised to call Kathy Upchurch first thing Monday to set up an appointment.

Out of the corner of my eye, I noticed a car working its way up the street. "Hi, Sarah!" yelled the driver. It was Parker. "I like your new house. I hope you're well. Good morning, ladies. Are you girls going to posse up today?"

"Indeed we are," I said. "And I'm fine and you?"

"I can't complain. Well, you girls have a great day. I'm late for an appointment," Parker said, waving as he drove away.

"Holy crap," I said crumpling into the closest seat. "I haven't laid eyes on him since the movers came to load up his stuff, and that's been, what, over three months ago? I think I might throw up."

Margaret handed me my cup of tea and Betsy held my shoulders.

I shook my head. "Plus, he's got a new car—I wonder if he's been by here before?"

In time, I regained a normal heart rate, and soon we were off to the barn for a much-needed ride.

Monday afternoon, attorney Kathy Upchurch and I got right to work. I was instructed to give her the facts in ABC order without emotion or sidebar information. After that, Kathy looked straight into my eyes and said, "Sarah, before you go to bed tonight, make a list of all your holdings—don't leave anything out. Review it several times, because what you think to be unimportant could actually be quite valuable. I'll do the rest." Kathy Upchurch was as tough as nails and hopefully worth the small fortune she charged.

That night as I began to work on the required inventory of my possessions and money, I began to feel a bit uneasy. Historically, I had always been a scaredy-cat when approached by an authority figure on topics I didn't fully understand. I would just agree to their suggestions or advice, thinking they surely knew more than I did. Thankfully somewhere during the listing process, I realized I was on my own now, and it was time I woke up, took a stand, and accepted responsibility for my own life.

Working down the list, I smiled, again appreciating the

saving grace of my late father's wisdom.

The old Sarah had been easily steered in any direction, but the new Sarah questioned things. I would never have changed the decision to have children or go into teaching. But going forward, the independent Sarah had a chance to shine. I wouldn't have been open to the opportunity had Parker stayed.

I was beginning to find the new Sarah—or was it the real Sarah? Either way, I liked her very much.

CHAPTER 7

Over the summer, Parker and his cutthroat attorney did try to go after some of my more valuable holdings, but that effort was denied. During the two meetings of mediation, I sat motionless and absolutely silent as Parker's attorney read their request of what my estranged husband considered to be his. Fortunately Kathy Upchurch earned her outrageous fee in putting the kibosh on Parker's greed fest, and an agreement was eventually reached. With a mutual understanding, our previous separation months counted toward the required year of separation before a divorce in North Carolina. The papers were signed, and in a strange way, that day in September brought me peace, not just because everything was 'on the books' and pending divorce the following spring, but that all that legal ugliness was finally over.

I was very disappointed in the person Parker had become. He had always been such a kind soul, but now he sat across the table from me with a stone-cold expression I had never seen before. I jumped when he hammered his hand on the table when a request was denied. His tone and aggressive behavior were so surprising, especially considering the divorce was his idea. I wondered if Pam had pushed him to be so nasty. With a shrug, I decided it really didn't matter, and I really didn't care.

I was on frazzled overload. Once again, the barn, plus a ride with my friends, was the cure. After several calls, Betsy and Rose agreed to trailer over, as did Elizabeth and Jennifer. Margaret was already at our barn and agreed to wait for the rest of us. Within an hour or so we six were saddled up and ready to enjoy the afternoon.

As we walked our horses across the last meadow before the barn, I said, "I need to share something with you guys. I know that everything with the divorce is now legally all tied up and on the books, but emotionally, I'm kind of a wreck. This is unfamiliar ground, and I'm not quite sure what to do. Sometimes I wake up in a cold sweat about money. I know I'm capable, but still have trouble trusting my financial decision-making skills. There are times when I'm so angry with Parker that I can't breathe. I think I need help."

Jennifer and Elizabeth offered their suggestions on how to just let it go. Rose said I should take up drinking and that I was a fool to be a teetotaler, and Margaret reminded me of her solution involving a firearm.

Betsy suggested that I consider discussing my concerns with a counselor. Her husband was the head of a behavioral management group. "Frank's just added another psychologist to his staff, Dr. Deborah Baxter. I think she would be a good fit for you."

"Hmm . . . that's not a bad idea," I said. "It would be nice to talk things over with someone who's required to be totally objective. You know how worried I get talking about very personal stuff."

Betsy nodded. "I do indeed. But in therapy, you can share your thoughts openly with the understanding that everything you say stays in that room."

"I'll give the office a call tomorrow after school," I said.

CHAPTER 8

I'm Southern born and bred, so regardless of the circumstances, I understand that what one wears is very important. That nonsense goes back generations; even when a poor departed soul was lying in her casket for the viewing, I've heard people comment they couldn't believe she wore *that* suit. And remembering the Palm Beach fiasco years ago, I took a bit more time looking through my closet. Perhaps it was a form of protective armor: "I've lost my center, but please note that I am dressed appropriately!" In no way was I ashamed to go to a psychologist. In fact, I welcomed the opportunity. I just didn't want everyone to know about it, at least not right now.

Teaching art in high school is all-consuming, so I worked through the day with little thought about my afternoon appointment. It took about fifteen minutes to travel the distance from my school to the center of the city. Frank's practice was in a charming two-story building dating back to the 1880s. It had originally been a millinery shop and was furnished with period antiques. Betsy and I had shopped for most of the pieces early in our friendship. We, and occasionally Rose, often went antiquing on Saturday mornings after our weekly visit to the farmer's market. I was sworn to secrecy about the cost of most everything, especially the truly amazing Oriental rug in the foyer. Frank was a wonderful man, but to call him frugal was an understatement.

Once I'd signed in, the receptionist handed me the standard forms to complete. Soon after, a very attractive young woman of small frame, displaying a peaceful smile, called my name. She was holding a yellow legal pad in one hand and used the other to support the opened door. Gathering my things, I stood and followed Dr. Baxter down a short hall and into her office.

She closed the door, then turned and offered me a choice of any seat in the room. I sank deeply into the corner of a large, inviting beige tuxedo sofa whose design offered an immediate sense of security. The high back and sides allowed me to wiggle a bit, finding my comfort spot. I sat clutching a bright-red beanbag pillow and never stopped rolling the bits and pieces between my fingers.

"So, Sarah—what brings you here today?"

I hesitated a bit before I answered, "I'm lost. I don't know how to move forward, and I cannot fathom going backward. It's like being stuck in quicksand, but I'm not sinking. I'm just stuck."

She nodded. "Okay, so let's start with the catalyst: the event that launched you into your current mental quagmire."

After a few minutes of dry-mouthed rambling, I found a rhythm to my racing thoughts and began my story with that early February afternoon and Parker's announcement. I had gotten up to the point of working on my new house when an annoying buzzing sound interrupted my train of thought.

"I'm sorry," Dr. Baxter said, "but our time is up for today. I think you've made real progress. I know it's hard to get started, but now that you have, I think we should continue our conversation next week or, at the latest, in two weeks. In the meantime, I would like for you to keep a journal—record-keeping is extremely beneficial for the mind and the soul. Writing down what you're thinking and feeling at the time is often a more genuine account of your emotions than discussing it for the first time weeks later. Would you be open to doing that sort of thing?"

"I'll try," I said. "I've never liked the idea of a diary. I've always worried that someone would come across my writings and take issue with my thoughts. But, except for my dog Annie, I now live alone, so clearly that's no longer an issue."

"Great," Dr. Baxter replied, "and we'll talk about those concerns in our coming visits."

While I waited for the crosswalk light to change, I was surprised to find that I actually did feel a bet better.

CHAPTER 9

Choosing my favorite perch on the patio, a 1940s mint-green metal rocker I salvaged from a junkyard, I sat swaying in and out of the long shadows of the afternoon, thinking about my conversation with Dr. Baxter. The soft squeak of the metal against the patio bricks became a metronome for my thoughts. Dr. Baxter had a very easy way about her and never rushed me to talk. It had taken all my courage to finally speak, but once I had, it was very liberating. I was emotionally drained for about an hour post-visit, but I was honestly very excited about my next appointment.

Annie was entertaining herself by running the fence line in full chase of a feral cat that was quick enough to elude capture. The children in the yard that backed up to mine were having a who-can-swing-the-highest contest. Lillian, my next-door neighbor and new good friend, was planting annuals in the beds along her side of our shared fence.

It was getting close to supper time, and pressing her chin on my knee, Annie let me know she was a hungry dog. I gathered the mail from the glass-top table, also a refurbished rescue item, and we headed for the back door. Inside, I fixed her dinner and, sinking into my desk chair, began to separate the bills from the junk mail. "Okay, best dog," I said as she inhaled her kibble, "let's check our email, and then we'll give this journal nonsense a go."

Annie wagged her tail in response, and I began to click my way into cyberspace. I deleted the offerings for performance-enhancing medications and vacation opportunities, read a note from a friend, and reviewed several items from my publisher. My books were nonfiction texts about the strong bonds women create with their horses, how-tos on stable care and horse care, the evolution of horses, and the exceptional women who broke the competitive gender barrier in our sport. My second manuscript was in the final stages of editing, which generated volumes of electronic correspondence, but was one of my favorite parts of the publishing process. The final steps to make your book the best it could be.

Then I opened up a new file called "Dear Debby" and began to type. . . .

September 15, 2008
Dear Debby,

I've decided to give your journal idea a try. However, I have chosen to address my entries to you, as opposed to someone named "Diary," or even worse, "Journal." Verbalizing my thoughts and feelings has never been easy for me. I've always worried I would say or do the wrong thing. Routines make me happy, and I find comfort with order to my life and surroundings.

I know I need to come to terms with Parker's leaving. It's the first time in my life I've ever been alone. I know I can do this, but the realization that I have allowed a man to run the majority of my life is shattering and disappointing. I feel like I have been stripped naked and am left standing alone with the forest of male security burned down around me.

Parker took half of our money, and I know he was entitled to that, but it was the way he said he was taking it that still rattles around in my brain. I worry a lot about money. I have enough . . . I just don't think I do.

Additionally, and sadly, I have come to absolutely despise that lyin', cheatin', son of a bitch whom I once loved to the depth of my heart. . . . This is gnawing at me like a cancer.

With all good wishes,

Sarah

P.S. Our first meeting has given me hope for an eventual sense of peace and resolve. I will need time to digest pieces of our discussion, and fortitude to confide in you my darkest fears. Bravery has never come easy to me; I have always needed a bit of a nudge. However, I promise to try.

Resting my head against the back of the chair, I closed my eyes and took a cleansing breath. As I exhaled ever so slowly, my mind drifted back to an earlier time in my life.

My childhood was spent in Iron Springs, a town of around twelve thousand. Everybody knew most everyone, their business, and at least four neighbors knew where you kept the spare key. Anything worth knowing was old news by noon and a fish tale by dinnertime. It was a glorious way to grow up, and I had only the best memories.

From this sheltered beginning I packed my things and those

of my first horse, and we were off to college: Appalachian State University, in the Blue Ridge Mountains of North Carolina. I was an art major from day one and fell instantly in love with college life. Having total responsibility for myself was foreign territory, but I got the hang of it in the blink of an eye.

Parker and I met at a football game during our junior year. He was slim but muscular, of medium height, handsome, and looked like he had just stepped out of *GQ* magazine. From the beginning, he seemed very comfortable in a group and easily moved in and out of conversations, which offered me the opportunity to join in. I loved that he was well mannered, intelligent without being a know-it-all, and easy going.

It wasn't long before we became exclusive, and we were married a year and a half later, in June. I took the art teaching position at Hadley Falls High School, and with some financial help from his parents, my new husband went into the lawn and landscape business. Our home, and the main reason we settled in Hadley Falls, was my inherited house on Washington Street.

Those first several years were full of ups and downs, but Parker and I weathered each storm, one at a time. The next twenty-five years were filled with the lives of our two daughters, our jobs, and hobbies—I rode horses and he played golf. So where during that time did it all fall apart? Why had I not seen this coming? How was I so blind to what was going on around me? These and other questions were on my list of hot topics for Dr. Deborah Baxter.

Annie brought me back to reality with a nudge, signaling she wanted some attention and her nightly walk. I knew I could get through this—I just needed some direction.

CHAPTER 10

𝒯wo weeks later, at my next appointment, Dr. Baxter and I went back in conversation to the beginning of my living alone and how it had made me feel: the chaos of selling my home, sorting through a lifetime of possessions, and the feelings of total abandonment. During a brief pause, I reached down and pulled a hot-pink folder out of my tote bag and removed several typed pages. "These are Dear Debby letters," I said holding them out for her to see. "I find myself spending a great deal of time at my computer trying to express my feelings, and I'm amazed at how helpful it is."

"I'm so proud of you, Sarah," she said, taking the letters from my hand. "I wasn't sure you would actually give it a try, but you did. This is excellent!"

"I'm proud of me too, and I think there will be many more pages to come," I said with a smile.

"Before you go to bed tonight, I want you to truly and honestly take a look at what you have," she said later, as we finished up. "At some point, and when the time is right, go to your computer and write the truth. I'll see you and your hot-pink folder in two weeks."

That night, sleep would not come. Flipping back the bed covers, I put on my robe and went to my computer.

September 29, 2008
Dear Debby,

When I got home today, I did as you suggested, I stood in every room of my house and reviewed what I had and tried not to think about what I had lost. Not one room of my home is empty or lacking. So my loss is not the tangibles, but the trust and security I once had in others, Parker in particular.

The abruptness of the abandonment was the scary part, and I now understand what you were talking about. You were so right when you said that my personality needs time to think about change.

We need to talk about my future, and what I can do to help myself. I also want to discuss my feeling that I was simply cast aside like yesterday's garbage, used up, and abandoned for someone else, a newer model.

With all good wishes,
Sarah

P.S. Progress . . . I can now just say son of a bitch, leaving off lyin' & cheatin'. Peeling back the onion. It may actually be getting smaller!

Over the next few months most of the basic "you can live here without fear of freezing to death or being electrocuted" work had been completed. I decided to stop all construction from December to February.

Christmas of 2008 was not going to be easy for my children, and I needed to focus most of my energy on trying to make that handful of days enjoyable for all of us. It was important to acknowledge the past but equally to embrace the future. Their stockings hung on the new mantel just like always, but clearly one was missing. I turned the gas logs on full blast and reminded them of the first time they'd seen this house and the mention of bags of pot possibly stashed in the chimney. We laughed and had a wonderful discussion over breakfast about creating our "new" Christmas. Scott joined in and offered several suggestions as well.

Emma, Scott, and Sidney had to leave two days after Christmas but not before mentioning that I would be celebrating my fiftieth birthday on February the seventh.

"Ugh," I moaned. "Don't bring that up. Fifty years old—how on earth did that happen?"

"Well, Mom, the good thing is that you don't look like you're a half a century old," Emma offered. "Do you have any plans for your big day?"

"Since it's on a Saturday, we're all going to Virginia for the day to ride and have a late lunch. Betsy is the mastermind for the whole thing, so you know it will be great fun."

"Fifty years—wow, that's a lot," Sidney chimed in. "Think of all the stuff you've seen. I'm serious—you've gone from manual typewriters to computers, black-and-white TV to color and more than three channels. Amazing!"

"And I survived the teenage years of two daughters—even more amazing!" I smiled.

After they'd all gone back home, my house seemed so empty

and quiet, and it took some doing to work through my loneliness. But I couldn't depend on others to fill the void—that could only come from me. With the washer and dryer going, running the vacuum, and cleaning up the kitchen—all of which made me happy— I slowly returned to my new normal and was delighted that I could find that peaceful place all by myself.

My birthday was as fabulous as I knew it would be. My friends made it a very special day—riding at Moss Creek Farm was always exceptional—and lunch at a trendy little bistro in town was delicious. The icing on my cake even supported fifty candles. I was concerned that the blowtorch of heat they created might activate the sprinkler system, but thankfully that embarrassment was avoided. We made plans to come back one weekend in April and toast spring with two days of riding and a girls-only sleep over.

I was still very nervous about my cash flow. With every one thing I fixed, two more fell apart. The house remodel was costing twice the original proposed amount and creating a virtual hemor-rhage of money, to my way of thinking. I had gotten estimates for everything I wanted to do by each individual contractor, but every time they opened a wall or dug a footing, a surprise presented itself.

I suffered my most serious panic attacks during the nighttime hours, when the world stood quiet. One evening, after having received the electricians' final bill for rewiring my cottage, I woke up dripping wet and in an absolute cold sweat. That panic attack had made me nearly breathless, and the crushing feeling on my chest was horrifying. Resting on the side of my bed, I began to calm down and find some internal quiet. Writing relieved my stress and was becoming more and more necessary.

March 17, 2009
Dear Debby,

The electrician finished rewiring the house last week, and his bill came today. What began as adding two exterior outlets grew into over two thousand dollars' worth of work. I do sleep better at night, though, knowing I no longer have the threat of being reduced to ashes while mowing my yard or getting launched into space when turning on a light! I told Lester (the electrician) that there were several switches in the house that should operate the lights in the detached garage, but clearly did not. Like a ferret scout, he found the reason why and continued to burrow into every nook and cranny of my house, and actually did locate two additional dangling hot wires.

In the end, I have a house up to code, with all new outlets, fixtures, wiring, and a bill ten times greater than the estimate. Good Lord!!!

I realize that while I have more than enough money to get by, I am still horrified of being totally responsible for these decisions. You were right, it really isn't the money—I have to learn to trust myself.

With all good wishes,
Sarah

P.S. Soul searching and unbridled honesty is a huge undertaking. It's like eating an emotional elephant: one bite at a time, realizing a clean platter will be a long time coming.

The demolition and rebuilding of the addition to the back of the house was the final major thing on my to-do list. I had saved that project for late March. Glancing at the calendar for the start date for construction, I was reminded of the finish date for the divorce. I was sad and glad all at the same time. But mostly glad. The sad couldn't go on forever—I needed to accept the past and embrace my new life. With a deep sigh and a few tears, I decided to work in the backyard flower beds. Digging in the dirt and planting things was an absolute catharsis for me.

True to form, the two-week project took nearly two months. The roof of the addition had to be replaced, which also meant re-shingling the entire house so it would all match. When the floor was removed, new footings and floor joists were necessary to bring it up to current building code. I felt like I was on an episode of *This Old House*. It was beautiful when it was finally completed, but naturally twice as expensive as the estimate.

CHAPTER 11

School was out, and for more summers than I could count on one hand, we six had attended a Monday-through-Friday horse camp during the third week in June. This annual pilgrimage offered us the opportunity to up our riding skills, relax, and enjoy five days of "girls-only" fun and fellowship. Moss Creek Farm was situated in the gentle rolling hills of the Old Dominion.

The equestrian facility was owned and operated by a no-nonsense horsewoman, Susan Tillman, whom I adored. For five days, I would do nothing but ride my horse, laugh with my friends, enjoy wonderful meals, and sleep like a baby. I knew I needed some time away from worrying about the house, or that I might end up living alone in one room with nothing but a black-and-white TV and a space heater, eating cat food. A trip to Moss Creek Farm was just the ticket, and an affordable one at that. Susan all but gave us her time and there was only a minimal charge for boarding our horses. Our lodging was also free, and we brought our own food.

The two days before we left were devoted to cleaning our tack, packing trunks, clipping and bathing horses, and loading our trailers. On our departure day, we met at a church parking lot just down the road and headed northwest. Susan demanded that her riders be on their horses and in the ring by one o'clock Monday afternoon; tardiness was unacceptable. When we were lagging behind, she would bellow, "Ladies, this is not Miss Pity Pat's Riding School. Get ready and in the ring in five minutes." There was always a tone of "or else" to her voice, and I chose to never realize the mystery consequences.

After putting Annie in for her spa-like boarding early that Monday morning, I headed for the barn. Margaret and I used her truck and trailer. Our horses, Rascal and Louie, went everywhere together. Betsy and Rose always trailered with their horses, Charlie and Beau, traveling side by side. Rose had kept her mount at Betsy's farm for years. Those two women were the connection and the initial invitation for the rest of us to attend Susan's horse camp. We earned the return invites on our own merit. Elizabeth and Jennifer were the final link in our equestrian caravan, pulling Sonny and Romeo.

On our way down the highway, Margaret said, "Sarah, you are not allowed to mention any of your worries. You've been divorced for nearly three months now and your house is basically finished. We're going to have a great time as long as Susan doesn't kill us."

I laughed. "You're on; I promise to try. I probably won't have the strength to worry about anything anyway. But the good news is I'm worrying less and less: Dr. Baxter was one of the smartest things I've ever done."

In the absolute middle of nowhere, and about two thirds of the way into the trip, we usually stopped for lunch at what appeared to be your basic truck stop, and that's actually why we stopped the first time. Between the six of us, we were pulling three loaded horse trailers that required serious parking space and easy access back onto the highway. Our expectation was to dine on pre-packaged sandwiches, but there it was, a virtual oasis in the midst of bottled motor oil, boiled peanuts, and lottery tickets. The wall-mounted menu board of the mini café offered homemade sandwiches, salads, and burgers. And working in perfect harmony, the staff of two delivered your surprisingly delicious order in less than ten minutes.

Our lunch conversation was all about horses and camp. No one was quite sure if there would be other riders in attendance, but we all hoped it would be just us. We knew it was selfish— but it was our truth. Over lunch we tossed around ideas of what might be asked of us this summer. We knew it would be harder than last year—it always was—but how much was the question.

A refreshing breeze welcomed us as we walked across the parking lot and back to the trailers. Rascal lifted his head, and his soft nicker demanded a treat that he knew I had stashed in my pocket. I stroked the length of his handsome face as he devoured two baby carrots. I was lucky enough to have bought Rascal ten years earlier, and it had been a marriage of two hearts from that day on. Over the years we had grown a bond of trust that was unbreakable. It was hard to explain, nearly impossible, actually, but he just knew how to take care of me in and out of the saddle. Now eighteen, Rascal was starting to show his years, and I under-stood the day would come when he could no longer work so hard—the day he would be retired, or worse. With one last pat and a kiss on his nose, I said we had to get back on the road.

We turned off from the divided highway and traveled four of the final seven miles along the spine of Butler's Mountain. Margaret shifted the truck into low gear as we began to descend the steep downhill grade, and said her annual prayer for the brakes to hold. In the distance, you could see the white barns with green metal rooftops surrounded by black slat fencing. The pastures dotted with horses rolled gently over land that had belonged to Susan's family since the earliest settlers acquired land grants from King Charles II.

Moss Creek Farm was the pinnacle of training facilities for hunt seat and cross-country riding. We worked in the hunter ring, going over jumps, usually eight total, set at a measured distance apart to hone our skills in creating the correct canter to find the pre-determined distance from jump to jump. Hunter jumps were mobile, and Susan would set them in different patterns each morning before our class. Cross-country however, was a whole different ball of wax. Those jumps were bigger, totally stationary, up and down hills, and through water. At Moss Creek, the cross-country course consumed a large field and the edge of the woods. This discipline was a test of speed and sheer guts to vault something that was absolutely unforgiving.

Pulling into the parking area of the main barn, we spied Susan smiling warmly as she motioned us to a spot. With our annual hellos and hugs taken care of, Susan said we had forty-five minutes to get organized and into the indoor ring.

"Is anyone else coming this year?" Betsy asked.

"No," Susan said. "It's just the six of you."

"Excellent," Rose said.

"You might not think so by the end of the week." Susan grinned.

The walk to the barn gave everyone, including the horses, a chance to look around and stretch their legs. Each stall was labeled with the name of a horse, piled deeply with shavings, had two hanging buckets of water, and a leaf of hay. The center section of the main barn had been raised just after the end of the Revolutionary War and was a handsome old structure. You could feel the history radiate from the enormous hickory timbers standing strong down both sides of the center aisle.

The indoor ring was an add-on to the back of the main barn, but you never would have known to look at it. Susan and her husband, Roger, took great pride in historical preservation and were very careful to make any new structure outwardly resemble the past. It looked as if George Washington or perhaps Thomas Jefferson might join us for a quick gallop across the fields.

We led our horses down the central cobblestone corridor, made smooth by the addition of concrete, and into the indoor arena. It was a large space, perfect for hunter work or dressage. Susan had set up the jump course, and I tried to guess what we were going to do. I always felt like a sacrificial lamb of sorts as she would shout, "Sarah, you go first." I once asked why I always had to be the first to ride the course. Susan answered, "Because I am in charge, and I said so."

"Excellent reason," I replied, striking a canter and looking toward the first jump.

After an exhausting afternoon of riding, we headed to our guest quarters—an old farmhouse that had been on the property for several generations. Three enormous oaks stood guard in the front yard of the two-story gray hardboard structure and a set of deep hunter-green doors welcomed you inside. I loved the smell of the boxwood hedge that lined both sides of the brick sidewalk that led you to the front entrance.

We spilled through the double doors and plopped down on either of the two facing parsons benches and began to remove our tall boots and socks. From there you could see the spacious great room that was the center of all activity. A beautifully remodeled kitchen was in the back, with an exterior door leading to a shaded slate patio. Also off from the kitchen were a half bath and the laundry room. Sitting squarely in the middle of the open space was an enormous round dining room table with twelve ladder-back chairs. Dragging ourselves into the den, we collapsed onto the overstuffed chintz sofa and pillow-ticking chairs that faced a stacked stone fireplace. The bedrooms were upstairs, and it took us an hour or so before we even had the energy to make the climb.

We stayed up entirely too late that night, so that when the alarm blasted early the next morning, we winced with stiffness, and stretched in all directions trying to get out the kinks. The two upstairs bathrooms were laid out such that at least two of us could occupy that space at a time.

Breakfast was all hands on deck, and collectively we created a buffet of protein, fruit, and carbohydrate options. Each year we planned our menus for the first three days, and shopped for the groceries the day before leaving Hadley Falls.

As united as the armed forces on D-Day, we stood firm in our conviction that we were not going to participate in any exercise too risky, too demanding, or too dangerous. Because I was ganged up on, and my teacher's voice was mentioned as a positive, I was appointed spokeswoman, and practiced my delivery over a bowl of granola and yogurt. "Okay, but let the record show," I announced, "you claim to be my dearest friends, and yet you're all willing to throw me under the horse trailer. I'll do this, but know it's with great protest, and an element of fear. Susan will make me pay for my comments, and you all know this to be true!"

Hearing us walk into the main aisle of the barn, Susan stuck her head out from the office door and told us to get ready quickly. We were to go to the cross-country field for the morning portion of our instruction. Elizabeth poked me in the ribs repeatedly and whispered for me to tell Susan our plans.

Clearing my throat, I said, "Susan, over breakfast we were discussing our thoughts for the morning part of today's agenda. Considering we haven't been here since April and are a bit out of shape, maybe we could have a lighter workout today?"

Susan smiled, nodded, and drew her index finger upward saying, "I will see all of you in the field in forty minutes. Heaven help the poor soul who's bringing up the rear!"

Nearly knocking each other out of the way, we scrambled to ready ourselves and our mounts. What had just happened? Where had we gone wrong? How could something sound so good one minute and be reduced to ashes the next?

I was first out of the barn, followed quickly by Betsy and Margaret. Jennifer had to work a bit to get Romeo to walk past the apparent horrifying manure spreader—but success did come. Rose had a system of sorts to pre-mounting, and worked with her horse, Beau, while the rest of us inched our way down the road. Elizabeth, the perfectionist, took forever to do anything, and today proved no exception. Five minutes had passed, and still no sign of her. Betsy suggested I trot back to the barn and check on things.

"Why am I always the one to do that sort of thing?" I asked. "First this morning with Susan and now with Elizabeth. It makes me look so bossy."

"You are bossy," Betsy said, turning Charlie toward the barn, "but you manage to do it without hurting anyone's feelings. So go see what she's doing."

With a gentle tap of my heel to Rascal's side, we struck a trot back to the barn. Pulling up short of the double barn doors, I could see Elizabeth fussing with the keepers on either side of Sonny's bridle. She stood, sliding the tiny leather loops on both sides of the cheek straps up and down in an effort to make them uniform. Using my best people skills, I announced that we were going to leave her, and she would be raw meat with Susan. Returning to the group I said, "She's on her way, but we're going to need to book it down the trail to avoid being late. I don't know about the rest of you, but I have no intention of being *the last poor soul* to arrive in the field."

"Here she comes now. Tally ho, everyone!" Rose said, turning Beau around and holding her riding crop high in the air.

Just before making the final turn and spilling onto the jump field, we stopped, counted noses, and walked side by side to where Susan was standing. Our equestrian mentor applauded our team's effort to arrive as a group. I gave a quick glance from hurdle to hurdle, and was doing splendidly until my eyes rested on the final jump. It was a new addition to the course from last year, and loomed high on the horizon.

"Holy too-high, Batman," I yelped, turning my head in Betsy's direction. Having already spied the final obstacle in the jump sequence, she nearly fell from her saddle with laughter. "I'm sure Susan doesn't expect us to go over *that* jump? It's the size of your Suburban!" I whispered with concern, or perhaps terror.

Rose was standing the next horse over and said, "Rascal will jump anything; he'll pop right over."

"That jump is not 'pop' friendly," I said, "It's gigantic—look at that massive thing! It must be at least three feet high and wide—and rock solid. Sweet Jesus!"

Before Betsy could respond to my original question, Susan walked in our direction. "What's going on, ladies? Is something wrong?"

"Sarah's worried about the height of the final jump," Betsy said. "They don't jump that high at home."

Looking around, Susan paused and said, "Does this look like 'home' to any of you? The purpose of this camp is to push you a little and offer you the opportunity to grow as a rider. I wouldn't make you jump it if I didn't think you could." She waited briefly for a response; when none was offered, she turned on the heels of her tall boots and walked to the center of the field.

Flat work was always first in any lesson and we went at the walk, trot, and canter for the better part of fifty minutes. There were times when each rider did the exercise alone, but for the most part we worked as a group.

At the end of the final canter sequence, Jan, Susan's closest friend, appeared driving the Ranger, carrying coolers filled with water and assorted energy drinks. Jan was a top competitor, and second in command at Moss Creek Farm.

Susan announced our break was over and that we were to line up beside the water obstacle. I loved flying through the water, taking the jump, and climbing the hill. But I absolutely hated dropping down the cliff on the other side. It was so steep I was sure at any given moment I might simply slide right past Rascal's ears on the way down.

Once all of us were within earshot, Susan explained the course and our order of go. Naturally, I was first. Not because I was extraordinary, but because my horse was. He really would jump almost anything. I, on the other hand, was terrified and had never gone over anything that high or wide. As Rascal and I moved past our mentor, I mentioned that I was not sure we would be taking the final jump.

Susan used her calmest voice, reviewed the course, and insisted, "The last jump is the last jump, and you will go over the last jump."

Striking a trot, I drew in the deepest breath possible, with a gentle nudge asked for the canter, and turned my head in the direction of the first jump. We were as smooth as butter over the pyramid shaped stack of logs, up the hill, and down the cliff on the other side. Next was the hurdle built to resemble a barn, Rascal twitched his ears with curiosity, but over we went, and we were off and over the huge section of a fallen oak. Rounding the curve, I cantered up to take the next water jump. The splash from Rascal's hooves felt refreshing as it dotted my face. Up the hill, over a stone wall, and there it was: the biggest jump I'd ever seen.

From the corner of my eye, I could see Susan and Jan. They had driven the Ranger up the hill and parked in a stand of scrub pines near the final jump. Rascal and I were about seven strides out, roughly eighty-four feet, and I could hear Susan yell for me to sit up, squeeze with my lower leg, and grab a handful of his mane.

There was no turning back now. Rascal celebrated the challenge, rocked back on his hocks, and we were airborne. As we sailed over the enormous obstacle, my heart took flight as well, and for one brief moment, I was free. I don't think I drew a breath until we had cantered out six or seven strides on the backside of the jump.

Everyone applauded as we returned to our place in line. I could not contain my euphoria and beamed with pride as the tears streamed from my eyes.

"I'm very proud of you for standing right up to Susan and refusing to take the final jump," Betsy said.

"Oh, shut up," I said with a giggle. "I planned to ride that jump all along." With a whisper, I continued, "I nearly wet my pants, but holy cow, I did it!"

One after the other, my friends rode the course, and no one turned down the challenge of the final jump. The second and third trips over that enormous hurdle were without fear by any of us, and we accepted the challenge each and every time.

Before falling asleep that night, I mentally rode the course over and over. My smile widened as my memory drew us closer to the final hurdle. That jump was an epiphany, a sign of things to come.

CHAPTER 12

 *T*hursday night was always peel-'n'-eat shrimp, served at the big house. Susan would spread an enormous oilcloth over her dining room table, and bowls piled full of steaming hot shrimp were placed on top, running the length of the heart-of-pine family heirloom. Susan was a self-professed bad cook and never pretended to be otherwise. The seafood was delivered in the afternoon, and Deacon, the barn manager, did the rest. He was from the Tidewater area of Virginia, and he held his secret recipe close to the breast.

Deacon was very easy on the eyes, and watching him cook was somewhat spiritual in nature. He wore well-fitted faded blue jeans, and a polo shirt that left little to the imagination. Who knew that ripped torso was in the shadows of the work shirt and heavy-duty overalls he wore during the day? Minus his sweat-stained John Deere ball cap, Deacon's now-clean and curly mahogany hair softly framed his hazel eyes. All six of us appreciated how kind God had been to this unmarried, very well mannered, and usually quiet man.

Showered and dressed in jeans and tops, the six of us walked up the hill to Susan's about an hour and a half before dinner was to be served. We were the sous-chefs for Deacon, and believe me when I say the pleasure was all ours. Sitting on stools grouped around a large wooden table, we worked diligently on the side items for the evening's menu. Rose made the most fabulous potato salad you've ever eaten, and her hors d'oeuvres were to die for. Betsy was in charge of making coleslaw using her special dressing and corn on the cob boiled in water, half a stick of butter, and a pinch of sugar—holy heart attack, but so good! She was also in charge of mixing the cocktail sauce. Margaret, Jennifer, and Elizabeth had their annual heated discussion on the correct way to snap green beans. It was perhaps the most ridiculous conversation I've ever heard, but it happened each and every year. The end result was a bowl of deliciously prepared green beans, snapped three different ways. I made a special spread of butter, Bearnaise, and parsley to go along with my cheese biscuits. Which put me at the corner closest to the Bisquick—and Deacon.

Rose caught me looking in his direction and later suggested that I might give him a wink when I was feeling down. She whispered, "You know Sarah, a roll in the hay might do you a world of good."

I blushed as my eyes rolled back. "For God's sake Rose, I am at least ten years older than he is, and I haven't had sex in a long time." *Wow*, I thought, *it really has been over a year.*

Rose laughed and said, "My dear friend, it's rather like riding a bicycle, one never forgets."

With dinner ready, we sat down in front of newspaper place mats, damp cloths, and saucers of drawn butter and cocktail sauce. We each recounted all the funny and not-so-comical things that had occurred during the week. As the evening progressed, the jumps grew to monumental heights, the pain of our sore muscles increased to unbearable, and the demands of our fearless leader had no equal.

Our physical pain led us to conversations on the topics of aging and retirement. I was the oldest by about nine months, Margaret would turn fifty in November, and the rest were somewhere in their late forties, so depending on each person's occupation, retirement could come within the next ten years. We also talked about trips we'd like to take and things we'd like to do post-retirement. Rose traveled a great deal and was rarely short of a companion, and she never chimed in on the "going hand-in-hand into the sunset" conversation. I, on the other hand, became very melancholy thinking about my current very-alone status. *Where does one find Mr. Right?* I thought. *I don't want much: kind, tall, no older than sixty, loves horses and dogs, good-looking.*

That night, after everyone had gone to bed, I slipped my laptop from the bottom of my duffel bag. I tiptoed past Margaret and into the walk-in closet, plugged my computer into the outlet, put a blanket over my head to diffuse the glow of the screen, and began to type. There were a few things I could not get off my mind.

June 18, 2009
Dear Debby,

I'm having a wonderful time at camp, and if you were my mother and I was ten, I would ask if I could stay another week. I actually did that when I was ten. Seriously, everything is going great, but I felt like an outsider during this evening's dinner conversation. Everyone was talking about their husbands and their plans after retirement. My sense of alienation was not created by my friends, but by my internal reaction.

I told you about my worries that I would die alone, and my final resting place would be who knows where. My concern is going forward.

You'll remember our discussion of my wanting to take trips to New England antiquing with a wonderful man and my Annie. Trailering Rascal along with the horse of "Mr. Right" to the mountains of North Carolina for romantic weekends was also a hope of mine. I refuse to surrender my dreams, but I'm not sure what to do.

Rose is a sophisticated, self-assured, unmarried woman who was not bothered in the least by the conversation. She is truly the strongest woman I have ever known. As a result of her literary/culinary career, she spends a great deal of time traveling all over the world. Along the way, she has found the company of men fulfilling without the cumbersome restraints of marriage. I'm not sure that I ever want to retie the knot, but I would enjoy the companionship of a gentleman. On the flip side of that coin, I think I am too insecure to enjoy life as Rose does.

I wish I could live my life the way I rode that course two days ago. When Rascal and I were in the air, all my worries were behind me. I spat in the eye of fear, and I was victorious. My mission is to find the courage to believe in my ability to handle situations on my own. I don't understand how I can be so dauntless at the barn and in my classroom, and resemble a deer caught in headlights everywhere else.

With all good wishes,
Sarah

The last day of camp was always bittersweet. The final lesson ended with a long trail ride along the narrow banks of Moss Creek. Preparing our horses for travel and collecting our things was the first order of business and in that order. Once all chores were completed and the trailers were tightly packed, we enjoyed lunch at the barn. All the saved bits and pieces from the refrigerator morphed into our own all-you-can-eat buffet.

We grimaced with physical pain and emotional sadness as we climbed into our trucks and started to make our way home. Margaret and I talked non-stop about the past week as we traveled down the road. Somewhere along the way, I said, "I have to tell you the truth. I know on the way to camp, I promised you that I wouldn't, but last night I spent a few minutes in the closet with my computer. And yes, it was a *Dear Debby* letter—I needed to record my thoughts so I could go to sleep. Anyway, I have another confession, too, but you have to swear you'll never tell anyone."

"I swear," Margaret replied, holding up her right hand.

"This is absolutely ridiculous," I said, "but remember last night when we were cooking dinner with Deacon, and Rose whispered her suggestion that he and I have a good ol' roll in the hay? I actually thought about that—not asking him, but what it would be like to have some wild fling. I think I would rather have a forever than a fling, but you know what I mean."

"Yes, of course I know what you mean, and maybe not with Deacon, but "your forever" is out there somewhere. Be patient. You'll find him, or he'll find you," Margaret said. "But I have to add—in the meantime there's no rule that says you can't have a fling—you're a free woman, you know—and fifty years old, for Christ's sake. But Deacon is gorgeous, isn't he?"

"Lord have mercy, he is!" I said.

CHAPTER 13

Saturday morning, after collecting Annie from the spa and in between loads of laundry, I sat at my computer catching up on my correspondence, most of which was from my publisher. The manuscript for my latest book was due to her in September, and I was in the final stages of editing. *Happy Horse-Happy Human: the Four-H Theory* is about the anatomy of the horse and why proper nutrition and general care are so critical to its longevity. There's even a recipe section for horse treats and human snacks to keep both at top performance.

Historical horsewomen, the evolution of horses, how to ride, and proper care of the rider and her mount are the topics of my books. My premise is that I'm no one you've ever heard of, but as a working mother, I truly know how to enjoy this sport without going broke. For example: in the show ring, it is essential that the exhibitor is properly dressed from head to toe. Most tack stores have a consignment area, and those gently worn clothes are perfect for the rapidly growing child rider. The cost for boarding and horse care can vary from barn to barn, but making sure your mount is safe is of the utmost of importance. If the board is super cheap, something might not be quite right. You need to be sure you're getting your money's worth, and that your horse is in good hands twenty-four/seven.

Occasionally I freelance humorous—personal observation—articles for one of the oldest equestrian periodicals in the country. I love to write, but not for the money or notoriety. In my case, the sum of a royalty check is usually absent double digits to the left of the comma, if there even was a comma. The revenue isn't important; it's the peace writing brings my way that gives me such joy. I guess the same mental clarity could be attributed to the *Dear Debby* entries, which were really helping me to put my thoughts in order about what I wanted out of life.

Aside from the work emails, there were some personal ones, including a note from one of my closest teacher friends, Laura, who wanted to set me up on a date with a man named John. I tried to tamp down the butterflies that fluttered through me as I wrote back that she could give him my number.

Sunday morning, John called. We had a nice phone conversation; he was charming, funny, and polite. We agreed to meet for dinner the following Tuesday, but Tuesday came and went, and he never called to confirm a time and place. I was confused, a touch angry, and embarrassed. *What had I done wrong? Side of a ditch!*

Wednesday afternoon found me anxiously awaiting my appointment.

"Hi, Sarah, come in," Dr. Baxter said with a smile, offering me a seat. "How are things? I know we had to skip our last session for your horse camp, so bring me up to date."

"I don't even know where to start," I said. "Camp was great, and I have a page about that, but my most recent letter is about John, the man who never called back."

"All right," she said, "let's start at the beginning. If he didn't call back, then he did call at least once. Show me the letter about that experience," she said, holding out her hand.

"Okay," I said pulling out my folder and laughing.

"Progress—in an effort to clean up my potty mouth, I've replaced SOB with 'side of a ditch'. It's not quite as strong and the presentation is softer."

"You laugh, but that is progress—good job." Dr. Baxter said taking a moment to skim the single sheet of paper and looked up, saying, "Let's start with your last sentence. I'll read it aloud: 'For some reason I feel the need to know why John never called back . . . even if it's hurtful.'"

Over the next forty-five minutes we discussed not getting a call back, horse camp, sexy Deacon, and touched on my concerns about living alone for the rest of my life. We agreed that John fell into the category of "kissing frogs to find a prince," and he clearly was just a frog. It was strange to realize that sometimes rejection could be a blessing.

Returning my folder to my tote bag, I said, "I love writing these letters. I'll be glad when I no longer have the need, but for now, they do more for me than I could ever explain."

"Remember to keep writing down what you feel when things happen," she said. "Again, I'm very happy with your growing self-confidence, and I hope you are."

"Yes, I am. I'll see you in two weeks," I said.

I left her office with a smile on my face and a much lighter heart. During our discussion of the "frog" who didn't call back—which would always feel like an unfinished sentence— we revisited prior appointments concerning Parker and my lack of honest and open communication. I hadn't realized until that day's session that, except for the "please pass the salt" level of conversation, somewhere along the way Parker and I had stopped talking to each other. Going forward, Mr. Right and I would need to keep all lines of communication open, even if the topic was mundane, unpleasant, or somewhat controversial—no more stuffing my feelings in the catacombs of a metaphorical backpack and pulling the zipper closed like you did when you made a fifty-seven on a math test, hoping it would never resurface!

CHAPTER 14

$\mathcal{S}$chool had been in session for nearly two months now, and I found myself face-to-face with the issue of misinterpreting a gentleman's intentions.

Wednesday afternoon found me planted firmly on the edge of my seat in the waiting room of Dr. Deborah Baxter.

"Hi, Sarah. Please come in," she said turning to close her office door. "How have you been?"

"I don't know where to start," I said, dragging the ever-thickening hot-pink folder out of my bag. "Remember my telling you about the football coach—moved here from Kentucky and new to the staff—who's been flirting with me since the beginning of the school year?"

"Yes," she said smiling. "What's happened with that?"

"Ugh," I sighed, handing her a long letter. "Let's see if I can make this short. Apparently Larry was not flirting with me at all, but simply enjoyed my company on a colleague basis only. I know this because my two best teaching friends and I attended last Friday night's home game. Just before the opening kickoff, he looked up to where we were sitting and waved. I almost returned the gesture but realized it was not for me—it was for the ponytailed thirty-year-old wearing tangerine earmuffs and sitting three rows in front of us. Hadley Falls won the game, and she bolted down to the field—jumped into his arms and nailed him with a victory kiss that nearly knocked him over."

"Oh dear," Dr. Baxter said. "Give me a minute to read your letter and then we'll begin."

I watched her eyes race back and forth down the page. As she neared the bottom, I could no longer contain myself. "Oh dear is right, and I'll add what the hell? I may just give up on men all together. I don't really mind being alone until around nine o'clock at night, and even that is getting better with time," I said, taking a breath.

"Goodness. Is that really what you want to do?" she asked with raised eyebrows.

"No—not really," I said dropping my shoulders. "But I've apparently lost the ability to read men. Perhaps I never had that gift. Anyway, this time I found myself replaced—no, *replaced* isn't right at all—I truly never was."

For the remainder of our time we discussed the whole football coach situation, and things to look out for going forward. It was wonderful to have the verbal freedom Dr. Baxter's office allowed. She would pull out a phrase here or there from the letters, and off I went. By the end of our hour, I felt much better and promised to keep an open mind—and to keep writing.

CHAPTER 15

$\mathcal{L}$ate fall came, and with it the last hunter pace competition of the season. It was one of our favorite courses to ride and not too far from home. The object was to finish closest to the time set by the pace rider the day before or the morning of. The riders followed a marked trail that took you across meadows, in and out of the pine forest, and over an abundance of immovable jumps. Riders were not permitted to study the course, or carry a timepiece of any sort, and were competing against at least a handful of other teams in the same division. There were several course options that varied in length and degree of difficulty, and teams were required to declare their choice at the sign-in table. Our team rode the six-mile course, which allowed each participant the option of jumping the obstacle or going around. Some of the jumps loomed high on the horizon, and Betsy and Jennifer were usually the only takers for the giant ones.

Betsy and Rose were the seasoned fox-hunters, so they were one to each group. Margaret and Elizabeth were distance runners, and each had a mental clock. Jennifer and I had a good sense of direction and distance traveled. It was also helpful that Rascal could recognize when we had made our turn for the finish line. I always knew when he twitched his ears and quickened his trot that we were headed home. As a group, we would decide if we needed to make up some time or back off just a bit.

We had a two-hour travel time from Hadley Falls to the competition, and added about forty-five extra minutes for checking in, tacking up, and schooling our horses.

Jennifer and I were elected to collect our competition information packets, which included our team numbers, time cards, and lunch tickets. While standing in line, I noticed a man staring at me from the back of the line. I nudged Jennifer and asked if she knew who he was. She studied his face and said she didn't recognize him, but mentioned how nice-looking he was. I agreed.

With manila envelopes in hand, we returned to the trailers, where Betsy was handing everyone cups of coffee in an effort to keep us warm. Everyone except for me, that is; I love the smell of fresh brewed coffee, but never acquired a taste for it.

I went around to the tack room of Margaret's trailer to unload our things. I turned to offer Rascal a carrot, and I saw, two trailers down, the nice-looking man I had seen earlier. I recognized the name on the side of the trailer: Long Leaf Farm, a barn not too far from Hadley Falls. I wondered if he was an employee or a boarder. I knew I had never seen him at any hunter/jumper shows, so he must have been new to the area.

At one point our eyes met, and he offered a gentle smile and a wave of his hand. For a split second, I had a flashback to the fifty-yard-line situation not more than three weeks prior. I waved back, and quickly got back on task.

Betsy, Margaret, and I were in the first team, with Rose,

Elizabeth, and Jennifer making up the second. Start times were in four-minute intervals, so our group left at a canter but slowed to a trot when we entered the woods. The second team maintained the canter until they caught up, and we traveled together during a short walk stretch. It wasn't against the rules, and even if it had been, we'd have done it anyway. It gave us the opportunity to check on one another and make sure all was well before going on.

During that brief walk stretch, which was not only good for us, but important for our horses to take a breath, I mentioned having seen "the man in line" two trailers down, the name of the barn, and the wave. He became the subject of choice for the next quarter mile or so. With our horses rested, we once again parted company and cantered off, telling the second team we would see them at the designated halfway point, in a large clearing surrounded by a thick stand of tall long-leaf pines. All participants were required to stop for a rest period of ten minutes. During this time riders could dismount, use the porta-john, or have a snack. A member of the host hunt club checked each team's time card and told the team to remain in the area until instructed to continue.

There were two older ladies from the local organization whose job it was to offer each rider cookies and juice. Carefully choosing their steps and pace through the deep sand, the two women shuffled in our direction. Once close enough, our horses extended their heads to help themselves. Margaret suggested the ladies move their trays to their opposite hands. Our guys loved cookies and juice, and they would have emptied the trays in a heartbeat.

With sand flying, a group approached the rest area at a full canter. Through the cloud of settling dust, I recognized the man from earlier that morning. As I took the last sip of juice and moved over to the trash bin, he pulled his horse in line with mine. He really was quite handsome, and his red hunt coat put the polish on the total package—yum, yum! *Breathe, Sarah,* I told myself.

This tall, trim stranger had the most alluring azure eyes I had ever seen, and his sandy-blond hair tickled the back of his coat's black velvet collar. My first thought was actually a prayer that I not say or do something stupid.

Tossing his trash in the bin, he said, "Hi, I'm Nick Heart. It's a great day for a ride, don't you think?"

"Yes," I said. "I love this piece of property. I'm having a wonderful time. Oh, and yes, it's a great day for a ride."

"Your handsome boy looks like a seasoned veteran who loves his job," he said.

I could never contain my love for Rascal. "Absolutely, and thank you. I have zero objectivity when it comes to this guy. I consider him to be the best horse ever created. Oh, I'm sorry to rush off, but our time is up. I've got to go," I said, looking over my shoulder as I turned to rejoin my team. "Good luck, and have fun."

With a nod, he said, "Be safe. I'll see you at the finish line."

Once our second team caught up, Margaret took a minute to launch a group discussion concerning the man in the scarlet coat. I was given more suggestions in the next quarter mile than I could possibly digest. Their pearls of wisdom ranged from how much lunch to put on my plate to try hard not to babble on about anything, which was a nervous habit of mine.

We really did need to try and at least place in this competition. Rascal had quickened his trot, and I knew we had turned for home. Reorganizing into the two original teams, Betsy, Margaret, and I cantered away, and our second team continued to walk for a while. Rose's horse was still a bit winded and needed some additional time.

"We'll wait for you after we cross the finish line," Betsy said over her shoulder. "Send Elizabeth on if you run into trouble."

What a rush it was to fly across such a large field with nothing in our way. The pine thicket stood as a backdrop for the meadow, and that was our time to return to the trot and one last walk.

Through the long needles of the towering pines we could see distant bits and pieces of color from parked trucks and trailers, and knew we were nearing the end of the course. The finish line was not far away, and the three of us prepared for the final canter stretch and taking the last jump. Betsy's horse, Charlie, was always terrified of the photographer waiting on the other side of the jump. Sporting a wide-brimmed hat made from bright yellow canvas, she would pop up from her lawn chair at the sound of hoof-beats, camera in hand. If Rascal was in the lead, Charlie and Margaret's horse, Louie, usually paid less attention to the jack-in-the-box in the hedges.

Two strides before leaving the woods and spilling into the meadow, I gave my horse a tap on his shoulder, pressed my hands to his neck, and we were off. Betsy and Margaret were on our heels, and the final jump was in view. One after another, we all cleared the jump with inches to spare, and cantered the field to the finish line.

Margaret and Betsy pulled their horses over to the side and

turned facing in the direction of the woods to wait for Elizabeth, Jennifer, and Rose. I trotted over to the gentleman collecting time cards, relinquished the now-rumpled piece of paper, and told him how much we had enjoyed our day. Walking back to the group, I could see a team approaching from the south end of the meadow, the lead horseman wearing a scarlet coat.

I watched with excitement when he called for his teammates to gallop the field. As the three horsemen sailed over the final jump in perfect unison, it was obvious Nick and his teammates had put in some serious practice time. He threw up his hand as they flew by and said, "See you at lunch!" I nodded, and my cheeks flushed. I was once again—if only briefly—sixteen, and the class dreamboat had given me a nod.

With our feet back on the ground, we went about the business of taking care of our mounts. Attention was always given to the horses first, untacking and covering them in a blanket called a cooler, walking them dry, and then giving them water and hay. Rose's horse, Beau, had improved greatly, which generated a group sigh of relief.

The meal was catered by a local barbecue restaurant and was not bad, considering it was served in the middle of a field on a cold day in November. With a full plate in one hand and iced tea in the other, we stashed the plastic-ware, napkins, and brownies in our coat pockets.

Bales of hay were our seats. I quickly realized I had been strategically placed on the end, with empty bales beyond. Leaning forward, I looked down the line of my dear friends, smiled, and said, "You're shameless, all of you. I understand what you're doing, and it's very sweet, but you're shameless."

There he stood in the lunch line, about two-thirds back from the front. He was having an in-depth conversation with his teammates, both of whom were women. Another gentleman walked over and offered his hand in congratulations. The usual male posturing followed, with arm slapping, adjusting of their hats, and the widening of each man's stance.

Jennifer said, "Holy cow, he is a good-looking man. I'm surprised he's single. Maybe he's gay."

"Don't tell him you're divorced, or refer to most men as—using your new phrase—a 'side of a ditch'—while cute—it's still understood," Betsy said.

Elizabeth chimed in with, "Take small bites and sip your tea before you speak. Oh—and try not to talk too loud."

Margaret shushed everyone. "Y'all are going to make her nervous. Sarah, just relax, be yourself, and don't bite your lip. And Betsy's right—don't call anyone something ugly."

With his full plate in one hand and iced tea in the other, Nick Heart looked around, spotted me, and headed straight for the empty space on my hay bale.

Rose leaned over and whispered, "Remember, *think* before you speak."

He motioned toward the empty spot beside me and asked if he could have a seat. I replied with a confident but not overly excited "Certainly." He reintroduced himself and asked that I call him Nick.

"I'm Sarah Sams, and you can call me Sarah," I said with a smile.

He laughed, and we went directly into conversation about the just-completed competition.

As we talked, I studied the chiseled contours of his face, and appreciated how his eyes were completely engaged in our conversation. The artist in me would have loved a sketchbook and pencil to document his deeply furrowed brow and weathered good looks.

I could hear Margaret and Betsy whispering for me to ask some questions. With a break in the conversation, I excused myself for an obvious display of bad manners in not having introduced my good friends. Nick stood beside me as I called roll, beginning with Margaret and continuing down the line. He extended his hand to each woman, adding a short comment to each. Soon it was time for the competition results, and we gathered our dirty plates, tossed them in the trash box, and drifted toward the announcer's tent.

The gentleman in charge of the competition used the stem of his pipe to tap on the aluminum tent pole. "Folks, if I could have your attention, I would like to announce the winners of today's competition."

He began by pinning the longest and most difficult course. Nick stood up tall with arms crossed to pay attention; this was his division. "First place honors, with a time of one hour and forty-six minutes, goes to Nick Heart, Nancy Wall, and Linda Vance of Long Leaf Farm in Greenway." Before moving toward the announcer, Nick reached his arm around my shoulders and gave me a quick, strong hug. Rose happened to be looking in our direction, caught my eye, and offered me a thumbs-up. I smiled, blushed, and continued to clap along with the rest of the competitors. The winning trio stood on either side of the master of ceremonies, holding their blue ribbons and wrapped gifts while the photographer took several snapshots.

With one final handshake, Nick and company returned to where we were standing. He asked if I would hold his ribbon so he could open his gift. It was a handsome set of green marble fox-head bookends. "They'll be perfect in my office," he said, putting them back in the box. *Hmm,* I thought, *he has an office.* But by the looks of his tanned face and somewhat weathered hands, he spent little time there.

The master of the host hunt continued to call out the ribbon winners from first place to sixth in each division, finally arriving at ours. Nick stopped talking to his teammates and stood quietly as the gentleman announced the Gray Fox Division. I had never cared a thing in this world about ribbons, prizes, or trophies, but all of a sudden I wanted to win more than anything. I couldn't explain why exactly, maybe to appear as accomplished a rider as Nick; I didn't know, but at least placing was paramount. The pinning of this competition was not a yardstick of skill; it was sheer luck. I knew all that, but I also knew it was suddenly very important for me to be just as fortunate as he.

"First place and the blue ribbon, with a finish time of only ten minutes off the pace time, goes to the team of Sarah Sams, Betsy Henderson, and Margaret Green of Hadley Falls." Nick grabbed my arm and offered his congratulations. The three of us worked our way to the front, where we, too, had our picture taken with the master of the host hunt. Returning to our group, Nick suggested I open my gift. I told him I would, but after I listened to the pinning of the rest of the division.

The master of ceremonies continued by announcing the second-place team and then saying, "Third-place colors are awarded to the other half of the women from Hadley Falls, with a time of one hour and twenty minutes: Rose Mills, Elizabeth Peters, and Jennifer Hughes." We all began to jump up and down, elated to be in the top three in a field of six or more teams. After a brief celebration, it was time to make our way back to our trailers. It was getting late, and we had a two-hour drive ahead of us.

Nick spoke up, reminding me that I had not yet opened my gift. The ribbon was tied so tightly I couldn't wiggle it free. Nick dug into his pocket and drew out a Swiss Army knife capable of opening that package, cracking a safe, or perhaps changing a tire. Briefly I thought, *Men and their toys, good grief.* Nick slit the ribbon on Betsy and Margaret's packages as well. In all three boxes, buried beneath oceans of tissue paper, was a lovely silver Revere bowl. Nick asked what we would do with them, and I am sure the next two or three minutes were more answers than he had anticipated. As I pressed the wrapping paper between my hands, the wind caught the hunter-green ribbon, sending it to the ground. Nick leaned forward and used his foot to keep the ribbon from blowing away. He grabbed it and, while twisting it around his index finger, said that he wanted to give me a call sometime next week, if that would be acceptable. I said I would like that, adding I was never home before seven thirty in the evening. I offered to give him my telephone number.

He quickly replied, "I don't have anything to write on or with, but I imagine there could only be one Sarah Sams in the Hadley Falls phone book."

Betsy laughed out loud. "In the book it's S. O. Sams. Too funny isn't it—SOS—get it?" She continued, "The *O* stands for O'Neil."

Nick answered, "Sarah O'Neil Sams. What a beautiful name."

"Thanks. O'Neil is my maiden name, and Sams belongs to my ex-husband. For professional reasons," I went on, "I decided not to change my name after the divorce. Google my name, and you'll understand why."

Walking back to the trailers, Betsy and I discussed the odds of Nick actually calling me. She was sure he would, but I took the safer bet that he would not. Nick was tall, good-looking, well mannered, and a horse person. He was quite possibly too good to be true.

"Sorry about bringing up the divorce and the ex-husband, but it just came out. Anyway, I've decided it's not a disease, just a fact. I don't know why I told him I kept my ex-husband's last name for professional reasons, though. What in the hell was that?" I shook my head. "That didn't come out right at all and sounds a bit sketchy. If he does Google my name, won't he be disappointed to realize the truth: I write how-to horse books that few people read. Just shoot me!"

We laughed, and I hunkered down in my seat, flushing. The day had given me a meeting with seemingly the perfect man for me, and I just had to enjoy the bubble of good feelings while I could.

CHAPTER 16

$\mathcal{F}$inally home, dinner from the microwave consumed, and Annie attention satisfied, I took a minute to jot down my thoughts.

> *November 15, 2009*
> *Dear Debby,*
>
> *I refuse to fall victim to wishful thinking, but this man, Nick, might actually give me a call. He could be a wanted felon for all I know, but on the surface, he seems very nice. I was very relaxed today as we shared lunch and conversation.*
>
> *I've also come to a monumental realization: I don't know that want to give up my newfound independence. I'm becoming comfortable with my new life, even after nine o'clock at night. I'm learning who I am and that I can stand alone.*
>
> *I worry I might latch on to someone for all the wrong reasons. I will need to keep my wits about me with Nick, or anyone who might come down the line, to avoid another disaster of the heart.*
>
> *Nick Heart . . . why is he, or is he, single? I think I will have my cousin Alex run a check on him. She's a private inves-*

tigator in DC and would love to find the dirt, if there is any.
Better safe than sorry.
   With all good wishes,
   Sarah

Alex Armstrong was my favorite cousin, and holidays or summer vacations were very special times. Our fathers were brothers, Irish O'Neil's to the bone, from loving a pint of Guinness, hunting and fishing, to dark auburn hair. Family was everything. When we were young, our grandparents' farm outside Iron Springs was the gathering place. They would travel from Newport News, Virginia, for whatever occasion, and stayed at the farm. Because Alex was every bit as horse crazy as I was, my parents allowed me to move to Grammy's while Alex was there during holidays and vacation time. We spent every day at the barn, doing chores, riding, cleaning tack, and having a wonderful time.

Alex answered on the third ring.

"Hi, Alex! It's Sarah."

"If you are calling to rub in the fact that my birthday is next week and how old I'll be, I'm hanging up on you."

"No!" I laughed. "I wouldn't dare. This is going to sound ridiculous, but I need you to run a check on a man I met today at a hunter pace competition. He is very handsome, polite, appears educated, is well mannered, and hopefully isn't married. He said he was going to call me this coming week, and I want to make sure he's . . . okay."

Alex went on to ask questions, from his full name to where is he living. It was really quite interesting to see the professional side of my chocoholic, nail-biting favorite cousin. She didn't make any jokes about my being paranoid; rather she reinforced my desire to know the truth about this man. Her husband had died from a massive heart attack five years before, and she admitted to running a check on anyone who asked her out.

"This has to be our secret," I added. "I'll pay you a dollar at Thanksgiving to buy your silence."

Alex laughed. "My rates are a good bit higher than that."

"I'm sure you deserve every penny. But remember the secrets we've shared over the years, and for the price of one dollar, my lips are forever sealed."

With business out of the way, we continued to chat. Alex promised to have an answer to me on this mystery horse rider sent by the end of the next business day. Before hanging up, I said, "Happy birthday, and I hope fifty-three brings you joy and happiness."

Alex growled her goodbye, but giggled before hanging up.

I asked God for a little help. "Please let Nick be an honest man. If he is married, gay, or lives with his mother, I'll just die. If Alex finds out he is a sex offender, porn star, or on the work-release program, I'll just die. If he is as nice as I think he is and never calls, I'll just die. I know that's a lot of dying, so to avoid my children having to bury their mother long before her time, could you please let this one work out? Thanks. I appreciate your time. Amen!"

While standing at the teachers' mailboxes on Monday morning, George Finch, the chemistry teacher, said, "Well, Sarah, did you find a man at your horse thing this past weekend?"

What a strange thing to say, I thought. "As a matter of fact, George, I did. He's drop-dead gorgeous, can ride like nothing you've ever seen, and I think he thought I was cute. How was your weekend?" George nearly choked on his coffee. "You can get back to me when you catch your breath." I smiled, piling my new mail on top of my already full arms.

A hush fell over the crowd, and the expressions of my fellow staff members spoke volumes. I filled Laura and Molly in at lunch, and apart from cringing over the details of the high jumps I did on horseback, they were eager to hear every detail of a close encounter with Mr. Might-Be-Right.

Mondays were exhausting, especially this one, since the hunter pace was yesterday. The school day was over, but tired or not, I had to go home, change into my riding clothes, and get Annie. Then we'd go to the barn so she could run around and I could organize my stuff from the day before. Rascal would also need a quick ride to stretch him out.

Coming through the front door, I was greeted by a very happy dog and a moaning noise from the fax machine in my office. I put my barn plans on hold long enough to read what Alex had to say.

Hi Sarah,
Here is what I have dug up so far. If I find anything else, I will send it to you ASAP.
1. Nicholas F. Heart was born in Pennsylvania on October 31, 1957
2. Went to Yale, was in ROTC, and did his time in the military after graduation

3. Was married . . . wife divorced him early on. She found someone with a lot of money (she died five years ago from ovarian cancer)

4. No children. He never remarried, but had a serious girlfriend for years . . . I'll see what I can find on her

5. Parents died in a plane crash. He and his older brother (only sibling) inherited family property in different parts of Pennsylvania—Nick's was a farm, guess what kind? Surprise: horses

6. Bought up huge amounts of surrounding acreage, made a fortune in real estate

7. Sold off most everything last spring, bought Long Leaf Farm in Greenway

8. Wants to breed horses and loves to fox hunt

9. Oh, one side note: I almost missed the most interesting bit of information. I checked into his family tree. He has an older cousin from his mother's side who lives in Hadley Falls. He is a chemistry teacher at the high school, a George Finch. Do you know him?

I hope this helps you out, and I hope he calls. Let me know what happens. See you at Sibby's for Thanksgiving.

Love,

Alex

I sat as limp as a dishrag in my computer chair, reading the fax one more time. I could not believe Mr. Finch was Nick's cousin: what were the odds? Suddenly, I realized Nick must have had some sort of prior knowledge about me. "Holy conspiracy, Annie," I said aloud. "I have been one-upped. Oh my God." I gasped. "This morning at the mail boxes—what did I say?" George Finch would hereafter be referred to as the mole. Excluding Laura and Molly, I would need to be careful what I said to everyone at school. But it was clear that Nick and I had a lot in common, both good and bad, and trusting in others might well be an issue for both of us.

But I was jumping the gun. He hadn't even called yet, and I was worrying about issues our relationship might have. "Come on, Annie, let's go to the barn." She didn't need to be asked twice.

CHAPER 17

Clambering through the front door for the second time that afternoon, Annie and I were treated to the aroma of a pot roast that had been cooking in the Crock-Pot since early morning. I lifted the lid and gave everything a stir, realizing that I hadn't even noticed that wonderful smell earlier, I'd been so overwhelmed by Alex's fax. Giving my head a gentle shake, I looked in the pantry and grabbed a loaf of French bread. Within twenty minutes, dinner was served.

My home phone rang just as I was sitting down to enjoy my meal. It took three rings before I was able to locate it buried beneath a dishtowel, and one more for me to push talk. "Hello?" I said, half expecting the person to be gone.

"Hello, may I please speak to Sarah?" asked a man with a pleasant voice.

"This is she."

"Hi Sarah, this is Nick—Nick Heart—from the hunter pace yesterday. I hope I'm not disturbing you."

"No, actually, I just sat down to dinner, but don't worry," I replied, blinking fast. I was stunned; I hadn't even allowed myself to hope he might call before Wednesday. "I can talk and still enjoy my meal."

"Oh—what's for supper?"

"Yankee pot roast with carrots, peas, onions, and potatoes. Oh, and French bread."

"Sounds delicious," Nick said.

Without thinking, I said, "It's fabulous—too bad you're not here to enjoy it with me."

His response was totally unexpected. "Actually, I'm in Hadley Falls right now. I came to see my cousin. Are you still sure about that dinner invitation?"

"O-of course," I replied with a bit of a stammer. "Where are you now? I live in the historic downtown area, which can be very confusing, especially at night."

"I'm at the corner of Westbury and Long."

"You're only about two blocks away," I said.

With Nick on his way, I tried to suppress any sense of panic. *Me and my big mouth.* Luckily my house was in order, as I'd cleaned the night before, and it smelled divine thanks to the roast. I, however, was a wreck with dirty riding clothes and purple hoof-treatment stains on my hands. This would be the second time in as many days that Nick had seen me filthy, but at least the clothes explained why I was in disarray. I reminded myself *what you see is what you get.* Here was my chance to embrace the unexpected, and I made no effort to rectify the outfit, though I did brush my teeth and my hair.

The doorbell rang. It had been a long time since I had had a gentleman caller, and I nearly passed out on the way to the door. Inhaling to my toes, I put on my very best smile and unlocked the deadbolt. There he stood, immaculate, very handsome, and taller than I remembered.

For the first few seconds, it was a game of who goes first in finding something to say. I had a habit of speaking at a very rapid pace when I was nervous, so I consciously tried to slow down. Sadly, it was a bit too drawn and resulted in an extended syllable. "Hiiiiii . . . . please come in. Let me take your coat."

Walking into the kitchen, Nick saw my partially eaten supper and offered his apologies for having interrupted my meal. I quickly told him it was not a problem, and I was delighted to have company for dinner. My kitchen had an island bar in the middle, where I always ate unless I was entertaining. I served his plate and gestured for him to have a seat. We engaged in small talk about the competition, my house, Annie, and my afternoon at the barn. I reminded him that I had said I was never home before seven thirty. He smiled, calling me a barn rat, which is actually a nice thing to say to someone who loves to ride.

I cleared the table after he finished his second helping, placed the dishes in the white farm sink, and asked if he would like dessert.

"Yes, if it's that apple pie I see cooling."

Holding the pie server in my hand, I replied, "It is, and, if you ask nicely, you may also have vanilla ice cream."

"Did you make that too?" he asked with a hint of sarcasm and a smile.

"Actually, yes, I did. My mother gave me an electric freezer last Christmas, and I love to make homemade ice cream—it keeps me off the streets. I canned the apple pie filling too. Look out Martha Stewart. One Saturday, every fall, I can apple pie filling—what a mess but it's such fun. Easy and yummy, just dump it in a deep dish pie shell, lattice the top, bake for twenty five minutes and voila—instant dessert—so what will it be: pie, with or without?"

"Definitely with," he answered.

"Would you like a cup of coffee to go with your pie?"

"If it's not too much trouble, I'd love one," Nick said with a smile. The smile that couldn't help but dazzle me. He asked about a few local riding facilities, their policies, and their rates for boarding & lessons. I told him what I knew, but added that it was dated information. My youngest daughter had ridden at a local barn before she went to college, but now that she was grown, I was out of the loop on lesson fees and availability.

Suddenly, curiosity got the better of me. I stopped in the middle of my dessert and said, "How is it you just happened to be in Hadley Falls tonight, and just two blocks from my house? I happen to know that George Finch lives way out on Grover Church Road, which is at least twenty minutes from here."

Startled, Nick nearly choked on his coffee, "I asked yesterday if I could call, and you said yes."

"Yes, and I meant it. But you didn't call until you were nearly here. That's not exactly what I was expecting," I said, interrupting.

"I've gotten the cart before the horse, haven't I?" Nick asked. "But I can explain. I was leaving George's house, thought about you, and asked if he knew where you lived. He gave me directions, but I made a wrong turn somewhere after the bridge. I remembered the SOS conversation and dialed information. Have I done something wrong? Hey, wait a minute—I never said my cousin's name. How did you know it was George Finch?"

"I—well—I'm just thrown a bit off center. I apologize for

barking. I'm as transparent as cellophane, and you can read my face like a book when I've done anything that's not quite on the up-and-up."

He raised his eyebrows, and I was fairly sure he was fighting a smile, but he waited for me to continue.

"Confession has always been good for my soul, so here goes. When I finish you will probably think I'm insane and vow never to see me again."

"Well, this is getting interesting," he said, filling his cup to the brim and nodding for me to continue.

"Perhaps, but anyway, I teach with George Finch, and I think you knew that. In fact, I believe you knew about me in advance." I checked his face for a reaction, but if there was anything there beyond the mildest surprise, I couldn't see it, so I went on. "I'm not innocent of a bit of spying either. My cousin Alex is a private investigator, and I called her last night and asked that she check you out. The last item on her list of nine was the biggest surprise of all—George. I feel weird now that I did that. I just want us to be honest and put our cards on the table, so we have no ghosts in the closet, so to speak. You are free to leave if this is too much."

Staring at me over the lip of his cup, he said, "Are you finished?"

I thought about it for a second before nodding. "Yes."

"My turn," he said. "I should've just called you like we agreed, but I was close by, and I wanted to see you. I hope I haven't scared you off. As for the spying issue, assuming your cousin did her job and earned her fee, I don't need to tell you anything except that George called about a week ago and asked for some help with a piece of property he owns. I told him that I would be more than happy to help, but I couldn't come until today. I mentioned that I was going to a hunter pace over the weekend."

I had a feeling I was about to wish I'd held my tongue.

"George jumped right in, telling me about the art teacher at his school, saying that she was nuts about horses, and he'd heard her say that she was going to a hunter pace. He went on to say you were single, very tall, and very pretty. He added that he'd try and get the name of your barn, so maybe I could find you in the crowd."

I felt the color rising in my cheeks.

"He was very complimentary about you, said you were a gifted teacher, and an asset to the faculty, but that you are also the definition of an art teacher, which to him means that you wear weird clothes and have totally unorthodox teaching methods."

"He's not wrong," I admitted with no small amount of pride.

"To be honest, I find your . . . let's call it enthusiasm to find out more about me flattering, and somewhat refreshing. Honesty is becoming a lost trait in humankind, and I think perhaps you, Sarah Sams, are truly one of a kind. Does that explanation suffice?"

"Uh—yes, I think so," I answered, trying to breathe. "I also think we need to share cell phone numbers. It will make things easier, don't you think?"

"Absolutely," Nick said, holding his phone and putting on his readers. We exchanged phones and added our numbers.

Nick pushed back from the bar, saying this was the best meal he'd eaten in a long time, but he had to be getting home. He offered to stay and help me clean up, but I assured him it was not necessary. At the front door he paused, saying, "Oh, I almost forgot: thanks for the compliment. George told me that you said I was drop-dead gorgeous, and you're right: I do think you're cute. What'd you say we clear the air about our investigating into each other's pasts over dinner Saturday night? I'll pick you up around seven o'clock?"

I must have just stood there gaping like a fool, because in a minute Nick said, "Well, are you?"

"Am I what?" I asked.

"Are you free for dinner Saturday night?"

"Yes! Yes, I am, and I would love to go out to dinner."

Nick suggested I choose the restaurant and make a reservation for seven thirty. He said he was going to Virginia tomorrow to look at some horses and would give me a call on Wednesday.

I offered the standard, "Sounds good!" and asked that he be careful driving home.

Tossing his hand in the air, he thanked me again for dinner, adding, "In case your cousin left this out of her report: peach is my favorite flavor of ice cream. I'll see you Saturday night."

As I watched him drive away, I whispered. "I certainly hope so."

November 16, 2009
Dear Debby,

Nick came to dinner tonight, and his presence added a level of warmth and excitement to my home that I realize has been sorely missing. The fact that he thought about me and coming to see me on his own just one day after we met is flattering. I cannot allow myself to get too excited about this man for fear of disappointment.

He didn't seem to be at all upset that I ran his name past my cousin. Nick confessed to a conversation with his cousin George—a cousin conspiracy.

He said I was cute. No one has told me I was cute in years. Well, Miss Madge, the elderly woman who lives next door does, but that is just because I mow her yard.

With all good wishes,

Sarah

Sliding into bed, I knew there was no point in my trying to go to sleep without sharing my news. Margaret goes to bed very early, so Betsy got the call. She answered on the second ring, and I launched into a short review of my evening.

"What are you going to wear?" Betsy asked. "You haven't had an actual first date since Jimmy Carter was in office. We'll go shopping so you can buy something special, including matching underwear."

"Matching underwear is ridiculous, and a waste of good money." I said. "We can talk more tomorrow, but I just had to tell you the news tonight."

Wiggling the comforter up around my nose, and closing my eyes, I thought, *Matching underwear—ha! I've never had matching underwear. Well, I guess it might be nice.*

CHAPTER 18

Wednesday morning found me wide awake and wondering if Nick would keep his word about the promised call. Annie and I finished our mile walk shortly after sunrise in the bone-chilling cold. It was heavenly to be back inside. My cell phone rang just as I was coming out of my top layer of clothes. I retrieved the phone with one hand and offered a quick hello while shaking the remaining sleeve with the other.

"Good morning, Sarah. This is Nick. Is everything all right? You sound winded."

"Yes, I'm fine. Would you hold on for just a second, though?" I asked. After freeing my remaining limb, I returned the receiver to my ear. "Sorry for that; I was trapped in my coat. What's up?"

"I wanted to catch you before you went to school. I bought two horses yesterday, and they're scheduled to arrive just after lunch. I'll be busy with that and didn't want you to think I'd forgotten. I'm sure you're going to the barn after school, so I hope now's not too inconvenient. Have you decided on a restaurant?"

"I haven't made a reservation, but there's a wonderful Greek restaurant in the heart of old downtown. It has terrific food, a fun atmosphere, and overlooks the river. It's casual, but it's pretty.

Does that sound interesting?" I asked.

"Excellent choice," Nick said, adding I should go ahead and make the reservation. He said he'd call on Friday to make sure everything was still on go.

Before I could harness my tongue, I asked where he had gone in Virginia, and what kind of horses he'd purchased. Not that I had said anything wrong, it was simply none of my business and perhaps a bit too personal. "I'm sorry," I apologized quickly for my obvious meddling. "It's just that I know a good many horse people in Virginia, and we may possibly have some friends in common."

"No need to apologize. I can talk horses all day. I bought two Thoroughbreds and have first rights to an eight-year-old Dutch Warmblood. The Thoroughbreds are for two of my boarders, and I think the Warmblood has great fox-hunting potential."

Glancing at the clock, I realized time had gotten away from me, and I was going to be late for work. Nick was very under-standing and said he hoped I had a good day.

Just before hanging up, he said, "Oh, you asked where I bought the horses. Have you ever heard of Moss Creek Farm? The owner, Roger, and I go back to our Yale days."

I was momentarily unable to speak. "Oh my gosh—you're kidding! I've known Susan and Roger for years. My buddies and I go to Susan's summer horse camp every year. What a small world! Put that on our list of things to talk about over dinner Saturday night."

Nick chuckled, saying, "You must be one of the Hadley Falls Rowdy Girls. Susan has a picture hanging on the wall in her office of six women standing side by side, holding the reins of their horses, with a plaque that reads, 'Rowdy Girls.' I met all six of you this past Sunday, didn't I?"

"Yes, you did," I said, "but we really aren't that bad."

"Remember, before you say another word," Nick cautioned, "I met and had lunch with all of you just four days ago. I believe your title was perhaps earned, and I'm sure well deserved."

"Well, my goodness," I said with urgency and an extra Southern twang, "would you just look at the time, I am going to be so late to school. Thanks for calling me this morning, Nick. That was very thoughtful, and I will be sure to make our reservation today during my lunch break."

Hanging up, I thought *Holy Moses. He knows Susan, went to school with Roger, and saw the picture. I would be late, but I had to write this down.*

November 18, 2009
Dear Debby,

I've decided to purchase matching underwear. Aside from accidentally turning my hair orange fall semester of my freshman year in college, this is possibly the silliest thing I have ever done, but who knows, maybe my friends are on to something. Margaret said I had to shop at a boutique and was forbidden to buy underwear that came three to a package. She also said it could not be white and had to match the color of my outfit. I think I like the idea, and it's a bit exciting, but I will never tell them that.

Nick called this morning and we have a mutual friend in Virginia. Remember Susan my summer camp riding instructor, and the lady who owns Moss Creek Farm? You'll never believe this—Nick and her husband went to college together.

With all good wishes,
Sarah

CHAPTER 19

We would be out of school in a week for Thanksgiving, and I had forgotten about the annual excursion of the freshman class to the Raleigh Civic Center to enjoy Dickens's *A Christmas Carol.* Their absence left me with two free periods back-to-back on Wednesday morning. I had finished organizing my students' pieces for the annual Holiday in Art show just the day before, so I decided to take advantage of my free time to deliver their work to the county office. As I was backing out of my assigned parking space my cell phone rang; it was Emma.

"Hi, Mom. Can you talk?"

"Usually no. You know this is during my school day. Are you at your office? Are you okay?" I said. "What's wrong?"

"Yes, I'm at my desk. I just took a break to give you a call," she said. Emma didn't care a thing in this world about horses. She thought they were pretty but that's as far as it went. Emma was my educator child, and had taught English right out of college while getting her master's in administration. "You know we've got that big university fund-raising event this coming weekend, and I'm up to my eyeballs in paperwork. But I just needed to talk to you. Speaking of absences, why *did* you answer? Aren't you at school?"

"I have some free time this morning, so I happen to be on my way to deliver twelve pieces of work for a student art show. So what's wrong?"

"Well, Scott talked to his mom this morning. She is insisting that we spend Thanksgiving at their house. He won't listen to anything I say. He says we have to go because we never spend any time with his family. Um, could that be because his father drinks too much, his mother can't cook, and they hate dogs? He says he's their only son, blah, blah. So, I just wanted to let you know I'm going to miss Thanksgiving with you for the first time in twenty-six years. I am *not* happy about this."

"My precious Emma, you are so dramatic," I said with a chuckle. "It will be fine, and you'll have a great time. Your sister can't come either; she has to work. I'm sad about that too, but it's just the give and take of life. Annie and I will go to your grandmother's, cook Thanksgiving dinner, and spend the night."

"Okay," Emma said. "If you're sure you'll be okay. But I refuse to give an inch on Christmas!"

"I wouldn't let you. Oh, and . . . speaking of dinner," which we no longer were, but I had to get this in somehow, "I have some news of my own: I have a date this coming Saturday night."

"Mom!"

"Yes, that's right, with a very nice man from Greenway. I met him at the hunter pace last weekend."

Emma stammered, "A date—what kind of a date?"

"A date date. You know, where a man comes to your door, helps you on with your coat, you get into his car and go somewhere? He's already been to the house for dinner." I could practically see Emma sputtering seven hundred miles away. "His name is Nick Heart, and let me see . . . he's tall, six feet or better, very nice-looking. He bought Long Leaf Farm in Greenway. Oh, and another interesting tidbit: Nick is Mr. Finch's cousin. You remember Mr. Finch, your chemistry teacher? Anyway, I need to hang up—the traffic is terrible, and I can't miss my turn."

"Okaaaay," Emma said. "Well, I guess I'll call you later. By the way, saying that a gentleman helps you on with your coat is cute. This isn't 1962, but it's cute."

I was positive she would call her sister the second we hung up, and that Sidney would call me shortly. Sidney was an on-location junior reporter for a TV station in Raleigh. She dealt well with factual information and was seldom emotional. My having a date would likely elicit a *I hope you have a good time.* She had ridden and shown horses nearly all her life, so she would surely find the fact that Nick owned Long Leaf Farm to be the most interesting piece of the news.

With the artwork delivered and checked off by the curator, I worked my way back to my car. Before backing out, I rummaged around in my purse, found my cell phone, and saw I had a message. "Hi, rowdy girl, this is Nick. The horses will be here early, and Susan is sending you a present. Can you come to Greenway this afternoon after school? You'll need to wear your riding clothes. Call me."

Nick picked up on the second ring, "Hi, Sarah. I'm glad you got my message. I am sworn to secrecy about the gift, and Susan threatened me with my life if I can't get you here this afternoon. So, will you please say yes and spare me a terrible tongue lashing?"

"Yes, I think I can be there around four thirty. Don't I even get a hint? And may I bring Annie?" I asked.

"No, you may not have a hint, but yes to your bringing Annie. I'll cook your dinner this time but don't expect much. How do you feel about peanut butter?"

"Peanut butter is fine," I said. "You know this will drive me crazy. Come on, just one hint. I swear I'll never tell Susan."

"Nope," Nick said, stubbornly. "I'll see you this afternoon."

Wow, another dinner date with Nick, and he's cooking. How romantic, I thought. I don't think I've ever had a man cook for me, peanut butter or otherwise.

$\mathcal{I}$ couldn't imagine what Susan might possibly be sending my way. We had been friends for years, but gift giving for no reason was a new twist.

Flying in the front door after school, I dropped my purse on the bench, patted Annie, and scooted her out into the backyard. I quickly called Margaret and asked if she would take care of Rascal this afternoon. We did that sort of thing for each other, but usually with a little heads-up. She asked if I had changed into my riding clothes.

"Are you going to start that underwear conversation again?" I asked.

"No," Margaret said, "but if you haven't changed your clothes, why not give it a try? At least the colors could match."

"Fine, I'll see what I can do. Kiss Rascal, please, and give him extra hay. I'll call you on my way home. I expect for you to still be awake, even if it is after nine o'clock," I said.

I pulled out my best pair of black riding pants, a matching turtleneck with no holes, and a hunter-green sweater. Just before putting on my breeches, I glanced in my lingerie drawer. Sitting right on top was my black sports bra. I took it as a sign and dug around to find a pair of black underpants.

Then I was on my way to a man's house to collect a surprise gift, ride horses, and have dinner on a school night. I smiled, thinking, *Perhaps I really do have a free spirit. Rose would be very proud.*

Turning into the driveway of Long Leaf Farm, I could see Susan's trailer in the distance and a group of people milling around. I broke out in a panicky sweat—*this is really happening.* Nick was waving and walking in my direction, Annie's head was hanging out the window, and I was hyperventilating. I had about forty more yards of asphalt to get myself together.

Just over Nick's shoulder, I spied Deacon walking the most beautiful paint horse I had even seen. He was brown and white with just a whisper of black in his mane and tail. It was strange to see Deacon somewhere other than Moss Creek Farm.

Nick motioned for me to park up near the barn just beyond Susan's trailer. Deacon threw up his hand to wave and smiled as I drove by, and I returned the gesture. With nervous tension, I tittered, thinking, *Calm down, Sarah. You can do this: you have on your power underwear.* With one deep breath, I got Annie and myself out of the car and began to walk in Nick's direction.

Leading the surprisingly calm horse, Deacon walked toward me. I extended my arm, and the gorgeous paint softly nuzzled my hand.

"Hi, Sarah. How are you today?" asked Deacon.

"I'm fine! I hope you are. Look at this guy! Where did you find this handsome horse? I don't remember seeing him at Moss Creek."

Deacon looked in Nick's direction. "He was never at Moss

Creek. Uh, Susan found him somewhere."

"Found him—what do you mean found him? Was he just walking down the road?"

Nick took over the conversation and the lead rope. "Sarah, the first part of this story is going to upset you. I don't know you that well yet, but I do know you well enough to be sure of your heart when it comes to animals."

That was a compliment, but I was afraid of what was coming.

"Susan truly did find this horse about a month ago in the middle of Butler Woods while fox hunting. He was grazing in a clearing as the hunt flew by. Naturally, she stopped and checked the horse, then called Deacon to bring the trailer. Roger went to work trying to find any information about the horse and possibly his owner. Dr. James came to the farm that day and did a complete physical on him."

I interrupted, "Well, what happened? Was he healthy, did he vet out? Who does the horse belong to?"

"I'm getting to that part. Anyway, Buddy, that's what Susan named him, passed the vet exam, with only a few minor exceptions. He has a tattoo on the inside of his upper lip, and after a bit of digging, Roger was able to find the owner's identity. He also discovered, or should I say uncovered, the reason the horse was in the meadow. The owner owed money all over the place, and Buddy was the only thing of value he had left. So he dumped him in the middle of nowhere in hopes of collecting on the insurance. We understand from the detective who took the deposition that the owner didn't want the horse to die, and just hoped he could survive in the wild until someone found him."

"What on earth? Was he hoping that whoever found the

horse would pretend it was like finding a puppy or a litter of kittens, and wouldn't think to alert the authorities? I think I might be sick." I clutched my stomach. "At least there was plenty of grass and that tiny stream runs close by there. But how could someone do that? What is the matter with people? Why didn't he just sell the horse?"

"I don't know—possibly overwhelming desperation," Nick said, sitting me down on the tack trunk. "Remember, much of this is third-hand information, and the investigation is ongoing. But apparently the horse was worth more stolen than sold. Anyway, it will all be worked out. The local facility doesn't have the space required to care for a horse, but they knew Susan and gave her temporary guardianship. For whatever reason, Buddy is unhappy at MCF. I have asked to purchase the horse. So Susan and I talked to the authorities and offered a solution. After I signed some paperwork and they ran a background check, they've agreed to let us bring him here. That's where you come in."

"Me? What do you mean *me*?" I asked.

"Susan knows you, how you ride, and the way you work with horses. Just look at him: he hasn't taken his eyes off you since we started walking. He has animation in his step that wasn't there before you got here. I know this is a lot to digest, but I need—no Buddy needs—for you to give this a try." Nick handed me the lead rope.

"You're giving me entirely too much credit," I said. "It's probably that he likes the energy of this place." Turning to Buddy, I placed the palm of my hand between his eyes and rubbed gently up and down. "You sweet boy, I am so sorry all of that happened to you. It'll be all right; you have to trust me. Let's go for a spin and see how we do." Looking in Nick's direction, I asked if Buddy had come with any tack, and if we could ride together.

Nick's smile widened as he directed me toward Buddy's stall and belongings. "Don't smile just yet—this is far from a done deal where I'm concerned. There's a lot that needs working out—the biggest of which is money. My budget can't afford to board, vet, and shoe *two* horses. Rascal will never accept my loving another horse, and I would never break his heart, so they couldn't be at the same barn. And it's all I can do to ride one horse on a regular basis, much less two."

Tossing his head back in laughter, Nick said, "Susan and I have been back and forth on the phone all day. We have everything worked out. All we need is for you to agree to help Buddy, and I think you have. So let's ride!"

"Wait just a minute," I said. "I still have some questions, and they need answers. Rascal is number one, and money is number two. I fall in love with animals on sight, and, unless he throws me off, I'll be completely hooked once we ride. So before we go any further, please tell me how everything is 'worked out.'"

"Buddy will live here at Long Leaf Farm, and I'll pay all of his expenses. We'll set up a schedule for you to hopefully bring him back around, and maybe Rascal will get a few days off during the week. For example, you could come here every Tuesday and Thursday and maybe Saturday or Sunday. It's only a forty-minute drive, so that's not too bad, and with the indoor ring, weather's not an issue. How does that sound to you?" Nick asked.

I was still skeptical, but I wanted so much for it to work. "Well, I'd say that sounds like a fairly good plan," I said. "But it's not written in stone. I'll need time to think about how this will affect Rascal. But for now, let's ride."

Walking into the indoor ring, I led Buddy to the center and allowed him a few minutes to take a look around and smell the dirt. I had been very fortunate in my life to have learned from some of the best horsewomen around, and Buddy would benefit from that piece of my training. Nick stood with his horse at the gate and watched me work without saying a word. At first, I was very conscious of his presence, but after a few minutes it was just Buddy and me in a world of our own.

My traditional groundwork warm-up was a type of yoga for horses, and once he understood what I was asking, Buddy did an excellent job. "Good boy," I said with a pat on the neck. I led him over to the mounting block, tightened the girth, and lowered my stirrups. "Okay, big guy, let's see what you've got," I said, placing my left foot squarely in the iron.

Nick brought his horse Chance into the ring, and directly behind him were the two ladies from the hunter pace. "Sarah, you remember Nancy Wall and Linda Vance from last Sunday?"

"Yes, I do! It's good to see you again. It's also good for Buddy. He'll remember your horses tomorrow when they go out," I said, as if presenting a new student to my class.

For the next thirty minutes, we all worked on flat work, and Buddy softened into a very willing horse. From the corner of my eye, I saw Deacon leaning on the railing just to the right of the gate. I trotted over and asked if he would mind setting up a few jumps.

Deacon nodded and walked over to a pile of poles and standards. While rummaging through the options, Deacon said he'd seen Buddy go just once, and it was terrible at best. It was right after the horse had been found, which might have had something to do with his poor performance. "Please be careful," he said.

With a few small verticals and a medium cross rail, we were set to go. "Are you sure you want to jump Buddy on his first day?" Deacon asked, his eyebrows knitted with concern.

"It doesn't matter what day we give it our first try, so it might as well be today," I said. "These jumps are so small I don't think he'll hesitate to pop right over."

And he didn't. After about thirty minutes of nearly flawless jumping on Buddy's part, I decided we were finished for the day. He had earned his supper and a handful of carrots. I dropped my irons, and we walked back to the in-gate on a loose rein, my legs dangling alongside. Buddy knew he had been a good boy, and my posture reinforced his performance.

Nancy and Linda worked to clean their mounts, and with a quick and friendly goodbye, they were gone.

Since it was a new barn to me, I wasn't quite as efficient. Finally, with Nick's help, all my chores were taken care of, and Buddy was settled. I turned to Nick and said, "I'm starving— bring on the peanut butter."

"I think it should be ready," he said. "Give me one minute to check on two things in the office, and we'll walk to the house."

"Okay," I said, thinking, *Ready—what does he mean ready? It's peanut butter.*

CHAPTER 21

Nick's house was very old; my guess was it had stood on that property for at least two hundred years. The Georgian Revival style was impressive, with double chimneys climbing up each end of the center two-story section and a wing on either side, the visual symmetry helped to balance the home from the towering roof to the ground. I was fairly certain the kitchen was an addition. Back when the house was built, the cooking would have been done in a building separate from the main house.

I gave Annie a whistle, then paused to appreciate the unusual and eerie pink-and-gray sunset. My girl came running, and flying up beside her was a huge, hairy black dog with a very sweet face. "Goodness, what a big dog!" I said, finding my balance.

Nick laughed and introduced us.

"Well, hello, Caesar," I said holding my hands on both sides of his face.

Caesar returned the greeting by licking the full length of my face, then trotted off to catch up with his newfound friend.

Wiping the canine smooch from my face, I laughed, and said the hairy emperor was a very sweet giant of a dog. "Exactly what breed is Caesar?" I asked.

"A Newfoundland," Nick said, adding his apologies for the zealous, wet dog lick. Reaching for the handle of the screened door, Nick placed his hand in the small of my back, suggesting I go first. A warm shiver ran the length of my spine from his touch, and I could feel a Mona Lisa smile come over my face.

As we walked across the screened-in back porch, and to the back door of the house, Nick said, "I hope you're hungry. It was decided that anything to do with peanut butter was not a fair exchange for the dinner you offered me the other night. I can't cook worth a lick, so I hope you don't mind, but I had our dinner brought in." Nick said while we removed our tall boots and left them on the porch.

"Mind? Of course I don't mind," I said. "I think it's very thoughtful that you cared enough to go to the trouble."

Stepping sock-footed into the kitchen, I was greeted by an elegantly set table complete with crisp linens, silver flatware, and a single candle surrounded by greenery. I stood momentarily frozen by the beauty of the table and the unexpected surprise of such a treat. "Nick, this is absolutely lovely," I said. "I don't know what to say, other than that I am obviously seriously under-dressed."

Nick smiled and offered me a seat by pulling out my chair. "I can't allow you to think I did any of this on my own," he said with the grin of a schoolboy. "Nancy and Linda were at the barn this morning. Actually, they're here most every weekday morning— they don't work."

"Anyway, those two overheard me invite you to dinner, and also my suggestion of peanut butter. Well, they tore into me the second I hung up, and insisted I call River's Bend in Hadley Falls.

The meal was delivered about thirty minutes ago, and Nancy and Linda set the table for me. That's the real reason they were here this afternoon. I must say it is very pretty, and there's no way I could have pulled this off."

"River's Bend is wonderful, and I happen to be good friends with the owner," I said. "You met her—Jennifer. She's one of the Rowdy Girls," I added, instantly putting my hand over my mouth and blushing.

Nick's face ignited. "I am so glad you brought that up—I was hoping there would be time to address how you ladies came to be so named."

I tried to change the subject by suggesting we not allow our catered dinner to get cold. I told Nick it really wasn't at all what he thought, just a funny camp thing. He ignored my lame attempt to brush the subject aside, and went on to say he had all night for me to fess up.

"All right, but you need to keep an open mind," I said, moving my salad of fresh greens around the plate. "It was the first year we went to camp as a group. Betsy and Rose had gone for several years prior, but all six of us began as a team seven years ago. We decided to break the "early to bed" rule and go to the local steakhouse for dinner the first night. Susan and Roger decided to come along as well. Susan told us to go ahead and they would meet us there.

"The restaurant was packed for a Monday night. We threaded our way around the bar area, where a group of men in cowboy hats stood around a mechanical bull, gawking at the scantily clad young woman trying to ride it. We all laughed and wondered just how much alcohol one would need to ingest to give that a try. Well, I don't drink, but I said I had always wanted to try it and would consider taking a turn.

"I asked our barely-old-enough-to-vote server to explain the rules for riding the bull. She rolled her eyes at the idea that six women somewhere between ancient and the grave might consider running the risk of breaking a hip or worse. It was her facial expression that sent me around the bend, and I stood up and announced that we were all going to mosey on over to the corral and give it a try."

"Oh, no," Nick said, already laughing.

"Oh, yes," I said. "Just you wait. We stood up and walked six abreast, like we were headed for a shootout at high-noon. The Bonanza wannabes in the bar gaped as they realized we were serious. From the corner of my eye I saw Susan and Roger coming in the front door of the restaurant. Susan howled, and yelled, 'Sarah, you go first!' I shouted back, 'Why do I always have to go first?'"

"Do you always have to go first?" Nick interrupted. "And if so, why?"

"I do. I'm the official sacrificial lamb of the group," I answered. "It has absolutely nothing to do with my abilities and everything to do with those of my horse. Rascal really will jump anything. Anyway, Susan yelled, 'Because I said so, that's why. Now get on that thing and ride!' So I swung my leg over the back and wiggled to find my comfort spot. A very eager young man helped me secure my right hand and raised my left arm over my head. I yelled, 'Let 'er rip!' and we were in motion. It might have taken all the leg I had, but I managed to stay on. It was totally out of character for me, but hell's bells, it was fun, and I was proud of myself. Everybody had a turn, and we all stayed on."

Nick smiled as I told my story. With both elbows resting on the table and his fingers intertwined, he lifted his chin and said, "I'm sure there's more. Keep going."

"There is," I said taking a sip of my water. "So after we completed six almost-perfect rides, in that we didn't fall off, the crowd stood in amazement as the owner of the steakhouse presented us with the handsome plaque. We had no idea that Monday night was host to the official 'Rowdy Girl' contest, and we had crashed the party. All the local yee-haw girls were pissed beyond definition that a bunch of over-forty prissy equestrians had taken the title."

"That's really funny," Nick said, sitting back in his chair.

"It was hilarious. The next day, at the end of the morning's lesson, we were standing in a row for a camp photo. Deacon worked to organize us with our horses according to height. When everything was to Susan's liking, she took some pictures. None of us thought a thing about the picture or the plaque until the next day, when there they hung on the wall behind Susan's desk. And that is how we became known as the Rowdy Girls."

Nick looked at me from across the table, his blue eyes flashing, and said, "I wish I could have been a fly on the wall. I bet those cowboys never expected any of you to stay on for a second."

"It really was fun. I'm certain that machine was nowhere near even half throttle, but the cowboys sure clapped for us. On our way back to the table, one young cowgirl made some snide remark in our direction, and it took all I had to contain myself. Ordinarily I would have volleyed back, but we were carrying the plaque, not to mention greatly outnumbered, so I chose the high road."

He took my hand and brushed it lightly with his thumb, saying he was glad I had escaped the wrath of the angry cowgirl. It was hard work trying to maintain my composure as he stroked my hand, which I had forgotten could be so sensitive, with such a soft and gentle touch. I was thankful to be sitting down and prayed he didn't realize his touch had reduced me to butter.

Nick removed our salad plates and replaced them with a beautiful dinner of Cornish game hens, cranberry stuffing, wild rice, and green beans, which was absolutely delicious—of course. We took our time enjoying the food and conversation about our past jobs, families, college, and naturally, horses.

Annie and Caesar had taken their places on the floor beside our chairs. Caesar barked at the sound of something bouncing off the tin porch roof. His furious bark broke the silence and the grasp of Nick's hand to mine, and made me jump. Nick chuckled while asking Caesar to quiet down and offered that it was most probably a limb from a tree or a squirrel darting from one place to another.

"I really do need to be getting home," I said, finishing my piece of chocolate cake. "I've had a wonderful time. Dinner was marvelous, and the company delightful. But I am a working girl, and the clock doesn't lie."

Nick stood to take the back of my chair. "I hate to see you go, but I do understand." He put my hand in his as he pulled back my seat.

I was grateful for the attention, and especially for the steadying hand. This entire evening had thrown me off balance in more ways than one. "Thanks again for dinner . . . it was an unexpected treat. Let me help you with the dishes, and I'd also like to say goodbye to Buddy," I said, hoping Nick couldn't detect my nervousness.

"I'm glad you enjoyed it, and no to the dishes. I'll take care of them later. Nancy and Linda will be happy to know you were impressed with their idea. I really do think you are worth more than peanut butter—I just can't cook," Nick said. "Now let's take the dogs for a quick run to the barn and check on Buddy."

As we put on our coats and made our way from the kitchen to the back porch, I thought about Nick's gentle touch and how wonderful it was to have a flutter in my stomach . . . and other places. Placing his hand in the small of my back, Nick once again guided me through the back door and onto the porch.

"Ack, what's that?" I asked zipping up my tall boots and looking out over the landscape of Long Leaf Farm.

"Oh, it's snowing! Looks like about two inches so far. The weather forecasters were right and wrong on this one."

"Good grief," I said. "I forgot all about that—and you're right. This morning they said 'the possibility of snow' but I thought not until after midnight. I need to be headed home."

"Do you know how to drive in the snow?" Nick asked.

"Actually, I do," I replied with pride, and perhaps too much zeal. "I went to college in Boone, North Carolina—Appalachian State University—Go Mountaineers! Sorry", I blushed. "That was entirely too loud."

"That's okay," Nick said. "I'm proud of my school too. Go Bulldogs! Just in case you don't know, his name is Handsome Dan."

I was grateful for my tall boots and warm riding clothes while we walked from the house to the barn. Annie and Caesar bounded across the closest paddock in sheer delight with the fresh pallet of new-fallen snow under their feet. Nick and I walked next to each other to the barn. The light from the aisle cast amber shadows across the zinc-white ground cover. From a distance we could hear the nicker of each horse as they welcomed us into their space.

With a rub over each of Buddy's eyes, I promised to be back as soon as the weather permitted. Nick extended his hand, and I laced my fingers in between his as we walked toward my car. Somewhere along the way, I broke the silence with a whistle to Annie. From the far pasture we could see two silhouettes streaking in our direction.

Nick opened the car door for me. I paused for a moment and thanked him again for the afternoon of riding Buddy, and the wonderful dinner. Smiling, Nick wrapped his arms around me and gave me a kiss that buckled my knees. Slowly taking his lips from mine, he added a soft peck. "Wow," he said.

"Wow is right," I said tucking my hair behind my ears.

Nick opened the back door and allowed Annie to take her place in the back seat. After I was situated, he leaned down and insisted that I give him a call when I was safely home, and to please call him if I had any trouble along the way.

As I drove down the lane, I had the most wonderful feeling of happiness and serenity. My car fishtailed a bit as I accelerated onto the highway, which brought me back to reality. I also remembered having promised Margaret a phone call on my way home. After only two rings, Margaret was on the other end of the conversation, worried about my drive home, and excited to hear all about my adventure. I told her this would need to be short and sweet, but that I had had a wonderful time, a great ride on a new horse, and felt that Nick and I had a possible future. "Oh, and have I mentioned that he kissed me?" I said.

"What? You know you haven't. So how was it? I'm going to be absolutely devastated if the answer is mediocre!" Margaret said.

"Far from it," I answered. "It was knee-buckling, but now I need to pay attention to getting home in one piece."

The snow was beautiful and still coming down when I backed into my driveway. Annie collapsed two steps into the den, and it took me a few minutes to shed some of my clothes before giving Nick his promised call.

He answered on the first ring and sounded genuinely relieved to hear that I was safely home. "Thanks for coming this afternoon, and for agreeing to work with Buddy. I think it will be a wonderful friendship. And I hope I'm not getting ahead of myself, but I think you and I have the chance for a long and lasting relationship as well. Don't you—I hope?" Nick said.

"Yes, I think we just might."

"Sweet dreams," he said.

"Sweet dreams to you too," I replied, thinking, *if I'm ever able to go to sleep.*

November 18, 2009
Dear Debby,

I think Nick is no longer a "what if" and has taken on the flavor of an "is," and I like that very much. I do have a tendency to overreact and read way too much into a situation or conversation, but he did say he thought we had the beginning of a great relationship. What does that mean: friendship . . . lovers

. . . what? The lover part really does unravel me. It has been a long time since I went to bed with someone for the first time, and that thought sends me into cosmic hysteria.

Over dinner we talked about everything under the moon, from our childhoods to our current status of single and available. We are miles apart on some fronts—the way we grew up, he's a city boy and I'm from the sticks to mention a few—but I think that makes things interesting. Our similarities are the important points . . . we have both been divorced . . . so we understand how that feels. He doesn't have any children but played a big role in the lives of his brother's kids, so he must like the idea of children.

He is everything I have ever wanted, or so it would appear. When he held my hand, I was reminded of feelings I thought lost forever. His touch also brought up my years with Parker. I questioned when exactly, and more importantly, why did Parker and I stop making each other wilt with desire?

I am terrified of being hurt, deceived, having my heart broken, and God knows what else. What do I do? This man is handsome, kind, well educated, is an excellent horseman, and, as tacky as this sounds, I think he's pretty wealthy. He has a gentle tone, style, is interesting and funny, is well traveled, and doesn't mind that I kiss dogs and horses. Oh, and he thinks I'm cute. Plus, he's HOT. I'm serious, he's just killer handsome!

Today was an absolutely beautiful day! The hot-pink folder has another twist!

With all good wishes,
Sarah

CHAPTER 22

A four-inch snow had fallen during the night, which was quite rare at any time in our part of the state. The coastal south is ill-prepared for serious frozen winter weather, and anything more than a dusting is considered catastrophic. I clicked on the television to find that, as expected, all county and city schools were closed for teachers and students. The on-location reporter kept us up-to-date from the empty bread aisle at Walmart. Apparently, if you had a stockpile of milk and bread, you would live to tell your grandchildren about the freak storm of 2009.

Standing at the end of my sidewalk and collecting the newspaper, I admired the beauty of the freshly fallen snow, which, at slightly past sunrise, was undisturbed by cars or excited children. My moment of reflection was quickly interrupted by the sound of my cell phone ringing just inside the front door. Quickening my pace back up the steps and hoping not to fall, I scooped it up on the fourth ring. "Hello?" I said sounding slightly winded.

"Good morning, Sarah. This is Nick. I hope it's not too early to call, but I was just checking on you to make sure you still had power."

"Yes, everything is working here. Are there power outages around? I've only watched TV to check on school closings."

"Yes, half the county is without electricity, and it's not likely they'll have service before tomorrow. I'm glad you're not in the unfortunate group of shivering souls this morning," Nick paused. "What do you think about your being able to come to Greenway this afternoon?"

"My car has four-wheel drive, so I'm good to go in the snow. Annie and I were just discussing the possibility of my riding Rascal later this morning, and Buddy in the afternoon. How soon do you need to know if I'm coming, and do I have blanket permission to bring my dog?" I asked.

Nick replied that he didn't need a set time, Annie was always welcome, and Caesar would be very disappointed if I came alone.

"I'll be there around one, weather permitting. Tell Caesar to rest up; Annie is on her way."

"Great, I'll see what I can find in my refrigerator. We can have a picnic in the office before leaving for our ride. Do you like picnics?" Nick asked.

"Who doesn't? What can I bring? Better yet, how about I'll organize the picnic, and you supply the beverages. Please don't argue this point. You did dinner last night, so I can make a sandwich today."

I needed to get cracking if I was going to get all of this done, ride Rascal, and be in Greenway by one o'clock.

After a brief moment of thought and a quick look at the clock, I decided to add a pecan pie. I had plenty of time to make a special dessert, especially if I used my mother's foolproof

125

recipe; you simply measure and dump all six ingredients in a bowl, mix, and pour it over a blanket of chopped pecans resting in the bottom of two regular Pet-Ritz pie shells. I divided the filling between two shells, because one was too thick and gooey for my taste. I'd give the second pie to Miss Madge on my way to the farm; she would enjoy the treat and the surprise.

During the forty-minute bake time, I made turkey sandwiches, bagged some chips and pickles, changed my clothes, straightened up the kitchen, and cut apples and carrots for the horses.

I rummaged around my pantry looking for paper plates, plastic utensils and cups, and napkins. With all items tucked neatly in my picnic basket, I added two large beef-flavored dog bones. Annie loved them, and I felt certain Caesar would too.

We were out the door by nine thirty and pulled into the parking lot of Falling Creek Farm without having any trouble on the highway. Rascal loved to be groomed, and the more fuss you made over him the better. Carrots, apples, and Mrs. Pasture's horse biscuits were some of his favorite treats. My pockets always contained an assortment of goodies, and he knew it. Today was a carrot day, and I made him work for them. He was getting older, and bending and stretching him in every direction before riding was very important to keeping him as supple as possible.

With both of us ready to ride, I led him to the indoor ring, and we took our usual ten minutes to work on horse yoga. He always argued a bit in the beginning because it was hard work, and perhaps slightly ouchy to his aging body at the outset. By the end, however, he was as loose as a goose and ready to ride. Several of my riding buddies, including Margaret, had ventured out for a morning jaunt as well, and we enjoyed the next hour to its fullest.

About halfway into the hour ride, Inez Biddle, owner of the barn, appeared center ring and built a very challenging jump course. It was a wonderful thing for her to do, but curious considering she had never before been so generous with her time. Inez ran her barn in a pay-me-but-don't-talk-to-me fashion, giving her barn manager almost full rein over most barn decisions. She stayed for a while, watching as we warmed up over the cross-rail. She also worked hard to not miss a word of Margaret and me discussing the pending ride and picnic with Nick. At one point she yelled, "Sarah, the man you're talking about—would that be Nick Heart over in Greenway?"

"Yes, it is. Do you know him?" I replied.

Before Inez could answer, Margaret yelled, "It's not Nick Heart, it's Nick *Hot*. He thinks Sarah is cute, and he served her a gourmet meal last night."

Inez walked over to stand out of the way beside a brush jump. "Yes. Well, actually, I only know of him, but I understand he's a very nice man. I'm surprised he doesn't have a girlfriend."

"He does, and it's Sarah," Margaret offered on her way to the jump.

"Oh, I am not," I said, "but I do like him. We have a great deal in common, and hopefully our friendship will continue to grow," I said. I could feel myself blushing.

One final hand walk returned Rascal to a standing body temperature, and with his blanket back on, he was in his stall happily munching on a fresh pile of hay stacked in the corner. I rubbed the length of his face and told him no one could ever take his place in my heart, but I did need to ride Buddy. He always seemed to understand my every word. Annie came running with one, perhaps two sharp whistles, and hopped directly into the back seat of my car.

Leaning against my car door I said to Margaret, "Don't you think that whole Inez thing was weird? She never comes in the ring, rarely talks to us, and all of a sudden she builds us jumps and knows *of* Nick. I've got to go, but we need to get to the bottom of this. The horse world is small, but no one knows everyone."

"I absolutely agree," Margaret said. "Call me on your way home, and have fun."

My hands began to sweat as I turned into Long Leaf Farm, and I could feel my pulse increase as well. I was so excited to be sharing the afternoon with Nick. A picnic anywhere was very romantic, as was riding horses together. I realized what Nick and I had enjoyed for the past several days was everything I'd dreamed of.

Pulling into the barn parking lot, I was surprised to find another car in what I now considered to be "my" parking space. Full-color car magnets attached to both sides of the SUV proudly displayed the name and address of the owner of said vehicle. In bold hunter green print, it read: *Reagan Wrenn ~ Equine Photography.*

I knew Reagan Wrenn, or Rea, as most everyone called her— she was usually one of the photographers at the bigger horse shows up and down the East Coast. I hadn't seen her in years. I wondered what she was doing here? I would have thought she'd be wintering in Florida, preparing to photograph the Ocala or Wellington shows.

Annie was gone the instant I opened the car door, and it was game on with Caesar. Grabbing my coat, I decided to check with Nick before hauling in the picnic basket. From the barn doorway, I saw the silhouettes of a man and a woman in full embrace in the middle of the aisle just outside Buddy's stall. This was not just a hug between old friends. With my final step, they separated from one another as if having been caught with their hands in the proverbial cookie jar. Nick and Rea were obviously not just friends. *Damnation,* I thought, *Reagan Wrenn is #4 on Alex's list: the old girlfriend.*

"Hi, Nick. Sorry to be running late, but I took a little extra time at Falling Creek," I said, wiggling my fingers against Buddy's nose. "Hi, Rea. Sarah Sams. I haven't seen you in years—you probably don't remember me, but I've written you a good many checks over the years. My daughter Sidney rode Summer Sunrise and I showed Teacher's Pet."

Using her signature wide-as-Texas smile, Reagan said, "Yes—of course I remember you Sarah! It's fantastic to see you. Where is Sidney? I haven't seen her around in a while, or you either for that matter."

"Sidney graduated from college two years ago. She's in Raleigh now, working for a television station. As for me, I've been very busy with other things for the past several years, and I just haven't had the time."

Nick moved around to the opening of Buddy's stall. I thought the expression on his face reflected an anxious smile, and his worried eyes confirmed my suspicions. Nick handed me the leather halter and asked if I wanted to ride before we had lunch.

"I'm flexible," I responded, probably a little stiffly. "I can work Buddy while you and Reagan finish whatever you were doing." Glancing between the bars of the stall door, I said, "Rea, Nick and I were going to share a picnic lunch, and you are more than welcome to join us. I'm sure there are few, if any, restaurants open today."

She paused momentarily before answering, "Thanks, that would be great." Collecting her camera bags, coat, and gloves, she and Nick turned to walk in the direction of his office. Over his shoulder, Nick said he would be right back and for me to continue getting tacked up.

Buddy crooked his neck around to smell my hand, and I quickly turned my attentions in his direction. I wished I had three eyes: two for what I was doing, and a third to watch the office. I was coming unglued, and I knew it. The sooner I got on the back of this horse the better. Nick did not owe me a thing, but I would not play second fiddle to a ponytail again. I pressed my head against Buddy's side and whispered, "I cannot do this again. I simply cannot."

With all systems on go, I led him from his stall to the indoor ring. This being only the second time he had been ridden at LLF, I thought it was fair to give him a minute to remember where he was. Buddy snorted and blew out to let the imaginary ghost of a new place know he was there, and then quietly lowered his head, telling me he was ready to ride.

Somewhere during the first few laps, Rea appeared at the gate. "Wow, Sarah, he really is a good-looking horse. Nick told me about him just before you got here. I wish someone would give me such a handsome gift. Do you still have Rascal?"

"Buddy is a pretty boy, isn't he? But as you and I both know, beauty's only skin deep, and ugly behavior goes clean to the bone. I haven't ridden him enough yet to know if we're a fit. Yes, my Rascal is still at Falling Creek. He'll always be my dream come true. So, how have you been? What brings you to our neck of the woods? I would have thought you'd be in Florida this time of the year," I asked, changing my direction and diagonal.

"Ordinarily I would be, but my mother is quite ill, and I'm taking a few months off to help her out. I just drove down today from Virginia to visit with Nick. My mother lives on the coast so it's not a long drive. Anyway, I heard by way of a friend about his buying this place, and thought I would surprise him with a visit. Nick and I were very close for a long time, but I'm sure you knew that. My photographs are probably all over his house," she explained, twisting a section of hair from her ponytail.

Using my sweetest Southern voice, I responded, "To be honest, I've only seen Nick's kitchen. I'll be sure to notice the next time I'm there. Your pictures are in half the horse show homes up and down the East Coast, though, so I doubt seeing them here would have told me anything about your relationship."

With pursed lips she said, "Sarah. I'm sure you know that Nick and I once lived together and almost got married, but the death of the baby was more than our relationship could stand." Rea dropped her head and clasped her hands.

"No, I didn't know that," I replied, trying desperately to remain calm and keep my voice steady. "Oh, my, I'm so sorry to hear about the baby."

"Excuse me, Rea," Nick said, entering the ring area, as she worked her way to sit on the bleachers. "Okay, Sarah, let's ride. Have you done your flat work?" he demanded with an instructor's voice.

Caught completely off guard, I stammered, "Yes—some. I was talking with Reagan." I couldn't be certain, but I didn't think

Nick had heard any of our conversation. The noise of his horse walking on the concrete aisle would have drowned us out. His expression was completely void of surprise.

"Let me see you canter some figure eights, but I want you to trot the center and pick up the correct lead two strides from the center both ways," Nick said.

I tried my best to put the past few minutes of conversation in the back of my mind, but it was proving to be an impossible task. Inhaling, I turned Buddy into the center of the ring and came to a stop.

Nick trotted up to me and asked, "Is there a problem?"

"Oh, goodness me, yes, there is, and I'm afraid I have to leave," I said quietly.

"Leave? What do you mean leave?" Nick asked with a look of utter surprise.

"I mean I'm going back to Hadley Falls. You and Reagan have things to discuss, and I have no intention of being a part of the conversation. Sorry about the picnic, but under the circumstances it's out of the question."

"Wait a minute," Nick demanded. "What the hell is going on?"

"Ask Rea," I replied. "I'm going home," I said, leaving the ring. Reagan had a very strange look on her face as I led Buddy out of the ring. I couldn't tell if it was *kiss my ass* or *oh, hell, what have I done?*

"Why? Why are you leaving?" Nick said, following closely behind.

I paused at the stall door. "Nick, Reagan shared some interesting information with me. We all have a past, and I don't delude myself in thinking you just sat in the corner until you met me. But I don't know you well enough to be the third set of ears today. I mean—the two of you living together for years—almost getting married—and a baby? That's just more than I choose to hear right now. So I'm going home, and you and Rea can take care of your business."

Nick stood white as a sheet and watched as I brushed the saddle marks from Buddy's coat and picked his hooves clean. "There you go," I said, "good boy. Sorry about being in a rush today—next time I'll give you more attention." With his blanket back in place, and a pat of his neck, I picked up my groom box and left his stall.

I walked down the center aisle and gave a whistle for my dog. I could see her in the far pasture and whistled once more for her to come. I was beginning to feel myself falling apart. I was fighting back the tears, and my dreams of a future with Nick were rapidly dissolving. I needed to get out of there and fast. As I reached to open the car doors, Nick appeared and placed himself against the car door.

"You cannot leave. You just can't. I need to talk to you about this," he said.

Clearing my throat, I said, "I am leaving—probably not for good, but certainly for today." Annie appeared from around the corner and hopped into the back seat. "Good girl," I said. "Nick, I have to go. Here is your picnic—you and Reagan enjoy."

Nick took the large brown woven basket full of what was supposed to be our romantic lunch and stepped back from the car. Just before sliding into the driver's seat, I added the pecan pie to the top of the basket.

Nick said, "I'll call you tonight. Sarah . . . you really don't understand what is going on."

"You're right about that. And again, I am not mad. I have no right to be mad. I just need to leave," I said, getting into my car and buckling my seat belt.

As I drove down the lane, I could feel the tears welling in my eyes. I realized how much I must like this man to be so upset over an old girlfriend. I didn't know Nick that well, but I was more than surprised that he had never mentioned having a child, especially since I had discussed my own children on several occasions. I would have thought that to be common conversational ground.

Dear Debby, I thought. *Why does life have to be so complex? I knew this was too good to be true.*

CHAPTER 23

The ringing of my phone sent me about three feet in the air. "Hello," I answered.

"Oh, hi. I was just going to leave you a message," Margaret said. "I needed to tell you that I was going with Bill to Raleigh for a business dinner and won't be able to talk until tomorrow. Why aren't you riding? Sarah, what's the matter?"

"To be perfectly honest, I don't know enough to even start the conversation. But here's what I do know: Nick's old girlfriend showed up, the ride lasted about five minutes, and the picnic is not happening. But I'll talk to you tomorrow, and please don't worry . . . I'm fine."

Margaret said sternly, "You're not fine, and you had better call me tomorrow."

"I will, I promise. I'm just completely unraveled. You know how I am. I get so excited about things and then poof—they disintegrate. I'll call you tomorrow, and have fun in Raleigh, and please be careful in the snow."

I decided to write just a few words before taking a calming bath. At the end of each session, Dr. Baxter would remind me that making short notes was good practice in cataloging my true thoughts.

November 19, 2009
Dear Debby,

My hot-pink folder is going to be overflowing at our session next week!

I have sailed into uncharted territory . . . I think I am jealous (I'm not sure that is the right word, but I'll use it for now), and I know I'm very confused. Today I met the old girlfriend. We all have a past, but the information given to me by Reagan Wrenn was quite extraordinary.

I've never in my life been so embarrassed, put on the spot, or speechless! There I stood (well, actually I was sitting on my horse, but you know what I mean) gobsmacked in my tall boots, and let me tell you, Reagan loved it. She knew exactly what she was doing, and it was purpose driven . . . what a vindictive bitch! I hope she chokes on my pie!

Occasionally, I wish I drank.

With all good wishes,
Sarah

Slipping into the steaming bath water, I inhaled deeply, enjoying the calming effervescence of lavender rising from my antique tub. Occasionally I would turn on the hot tap in an effort to keep the water just below a gentle boil. I loved hot baths, and this one was definitely therapeutic. With the last sip of my Earl Grey tea, I pulled the chain and wrapped up in a fluffy towel.

I needed comfort clothes, and they needed to be warm enough for Annie's after-dinner walk. Slipping on my favorite sweats, I brushed through my hair and made a ponytail of my own.

With the kitchen ship-shape, Annie and I headed out for our nightly constitution. Walking was therapy for me as well, and I would have gone regardless of the weather. It was a time when I could think and sort things out in my mind, and I had plenty to think about tonight. Rounding the corner of our final leg home, I could see a car parked in front of my house. Nick's car.

"Oh my God, what's he doing here?" I glanced at my faded black sweats with tattered gold letters that once spelled my alma mater, but now had more gaps than jack-o'-lantern teeth: *AP AL CH AN.*

Nick stood up from the front porch steps and smiled nervously. Annie wagged her tail in recognition as Nick bent over petting her head. "Hi there. Did you girls have a good walk?" Looking into my eyes, Nick said, "I wasn't sure you would answer the phone, and this conversation really needs to happen in person."

"Truthfully, I'm not sure either, but come inside. It's freezing out here," I said as we walked up the steps to my front door. "Would you like a cup of coffee, or tea?"

Nick rested my picnic basket on the island in the kitchen, and said, "Yes, I would love a cup of tea. But what I really want is to talk to you about this afternoon. I take no responsibility for Reagan's behavior, but I do want to tell you about our past relationship."

"I'm happy to hear what you have to say," I said, filling the kettle with water.

I poured our teas, and we made our way from the kitchen to the den. Nick positioned himself in the center of the sofa and I squished myself once again in the corner of my favorite chair. "I think I'll go back to the beginning, so get comfortable; this could take a while."

"I've got all night," I said.

"Reagan and I met over twenty years ago at the Devon Horse Show just outside Philadelphia. I was showing in adult hunters, and she was the photographer for the week. That was her first big show, and she was trying to get her business off the ground. My hunter horse was a large gray that stood about seventeen hands and had an intense presence. From the beginning, she latched onto him, and took a bunch of pictures.

"The next day, I went over to her booth to take a look at the photos, and there we were, plastered all over the place. The pictures were amazing, and I was very proud to be the owner of such a handsome horse. Admittedly, I was also a bit puffed up to be the premier rider and found a new strut to my walk.

"As the week progressed, so did our friendship, and her business. She always gave me credit for some of her good fortune. Before I knew it, we were together. Rea was always very possessive, but I didn't mind in the beginning. She's a beautiful woman, and I was the envy of many men. My first wife had left me for another man, and this attention was a real boost to my deflated male ego."

I couldn't help chuckling, and I was surprised to see a blush creeping up his cheeks. "I know what it feels like to be left for someone else, as you know." I said. "Go on."

"Well, after about two years, she started to talk about marriage, and I made it clear that I didn't want the constraints of holy matrimony, but would consider living together. After several months of hashing and rehashing, she decided to move in with me at my farm in Pennsylvania. For the next year every-thing was great. Rea was off to horse shows all over the country, and I was busy building my real estate business. When we were together, it was good, and things seemed to be moving in a positive direction. Then it all fell apart." Nick paused to clear his throat, and take a sip of tea.

"What happened?" I asked, anxious to hear the rest.

Nick stood up and put his hands in his pockets. "It was the end of September, and Reagan had been away for two months, shooting shows in New England. I noticed when she came home that she didn't seem to feel well, and I suggested she see a doctor. When she got home from the office visit, she said it was most probably fatigue, and a few days' rest was the cure. She added that her doctor had run several tests, done some blood work, and had given her the go-ahead for the remaining shows she had scheduled.

"Two days later she left for the Gulf States, and I had a huge real estate deal in the works, so my mind was preoccupied. I received a phone call later that week. A very nice voice announced that she was calling from Dr. Putnam's office with the test results. The nurse went on to say that Ms. Wrenn had given their office permission to give the results to me, knowing she would be out of the state at the time."

Oh, dear. I had a feeling I knew where this was going, and it wasn't good.

"I said something profound like, 'Okay, let's have it,' and she said with absolute delight, 'Congratulations Mr. Heart—you're going to be a father.' I said, 'That's impossible.' And she said, 'Well, Mr. Heart, I don't know what to tell you, but Ms. Wrenn is about seven weeks pregnant.' I said I was sorry but I was just so surprised, and that was the end of the call."

All these years later, I could still see the shock on his face as if it were happening all over again. He shook it off and continued.

"Well, it was impossible that I was the father of that baby for two reasons. The biggest is that I'm not able to have children. My first wife and I tried to get pregnant but with no luck. We both went for fertility testing and the results showed I was the problem. Second, if Rea was seven weeks pregnant, she was somewhere in New England at the time of conception, and I was not."

I put my hands over my mouth, eyes wide. What a nightmare.

"That was the beginning of the end for us. She called that night and I gave her the news. There was total silence on the other end, and I heard a click followed by a dial tone. She never called back, but she did come home the following Monday. When we finally spoke, she began with a trumped-up story about some man she met in upstate New York. I stopped her mid conversation and told her I really didn't need to hear anymore. Tears started to flow, and I suggested they were also a waste of time.

"The next day I offered for her to continue to live at the farm until the baby came, but stood firm that I wouldn't take responsibility for her child. I also suggested that she notify the real father and give him the opportunity to participate in the life of his baby. About a week later, she came to me and told me the father's identity."

"Nick"—I stopped him—"you really don't need to finish this story if you don't want to. I can tell this is painful for you, and seriously—it's not necessary," I said.

"No . . . no, you really do need to hear all of this," said Nick.

"If we're going to have a relationship, then you have to know. I don't expect you to understand how I could have such strong feelings for you in so few days, but I feel a closeness to you that has been absent in my life for a long time, perhaps forever. We cannot have a future with this shadow hanging over us." Nick paused and took a breath. "The father . . . was my brother, Jack."

"Your brother? Damn!"

"I told you this could take a while. Jack horse showed maybe twice a month to get away from home. His barn traveled the northern-states circuit during the summer and early fall before heading for Florida. Apparently, Rea and Jack hooked up at one of the early shows during that summer, then she followed him around from show to show, and it continued until the early fall.

"Jack was married, already had three children, and had no intentions of leaving his wife or caring for Rea and the baby. His wife was from a prestigious family in Pennsylvania, and her family money and connections were the world to my brother. He wouldn't have given that up for anything.

"About a month after all the cards were on the table, I insisted Jack come for the weekend, and the three of us sat down to figure things out. Jack stood firm that he would not leave his wife, but he agreed to help Rea financially. Remember, this was a long time ago, and those were the early days of Rea's career. She made okay money, but not enough to support herself and a child. My farm was her only address, and I caved and said she could stay at the farm until the baby was born, and for several months after that. To be perfectly honest, I was building a business and didn't need the bad press of throwing a pregnant woman out on the street. The truth would have hurt too many people, especially

Jack's innocent children.

"In late March we had two foals born, and Rea and I went down to the barn to see how they were doing. She wanted to take some pictures of the babies, so she brought her camera bag. In the barn, Rea propped herself up against a wooden saddle rack and worked with her camera. Emory, my barn manager, opened the stall door of one of my yearlings to give him hay, and in the blink of an eye the horse bolted from the stall with Rea sitting directly in his path. She suffered broken ribs, contusions, and yes—she lost the baby. Rea was in the hospital for about two weeks, and during that time made all the arrangements for a funeral and also named her son after me."

"What the . . . ?" I shook my head.

"I know. It was crazy. But I let it go—she was obviously suffering, and I saw no need to make things worse. Everyone assumed the child was mine anyway, and it seemed to make the whole situation easier for everyone—that is, everyone but me. While I felt deeply sorry for Rea, I obviously felt deceived and betrayed. She had an affair with my brother, for God's sake. It was too much to forgive, and we parted ways about four months later.

"She has twisted the truth in her mind to make me out to be the villain in this story. Because I never denied fathering the child, everyone thinks I'm a despicable human being. The truth would ruin a good many lives, and I will not do that. I'm not trying to make myself out to be a saint of some sort, but you need to know the truth. I swear to you Sarah—that is the truth."

I nodded. "I believe you," I said.

"I can't tell you how much that means to me. I'm so sorry about today—I'm not sure why she showed up. She said she never found anyone else, but the fact that I was still single made it all okay, in a weird way. The woman who owns the barn where you keep Rascal—Inez? Well, apparently she and Reagan have known each other forever, and I guess Inez called Rea after you got back from the hunter pace and said you'd met me. She said that set her off."

"I knew it!" I said, and Nick looked confused. "I knew something was going on with Inez—but never mind. Go ahead."

"Well, I guess I'm about done. Rea did spend a great deal of time this afternoon apologizing for the whole thing. She admitted it was nothing short of insane. She said she has moved on, but the news of you and me hit her like a sickness. She decided this was her chance for revenge—for what, I don't know—and she wanted me to feel her pain."

For several ticks of the clock I sat in disbelief thinking, *Wow, I thought my life with Parker and Pam the Chiropractor was a soap opera . . . but good grief . . . my story can't hold a candle to this!* Nick looked at me for some sign of how I felt. Standing up, I wrapped my arms around his neck, hugged him gently, and said, "I believe you. Sincerely I do. I must also say that I feel sorry for Reagan. It's not right that she's turned it all around on you, but I suspect she uses her misplaced anger to survive. She loved you, your brother, and her baby, and in the end she lost all of you— how tragic."

Nick held me close, and I could feel his heart racing. He kissed the top of my head. "What a day. I should have put a stop to that lie years ago, but I couldn't figure out how to do it without destroying so many lives."

"Hindsight is 20/20," I said taking one step back, "and if

frogs had wings, they wouldn't bump their behinds."

Nick laughed. "That's a very funny thing to say."

"Well it's true. You can't do anything about the past but let it go. Listen to me," I continued, "I hold so much resentment for my ex-husband that there are days I can't see beyond the veil of disdain, but I am trying to move on. You've had your say with Rea, and what she does from here is up to her. What else can you do? As far as I can see—absolutely nothing! She says she's found someone, so maybe her trip was just a last-stab effort to hurt you. Agreed, it's twisted and crazy sick, but maybe it will bring her some closure and peace."

"Sarah, thank you for being so understanding," Nick said, giving me a long and deep kiss that curled my toes.

"You're welcome," I replied when I could breathe again, "and thank you for telling me everything. But I need you to remember that lies, the shattering of trust, and calculated deception are things that don't just go away with the flip of a switch. It's been almost two years since my marriage fell apart, but with the right trigger, the memory is all too fresh."

There was a moment of *now what*, and then Nick looked into my eyes and said, "Next fall, you and I are getting married! You pick the spot."

"You're funny," I replied, playing along. *He can't be serious. Can he?*

"You think I'm kidding, but I'm not. I don't want to scare you, and I hope you don't think I'm crazy. You may not believe in love at first sight, and I was skeptical before I met you, but my dear Sarah, I think it's a very real thing. I'll be patient, and you'll see."

"Dear Debby, what a day."

Totally perplexed, Nick said, "What? Who's Debby?"

"Uh—it's just an expression of mine. I'll explain it to you later," I said, giving myself a mental slap for that slip of the tongue.

"Okay, but that is a very odd thing to say," Nick replied.

"Odd for me, or the rest of the world?" I chuckled.

Nick smiled and said, "I'm guessing you have sole ownership of this oddity."

Standing with the front door half open and getting ready to say goodbye, Nick noticed a large unopened cardboard box resting just outside the front door. "What's in the box? I'm sorry," he said quickly. "That's really none of my business."

"No, don't be silly. And to answer your question, I don't know," I said. "It was sitting there when Annie and I got home this afternoon. I gave it a glance—but was too upset to care—so there it still sits."

Nick reached down and tried to lift the box. "This thing's as heavy as lead. Where would you like it?" he asked, dragging the carton inside.

"Just put it on the living room rug," I said, closing the front door. "Mercy, there's a lot of tape. I'll need a knife to open this."

Nick reached into his pocket and offered me the use of his combat-ready Swiss Army knife. Rummaging through the packing paper and Styrofoam peanuts, I could see the top of what appeared to be a bronze horse's head. "I think it's a sculpture," I exclaimed, trying to pull it out of the box.

"Here, let me help you," Nick said, grabbing the bottom of the piece.

"Oh my gosh, it's Rascal and me! This looks just like the picture on the jacket of my first book. Wow, it is absolutely incredible—the expressions are breathtaking."

"Who's the artist?" Nick asked, admiring the three-dimensional work of art.

"There's a note. Have a seat, and I'll read it." We sat down on the living room sofa with the sculpture resting on the floor in front of us, and I read aloud:

Dear Sarah,

It's been a long time since we have spoken or seen each other, but I hope you remember me. I recently saw a copy of your book and the picture on the back jacket was so inspiring that it took me back in time. As an artist yourself, I'm sure you can understand the overwhelming power of inspiration.

Enclosed, you will find a piece I made for you. I hope you like it, and I hope to see you soon.

Sincerely,

Stuart Branch

"I know Stuart Branch," Nick said, "I met him twice, I think. Both times were at hunt charity balls. He donated a piece for the silent auction. Nice guy. Very thick Southern accent, as I recall. So—the two of you . . . dated?"

I stammered, "Well—yes. But goodness, that was a long time ago. We met at an intercollegiate art exhibition. Our paintings were hanging alongside each other. We dated for about a year, and then I met Parker. I really don't know what to say about this gift—talk about out of the blue—holy cow. And I've got to say . . . a little creepy. This whole thing is very strange, and coming on the heels of Reagan, and her stalker behavior? I don't like it, not at all! Why would he send this to me? I haven't heard from Stuart Branch since halfway through college. And why now? How did he get my address?" I shivered.

"The internet, I imagine. You can find out most anything you need to know with one click of your mouse." Nick sighed. "I'm afraid I need to be getting home. The only one who can answer your questions is Stuart. You may want to consider giving him a call. His address and phone number are on his letterhead, and I guarantee you that choice of paper wasn't accidental. This has been quite the day for both of us," Nick said, leaning over and giving me a kiss. "Call me tomorrow?"

"I will," I said "Please be careful driving home."

"You bet! Love ya," Nick said, kissing my cheek and walking down the front steps.

I waved goodbye, and turned to walk back inside. "*Love ya?* Oh my God—did he say that?"

CHAPTER 24

The next morning, school was canceled again, and Nick called about me riding Buddy. I told him that, in light of the snow day, the Rowdy Girls had made a spontaneous decision to go out to lunch for Elizabeth's birthday. Before hanging up, I asked Nick if he had any plans for Thanksgiving, and if not, would he like to join me with my family in Iron Springs. I added that due to distance and the time of day, we would need to spend the night.

"Absolutely. I'd love to," he said, "if you think it would be okay with your mother."

"I'll call her after we hang up, but I'm sure it will be," I said.

My mother, who we called Sibby, was a bit taken aback by my wanting to invite a man I'd just met to Thanksgiving dinner. She was so shocked to hear I had met someone that she wasn't quite sure what to say. I spent thirty minutes bringing her up to speed about Nick, and I did mention Stuart Branch, reminding her of who he was, and his gift.

Before hanging up, I asked if Nick could spend the night. She cleared her throat and said, "Yes, I think that will be just fine. He can sleep in Ethan's old room. On the subject of your old college beau and his gift, do you plan to send him a thank-you note?" Sibby asked.

It is comforting to know that some things never change, and my mother's attention to "proper manners" was one of them. "No, actually, I don't. I do, however, plan to give him a call after I hang up with you."

"Well, would you please do me a favor?" my mother asked. "Would you try and be nice?"

"Nice—what do you mean by that? I'm always nice. I plan to thank him for the sculpture, but I also plan to find out why he sent it to me. I haven't heard from him in well over twenty years, and he sends me a piece of sculpture worth at least five figures— for no reason. That's strange, don't you agree?" I said.

"Yes, I do." My mother paused, and I could see her tapping her fingertips on the arm of her chair. "It sounds like you like this Nick fellow, don't you, Sarah?"

"Yes, Mama, I do. He is very nice and makes me laugh. He is also a wonderful horse person and kisses his dog. What more could a girl ask for? I can't wait for you to meet him."

"Please be careful riding that horse. Don't you think you're getting too old for such a dangerous sport?"

"Never!"

My mother sighed. "I love you, Sarah! Be safe!"

November 20, 2009
Dear Debby,

When I called Sibby this morning she said Nick was more than welcome to come for Thanksgiving and stay the night.

149

She was also very interested in learning all about him. I could hear my grandmother in the background of our conversation asking questions. Grammy O'Neil might throw him out when she finds out he's a Yankee.

My grandmother was an excellent horsewoman in her day, and she's the reason I was able to ride. When I was little, she put the squeeze on my father to wear down my mother's resistance (Sibby wasn't being mean, she just thought it was too dangerous and still does). Once I got the parental thumbs-up, Aunt Lucy and I rode every weekend at Grammy's farm. She even took me to my first horse show.

Hold on to your hat—there is a new wrinkle and his name is Stuart Branch!

At our session this afternoon, I will open my hot-pink folder to this and several other letters.

With all good wishes,
Sarah

"This message is for Sarah Sams," the automated voice announced. "Due to inclement weather, Dr. Baxter will be out of the office today. Please call to make another appointment. Thank you and have a nice day," and the phone went click.

Darn, I thought. I really wanted to talk to her, especially about how to share with Nick that I was going to a psychologist. Lots of people go for counseling and it's a good thing. I wasn't ashamed at all, but I wanted to present it in the right way. I needed her guidance.

The awkward phone call was next on my list. Taking a deep breath, I dialed the number printed on the letterhead. "Hi,

Stuart. This is Sarah Sams," I said when he picked up. "I'm calling to thank you for the amazing, and out of the blue, gift you sent me. It is fabulous."

"Hello, Sarah! I'm glad you think so," Stuart said. "I saw the picture on the back of your book, and I couldn't get that visual out of my mind. So, how have you been for the past, oh—twenty-five or so years?" he asked, sounding nervous.

"I've been great. I still teach art at the high school, I have two adult children, and you know about my horse from the picture. I continue to ride all the time, and I've just recently added another horse to my collection," I said.

"I'm glad to hear you are doing well," he replied. "How's Parker?"

There was momentary silence on my side of the conversation. I was more than surprised that he remembered Parker's name after all this time. He only heard it once when I ended our relationship.

"I don't really know. He and I haven't been together for a long time. I do know he married his chiropractor, and they live in New Bern."

"Oh my, I'm sorry to hear that, Sarah. I never knew Parker, and I don't know what caused the divorce, but he's an idiot for letting you go."

"Well, that's water under the bridge and no more sour grapes there. My new life is more like a freshly brewed glass of sweet tea, and I am very happy. So, how about you? Did you ever get married?" I said, not knowing what to say next.

"I was married for a very brief period to a dancer, Mary, but she said our legal status stifled her creativity. You know," he said with a sigh, "I have come to realize that I messed up when I let you go."

"Oh, Stuart, I don't know," I mumbled. "I never gave up my love of horses, and you didn't like that part of my life. And you refused to cut back on your drinking, which was a serious issue on my side of the ledger. You know we would have never withstood the test of time.

"Oh, I don't know about that," he protested.

"Plus," I continued, "I chose the teaching direction with my art, and you went professional. But it sure is nice that we can visit over the phone," I said, trying to wrap things up. "I can't thank you enough for the sculpture. It is magnificent, and I can tell everyone I own an original Stuart Branch."

"Why do I get the feeling that you are trying to hang up? Is there somewhere you need to be?" Stuart asked.

Clearing my throat, I said, "Well, actually, I do need to get to the barn. My friends and I are going for a morning ride and then to lunch. See? I'm still leaving you to go to the barn. Our lives are better this way, don't you think?"

Stuart chuckled. "I'm not so sure about that, but I would like to discuss it over dinner. I'm going to be in Raleigh this weekend, and would love to come to Hadley Falls and take you out. What do you say, is it a date?"

I was silent for a moment, trying to think of how to avoid this unwanted reunion. "It would be wonderful to see you too, but I actually have a date for this weekend. I am seeing someone, and we are more than just good friends," I said.

"Oh, anyone I know?" he asked, as if he already knew the answer.

"Actually, when your package came, he happened to be at my house. We opened the box together and he said he's met you on several occasions—charity benefits I believe. His name is Nick Heart—perhaps you remember him?

"Nick Heart . . . how do I know that name? Is he related to Paige and Jack Heart?"

"Yes, Jack is his brother," I said.

"Nice guy. I remember he was in the horse business, wasn't he?" Stuart asked. "Are you two engaged?"

I told Stuart Nick had bought a farm in Greenway and that we were not engaged. In the next breath I mentioned that I really did need to be on my way to the barn and thanked him again for the extravagant gift.

Stuart repeated that he would love to see me and catch up on our missed years. "Take care, Sarah, and I hope to see you soon."

"You too," I replied.

Yikes, I thought, *why did I say that? I don't want to see him at all.*

I shook my head. This was such a nutty way to start out the day. I think good ol' Stu already knew that Parker and I were divorced. Why else would he send me that gift—and to my new address, no less? If Parker and I were still together, he wouldn't have been so bold. But who in the world could have given him that information? Who could possibly know the two of us?

CHAPTER 25

$\mathcal{M}$any of the local restaurants were either closed because of the snow or offering a very limited menu for our Rowdy Girl lunch. Jennifer suggested we go to her café, rummage through the icebox, and have a great time. Naturally, she took charge of the refrigerator raid, as we all knew she could truly make a culinary silk purse of a meal out of a sow's ear of scraps.

Within thirty minutes, we had pots boiling on the stovetop, bread baking in the oven, and Margaret happily snapping green beans *her* way. Elizabeth was denied kitchen privileges due to her birthday girl status and was given the task of answering the telephone just in case anyone called to see if the restaurant was open. Betsy stood at the counter, whipping up one of her famous sauces for the entrée, and Jennifer was setting the table. I was making my three cheeses, olive, and pecan spread to accompany the bread and apple slices. Rose was creating one of her famous desserts.

Throughout the meal, I kept my friends entertained with the details of my unbelievable week with Nick, Rea, and Stuart. We laughed and cried, then laughed some more. There were as many opinions on every subject as there were women in the room. I offered that Nick was an honest man and also a very good kisser.

Rose proposed that he was also most probably very good in bed and wondered when I might actually quit fooling around and find out.

"Rose, shame on you." I giggled. "I haven't even known him for a week."

"So?" she replied, while looking in my direction. "Oh, sorry—you were serious. Is there a timeline for knowing Nick before you sleep with him? Have you penciled in next Tuesday, or perhaps December twelfth, for example?" she continued, bringing down the house.

"No, I don't guess so. This is new ground for me. I just don't want to make a mistake," I said with my eyebrows closely knit.

The notion that Stuart Branch had an ulterior motive in sending me that piece of art was a theory shared by all. None of us had a clue where it was going, but we agreed that the surprise sculpture saga was far from over. We put our heads together trying to figure out who might have given him the news about Parker and me, but no one came to mind.

Before you could say boo, the conversation turned to my outfit of choice for my up coming date. Margaret said she thought we should all go shopping after we cleaned up from lunch.

Most of the trendy shops and boutiques along the river walk were open, even with the snow. Shopping with my five best friends, who all thought my outfit to be their decision, was hysterical. I stood firm that I did not want to buy the first thing I tried on. This evening was very important to me, and I wanted to wear something special since so far Nick had only really seen me in riding clothes and sweatpants. I wanted him to think *WOW* when he came to my front door. How hard could it be to find an outstanding ensemble that screamed *WOW* and was not too expensive?

After two hours of sliding hangers up and back aluminum clothes rods in half a dozen stores and finding nothing that fit the bill, it was as if suddenly an outfit jumped from the racks into my hands. There it was: a black-and-periwinkle, slightly funky jacket with ankle length black pants—absolutely me. I tried the outfit on, and it fit like a dream. The suit was dressy-casual and very sophisticated.

"Sarah," Rose said, "don't even look at the price tag—just buy it. It's perfect."

Pulling the dangling bit of cardboard attached to the sleeve of the jacket close to my face, I tried to focus my eyes on the price. Betsy offered me the use of her readers. I shrieked, and then said, "Well, no wonder I like it so much. Are you kidding me? You could buy this outfit or make your next house payment."

"Now, Sarah," Margaret chimed in, "this is no time to be cheap."

"I am not being cheap, but merciful heavens!"

Betsy took back her glasses and held the price tag in her hands. "It's expensive, but for God's sake, Sarah, when was the last time you bought an outfit? Riding clothes don't count, and neither does a buy-one-get-one free sale."

"It really does look good on me, doesn't it? Does it also say WOW?" I asked, looking at myself in the three-way mirror.

Jennifer said, "This outfit says 'I am an up-to-date kind of woman, and thanks for asking me out.' What more do you want? You have plenty of money; you're just as tight as a tick. Now get changed, and buy the damn thing."

Leaving the store, I turned right while the rest of the group made a left. "Where are you going?" asked Margaret.

"To my car," I replied. "Why? Did we have something else to do?"

"Yes," Margaret said. "Now we have to find the underwear."

"Oh, for pity's sake. I really don't think that's necessary. He will never know what is under this outfit."

"That's what's worrying us," Rose said. "It's not so much for him as it is for you. We are trying to help you. Wouldn't it be lovely to have a male other than your horse think you're fetching? Even if he doesn't get the chance, wouldn't you love to have Nick thinking 'let me at it?' Don't even try to tell us that you haven't given this some thought. We're wise to you, Sarah Sams. You want Nick Heart—you're just too scared to admit it. So get your knickers over here and let's get serious about undergarments." Rubbing her brow, she mumbled, "I cannot even imagine what you sleep in, and please don't tell me. I will need an exorbitant amount of alcohol to conquer that imagery."

Pointing to the mannequin in the front window of the boutique, Elizabeth said, "Hey, Sarah, how about that in several colors?"

I could feel my face flush as I glanced at the nearly-nothing robe covering a perfect body shape wearing practically nonexistent underwear. Letting out a nervous howl, I responded, "That's it, and I hope they have it in red and black."

"Well, every woman should own a red bra," Margaret offered. "And black too—that goes without saying."

"How is it that we have never before discussed your knowledge of lingerie?" I asked. "We've logged at least a million miles of conversation and never once has a red bra been mentioned."

"I never dreamed you didn't have one," Margaret scoffed, rolling her eyes as if I had just climbed out of the nearest cave. "But now that we all know how lacking you are in this department, we're here to right your lingerie wrongs."

Like a colony of worker bees, my friends scoured the store, picking up ideas and discarding them. Finally they each stood with their selections in hand. All my options were in black. I chose the underpants from Betsy's selection and the bra from Margaret. I was no fool; Margaret and Bill had been together since third grade, and it was obvious they knew how to keep a relationship fresh.

I refused to try anything on in the store, but I did promise to buy additional items if I found that I liked what I'd already purchased. I smiled the entire way back to the parking lot. Rose noticed and mentioned that it was wonderful to see that look on my face and a twinkle in my eye.

"The twinkle to which you refer," I said, "is trauma-level sticker shock to my outlay of currency today. Had I known it was going to cost me so much to go out to dinner, I would have offered to cook."

They all laughed and gave each other a high five. Margaret said, "This is the most fun I've had long time. I can't wait to tell Bill. My black bra is his favorite . . . he'll be pleased to know you have one too."

"You will not tell your husband about my underwear! And I'm so glad that my dropping hundreds of dollars is funny to you guys," I said, shaking my head.

"This shopping spree will probably make the Hadley Falls Herald," Betsy said. "Wait a minute, do they put divorces in the paper? Maybe that's how Stuart knew about Parker leaving you? Or maybe he saw the Maple Real Estate ad about your house being for sale?"

"How utterly depressing," Rose remarked. "I was hoping for a weird horse world triangle or something. You know—like Reagan, Inez, and Nick? Golly, Betsy, I hope you're wrong."

"You two are ridiculous," I laughed. "The newspaper idea is an interesting theory, but whatever; it still means he's a big-time stalker. Why would he read the Hadley Falls Herald anyway? Don't you think it would be easier if I just asked Stuart? If I ever hear from him again, that is."

"Oh, you'll hear from him, all right," Elizabeth said. "He didn't send you that very personal, not to mention valuable, gift for no reason."

Driving home, I beamed with excitement. The outfit was awesome, and I was very happy my friends had pushed me to make the purchase. I even liked the fact that I now owned fashionable lingerie, even if I would never ever admit it out loud.

CHAPTER 26

*H*anging up my new outfit, I stretched between my closet and my dresser to answer my ringing phone—it was Nick. "Hi there," I said.

"Hi, darlin'. How was your girls' lunch?" Before I could respond, Annie started barking. "What's Annie after this time?" Nick asked.

"There's someone at the door. It's probably the eighth grader who lives two doors down selling fruitcake—'tis the season for the annual middle-school band fundraiser. Hold on a minute," I said, going to the door. "Annie, hush!"

I opened the front door to a shock. "Goodness, Stuart Branch, I'd know you anywhere. What are you doing standing at my front door? You were in New York this morning!"

"Stuart?" Nick said. "What's he doing there?"

"Hang on just a minute," I answered Nick. "I can't have two conversations at the same time."

"Sorry," I said to Stuart. "Let's try this again. What are you doing here?"

"I came to see you," Stuart replied. "I told you I was going to be in Raleigh and that I wanted to see you. I couldn't get a firm yes or no from you, so I decided to ask in person. God, you look good! Do you have a dinner date for tonight?"

"Uh, no, I don't, but I do have things to do. I have to bake a cake, and my supper is already in progress," I replied.

"That's okay. I'll bet you have enough for two. All right if I stay for dinner and we can catch up on the past twenty-plus years?" Stuart asked.

"Hang on a minute," I said, returning the phone to my ear. "I'm sorry to keep you waiting, but I imagine you've heard most of this conversation."

"Yes, and I'm going to show you a new piece of my personality," Nick said. "I don't like this at all. I'm coming to your house tonight. I want to make sure you're safe with him. What time is dinner?"

"We'll eat around seven, but come earlier if you can so we can visit," I said.

"Okay," Nick replied. "You can count on early. I'll be there in an hour, tops. Are you sure you're all right?"

"Yes, I think so," I said still holding on to the front doorknob. "See you in a bit."

"Who was that?" Stuart asked. "And what's for dinner?"

"It's actually none of your business who was on the phone, but since he's coming to dinner as well, it was Nick Heart," I answered. "Come on in, and I'm, or should I say we're having rosemary chicken, wild rice, and something green. And probably leftover apple pie for dessert."

"Sarah, your house is lovely. How long have you lived here?" Stuart asked, stepping inside. His thinning salt-and-pepper hair made him look much older than he really was, and I thought I remembered him being taller.

"Hmm, let me think," I said. "It'll be two years next spring. Gosh, how time flies. Here, let me take your coat. Your feet must be soaked from standing in the snow—just put your shoes on the rug by the door."

Stuart slipped off his designer loafers. He wandered around my house in his stocking feet and reappeared in the kitchen to announce that the whole house was a reflection of my personality. Sliding onto the closest bar stool, he began to nibble from the dish of peanuts I had placed on the island counter-top.

"Would you like something to drink?" I asked.

"I'd love a beer if you've got one," he said. I'd forgotten how thick his Georgia accent was. "Boy, Sarah, whatever you're cooking sure does smell good."

"Thanks, but I haven't started cooking anything yet. You just smell the fresh rosemary. So Stuart, what are you doing here?" I asked, pulling out the chicken from the fridge along with a beer.

"Well, after we spoke, I called the airline and asked if there was an earlier flight, and as luck would have it, there was! So I switched my ticket and here I am. I've got a lunchtime speaking engagement in Raleigh tomorrow, so it really didn't matter when I arrived. Can you believe people are willing to pay me an outrageous amount of money to discuss my craft and my life?"

"I'm sorry, Stuart, but I need to know," I interrupted. "How, who, or what prompted you to get in touch with me after all this time?" I asked.

Stuart rattled his handful of peanuts like a pair of dice and said, "Like I said in the note, I saw your book and the picture on the back jacket got me to thinking about you. I bought the book and went directly to my studio and began to draw."

"Okay, let's just stop right there," I said, my voice as authoritative as I could manage. "My how-to books are never promoted in a big way. They line the shelves of tack stores or are tucked away in some back corner of a bookstore. So how did you know I even wrote books?"

"To be clear, I never said where I saw your book," Stuart grinned. "I'm good friends with lots of folks and give smaller pieces of my work for charity auctions. I was invited to a horse rescue function, and a signed copy of your book was a silent auction item. I saw your name on the front jacket and wrote down one hundred dollars as my bid."

"Eight or nine weeks later the piece was finished, but my thoughts of you were stronger than ever. I only asked you about Parker to make sure you two hadn't gotten back together. The news about you and Nick Heart struck a sour chord, but since you're not engaged, I consider the playing field still open. Does that satisfy your curiosity?" Before I could answer, he pointed at his feet. "I'm afraid my feet are really freezing, may I please borrow a pair of dry socks?"

"Give me a minute and I'll go look." I said wiping my hands. "But I need you to understand: as I told you, Nick and I are more than just friends, so there is no 'open playing field.'"

"Okay," Stuart said with boyish grin. "But to my way of thinking, there is. You two have only known each other for a short time, so how close could you be?"

I stuck my knife in the chicken in frustration. "How in the world do you know how long Nick and I have known each other? That information could only have been gathered from someone you know who also knows me. Stuart, I'm two shakes of a lamb's tail from throwing you out the door you came in or calling the police, so cough it up, Branch: who have you been talking to, and how do you know about Parker and me?"

Stuart squirmed a bit in his chair, took a sip of his beer, and cleared his throat. Looking me straight in the eyes he said, "Your good friend Rose Mills has spent a great deal of time in Paris researching her culinary endeavors and enjoying the company of an artist buddy of mine. I don't want to freak you out."

"Too late for that, and I'm serious!" I said interrupting his explanation with my hands on my hips.

"Okay, maybe." He chuckled. "In a roundabout way, I've kept up with you for years by way of Henri DuBois. When I saw the book, I knew I had to see you again. I needed to know if you were available, so I called Henri and asked what he knew and what he could find out through Rose."

"Henri placed a return call with the information I needed, that being, you and Parker were divorced, and you and Nick hadn't even had a real first date. So here I am, and hopefully you won't actually throw me out. I do understand how you could think this is a little out of left field, but we're not getting any younger. I understand that you think Nick is the man for you, but you're wrong. *I'm* the guy you should be with."

I stood speechless behind the counter with a sprig of rosemary in one hand and a paring knife in the other. Frozen to the kitchen floor, I found myself paralyzed by the past few minutes of conversation. "Out of left field—that's an understatement. Rose would never have offered that information about me without questioning why. You've left something out, I'm sure."

"Rose talks to Henri. He knew all about your new house, the girls helping you with it, et cetera." Stuart answered. "They must have talked this week, because she told him about all of y'all going to a horse thing, what a good time you guys had, and your having met someone. It wasn't hard to fill in the gaps. Don't worry; Rose hasn't betrayed your trust. She doesn't know the connection between Henri and me."

I still didn't know what to do with this man. He was creeping me out, but when I'd known him, he was nothing but a stand-up guy. My mind was on overdrive.

I laid the fresh herbs and paring knife down on the counter and went to find him some dry socks. I tore through my sock drawer, unable to fully concentrate. I grabbed the first pair of riding socks I came to, returned to the kitchen, and handed them to Stuart.

"Thanks." He laughed. "Only a real man would, or could, wear pink-and-lavender argyle knee socks on a first date."

"This is *not* our first date. That happened light years ago, when we were nineteen." I added, still unable to calm down. "And it's not a date at all! Stuart, I'm going to be honest: I feel very unsettled and nervous with your uninvited presence, and it feels like you have been stalking me for years. I really will throw you out or call the police if this gets any stranger, and I need for you to understand that I'm not kidding! You might also share with your friend Henri that he can kiss his relationship with Rose goodbye. She will see this as an absolute conspiracy and betrayal on his part."

Stuart held both hands in the air as if to proclaim his innocence. "Sarah, I would never hurt you. I'm not a stalker.

Henri would mention seeing Rose and would tell me about Hadley Falls, and then I saw your picture. I got the news about your current single status, and I had a speaking gig in Raleigh. That's all there is to it," he said. "After Mary, I've never had a long-term relationship, and I thought I'd pay you a visit. What's the harm in that?"

"I refuse to get into a conversational taffy-pull over this, but your Aunt Alice just pays you a visit, Stuart," I said sternly. "An old beau from over two decades ago doesn't just happen to drop by. You can stay for dinner, but that's it!"

Stuart continued to munch on peanuts, sip his beer, and talk about his life in New York. After about five minutes of conversation, he announced that the socks were going to need the assistance of the slippers if I had any. He offered to find them for himself, but I said I would get them for him. There was absolutely no way I was going to allow him in my bedroom. Poking his nose in my room earlier on his self-guided tour was bad enough, but rummaging around in my closet was absolutely off limits.

"Well, now—aren't I just the picture of masculinity," he said with a chuckle. "These incredibly yellow fuzzy slippers along with the socks are quite something. You'll never believe this, but I gave considerable thought to my outfit this morning."

"That's your fault. You live in New York. Surely you know how to dress for snow," I said, as the doorbell rang.

"I'll get it," Stuart said leaping from the stool and scooting toward the living room. "That should be Nick, my new best friend."

I wasn't quick enough to beat him to the door and stood just feet behind as he opened it. This was the craziest day I had experienced in perhaps—forever? Mr. Right was on my front porch expecting me to greet him, and instead Big Bird with pink-and-lavender knee socks would be opening the door.

"Well, Stuart," Nick said with surprise. "I love your socks, man, and the slippers! They're so you."

"Thanks," Stuart replied. "I assured Sarah that only a real man would accept socks of any color over certain pneumonia or minor humiliation, and I gotta tell you, these slippers are really very comfortable."

"Hi, Nick," I said, stepping forward. "Just lay your coat over the back of the sofa and come join us in the kitchen. Stuart was just telling me all about his years in New York and how he came to know so much about me. The connection is Henri Dubois, a French painter and admirer of Rose Mills. Would you like something to drink?"

Nick walked with me to stand behind the island, reached for a handful of peanuts, and said that he would like a glass of wine. "How interesting—small world," Nick said leaning over, kissing my cheek and removing the corkscrew from my hand. "Thanks for letting me come to dinner. I love your cooking and your company."

"So you've eaten here before?" Stuart asked.

"Absolutely," Nick responded. "It was just this past Monday night, as a matter of fact. We had Yankee pot roast, French bread, and her gravy would have made dirt taste good. Can you believe she even makes her own ice cream?"

Smiling from the compliment, I excused myself to collect Annie from the backyard. With all that had transpired, I had actually forgotten I'd let her out after Stuart arrived, and it was her dinnertime. As I opened the back door I could hear the two men in my kitchen engaged in conversation. "Annie," I called, "where is my hungry girl? There you are. Come on, let's get your supper."

Walking back into the house, I heard Stuart say that he and I had history. Nick responded with, "We all have a history. The difference is that Sarah and I have a future."

"Okay, there we go," I said, my voice a little high. "Annie is eating her dinner, so let me check on ours. I hope you boys are hungry."

"I'm starving," Stuart announced. "I haven't had anything to eat since my sandwich on the airplane."

Grabbing two oven mitts, Nick opened the oven door, removed the baking dish, and said, "Me too—starving that is. I had breakfast and lunch, but I've been working in the barn all day. Where do you want this?" Nick asked, holding up the main course.

"I thought we would eat in the dining room since we're three. Just put it on the largest trivet, and thank you," I answered. "Everybody grab your drink, and let's sit down."

Nick took the back of my chair and Stuart rested my iced tea on the place mat. I motioned for them to have a seat and thought *God, this is strange—talk about guess who's coming to dinner!*

CHAPTER 27

That evening was a first for me: two men vying for my attention at my dining room table. Stuart spent a great deal of time dredging up the past, and Nick volleyed with discussions concerning our future. I was stuck in the middle of these two men, and listened intently to their combative conversation.

Somewhere over the last scrapings of dinner, Stuart asked if there was decent lodging in town. He said it was too late for him to drive back to his hotel in Raleigh, and that considering the weather conditions, it might be prudent to stay the night in Hadley Falls.

It sure as hell won't be here, I though, sitting back in my chair. *I think I've already blown up the generosity meter.*

Nick jumped right in with a list of national chain hotels, all of which dotted the interstate. He even knew which ones offered a complimentary breakfast. "It's getting late and I've had several glassed of wine. I think I'll give George a call—it's better road to his house. Excuse me for a minute while I give him a call?" Nick said, with Stuart leaving the table as well.

"Tell him that Sarah sends her best," I added with a chuckle.

As Nick moved in the direction of the den, I heard Stuart

from the kitchen thanking someone for their time, adding that he understood. "Understand what?" I asked.

"The guy at the Holiday Inn Express said there was a multi-car pileup on the interstate and the power's out everywhere. One hotel is functioning, but only on partial power and has no more vacancies. Hmm—what to do?" Stuart said with a sideways glance to me.

Not a snowball's chance in hell!

"You can bunk with me at my cousin's house," Nick called from the den. "He has lots of room. Hey, George, this is Nick. I hope I haven't called too late? Great, listen, I'm in need of a place to stay. Would it be possible for me, and my buddy Stuart to stay the night at Hotel Finch? Are you sure? We don't want to put you out, but it's too late to drive home." Nick paused, listening to his cousin's reply. "We're over at Sarah's—oh, and she sends you her best. Thanks—we'll be there in a little while."

Stuart thanked Nick for the favor, and turned and asked what he could do to help me clean up. "Nothing," I replied. "I have to make a cake, so I'll just clean up everything at one time. Plus, I don't mean to be rude, but I can do it faster with y'all out of my way."

"Well, I guess that's our cue," Nick said, "but I am not going until I have at least cleared the table, and I do remember your saying something about apple pie?"

"Oh, good Lord! I forgot all about dessert," I blushed. "Who would like pie and who wants vanilla ice cream on top?"

The right arms of both men took flight, and I smiled while reaching for three small plates. After nearly licking them clean, my guests placed their dessert plates next to the kitchen sink then scurried like mice helping me bring the few remaining dishes from the dining room into the kitchen.

With the kindest voice I could muster, I said, "Okay, now, I need for the two of you to leave. I have things to do and you are both equally in my way." Earlier Nick had asked if I knew of a bakery where he could get a coconut cake for a birthday party for Coy, his barn manager. I said I would bake him one, and it would take me no time.

I walked behind the two of them as they made their way to the living room. Stuart took a seat on the sofa and exchanged socks and shoes. Then he hugged me, thanking me for the wonderful dinner and the much-overdue reunion. The reunion was actually kind of sweet, and I sort of understood. It really was nice to see him again, but while he meant no harm, it was weird. I guessed it was possible to never truly get over a past love, but I wasn't interested, and he needed to understand that.

Nick took several steps toward the door, turned back, and gave me the most incredibly tender, knee-melting kiss I had ever received. Mr. Heart's intentions were also not to be confused and were twofold: *nice to meet you, Stuart, and Sarah's mine.* However Neanderthal that move was, I loved that Nick would be so bold as to mark his territory in such a passionate way. I didn't need for him to, but it was heart-warming all the same.

"I'll see you in the morning," Nick said. "I really do appreciate your making the cake. Please don't stay up too late."

"Oh, I won't," I whispered trying to catch my breath, "Remember, it comes from a box, but don't tell anyone. Annie and I will be there in the morning. Be careful driving. It was very good to see you, Stuart. Good luck with your lecture. I'm sure it will be well attended and reviewed."

Standing in the open doorway, Nick turned, and while nibbling my ear, said, "See ya tomorrow."

"Absolutely," was my only reply.

November 20, 2009
Dear Debby,

Lord have mercy . . . this has been a hell of a day!

Earlier today I spent a fortune on an outfit for my date with Nick and allowed my friends to tack on another hefty chunk of change for lingerie. I stood in my bedroom and reviewed my purchase and smiled thinking . . . it really is pretty. I've never known this feeling and it is nice, but it will take a while for it to be a part of me.

I ended up having dinner at my house with Stuart, an old boyfriend, and Nick. Holy mother of pearl! It's way too much to write, but suffice it to say, some questions have been answered and we need to talk about things. I've seen a new side to Nick, and I like it very much. He stood his ground with Stuart, and fought for me, and our future . . . that was amazing. I really didn't need for him to fight for me, but it was wonderful that he did.

More later... but this is an interesting reaction—I'm also more than curious as to how a signed copy of my book found its way to that silent auction table. Who donated it? Was it a famous horse person? Maybe I'll ask Stuart—maybe not— curiosity killed the cat, but satisfaction brought it back.

With all good wishes,
Sarah

CHAPTER **28**

"*H*oly cats, it's cold," I said with rattling teeth as Annie and I set off on our morning walk. "It must be in the teens out here. Mornin', Miss Madge," I yelled, waving in her direction. Miss Madge had lived her entire life in Hadley Falls, and the last sixty plus years were spent in the house next to mine. She and her husband Walter bought the house soon after they were married and had never lived anywhere else. Miss Madge had been a widow for years but refused to downsize. She once told me the only way she was leaving her house was in a box.

"Hi, cutie. It's mighty early for your walk, considering how late you stayed up last night. Did all of those men stay for dinner?" she asked with a smile.

Somewhat surprised, I replied, "Yes, ma'am, they did. Luckily I had enough food to go around. I was not expecting either one of them. Actually, I had your name in the pot for half, but my unexpected company licked the platter clean."

"Well, damn the luck," Miss Madge said with levity. "What did I miss, and who ate my share? Was one of them that tall, handsome man who came around this past Monday? It looked like the same car."

"Why, Miss Madge, I do think you have been spying on me," I said with a chuckle. "Yes, the tall, handsome man is Nick Heart, and he lives in Greenway. The other gentleman was Stuart Branch, who was actually an old college beau of mine."

"Are you going to marry that good-looking one? Why do you want a man anyway? You know nowadays you don't have to marry anybody. Just let him take you to dinner and the movies and say good night. If he ever makes you pay for anything, drop him like a bad habit," she said.

"Oh, Miss Madge, you're so funny." I laughed. "I hear what you're saying, but I think I'm the marrying kind. Besides, what would the neighbors think? Not to mention my mother?"

Miss Madge picked up her morning paper and said, "Who cares what the neighbors think? As for your mother, you are old enough to make your own decisions with or without her approval. You know, Evelyn Farley over on Elm has had men in and out of her house for decades, and she still sits on the city council. Years ago, Blanche Snipes was more than just an account on Sycamore with the Fuller Brush salesman, and she's still singing in the church choir. So, I think you can have a gentleman friend and not get married."

"Well, Miss Madge, you have given me something to think about. Annie and I are going to need to get cracking—I have a date with a man and a horse."

"Okay. You have a good day, too, and remember: you're worth more than the likes of Parker Sams, so choose wisely," Miss Madge said, turning and walking back up her sidewalk.

Inside thirty minutes we were off to Long Leaf Farm. We had been there enough times that my dog knew where we were as soon as we made our turn from the highway. Annie stood up in the back seat and started to bark out the window. It took me a second to locate the source of her excitement, but there in the distance was Caesar, running parallel with my car.

I put the car in park and opened the back door, and a golden streak vaulted from the car. I watched as my carefully groomed city canine squeezed under the fence and blew across the field. She was met by a dripping-wet, filthy beast of a dog who proceeded to roll her around on the slushy ground for several turns.

Linda and Nancy stood waiting for me in the barn parking lot. Their smiles could be seen from a distance, and I had a rush of doubt about the quality of my birthday cake. I don't know why their opinion seemed to matter so much, but it did.

"Hi there," I said. "I hope I'm not late."

"No, you're right on time," Linda replied. "In fact, you're a little early, and that's great. Coy is in the back field mending a fence, and we can get everything fixed before he gets back. Sarah, you really are a life-saver. Oh my gosh," she said, taking a look at the birthday cake as I pulled it from the car, "look at this cake—it's perfect!"

"Thanks," I said. "Now let's hope it tastes good."

The three of us scurried around the office to create the perfect barn birthday party. My cake was the centerpiece, and I beamed at my handiwork. I peeked out the door and shrieked at the sight of my once-clean dog. Nick chuckled and said he would take care of cleaning her up before we left for home.

Walking the dogs to his house, Nick glanced over his shoulder and said, "Were your ears burning last night after Stuart and I left?"

"Uh, no—should they have been?" I stammered.

Nick smiled and said, "You were our topic of conversation for hours—and what a conversation it was!"

"Really?" I said, gasping.

"Yes, we talked long enough for the wine buzz to wear off. He carried on about the close and deep connection between you two—I said if it ended when you met Parker, it couldn't have been but so strong. But now he's sure he can rekindle the flame you two once had. I assured him that our fire burns hotter each day and appears to show no sign of burning out, plus we're no longer eighteen and actually do know what and who we want. In a last-ditch effort to get one up on me, he said you two had a special artistic connection. I said your love of horses and a man who kisses his dog trumped all. And I told him I would never give you up."

"Goodness," was all I could find to say.

Coy's midday birthday party was in full swing and the barn was brimming with people, most of whom I didn't know. In the horse world, an introduction to a human will almost always include a brief description of said equestrian's mount. It does help with identification and is never questioned or thought rude. Nick was at my side taking on the responsibility of names and adding a brief description of each person's horse. I would nod with recognition, not of the person but that of the mental equine image.

Nick whispered tidbits of information about a guest here and there. Suddenly I interrupted, saying, "Well, look what the cat drug in."

Nick stopped in mid-conversation and glanced in the direction of the office door. "What's she doing here? I know I didn't invite her. I wonder who did."

"Hi, Rea," I said. "What a surprise. We stood right here just two days ago."

"There's a good explanation, I promise. My date is parking the car," she replied.

"Well, we're glad to have you," I said with a genuine smile. "Let me take your coat."

Rea offered me her suede coat along with the Barbour scarf, and smiled to say hello to a lady standing on the other side of the office. I watched as she tacked her way in and out of the guests to find her apparent friend. *Hmm,* I thought, *this small world thing is getting out of hand.*

Nick had moved to the other side of the room to answer a boarder's question when the next guest arrived. He was a very tall, thin man whom I'd never met. I stepped in his direction, offering my hand and a pleasant hello. "I'm Sarah Sams. Welcome to the party."

"It's nice to meet you, Sarah," replied the stranger while holding my hand. "I'm Jack Heart, Nick's brother."

Standing more upright than I thought possible, I sputtered, "Well, this is quite a treat. Nick has told me a lot about you."

"I'm sure he has, and I doubt much of it was complimentary," Jack said. "Now where is my little brother?"

"I don't believe it," Nick said grabbing his brother's hand and pulling him close. "What are you doing here? Why didn't you call?"

With each brother slapping the other on the back, Rea reappeared. Weaving her arm over Jack's, she gave a slight but deliberate tug. Jack shifted his weight several times, cleared this throat, and began to speak. "I guess you're both wondering what we're doing here. We've come to see you, Nick, and it's just coincidental that we happened upon your party. Our news is big and best left for later."

Nick stood with his arms folded. "*Our* news? Well, this should be interesting." He looked back and forth between Jack and Rea; both smiled, but neither moved to speak. "Okay, then," Nick said. "Later it is. I look forward to hearing what you have to say. In the meantime, please join us to celebrate Coy's birthday."

The two brothers embraced once more, and it was easy to see how much they had missed each other. I, on the other hand, was about to die from curiosity.

Coy was more than thrilled with his celebration. He said that turning fifty-two was not so bad when you had friends, but that the heat coming from the field of birthday candles was almost enough to roast marshmallows.

Nick circulated throughout the office, giving everyone equal attention. Jack and Reagan were a part of the group in no time and seemed to be enjoying themselves. I just wanted everyone to go home so we could learn the reason for their unannounced visit.

With the last guest driving down the lane, Linda, Nancy, and I began the process of cleaning up. Nick offered to help, but Nancy quickly suggested that we really could do it faster without his assistance. Linda added that he should use the mule, an all-terrain vehicle, and drive Jack and Reagan around the property.

Nancy, Linda, and I had fun getting to know each other, and it seemed like hardly any time had passed before the door opened and in walked Nick, Jack, and Reagan. They found us sitting side-by-side on a tattered divan, one holding a crumb-covered cake server, the next clutching an overloaded large trash bag, and the last swinging a sleeve of cups. In unrehearsed unison we looked up and said, "Hi."

"Are you?" asked Nick.

"Yes, we're high on life. How was the tour?" I asked.

"Great," Nick answered turning to his brother. "Jack, we'll see you two later."

"Ladies, the party was fun and thanks again for allowing us to join in," Jack said, and with that they were out the door.

As Nick peeled off his outer layer of clothing, he said, "Now, if you and I are going riding, we need to get a move on. I'm going to let the dogs out for a run. Oh, we've been invited to dinner with Jack and Rea."

"Fabulous! I guess I'll need to call Zorba's and cancel our table for two."

"I've already called and asked them to move it to Sunday—assuming that's all right with you."

"Of course. But I don't have a change of clothes for dinner, and I really can't go anywhere looking like this," I said walking out the door.

"No problem," Nick chuckled. "They want to take us to the Tinker Inn in Hadley Falls. If you leave here by four o'clock that should give you enough time to do whatever you need to do, right?"

"That'll work. The Tinker Inn, how nice," I replied. "You'll need to wear a tie."

"I'd wear a tux to find out what's going on. Now let's go for a ride," Nick answered.

CHAPTER 29

$\mathcal{I}$ was about halfway home when my cell phone rang. "Hi, Mom. Are you getting ready for your big date?" Emma asked.

"Hi there, and no, actually we've postponed it until tomorrow. Nick's brother and girlfriend are in town and we're going out with them tonight. How sweet that you remembered," I said.

"It's hard to forget your mother's first date," she replied. "So I'll call you probably Monday to hear all about it. Have fun."

"Okay and love to all," I said.

Since I started living alone, one of my quirks was to carry my cell phone everywhere I went. Placing it on the bath mat, I stepped into the bank of steam rolling clockwise behind the shower curtain. "Ahhhhhhhhh," I sighed. "Now this feels good." I arched my back and enjoyed the hot water therapy as it pounded my torso.

The blaring ring of the telephone was an abrupt interruption to my tranquility. Reaching around the shower curtain, I dried my hand and grabbed the receiver. "Hello?"

"Hi Sarah, this is Stuart. What's up?"

"Uh, I'm in the shower. Can I call you back later?"

"I just wanted to see if we could have dinner. I'm on my way to your house."

I paused. This had to end and right now. "Stuart, I truly don't want to be rude or hurt your feelings, but I'm not interested in a relationship with you. That ship sailed a long time ago. The memories are wonderful, but you and I are past tense. It was great to see you, and the gift of your sculpture is something I'll treasure forever, but that's all there is. I hope you can understand. I really need to go now."

After a moment, he said, "I will take this as a momentary setback, but I won't give up just yet. I'll go back to Raleigh tonight, but I'll be back; you can count on that."

"Well, I'm telling you that I don't share the same feelings, and if you don't stop, and I mean right now, I might be forced to call the law," I said, agitated. Why wouldn't this man get real? "Have a safe trip back to Raleigh."

Then a strange high-pitched series of squeals came from the other end of the line, and Stuart bellowed the most horrifying scream I have ever heard. I was certain that I had heard his car crashing into something.

The phone was still on, but he would not respond to my questions. I could hear him moaning and what I thought to be a very faint whisper. "Stuart: listen to me. I am going to hang up and call 911. I'm sure you took Highway 64 from Raleigh, so I'm guessing you're on Woodland Road now to get to Hadley Falls. Hang on and I'll get someone there as soon as possible. Don't hang up your phone; they can track you by the signal. Don't hang up," I insisted one last time.

I was dialing 911 and trying to get out of the shower at

the same time. A woman took all the needed information and assured me that emergency services were on the way. I asked if someone could call me when they found Stuart and let me know what was going on. She asked if I was in anyway related to the person needing assistance, and I briefly explained the situation. After a moment, she said that they would be able to tell me if he needed medical attention and if so, where they were taking him.

At lightning speed, I dried myself off, raced around putting on some clothes, and brought Annie back inside. Within five minutes my phone was ringing. "Hello," I said anxiously.

"Sarah—is something wrong?" It was Nick. "I just wanted to tell you that I might be a little early. I need to stop at Home Depot before they close."

"I'm slightly frantic right now," I said, and explained the situation.

"I'll hang up, but don't hesitate to call me back if you need me," Nick replied.

"Thanks," I said. Trying to slow myself down both emotionally and physically, I took deliberate breaths and closed my eyes. *Who makes decisions for you at the hospital when you're alone and unable to decide for yourself?* That was a question for Deborah Baxter.

When my phone rang next, I heard, "May I please speak to Sarah Sams?"

With a deep inhale, I responded, "This is she; this is Sarah Sams."

"Ma'am, this is Officer Wright with the Highway Patrol,

and I am calling in regard to Stuart Branch. I'm not allowed to give out information over the phone, but I can tell you that he is being taken to County General Hospital in Raleigh. Would you like to speak with him?"

"Yes—yes I would," I replied quickly.

"Hi, Sarah. Don't worry, I'm fine," Stuart said with surprising calm.

"Are you sure?"

"Yes, I am sure," he said. "I just got a bump to the head, and I think I may have a broken ankle. I know you have plans for tonight, so don't change anything for me. I'm sure I'll be in the hospital for a few days, so you can come by maybe tomorrow? Bring my new best friend Nick and we can have a party. I'll supply the Jell-O."

Pausing for a minute, I said, "If you are lying to me, Stuart Branch, I'll have your head."

"Too late," he laughed, "the airbag beat you to it. Now go have a good time at dinner, and I hope to see you tomorrow."

Another voice cut in: "Ms. Sams, this is Officer Wright. I have to break this up; we really need to go." And with that, the phone went silent.

Before getting up to finish dressing, I closed my eyes and said, "Dear God, please watch over Stuart. I know our situation is very strange, but I don't want any harm to come his way. So please take care of him. Amen. . . . Yikes, look at the time."

I stood in the doorway of my closet, searching for my little black dress. I decided my new outfit was on hold for our just-us date tomorrow night. Finding the dress, I checked it for stains or wrinkles, and dusted off my only pair of black heels.

Forty-five minutes later, I was presentable. My hair had refused to cooperate, so I'd twisted it into a bun and run a metallic silver chopstick through it on the diagonal. My make-up was applied, and I was all dressed up and ready to go. Taking a breath, I realized I had about fifteen minutes to spare before Nick was scheduled to arrive. I took that time to give the hospital a call and check on Stuart.

"Good evening. County General Hospital, how may I direct your call?" asked the pleasant voice on the other end of the phone.

"Yes," I replied, "I'm calling to check on a patient of yours—Stuart Branch."

I was quickly transferred to the nurses' station.

"Mr. Branch is resting comfortably," answered the nurse. "Would you like to speak with him?"

"Oh, yes—yes, I would."

"One moment," he said, "I'm connecting you to room 416."

Stuart answered the phone on the third ring and sounded just fine. We talked for the next five minutes about the accident, his injuries, and the hospital food. I reminded him that since tomorrow was Sunday, I would be there around noon or a bit after. He said he couldn't wait to see me, and would I please bring lunch. I laughed and said I would try, then I said my goodbyes.

Several minutes later, the doorbell rang. The little black dress was apparently a good choice. I got my WOW from Nick—and thought *just wait until you see the new outfit—fingers crossed!* But not to give myself too much credit, this was the first time the man had ever seen me in anything other than riding breeches, turtlenecks, and fleece of some sort, along with helmet hair.

"You look amazing! I love your hair, and the chopstick—how you," Nick said.

With a smile on my face I said thank you, and off we went.

CHAPTER 30

$\mathcal{W}$alking toward the table at the restaurant, I felt the strangest shiver come across my body. *Weird*, I thought, *I have only felt that one other time in my life—the night my father died.*

I couldn't help remembering the last time I'd had dinner at the Tinker Inn, but I tried desperately to put those thoughts aside. I did love this beautiful old Inn—it was very well appointed and all the tables had king and queen arm chairs with matching side chairs resting on both flanks. The main dining room was especially well done, with dark wood wainscoting bellow the chair rail, and a rich linen hue on the plaster walls above.

Reagan greeted us with an exuberant hello while Jack sat pressed against the backdrop of the armchair upholstered in a rich English-hunt-scene tapestry. Nick offered me my chair before taking his. Working on the final adjustment of my seat, purse, and dress tail, I was once again consumed by that strange shiver.

"Are you all right?" asked Nick. "Do you need for me to get your coat?"

"Oh no, I'm fine," I said, "Just a shiver."

Nick and Jack shared the responsibility of ordering a bottle of wine. They reviewed the multitude of choices and settled on a bottle of Napa Valley cabernet sauvignon. Even if I drank wine, I'd still find the sniffing, twirling, and swishing of the grape climaxing in a string flowery adjectives ridiculous.

The waiter, who had introduced himself as Hal, turned in Nick's direction and asked if he had seen anything interesting in the starter section of the menu. Nick responded by ordering the crab cakes and the charcuterie plate—whatever that was.

As Hal left, Jack asked if I had ever been here before and if so, what I would recommend. "Yes, I have, and the beef and lamb are excellent. The chocolate cake is amazing if you save room for dessert."

"When were you last here?" Rea asked.

"Nearly two years ago," I said. "I had no idea that my ex-husband was plying me with a fabulous meal only to announce a handful of days later that he was leaving on the arm of another woman. All of the dinners I've had here were wonderful, but the grandeur of the last one fades significantly due to the circumstances."

Realizing my news found everyone momentarily speechless, I continued saying, "But never mind that! The Tinker Inn has been written up in several Southern magazines for their exceptional menu, service, and 'ghost sightings.' Many think Mildred Tinker still haunts this old house. She was the jilted first wife of the original Mr. Tinker, and she disappeared under the cloak of darkness one hot July night. Everyone knew he'd done her in, but there was never any proof, so some time later she was declared deceased. After a brief period of socially required mourning, Mr. Tinker married Iris Hadley—heir to her father's fortune. The Hadley family was huge in the farming of tobacco and thus our city bears their name. Interesting, right?"

Rea blew right past my short history lesson and launched into a barrage of questions about my past, and I answered only the last one on her list. "Parker left me for another woman, and I wish them all the best life has to offer, Rea. I don't really know why he made that choice, but when something is over—it's just over. I'd leave it at that and move on, which is what I am trying to do."

Taking a deep breath, Jack broke the silence by saying, "But when something isn't over, that moment should be celebrated as well, which is why we are here tonight. Rea and I have invited the two of you to dinner because we wanted you to be the first to know."

"Know what?" Nick asked, leaning forward in his chair.

Clearing his throat Jack said, "Rea and I are . . . moving in together. It's no longer the sex-crazed lover relationship it once was, but more of a loving companionship."

With jaw dropping silence, Nick and I sat paralyzed. Only two days before, Reagan had swooped onto the farm like a scene from a daytime melodrama and dropped her bombshell of information all over me, with the intention of causing irreversible damage to Nick's and my relationship. I thought Nick should be the first to comment.

After a long stint of silence, Rea said, "Well, don't you have anything to say?"

Still Nick sat stunned and unable to speak. So I blurted out, "Goodness, when did this happen? What was Thursday all about? You sat right there telling me all about your past with Nick—and by the way, left out a great deal of the story. Now, here we are just two days later, and you're making plans to live with Jack. That's quite a turnaround, don't you think?"

"Thursday was simply a case of bad judgment," Rea remarked.

"Bad judgment?" I said, my voice rising in volume. "Is that what you call it? I'd say it was more purpose driven, if not flat-out vindictive!"

Rea sat up very straight. "When you got back from the hunter pace, you and your friend at Falling Creek talked all about meeting Nick, hoping he would call, and a dinner that followed. Inez knew I would want to know, so she called and told me about it. I became absolutely enraged that Nick was going to fall in love with you in a way he had never loved me and have a forever life with you that he and I never had. I can't really explain, but that realization took me to a place I seldom visit. Jack knows," she said, reaching for his hand, "how worked up I can get and where my anger can take me. I know it was hurtful, and at the time, yes, vindictive, but please believe me when I say that I am truly very sorry for what I did."

"If I may," Nick interrupted. "Yes, Rea, your actions the other day were unfortunate, and that's being kind. I am not convinced that your intentions are honorable now, but that's not the most important issue at present. Jack, the bigger question is what about your wife and children?"

Jack displayed a nervous smile and said, "Nick, you know Paige and I never had a real marriage. She came from money, I was an opportunist, and there you have it. I only stayed for the kids. They're all out of the house now, and Paige agrees that we should go our separate ways—not that she's happy about the circumstances. There is much more to it than just me and Rea."

Nick raised his eyebrows. "Such as?"

"Apparently Paige found out about the affair and the baby years ago, though we never discussed it. She had also discovered that I had been unfaithful with a half dozen other women as well. When I announced several months ago that I wanted a divorce, Paige made her findings known. There was really nothing I could say, except that her information was correct and that, except for our children, I truly did regret that whole period of time. She called me every name in the book, slapped my face, and said that we would communicate only via our attorneys from here on."

Nick shook his head. "Good lord, Jack. Why didn't you tell me any of this was going on?"

"Well, I've had a lot to deal with. I kept trying to find the time to tell you, but . . . well, what Paige doesn't know is that I'm sick, and the prognosis is not good. I would like to live out my final years in peace, truth, and with someone I have always loved. Years ago I was too much of a coward to leave Paige for Rea. I wasn't going to make that mistake again."

"Sick? What's wrong with you?" asked Nick, placing his hand on his brother's arm.

"Advanced liver disease," Jack said, "and my kidneys are not in good shape either. Apparently my love for good scotch really is going to be the death of me. The doctors have given me five years at best. This is where you come in," Jack continued. "First and foremost, you are my brother, and I wanted you to know. Second, I have a proposition for you. I would like to spend the last years of my life at the coast, specifically at your house on Martha's Vineyard. I don't want to make any purchases at this point, and you never go there, so I thought you might consider renting it to me—no, don't argue. I won't live there for free. Rea is going to stay with me and work from there."

Nick nodded slowly. I could tell he was having a hard time taking this all in, so I chimed in. "I'm so sorry you're ill, truly I am, but to put a frame around this story, and if you don't mind my asking, how did the two of you reunite?"

"We found ourselves at the same horse show about a year ago, and it became obvious that we were not over," Jack responded. "We neither one knew exactly how to say hello on the first day. But by the third day, we broke our years of silence, and here we are." Jack said, once again squeezing Rea's hand and smiling. "It's been over twenty years, and the feelings are different, but they are still very strong in a new way. And as I said earlier, we need each other for lots of reasons."

Before the conversation could continue, Hal reappeared with selected bottle of grape and a corkscrew. With the grace of a wine master, he removed the seal, then the cork, and poured the moment-of-truth thimbleful of truth for Nick to sample. "Excellent," Nick responded to the delight of our overzealous server.

Resting the cork on the table, Hal reached for my glass. "No, thank you," I said. "I would prefer a glass of sweet tea, please."

"Of course, ma'am," Hal said, and finished pouring the wine for Rea and the men.

Nick turned to me and began to apologize for his forgetfulness. I could tell he was genuinely upset with my being overlooked, but Hal soon returned with our appetizers and my tea.

As Hal cleared our salad plates, Nick pushed back a bit in his chair and began to ask Jack about his health and the house on Martha's Vineyard. Rea chimed in now and again, but I just watched as the brothers caught up.

The balance of the evening went off without a hitch, and the discussion of Jack's health and Rea's presence became more palatable as the night progressed. Nick stood firm that he didn't want to charge his dying brother anything for the use of his house. But it was decided that Jack would indeed rent the house on Martha's Vineyard for the agreed-upon price of twelve hundred dollars a year. Using his realtor voice, Nick insisted that a higher dollar amount would involve all sorts of paperwork, and would be too much trouble. They hashed out the details during the meal and shook hands on the deal over dessert.

Hal offered the check to the center of the table and both men reached in unison for the leather folder. "This one is on me," Jack said, with conviction.

"Thank you, big brother," Nick said. "But you really don't have to do that."

"I know, but I want to," Jack volleyed.

The four of us worked our way toward the parking lot and exchanged one last round of goodbyes.

Turning the key in the ignition, Nick said, "How was that for the first meeting of my family?"

"Interesting—I'll give you that," I replied. "I am so sorry that Jack is desperately ill, but at least he won't be alone."

"No kidding," Nick said. "I never dreamed that I'd be grateful for Rea's help, but I think she'll be a true asset for Jack."

Nick walked me to my front door and stepped inside while I turned on some lights. "Would you like a cup of coffee of something?" I asked.

"No to the coffee, but to the something, absolutely," Nick replied. "I'm sorry about all the drama tonight, and want to assure you that our date tomorrow night will be a quiet one, and just us," he said, taking my face in his hands. He kissed me good night, and it was absolutely the most passionate to date.

"I'll be honest with you, Sarah," he said, when we eventually pulled away, "I want nothing more than to stay with you tonight, but it's not the right time, and I don't want to push you too fast," Nick said.

"I'll be honest with you as well," I said. "You're right we need a bit more time, but my feelings are probably just as strong as yours."

November 21, 2009
Dear Debby,

Nick and I joined his brother Jack and girlfriend at the Tinker Inn for dinner. Yummy food, all dressed up, Jack's girlfriend is none other than the old girlfriend from Nick's past (too crazy and more on that later in your office). The bigger piece of tonight's events is that Nick and I made it clear to one another that we want each other very much. It took all I had to let him leave. It's not just lust, and of that I'm sure. Dear Lord, I want that man in every way.

With all good wishes,
Sarah

CHAPTER 31

cAfter breakfast I turned my attention to the promised lunch. I thought, *all I've done recently is prepare special meals for two men. What is wrong with this picture? Was my generosity and love for cooking sending the wrong message?* It was too late now—for today anyway. I had promised something for Stuart, and I would never go back on my word.

Looking into the refrigerator, I decided that homemade chicken soup would be just the ticket to better health. I filled a pot with chicken broth, wild rice, a bit of onion, celery, carrots, peas, salt and pepper, and diced pieces of leftover chicken, then pulled on my frayed walking coat. Before leaving, I gave the soup one good stir and reduced the heat on the burner.

"Okay, good girl—are you ready to go?" I asked Annie, putting on her harness. She trotted out in front as far as her leash would allow, and I chuckled. "I'll take that as a yes."

As we walked up and down the uneven sidewalks of historic Hadley Falls, I thought about how in less than two years I had become an independent woman who had found a sense of freedom I'd thought unattainable. I realized that I also truly liked being on my own. Perhaps my actual adventure was finding myself. Maybe this whole thing was about recognizing my true identity. It was at that moment I understood what I really wanted. I realized that I didn't *need* Nick; I *wanted* him, and those were unquestionably two different schools of thought.

The smell of comfort greeted Annie and me when we finished our walk. My grandmother was a gifted cook, and every Saturday after Aunt Lucy and I finished our morning ride, Grammy O'Neil had lunch waiting for both of us. The soup, be it chicken, broccoli and cheese, or vegetable, was almost always accompanied with a basket of fresh cornbread and butter, never margarine. My grandmother was known to launch into a diatribe about the evils of whipped spread, artificial sweeteners, and other pretend foods. "If it didn't come out of the ground," she would say, slicing the air with her wooden spoon, "or from one of God's creations, then it isn't real food." In many ways, time had proven her right.

Annie wasn't pleased to be uninvited, but there was just too much going on this time. With one plop on the den floor, she licked my hand as I said I'd be back soon.

After a quick ride with Rascal, I dialed Nick's cell phone to let him know I was on my way.

"Hi, darlin'. How was your ride?" Nick asked.

My mouth dropped. "How did you know I went for a ride?"

"Sarah Sams, if you are able, you'll catch a quick ride before drawing your last breath," Nick said.

"Well, so maybe you're right, but I'm on my way now," I said. "The roads are much better today. I bet we'll have school tomorrow."

"I'll be watching for you," Nick said. "Just park where you usually do, and I'll drive the rest of the way."

"Okay, but I'll be happy to drive."

"I know," Nick hesitated, "but your car, well, and I say this with love and respect—your car smells like a wet dog. And the golden retriever hair rolls out like prairie tumbleweed when you open the door."

I hooted with laughter. "Yup—that's true! I carry a lint brush everywhere I go."

"I hope my honesty hasn't hurt your feelings," Nick said, "but I would rather take my car the rest of the way. I can hear the receptionist as she announces to us that they don't allow Wookiees in their hospital."

"My car is a wreck most of the time, and no, you have not hurt my feelings. Embarrassed me just a touch—but hurt? Not at all. Every time I take my car to the full-service auto spa you can see the men who work there running in every direction. There is always one new guy who draws the metaphorical short stick. The rest of the employees laugh."

"Will you forgive me?" Nick asked.

"No, I will not," I said, "because you haven't hurt my feelings so there is nothing to forgive. If we are going to have a relationship, then we both need to feel comfortable saying what we think. Besides, you have a much nicer car, and I love the heated seats. So gas up the Jag and I'll be there in about thirty minutes."

I needed to call Betsy, who I knew would be at the farmer's market. After I told her about Nick refusing my car, and when she stopped laughing, I asked if she could get me several pumpkins and gourds for my front porch, two butternut squash for Thanksgiving dinner, and half a pound of goat cheese.

"I'm very nervous about this trip, because I plan to tell Nick about Dr. Baxter. What if he thinks going to a shrink is unacceptable?"

"Why would anyone in this day and time frown in the direction of good mental health? Logging hours with a psychologist is considered to be quite chic in many circles," Betsy said.

"Maybe, but it still makes me nervous."

"Everything will be fine—you'll see. Just take it one activity at a time. Now hang up and pay attention to your driving," Betsy insisted.

"Okay," I said, "I'll talk to you later."

In an effort to calm down and divert my attentions, I turned the radio to my favorite country music station. Most of my friends didn't share my appreciation for country music, and especially bluegrass, but I loved it.

I could see Nick's handsome frame standing close to the corner of the barn, and the closer I got, the stronger my heart began to beat. Nick Heart was hot and a wonderful person all rolled into one, and I wanted him for myself.

I have about twenty yards to calm down and regain my composure, I thought. *Nope, it's not going to happen.*

CHAPTER 32

"It's good to see you," Nick said, giving me a gentle kiss and then another that said *I've really missed you.*

I was still trying to calm down, and his kiss finished me off. My legs felt a bit weak and my face began to flush. "It's good to see you too," I said, dusting myself off. "Do we have time for me to say hello to Buddy and make a trip to the restroom?"

"Sure. As long as we leave in the next thirty minutes, we should be at the hospital by twelve thirty or so. Are you all right?"

"Yes and no," I said tentatively. "Let me say hello to Buddy and go to the bathroom, and then I want to talk to you about something."

"Am I going to like this conversation?" Nick asked.

"I can't answer that question, but I need some sort of reply before we leave for the hospital. Give me a minute and I'll meet you in your office," I said, hurrying down the center aisle of the barn.

With my hellos to Buddy and the trip to the restroom completed, I cleared my throat and took a deep breath. Looking through the glass panes of the office door, I could see Nick sitting at his desk. He appeared to be anxious, twisting his leather chair right and then left. "There," I said as I entered the room, "that's much better. Now, I want to talk to you about something."

Nick sat upright in his chair as I positioned myself on the arm of the tattered sofa. "Sarah, what's wrong? Are you angry with me?"

"No! No, I just need to tell you some things before we go to visit Stuart. Hmm, where to start? As I'm sure you've realized, condensing a story is not easy for me, but I'll try. After my ex-husband left, I went to work on the remodeling of my current home, and took on extra responsibilities at school. I now know that all of that was an effort to avoid what really needed to be addressed, and that was me. On Betsy's suggestion, I began to see a psychologist in her husband's office, Dr. Deborah Baxter. Early into our sessions she suggested I keep a journal concerning my feelings and thoughts. I'm not ten years old, and Dear Diary seemed stupid, so I began each entry with 'Dear Debby.' Now when anything happens that is weird, out of the ordinary, very funny, or upsetting, I always say 'Dear Debby.'"

Nick chuckled. "Ah, that explains it." He stopped twisting in his chair and said, "I understand."

"I hope so," I said taking a breath. "I love going to Dr. Baxter and am thinking I might continue, just because I enjoy the time. I once stood silent on expressing my thoughts and feelings, but now I can say things out loud, and I walk away feeling lighter and rejuvenated. I'm telling you this to be perfectly honest about who I am and what I bring to the table. A relationship without honesty is doomed from the beginning. You and I won't live long enough to tell each other everything that has happened to us in the past gazillion years, but we can touch on the bigger events in our lives."

"That's very true," Nick replied sliding back in his chair.

"Secondly," I said, releasing my clasped hands, "I will never relinquish my independence. I have worked very hard to find my true identity and sitting before you is the real Sarah O'Neil Sams. I love country music and rock 'n' roll. I go to bed every night with Rod Stewart's *Great American Songbook* singing me to sleep. I get very scared about money and being thrown to the metaphorical wolves. I've learned how to truly take care of myself, and I'm rather proud of that."

"I understand it all," Nick said. "I've been on my own for a very long time, and I have no intention of relinquishing my independence either, but that doesn't mean we can't also be totally together."

"I agree," I said smiling. "Oh, and I'm a registered Democrat and a Presbyterian."

Nick rested his back against the brown leather desk chair, and I watched as a faint, then more pronounced, smile came across his face. "I have said this more than once, but I'll say it again: you are a piece of work, Sarah Sams. I appreciate your honesty, truly I do. I am very grateful to know these things, and I don't understand why you would have thought otherwise. I guess we don't know each other well enough yet to be able to see inside one another, but rest assured that I understand about the need to talk to an impartial listener."

"Are you sure?"

"Yes—when I got out of the service, I sought counseling and continued weekly visits for at least a year. I had what I thought was becoming a serious drinking problem. Alcoholism runs in my family—remember Jack's issue? So I knew I had to do something before it was too late. It did me a world of good and, now that I think about it, I went back to the psychologist after that mess with Rea, Jack, and me. I needed help with that situation, and I was worried that I would pick up the bottle again. I still have a glass of wine, maybe two, but that's where is stops—I promise."

I nodded, grateful that he had seen my disclosures as an opening to make his own.

"I understand it all, and not today, but there are other things to discuss as well. For example money—yours-mine-ours—I think there is an easy way to find middle ground especially when we're both in agreement. As time goes on, we can get down to the nuts and bolts of our financial situation, and devise a plan that works for both of us, together."

He walked over to me and sat on the edge of his desk. "I am in love with you, Sarah, and everyone thinks I'm some sort of a nut case for feeling that way in such a short time, but I can't imagine living without you. Oh yes, and I'm a registered Republican and a Catholic."

Staring into his azure eyes, I could feel the tears welling in mine.

"Don't cry. Why are you crying? We can work through the religious issues," Nick said with alarm.

"I don't care that you're Catholic. Republican maybe, especially if you vote straight ticket, but Catholic, no." I said brushing away a tear. "Nick, I'm as crazy as a bat and I will die that way. I don't think like anyone else. I have two-way conversations with my dog. I discuss jumps and courses with my horse, and I am beyond positive they both understand what I am saying. I could continue, but there would be no point. And here you sit telling me you know all of this, you don't care, and that you love me anyway?"

"That's right," Nick said with a smile. "It would take a serious emergency for me to ride in your car—but all the rest is wonderful. Now, if we're going to get to the hospital by one o'clock, we had better get a move on. Oh, wait a minute, I almost forgot." Nick said pulling me into his arms, kissing me deeply, and once again curling my toes.

Trying to catch my breath, I felt a huge wave of relief. *He didn't think I was crazy, or if he did, he loved me anyway.*

Hand in hand, Nick and I walked out of the barn. I gathered Stuart's promised lunch from my car and placed it in the floor behind my seat in Nick's car. "Prairie tumbleweed? Do you really think my car is that bad?"

"Yes, your car is a hairy wreck," Nick said. "I'm a neat freak. I don't care about dusting or dishes in the sink, but I like my clothes and my car just right. I don't allow eating or animals of any sort in my car either."

"Speaking of food, I am a funny eater. I prefer to graze through my day, rather than consume large meals. When you say no eating in your car, does that include travel drinks?" I asked, raising an eyebrow.

"What exactly is a travel drink?" Nick asked.

"You know, a soft drink or water from a fast-food restaurant with a top and a straw. I'm not sure I could go very far without one of those. And of course, travel drinks are usually complemented by cookies or a snack of some sort," I said with a grin. "Eating and snacking aren't exactly the same thing."

"Uh, I don't actually see the difference. I'll need to think about it," Nick said.

His car was very clean and smelled lovely; I'd give him that. I looked over at him, my heart swelling three sizes at how happy I was being with him. I said, "Nicholas Heart, I've waited a lifetime for you. I should write Parker a thank-you note for giving me the opportunity to find myself, and the man of my dreams. You know, Southern women write notes for everything—and usually on monogrammed stationery."

Nick reached over and grasped my hand. "I may have spent decades looking for you, but I can say without hesitation that it was worth the wait. We have things to do and a limited window of time in which to get them done. I strongly suggest we quit fooling around and get serious. I would also like to make my feelings clear to your family and friends. I plan to make an announcement to your family during dessert at Thanksgiving dinner."

"Announcement. What kind of announcement?" I asked.

"Oh, just your basic I-love-Sarah announcement." Nick said. "I'll wait a few months before speaking with your mother about making you my wife. I'm also pretty sure that I will have to go before the Rowdy Girls review board as some point as well."

"Just don't mess up—they'll serve you for dinner," I laughed. "Where are we going?" I asked as we turned from the highway.

"To McDonald's for a travel drink," Nick said. "Can you do this without making a mess?" he asked.

"Yes, I can," I said, surprised. "You are too sweet."

"I know, and I may live to regret my kindness," Nick replied pulling around to the drive-thru speaker. The voice on the other end asked for our order and Nick sat quietly. "Just a minute please," Nick said, looking in my direction.

"Oh, I'll have a large Diet Coke please—with a few extra napkins," I said, pulling a sandwich bag of sugar cookies out of my purse.

"Cookies? We didn't discuss cookies," Nick laughed. "Now what do I do?"

"Pull forward to that window with the number two sticking out. Have you seriously never been to a drive-thru?" I asked, my eyes wide.

"No, this is a first. I don't have children, I eat before leaving my house, and I don't have low blood sugar, but you apparently do. Have you ever had that checked?" Nick asked.

I couldn't believe what I was hearing, but in my shock, I did manage to pull out two dollars from my wallet and hand it to Nick. "Two dollars?" he shrieked. "A drink costs two dollars? I need to buy some stock in this place."

"No," I said laughing. "I just don't have the exact change."

"I'm concerned that you know the exact amount," Nick volleyed. "How often do you purchase this travel treat?"

"Oh, look it's our turn," I said, dodging the discussion. "Here you go."

Once back on the highway, Nick glanced in my direction and offered a few suggestions on reducing the possibility of crumbs in his car.

"I can put my head in the bag if that would make you more relaxed." And then I had a thought. "If we do get married and I become a grandmother, do the children get to ride in your car?"

"Only if they are wrapped in plastic, not sick, and you are also in the car," Nick said.

"You don't mean that," I said with a smile.

"Oh, yes, I do," Nick said quickly. "Small children always have something running out of their noses, mouths, or elsewhere. For some reason, no one under the age of ten is aware that they need to go to the bathroom or throw up until it is past tense. I may have never been a father, but I am an uncle, and I took care of Jack's kids a lot when they were small. How on earth someone so little can make such a mess and yell so loud is beyond me. I would love to be a grandfather, but they are not riding in my car until they have jobs!"

"You're funny, and you are also full of prunes," I said. "I can tell you're a soft touch, and they will reduce you to putty."

"Would you like to put some money on that, little lady?"

"You've got it, big guy. I'll bet you one hundred dollars and a car wash," I said.

"You're on, and I will hold you to that bet,"

"Easy money is headed my way!" I laughed.

CHAPTER 33

County General was on the north side of Raleigh, and I could never keep myself from giving unsolicited directions. Margaret had no idea how to get anywhere, and for the past fifteen or so years we had trailered all over the place with me riding shotgun. We were a great team; she drove that rig like a professional, and I would have been horrified to take the wheel. On the other hand, I had a natural sense of direction and never forgot the way to anywhere. Nick gave me a don't-tell-me-how-to-drive glance when I said, "You need to take the next exit."

"Thanks," he said. "I've been here before. Nancy took a bad fall once, and I brought her to this hospital."

"Ouch. I hope she wasn't hurt too badly. You know you take a left at the light," I said with a snicker.

"Left? Are you sure? I went straight the last time."

"You were going to the emergency department, but we're going to general parking, and that's to the left. If you go straight, we'll be sent around the moon and back before we get to the parking deck. Take a left at the light and a right on Elm, and the parking deck is directly in front of us."

With the car parked, Nick and I made our way across the

pedestrian overpass and into the main section of the hospital. I wanted to make sure Stuart was doing well, but I felt myself unraveling just a bit and was not sure why. The nurses' station of Fourth Floor West was all abuzz as we walked past. Looking up from a chart, a very attractive young nurse asked if she could be of assistance.

"No thank you, we know the room number," I said. I saw 416 and gently tapped on the door. With no response, I pressed down on the lever and opened to door to find an empty bed, no belongings anywhere, and no Stuart. Nick asked if I was sure about the room number, and I assured him I was. We went back to the nurses' area.

"Excuse me," Nick said. "We're looking for a patient of yours: Stuart Branch? We were fairly certain he was in room 416, but that room is empty."

"Yes, Mr. Branch has been moved to the intensive care unit," the nurse said. "Give me just a minute and I'll find out if he is able to have visitors."

"ICU? I spoke to him last night and he was fine," I said, feeling shaky.

"Yes," the nurse said, "last night around seven Mr. Branch suffered some complications and was moved to intensive care. That really is all the information I'm allowed to divulge. But he can fill you in on the rest."

"The rest?" I squeaked. "Oh my God—what's happened?" Leaning against the counter, I put my hand against the side of my head. "The shiver," I said quickly, looking at Nick. "That's why I had that shiver last night at dinner. It . . ."

Before I could continue, the nurse said that Stuart was able to have visitors but only for a limited amount of time. She gave us directions to the ICU.

With a quick thank you, Nick and I returned to the elevator tower. "I feel so guilty!"

"I am not making light of your feelings," Nick said sternly, "but Stuart Branch is a grown man who chose to drive on an icy highway. You didn't invite or encourage him to come to Hadley Falls. He made that decision, and a poor one it was, all by himself. You don't have any ownership of this situation."

"Yes, but—" I tried to finish.

"There is no but. Here we are," Nick said as the elevator door opened.

The smell of worry and day-old perfume was heavy as we passed the waiting room. Families sat close together, trying to console one another. Half-eaten food containers tumbled from the already too-full wastebaskets, and small children whined out of endless boredom. A few people were sleeping, while others paced back and forth. I had been in the same place ten years ago with my father. *That's why I don't like it here,* I thought.

"Are you okay?" Nick asked.

"Ten years ago my father's room was on this floor. You can smell death in this place."

"Do you want to go?" Nick asked.

"No. Well, yes, but no. I really do want to check on Stuart," I said.

"May I help you?" asked a nurse holding a chart.

"Yes," Nick said. "We're here to see Stuart Branch."

"Follow me," she said. "You may only stay for ten minutes, and whatever you have in that bag, Mr. Branch may not have.

Would you like to leave it with me?" she asked, glaring over her black half-moon-shaped reading glasses, which were obviously as dark as her soul.

"Please, have it for your lunch, and we hope you enjoy it as much as my Sarah did making if for you," Nick said.

"Why did you give that evil woman Stuart's lunch?" I said. "And it's in one of my favorite containers."

"You've got to be kidding," Nick replied with a disapproving look. "I know you wouldn't give a patient in ICU unapproved food. You'd worry for days that you broke the rules and would be sent to stand in the corner. As for your container, I can't believe that's an issue, but I'll buy you a new one if it is. Jesus!"

Stuart seemed to be in relatively good spirits, but you could see the past twenty or so hours on his face. His coloring was a bit off, and very dark shadows now rested below his eyes. He told us that just before seven o'clock last night, he'd had a blood clot, which we were relieved to hear was very small and had left no permanent damage. He said that he'd actually flat-lined for about a minute or so before they were able to revive him. I asked how he could be so certain of the time and he said that the last thing he remembered was the evening news anchor just signing off. I became very quiet, knowing that was the time I'd felt the shiver as I was sitting down for dinner.

If all things remained the same, Stuart was to be released in the next few days, and his cousin from St. Simons Island was on his way to bring him home. Stuart planned to spend a month or so with him to recuperate.

"The salt air has curative powers," I said with certainty. "It will be good for you, and the warmth of the sun will give you energy."

"I have a new lease on life since my near-death experience," he said. "I think I might move back to Georgia."

When we said goodbye, I felt fairly confident that would be the last time I ever saw Stuart Branch. He could tell how much I cared for Nick, and I could see that he had given up on rekindling our relationship.

"Let me know how you're doing," I insisted as we left. "You have my address."

"I'll do it. Nick, you be sure and take care of my Sarah. She is one of a kind," he said, waving goodbye.

"Not to worry—she's in good hands, I promise. You take care of yourself, Stuart. It was a pleasure getting to know you better," Nick said.

On our way out, I could see Florence Nightingale standing arms crossed, with her feet spread slightly apart and looking in our direction. I was somewhat frightened—until she held out my bag. "That was the best chicken soup I've ever eaten," she said.

"I'm glad you enjoyed it," I said sincerely, which more than surprised me. Perhaps it was because she returned my container.

As we rode down the elevator, Nick said, "What's wrong with you?"

"Do you mean right now, or in general?" I said.

"Right now, and you don't have to be a smart ass. I'm just concerned about you," he responded.

"Dear Debby! What a day, and it's not even two o'clock." I said. "I just need to process all of this: our talk at the barn, Stuart, memories of my dad, and that evil nurse. Are we still going out to dinner tonight?"

"Yes, but only if you can behave," Nick said with a chuckle.

"You know I can't do that, but I think you'll take me anyway. My uniqueness is part of my charm," I said with a sideways smile.

Just before getting into the car, Nick took my face in both hands, kissed me gently, and said, "Dear Debby."

"See?" I laughed. "It's the perfect thing to say when you can't find the right words. Oh," I said sliding into the car and fastening my seat belt, "I'd like to add something to what you said earlier about your drinking. There's not much of a gray area where I'm concerned; I either really like something or hate it all together. I smoked for years, and giving that up was a serious struggle."

"How'd you quit?" Nick asked, backing out of the parking space.

"I realized that my two children would be my primary caregivers in my old age, and that did it!" I replied. "They love each other to bits, but they would argue over the color of a blue sky. I can see it now: they would roll me out onto the patio of Sleepy Pines, get busy doing something else, and forget to bring me back inside. Small animals would nest in my hair, and the vultures would begin to circle. I took my last, very long drag on that final cigarette, and that was it. I was fairly amazed that my car would start without my lighting up or that cigarettes could possibly not be the dessert portion of my meals."

"You're hysterical." Nick laughed. "Do you even remember why you started?"

"Absolutely I do: peer pressure my freshman year in college," I replied.

Pulling out of the parking deck, Nick and I held hands and didn't let go for a very long time. We had become a team.

CHAPTER 34

*T*urning into my driveway after a very long day that was not yet over, I saw a gorgeous arrangement of pumpkins, greenery, and gourds on my front porch. As I got out of my car, the fragrance of fresh-cut evergreens permeated the air and took me to a wonderful place. I loved the holidays, and this was just the kickoff I needed.

"Betsy, my front porch is amazing," I said as she picked up her phone. "Wow—thank you so much. It's beautiful."

"You are very welcome," Betsy said. "Annie helped me cut the greenery in the backyard and work on the arrangement. There might be a little dog hair in the Carolina Sapphire."

"Texture, we'll call it texture," I said, thinking that I would need to try and get rid of that.

"The rest of your order is in the kitchen, and the goat cheese is in the fridge. Now go have fun, and don't be nervous," Betsy said with a chuckle.

With the final touches done to my hair and makeup, I declared myself ready. Standing in the bathroom, I closed the door and used the full-length mirror to take a look at the final product.

Not bad, I thought. *I clean up good.* I could not shake how much I'd spent for the total package, but it was worth it. I hoped Nick agreed.

I'd just sat down in the den to go through yesterday's mail when the doorbell rang. Annie always barked—she rarely got up—but she did bark. "Now remember, no hair on anyone's pants," I said.

Opening the door, I took a deep cleansing breath, hoping that Nick would approve of my outfit, and was greeted with, "Hi, Mom! Wow, you look fabulous."

"Sidney! What a surprise. What are you doing here? And thanks," I said, twirling to show her my outfit.

"Do I need a reason to just come to visit my mother?" Sidney asked.

"No, you don't need a reason, but you never do unless there is something going on. So, I'm thrilled to see you," I said, bringing her into a hug, "but why are you here?"

"I'm hungry," Sidney said, reaching down to pet Annie, avoiding my question.

"Sidney, this is your mother you're talking to. Tell me the truth: What's up? You are welcome to anything you can find to eat, and to stay the night, but you need to answer me and right now."

Moving into the kitchen, Sidney opened the refrigerator and shuffling items around she said, standing up straight and leaning her tall, thin body against the refrigerator door. "Okay, I'll tell you the truth. I want to meet this man you've been seeing. Emma told me your date got moved to tonight, and we both agreed that I should come home and check him out. We love you, and you haven't had a date in a very long time. Seriously, Mama, it's a different world out there now. When is he supposed to be here?"

"That's very sweet, and I love you for your concern. Nick should be here any minute. We have a reservation for dinner at Zorba's, so we can't hang around for too long. Are you going to spend the night?" I asked, not sure what I wanted the answer to be.

"Well, I don't have to be at work until late tomorrow. Do you mind?" Sidney asked.

"Well, no, of course not." I shook my head, trying not to roll my eyes.

"Oh, come on, Mama, can you imagine how strange it would be for you if your mother had a date? What if it was Sibby who was going out on the town? What would you do? I really do want to talk to this man, and by the time you get home and we talk, it'll be too late for me to drive back to Raleigh. So I guess I am staying. Oh, I love the sofa. When did you have it recovered?"

"Several weeks ago, and thanks. I really like it too. Now explain what you mean by talking—or do you mean grilling?" I asked, sitting her down on the new sofa. "And his name is Nick."

"I'm not *grilling* him. I just want to talk to the man—I mean Nick—ask him a few questions," Sidney said, and before she could finish the doorbell rang.

Again Annie barked, but she was so happy to see Sidney that she didn't care beyond that point. "Holy smokes—you look incredible," Nick said

"Doesn't she?" Sidney piped up.

Not missing a beat, Nick leaned over and gave me a serious kiss, and then offered his hand to the very tall young woman now standing beside the newly recovered sofa. "Hello! I'm Nick Heart, and you must be Sidney," Nick said in his warmest voice.

"How did you know?" Sidney asked, with her dark brown eyes looking directly into his.

"You are the spitting image of your mother. Plus, your portrait is hanging on the wall behind you," Nick said with a chuckle.

"Oh, I guess it is!" Sidney laughed, turning around to see her portrait staring back at her.

I stood frozen. Putting the past week into my kids' point of view left it hanging a bit askew. Emma's call yesterday had obviously been for the purpose of making sure that the date was still on. I shook myself back to the moment. "Sidney is my equestrian child. She rode Summer Sunrise."

"That's right," Nick replied, looking at Sidney. "Your mother showed me his picture—what a handsome horse! He must have been at least seventeen hands."

"He was." Sidney smiled with pride. "Wow, that seems so long ago. Rusty—that was his barn name—was the best. I was devastated when he stepped in a hole and had to be put down. I lost that horse long before his time."

"Oh," Nick's eyebrows knitted together in sympathy. "I am so sorry to hear that."

"Thanks. Me too," Sidney dropped her head and took a breath. "He was a great horse, but we all know that in the horse world you're always just one trip away from stardom or disaster."

"I'm sorry to interrupt," I said, "but we need to go. Now listen, you two, there is absolutely no eating in the living room or dogs on the furniture, especially my newly reupholstered sofa. Annie has been fed and walked," I added, walking toward the front door.

Sidney smirked in my direction and kissed me goodbye. As Nick opened the door, she said, "Now you kids remember . . . your curfew is ten o'clock, and only to the restaurant and back."

Nick and I laughed. I remembered having said the same thing to her when she had her first date. *How sweet*, I thought, *she remembered.*

CHAPTER **35**

"*I* need to tell you again how wonderful you look," Nick said, opening the car door for me. "I don't usually repeat myself, but holy smokes and wow!"

"Thanks, and you look especially handsome as well. That blue sweater is perfect with your eyes. I don't remember ever telling you, but you have the most beautiful eyes I think I've ever seen," I said, straightening my jacket. "I did make this insanely expensive purchase just for you, and I'm thrilled that you like it. My friends will be elated to know that their collaborative efforts were well received."

Nick said, "Sidney is beautiful."

"Thanks! She is also a mess, which is southern for 'usually up to somethin'." I assure you her showing up tonight was no accident—more like a covert operation between her and her sister. Emma sent her sister to check you out and make sure I was not in harm's way."

"I'm not sure whether to be offended or flattered," Nick said with a chuckle.

"When they were teenagers," I said, "I had a hard and fast rule that for every minute they were late, they were grounded one day. Their turning the tables on me really is cute."

"Well, we better not be late getting home. I don't think I could handle your being grounded."

"Yes, and we'll need some time, as I believe Sidney plans to engage you in some sort of investigative conversation when we get home."

"Do I take a left at the next light?" Nick asked.

"Is this one of those times that I can tell you how to drive?"

"Yes, ma'am. Well, not telling me how to drive, but giving directions."

"Take a left at the light, go two blocks, and the restaurant is on the right. You have to be careful about the parking . . . one false move, and we're in the river."

During the first course of our meal, Nick and I talked about the upcoming holiday visit to Iron Springs. I tried to soften the blow of meeting my entire family at once. "My grandmother has zero filter left and will say exactly what she thinks. My brother Ethan is a man of very few words, and his wife Meg is so sweet you'll think she's putting on, but she really is that kind. My mother is very protective and will study your face for the truth. You kind of know my cousin Alex, the PI; my Aunt Tess is a widow and Alex's mother, and is a hoot for sure."

Nick just laughed, saying he was so looking forward to the trip. "I'm sure I'll love them all."

"Oh, I hope you're not offended by anything Sidney might say tonight."

"Will you please stop worrying?" Nick asked. "I love you, and I don't care what she says. I'm not going anywhere. On that subject, I want to ask you a question. I realized tonight on my way to your house that you've never told me how you feel about me. Is there a reason for that?" Nick asked.

"Yes," I said quickly, before I lost my nerve. "The truth is I'm scared to feel the way I do about you. I have zero experience in the world of dating past the age of twenty-one. I know what I feel and what I think, but saying it out loud puts the period at the end of that sentence."

"Just tell me what you think," Nick said with a pleading look in his eyes. "I need to know."

Inhaling deeply and choosing my words carefully, I said, "I'm sure that I love you and that a life with you would be wonderful. But, I have another life that I am not quite willing to let go of."

"Your friends," Nick said.

"Well, yes, but that's not all," I said. "It's not as simple as just getting married and off we go. I've lived in Hadley Falls for nearly thirty years, and my roots are here. I've survived that jackass Parker Sams, taught art for my entire career, and I did them both here. My new house is very special to me, and I'm not sure I want to give it up. If we were to get married, I know I'll be the one moving—the farm is your livelihood. We just need to put it all on the table, take our time, and sort it out."

"I could not love you more than I do at this moment," Nick said, understanding that I wanted a life with him. "And yet somehow I imagine that I will love you more tomorrow than I do today."

I took his hand and kissed it.

Rolling the stem of the wineglass back and forth between his thumb and index finger, he said, "On the subject of marriage, I'm not suggesting that we go to a justice of the peace tomorrow,

219

just that we talk about the possibilities of our future collectively. I'm sure your family has no more nuts in the dish than anyone else—you don't need to worry about that. All I need to know for now is that you love me and that you want to be with me," Nick said, holding my hand. "Now, what is this I've heard about underwear?"

I blushed furiously. "All right, but this will be very brief." We both broke up laughing over my unintended pun. "Margaret said that matching underwear makes you feel better about yourself. That was the dumbest thing I'd ever heard, but she and Bill have been married for light-years, so maybe she's right. Anyway, all of my friends, both at school and the Rowdy Girls, seem to think alike on this topic, so I caved and upgraded my undergarments. And here I sit telling you this and dying on the inside. It is also the end of this conversation."

"You are too funny."

"I'm not trying to be," I answered. "I'm just trying to be honest. If things get to that stage, who cares what you have on? In five minutes at the most, all that fancy is on the floor."

"Yes, but what a sweet five minutes."

I could feel the blush running the full length of my body. "Well, I can't argue with that . . ."

The waiter in full Greek costume arrived at our table, carrying our entrees, and I welcomed the change of focus.

The rest of our meal was consumed over light conversation and the deeper realization that we had gently broached the subjects of both marriage and sex. Both topics rattled my frame, but I began to calm down as the evening progressed.

"That was a wonderful meal," Nick said, folding his napkin

and placing it neatly beside his plate. "We'll have to come here again sometime."

On our ride back to Brook Street, I took him on the scenic route, showing him River's Bend Restaurant and Maggie's Alley Bookstore. From there, we drove the entire distance of Front Street, which was about a mile along the river. I had always loved lights and the reflection of the street lamps as they danced across the water. With a turn here and there we drove by the homes of Margaret, Jennifer, Elizabeth, and Rose.

When we got back to my house, Sidney was waiting for us. "Well, how was the date?" she asked, popping her head around the corner of the den. "Did you two have fun?"

"We did indeed," answered Nick. "After dinner, your mother took me for a tour along the river and past all of her friends' homes. What have you and Annie been up to?"

"We ate dinner and watched TV. I never have the time to just vegetate on the sofa, so it was great," Sidney answered, looking in my direction. "Your face looks a little blotchy, Mom. Are you okay?"

"It's just the cold air," I said, blushing even more.

I could feel myself calming down the more I fussed around the kitchen tidying up behind Sidney. It really wasn't messy; I just needed the distraction. Annie went between Nick and Sidney in the den and the kitchen with me. I could hear pieces of the conversation, which was mostly about horses and Sidney's desire to have an adult jumper. I heard Nick say she was welcome at Long Leaf Farm anytime, and she could ride for the some of the owners. Here and there, the conversation would become very quiet, and I did not like that part.

"It's getting late," Nick said, standing up and reaching for his coat. "I need to be getting home. Sidney, it was a pleasure, and if you decide to drop by tomorrow, ring me up on your way back to Raleigh. As for you, my darlin', will I see you tomorrow?"

"I'm not sure, but I doubt it. I've got school, and I really want to spend some time with Rascal. But I'll give you a call," I said.

Sidney laughed and placed a hand on Nick's shoulder. "See Nick, this is what you'll need to learn: if you're looking for a yes or no answer, preface your question with the rules of reply or you may be in for a monologue."

"I love this girl," Nick said, giving Sidney a nudge.

"Yes, isn't she just precious?" I replied, tweaking her nose.

Walking Nick to the door, I asked if the one-on-one conversation had gone well. He assured me that it was fine, and Sidney had only my best interests at heart. With a deliberate kiss, and a smile after another one, he was on his way.

Walking back to the kitchen, I asked Sidney, "So, did Nick pass muster?"

Sidney smiled and said, "Yes, I like him a lot. I think you two make a cute couple. He sure was up front with how he feels about you."

"Oh, I'm glad," I said being careful with both our emotions. "What did he tell you?"

"He told me that he loved you, and that before the end of next year, he wanted y'all to be married," Sidney said.

"How do you feel about that?" I asked.

Sidney paused and said, "Like I said, I like him, and I think he makes you happy, but . . . you've known him a week, Mom. I just don't want you to rush into anything. There's been enough hurt around here; none of us need any more of that."

I agreed completely, and after some shared TV time, we were off to bed.

CHAPTER 36

With the Thanksgiving Holiday just a few days away, and having been out for the snow the week before, my students were not at their most focused. Be they eight or eighteen, children are children, and Monday was a test of my patience and disciplinary skills. But by the time I got home, the chili in the Crock-Pot smelled delicious, and I was glad I hadn't been able to resist inviting Nick for dinner once again. Just before he arrived, my cell phone rang.

"Mom, those horses are amazing, and Nick said I did a great job. He saved the hardest ride, but the best horse, for last and the owner also showed up to watch me ride. Mrs. Martin, the owner, gave me a hundred dollars and asked if I would ride her horse on a regular basis. I said yes, as long as I could work it around my job. After she left, Nick and I worked on a riding schedule for all three horses, and I'm so excited. Oh, and Buddy is very cute."

"That's great! What do you think about Long Leaf Farm?" I asked.

"Are you kidding me? It's incredible. If you marry Nick, you're going to live there, aren't you? You've always wanted your own farm, and they don't come any nicer than that one."

"I don't know," I said. "Yes, I've always wanted my own farm, but I love Hadley Falls. There is a lot to think about. Oh—gotta go. There's the doorbell."

Nick held a handful of white roses. Handing them to me, he said, "They are almost as pretty as you are."

"Thank you! They are gorgeous," I said, giving him a kiss that I hoped curled his toes. I had never been the instigator but was overcome with . . . let's call it appreciation for the thoughtful gift.

"Wow, what did I do to deserve that?" Nick asked with a smile, and his hand still under the hem of my sweater and just slightly above my waist, holding me close. "Besides you, what smells so good?"

"It's the chili," I said wrapping my arms around his neck, and changing the subject. "I was thinking about Thursday, and that we'll need to take my car to Iron Springs. Annie always goes with me. I promise to take it to the auto spa on Wednesday. That really does help—well, some, anyway—and I'll take Annie to the groomer too."

"All right, but please let me drive?" Nick asked.

"Why do you want to drive?"

"I refuse to pull into your mother's driveway and get out on the passenger side. It is not manly," Nick said. "I know is sounds old-fashioned, but I don't care. I really would rather drive.

"Fine with me, but I get to tell you where to turn."

"You're on. Now, let me tell you about your child and her riding . . ." Nick proceeded to review Sidney's abilities, the elation of the horse owner, and the schedule they'd worked out. I beamed that my child had bonded so quickly with a man who loved her sport and appreciated her natural gift.

"I knew the first time she rode—I think she was four—that she had *it*," I said. "There wasn't an ounce of fear, and she had a natural seat. Wait, I'll show you the picture. Here," I said, holding a silver frame. "That's my grandmother, then me, and Sidney with her first pony, Buttercup."

"Why is Sidney holding up four fingers?" Nick asked.

"She went in four walk/trot classes and won four blue ribbons. There was no stopping her after that." I watched as Nick glanced toward the den. "You don't have to stay in here with me. Annie will keep you company while you watch the news."

"Are you sure? You always do all the work at mealtime," Nick replied. "It's like you run a soup kitchen around here. Everyone eats from your table."

"Yes, and I love the clatter of flatware and conversation. Feeding people makes me very happy. I worry about Miss Madge not cooking for herself, and the good smells make me feel safe and warm. Oh, and just for the record, I don't like anyone messing around in my kitchen. I really would rather do it all myself."

Later, with the table cleared and the dishes in the sink, Nick gave me a hug and said how much he enjoyed dinner, but that he should be getting home. His hay man was scheduled to be at the farm bright and early, and I had school the next day. I thanked him again for the beautiful flowers. Just before leaving Nick said, "I have lived a very long and full life, but nothing can compare with the past nine days."

"That's a good thing?" I asked timidly.

Nick paused, then said, "Yes. Exhausting, but good. When are you coming to ride Buddy?"

226

"I thought I would ride him tomorrow and Thanksgiving Day. I'm cooking all my part of the menu before going to Sibby's. I'll get to the farm a bit early and have a quick ride, and then we're off to Iron Springs. What do you think about that idea?"

"Great," Nick said. "Sidney is riding early Thursday morning before reporting for work at three o'clock. I think she said she has to be on location at a church somewhere."

"To ride horses would be the only reason my youngest child would ever get up early. And yes, it's a church—I can't recall the name but every year they have a huge Thanksgiving celebration for anyone who needs a hot meal and fellowship. Be careful driving home." I said adjusting his collar.

"Good night," Nick said kissing me while his hands held the small of my back. "I could absolutely eat you alive, Sarah Sams. Leaving is getting harder and harder."

"Yes, it is, and so is letting you go," I replied.

Whew, I thought, closing the front door. *I need a cold shower! Dear Debby.*

CHAPTER 37

*E*ager to ride Buddy, I rushed home after school on Tuesday, scooted Annie out the door, and hurried to change into my riding clothes.

I was halfway into my sweater when my cell phone rang, "Hi there," I said. "Give me two seconds; I'm half dressed."

"Don't move. I'll be right there," Nick replied.

"Shameful," I said, using one of my grandmother's favorite words.

"Shameful nothing. I'm not sure how much longer I can wait," Nick laughed.

"Wait for what?" I tittered, red-faced and sweating.

"Right," Nick laughed again. "Anyway, I read where your Hadley Falls Hornets won their game last Saturday and have the home-field advantage next week. We should to go to the game and then out to dinner. What do you think about that?" Nick asked.

"I'd love to, and as luck would have it Coach Michaels gave me two tickets today at lunch," I said.

"Great, let's plan on going. I want to see the teacher side of Sarah. I know you're coming to ride this afternoon, but I have to go look at a new tractor and manure spreader, which brings me to the real reason I'm calling. I might not be here when you arrive, but I'll be back before you to leave. Have fun, but remember Buddy hasn't been ridden for a few days, and he might be a little fresh. I would rather you stayed inside," Nick said.

"I'll be careful. See you in a bit." I said, wiggling into my breeches.

Forty-five minutes later Annie and I pulled up to Nick's barn. "Don't get dirty," I yelled as she ran to find Caesar.

Coy was hard at work filling the stalls with hay, but stopped and kept me company while I got tacked up and ready to ride. I could tell Buddy was not as happy as before, and I could only assume it was because he was alone in the barn. "You will need to learn that you can be taken out of the pasture and function without your friends," I said as the horse danced a bit in the wash stall. "I won't have a herd-bound horse. You can still see and smell your friends."

"You know, Sarah," Coy said. "I don't believe he wants to ride today. You need to be careful."

"I think you're right," I answered, "I'll put him on the lunge line first and see what happens. I really don't want to eat dirt today. But we can't give in to this."

"Okay, but I am going in the arena with you. Boss told me to stay with you while you rode. He signs my checks, you know," Coy replied.

"That's fine. I may need your help, and I know I'll enjoy the company," I said.

"Okay, I got to go do two things. But don't you get on that horse till I get back," Coy said. "Boss will have my hide if anything happens to you."

On our way down the aisle and into the indoor arena, Buddy screamed to his friends in the pasture and walked sideways but did continue to move forward. With nostrils flaring, he blew out repeatedly, but he did continue to enter the ring.

"Good boy," I said with a gentle pat and a rub the length of his neck. "You're all right, I promise." When I let out on the lunge line, Buddy took off at a wild trot, twisting and turning, but completing a circle of sorts. He worked at a frantic pace for the next five minutes but began to calm down as we went along. Each time I changed directions, I talked to him, and slowly he began to lower his head and soften.

Coy stood up from his seat and suggested I ask for the canter. I agreed and asked if he could check that Annie was all right. Descending the bleachers two at a time, Coy left the arena, securing the gate on his way out.

"Okay, let's see the canter," I said, and with that, Buddy was off. I dug my heels into the footing, trying desperately to hold on, but it was no use. To avoid being dragged, I let go of the lunge line and moved to the center of the ring while Buddy flew around the perimeter. It was not the safest thing in the world to have the lunge line flying wildly around, but I didn't have a choice. Within a few minutes, I could see that he was settling into a more collected gait, and I encouraged him to calm down.

"Good boy," I said, motioning for Buddy to walk in my direction. I held out my hand and he took a few steps. "Good boy," I repeated, walking forward to meet him halfway. I gathered up the lunge line as I walked closer. "Now, let's see if you can go the other way without so much upset."

Coy shouted from the gate, "I found the dogs and put them

in the office. Are you okay? Was that scary?"

"Yes, I'm fine, but he's either become herd bound or he's just trying to push me around. Whatever it is, it's unacceptable!"

"Oh, I don't know, Sarah. I'm not sure you should ride," Coy said, moving down to the gate and holding on with a death grip. "That horse is wild today."

"He's fine; really, he is. I wouldn't consider getting on if I thought I would get hurt. We still have a lot of ground work yet to do."

After a bit more controlled lunging, I decided Buddy was ready to ride. Coy sat perched quietly on the risers and watched as I settled into the saddle. Buddy twitched his ears and we were off at a full canter around the edge of the ring. I was being run away with, which meant the horse was in charge and I was along for the hair-raising ride. Coy was as white as a ghost when I finally got the beautiful paint horse to stop.

"You need to get off that horse right now," Coy insisted, standing up and moving in my direction.

"No, he's fine, and we are going to settle this argument right now. If I get off, he wins, and that just can't happen. He's not trying to hurt me; he's trying to establish dominance. If it worries you so much, you don't have to watch."

I turned my attention back to the horse. "Okay, Buddy boy, we need to canter on the other lead," I said, giving him the signal to canter on, and we were off again, but not as frantic as the time before. As we flew by the gate, I could see that Nick had joined Coy. They were engaged in full conversation, and I was certain the new manure spreader was not their topic of discussion. Within a few minutes, Buddy had found that wonderful canter he had when other horses were in the ring. Working on figure eights, we found that pace I knew he had. I was exhausted; I hadn't worked this hard in years. Rascal was one in a million, and being run away with this afternoon was a reminder of both how lucky I was to have him and how much work I had to do with Buddy.

Walking on a loose rein, we stopped at the gate. Nick looked up at me, his eyes narrowed, and his face flushed, "Are you crazy?" he said. "You could have been killed!"

"He didn't want to hurt me; he wanted to control me," I said defensively. "If I had gotten off, he would have been declared the victor, and that would have been the end of us. He is a wonderful horse, and I like him very much," I added. "It really is okay. I know what I'm doing. I need for you to trust me. I wouldn't still be up here if he really wanted me off—you know that. Did you find a tractor you liked?"

"Uh, yes, but don't change the subject. I know you know what you're doing. It just really scared me to see you flying around the ring like that," Nick said, his hands cutting through the air. "Footing was spraying everywhere, and I could tell how hard you had to work to stay on. I know you're a seasoned rider, but you are absolutely forbidden—yes, I said forbidden—to ride that horse without me or Coy in the arena with you—do you understand?"

"Yes, but—"

"There is no but," Nick said firmly.

I straightened my posture. "Just so you know, I put him in that last canter to let him know it's fine with me if we go fast, but *I* just need to be the one who asks. But I am exhausted. I haven't had to work that hard in a very long time. Tomorrow I'll be sore as heck, but it was worth it. Just look at this wonderful horse," I said, giving Buddy's neck a pat.

"If you say so, but I'm really not happy with this," Nick said his voice low. "Before I say something I might regret, I'm going to do some paperwork in the office."

Later, I walked into Nick's office, and he looked up from his papers and over his reading glasses. "Is everything okay? Your ride today really concerned me."

"I'm fine, and I'll admit it took me totally by surprise. I didn't like it either, but I really do like him, so I'll just need to work on fixing that for sure. I was thinking about Mr. Goodbar for his show name, or maybe an artist's name since he's a paint horse. What do you think?" I asked.

"I think you're avoiding the issue, but I like it—short and sweet—all the best show names are," Nick answered. "I would sleep on it for a day or two. An artist's name—, hmm—what about Rembrandt?"

"Oh—I love that," I said. "Annie and I are going to need to be getting home. I have things to do for school and our Thanksgiving dinner."

"I don't want you to go," Nick said, pulling my body close enough to touch his. "I understand, but I wish you could stay." He nuzzled into my neck.

"Me too," I groaned, "but I can't. Thanksgiving and the day after will be great. We can have two days with no interruptions— well, that's not quite right, considering my entire family will be there. But you know what I mean. No driving back and forth."

Walking out of the barn, Nick gave a whistle and the dogs came running. Annie was once again filthy. I made a sideways face in Nick's direction.

"Is that look for me?" He made a face of pure innocence. "She loves to run this property. Surely you wouldn't consider taking her freedom away, would you?"

"No, but look at her! Good thing I booked a spa day for her at Paws & Claws tomorrow. Annie has to be clean and especially needs to smell good to go to my mother's. So she'll have to stay out of the fields on Thursday morning. Sibby's love for her has its limits," I said.

"I'm very excited about meeting your family and having a real Thanksgiving."

"To tell you the truth, I'm a nervous wreck about the whole thing. They are wonderful people, but—"

"Stop. You worry too much. All families are quirky; that's what makes them interesting."

"Well, okay, interesting it is," I answered with a giggle. "I'll see you in two days."

"I'm going to need just a little more than that," Nick said, putting my back against my car door. "Two days is a long time, and this kiss needs to last." It was all I could to do to stand up straight after that kiss and his body covering mine.

"Dear Debby," I said, brushing my hair away from my face. "Nicholas Heart, you are making this very difficult."

"I certainly hope so," he replied, nibbling my ear.

And with every inch of my body on fire and fighting to stay, Annie and I were once again on our way back to Brook Street.

CHAPTER 38

*T*hanks to modern technology, I had set the oven timer for the wee hours of predawn on Thursday, and the twenty-two-pound bird was nearing golden brown. The remaining offerings from my kitchen were assembled and only needed thirty minutes or so to be good to go. Grammy would make my favorite congealed cherry-and-pecan salad, while Sibby might argue that her corn pudding was our family's favorite dish. I would never tell my grandmother, but there was little better than homemade Southern corn pudding. A combination of creamed corn, milk, butter, eggs, flour, sugar, and salt and pepper, bake to a golden brown—Lord have mercy, that's good eatin'. My sister-in-law always brought sweet potato casserole and the stuffing, which was usually different every year and offered a yummy surprise to the traditional menu.

With everything packed and taken care of, we were on the road. I reminded Annie that she was not allowed to run all over the farm when we arrived at Nick's. She stood in the back seat and started to bark, which was rare. "What is the matter with you, silly dog?" I asked as the answer to my question came bouncing around the corner of the barn. "Oh, good Lord, I forgot about

Penny," I said. Penny was Sidney's giant Doberman, who at the ripe old age of two weighed ninety pounds, thought she was still little, and loved Annie.

Trying to contain my dog fell into the completely unsuccessful column, and in the blink of an eye, she was gone. All you could see were two tails and a nub as the three dogs disappeared over the rise of the first pasture. Nick leaned against the frame of the barn door, laughing while I yelled for my dog to come back to me.

He said that Caesar would return to the barn with one whistle, and Annie could stay in the barn office to dry. "It'll be fine. With a quick brushing, she'll pass the test, I promise," Nick said.

"You don't understand," I answered. "This whole day is so important to me. I put all this pressure on myself—I want everything to be as close to perfect as possible. Having a messed-up dog that my mother really doesn't want in her house just starts things off badly, so will you please call them back?"

"Look, here they come," Nick said, pointing at the three dogs galloping through the soggy grass. "Good boy, Caesar," Nick said, patting the giant head of his wet dog.

Annie and Penny flanked me with their tongues outstretched. "Oh my God, Mom!" Sidney called, walking her horse out of the barn. "Sibby will have a stroke. Annie is a disaster!"

"I know," I replied fighting back the tears.

Suddenly Nick realized that this was not a laughing matter and called for all the dogs to follow him. I watched as they disappeared into the barn. "What are you going to do?" Sidney asked.

"Pray," I replied, reaching into the front seat of my car and collecting my jacket. "I'll go tack up and meet you in the ring in ten minutes. I've never ridden Buddy in the outside ring, so this should be interesting," I said.

"After some flat work, if he still refuses to do as you ask, that horse is not worth keeping," Sidney replied.

"I kept you," I said with a smile.

"Ha, ha," Sidney said. "Hurry up, and don't worry so much about today. Nick is a very nice man, and he can take care of himself. Our family will like him a lot, especially Grammy. I only wish I didn't have to work. Now hurry up. We haven't ridden together in forever."

Walking into the barn, I could see Nick and Buddy in the tack stall. "Hi," I said. "What are you two doing?"

"I'm trying to save you some time, but he's not cooperating. Please stop worrying about your dog," Nick answered. "Your mother will be so happy to see you that she won't care. Stir into the pot that you brought a guest along with you, and your very proper Southern mother would never cause a scene over a slightly dirty dog in front of company. Feel free to correct me if I am wrong."

I inhaled and relaxed. "You're right."

"Now why won't this horse stand still?"

"Because you're doing it all wrong," I answered.

"I've been tacking up horses longer than you have," Nick said, pulling on the girth and getting nowhere.

"Okay, but you're still doing it wrong," I said, taking the girth out of Nick's hand. "Watch," I continued, going up one notch at a time. "He's a very sensitive guy and needs lots of TLC. Good boy, it's okay. Plus, he likes a rub on the side of his face."

"Really? Well, I want to ride with you and Sidney, so if you have this under control, I'm going to get Chance tacked up," Nick said.

Our group ride was wonderful. I beamed with pride as Sidney maneuvered her mount in and out of the jump course. I watched as Nick coached her over several obstacles and they exchanged constructive dialogue. Sidney was all business when she rode, and I'd always thought she never appeared to have fun; it was like a job for her. But suddenly it was clear to me that was how she enjoyed the ride. If she made repeated mistakes, then she was not doing her job correctly and therefore not having a good time.

We had ridden for about an hour when I glanced at my watch and realized we needed to stop and get cleaned up. Everyone agreed and added that our morning ride had been a wonderful start to the Thanksgiving Day. Nick suggested we make it an annual event, and Sidney jumped right in with her vote in the affirmative. "Riding always improves any day," I said.

Sidney finished up with her horse, kissed me goodbye, and asked that I calm down and just enjoy the day. With a thank-you to Nick, she and Penny were off. I smiled as the two of them turned onto the highway.

With Buddy back in the pasture and my tack squared away, I walked in the office to find a clean and dry golden retriever. I squealed with delight at the transformed dog standing before me, shining from stem to stern.

"What's wrong?" Nick asked, rushing through the door.

"Nothing," I exclaimed. "Look at Annie—she's beautiful! How did you do that?"

"I didn't," Nick replied, looking just as stunned as I felt. "But I bet I know who did," he said, turning in Coy's direction.

"Well, I couldn't let Sarah cry, or her mother be upset about Annie. So I worked on the dog while you rode. I think she'll pass the test; do you, Sarah?" Coy asked.

"You are a wonderful man, Coy Ingram," I said, giving him a hug and a kiss on the cheek. "I can't thank you enough."

"Well, if I were you, I'd put her on a lead rope to go to the house. Caesar will take her running again if you don't," Coy said offering me a tattered length of cording.

"Thanks again," I said, clipping the snap to Annie's collar. I left the office and joined Nick in the aisle of the barn. "That was so sweet," I said.

"Coy is a good man. I couldn't run this farm without him."

"I realize that someone has to be at the farm today, but how sad," I said. "Coy will be all alone on Thanksgiving."

"He's just helping me this morning. He's going to his mother's right after he drops hay around noon. I don't think I've told you he lives in the apartment at the back of the barn."

With a lighter step I said, "No you haven't, and I didn't even realize that there was an apartment at the back of the barn. I feel much better knowing he has plans."

The warmth of Nick's house greeted us as we walked into the kitchen. I needed to get into the shower, and we had to be on the highway in under an hour. Annie and Caesar found their spots on the braided oval rug in the den, and Nick said for me to follow him. The wide, hand-hewn timbers of the hardwood floor squeaked as we walked down the hall. The interior had an intoxicating bouquet of antiquity, which I absolutely devoured on the inhale.

"What do you know about this house?" I asked as we entered the downstairs bedroom.

"Not too much," Nick answered. "It's named the McMasters' House. Zeb McMasters bought up around a thousand acres about two hundred years ago. He made a fortune in materials made from pine sap. When the trees were tapped out, he sold the lumber. I'm required to keep most exterior things just as they were to maintain historic status, but I can upgrade basic items like the wiring, heat and air conditioning, plumbing, and that sort of thing. Going forward, if we wanted to change the exterior paint color for example, we'd need to submit a request.

"Here you go," Nick said, opening the bathroom door. "Just use anything you need, and don't worry about cleaning up. I know we need to get on the road, so just leave your towels in the bathroom and Adel will take care of it tomorrow. Now, how dressed up do I need to be?" Nick asked.

"Not very," I said. "Khaki pants, a shirt, and a sweater will be great, or whatever you want to wear, but certainly no more elaborate than that. Who's Adel?"

"My housekeeper. The hot water takes a minute, and I've hung the towels on the warming racks," Nick said as he turned to leave the room.

"Thanks," I said. "Now go away so I can get ready."

"Go away? Well that's a fine thing to say after I put your towels on to warm and turned up the heat in the house. If you think you're going to be allowed a travel drink this time, you can think again," Nick said with a smile.

"I have my own travel drink ready to go, and besides, McDonald's is probably not open today." I laughed, shutting the door behind my host.

"Where's the justice? Get told to go away in my own house." Nick chuckled on the other side of the door. I heard the floorboards squeak as he walked down the hall.

Stepping into the shower, I smiled, thinking how far we had come in so little time. Was I rushing things, or were we really getting this close?

CHAPTER 39

*N*ick smiled as we pulled into the driveway of my mother's house.

"What?" I said.

"It's perfect," Nick answered. "I can see you right now as a little girl playing in the front yard. You know, your house on Brook Street looks like a smaller version of this house, wraparound porch and all."

"I never really thought about that before," I said, "but you're right, it really does. Perhaps that's why I felt like I was home the first time I saw my little house. Uh-oh—we've been spotted. That's my mother coming out the door."

"What a striking woman," Nick said. "It's scary how much you, your mother, and Sidney look alike. Wow."

"You won't believe it when you meet Emma," I replied. "She actually looks more like my mother than Sidney and I do."

Sibby had worked her way down to the first step and waited patiently for the two of us to walk in her direction. "Hello, you must be Nick," my mother said, offering her hand.

"I am. It's a pleasure to meet you Mrs. O'Neil," Nick said.

"Please," my mother said, "call me Sibby."

Mama bent over and began to pat Annie's head. "How are you, Annie? You certainly do look nice today. I think perhaps your mother sent you to that fancy overpriced dog-care place for a Thanksgiving bath."

"I did indeed," I said, shocked that Sibby was giving my girl so much attention. "Is Ethan here yet?"

"You know they're never on time, but I'm sure they're not too far behind," Sibby said. "Come in and say hello to your grandmother, and then you can get the food out of the car."

We walked into the foyer, and there she stood, as neat as a pin in her shirtwaist dress and a cardigan sweater. I prayed I had her good genes. Grammy was ninety-seven years old, but she didn't look it at all. "Hi, Grammy," I said, giving my treasured grandmother a huge hug.

"How is my favorite granddaughter?" she asked, kissing my cheek. "Tell the truth, did you ride this morning before coming here?"

"You know me too well," I said. "Grammy, this is Nick Heart. Sidney is working some of the horses at Nick's farm, and the three of us rode for about an hour. It was a great way to start the day."

"Nick," Grammy said sharply, "I hope you're keeping my favorite granddaughter in line."

"Mrs. O'Neil," Nick answered, "it would be easier to herd cats than to tell this independent woman what to do. I have offered suggestions, but I realize it's probably a waste of time."

Grammy was holding Nick's arm by the time he finished his sentence. "You are a wise man, but there are a few things I need to tell you about my Sarah . . ."

"I will appreciate your wisdom," Nick said. "Let me help

bring in the food first, and then I'm all yours."

Walking down the front steps I said, "Well, Grammy loves you. And really, 'easier to herd cats'?"

"I don't know what you're talking about," Nick said, giving me a glance. "I was merely answering your grandmother's question."

"Oh, look! Ethan's here," I said, breaking out into a broad smile. "Hi there! You're just in time to help us haul all this stuff to the kitchen." My lanky brother got out of his car, and I introduced him to Nick. They exchanged handshakes and pleasantries as they juggled containers of all shapes and sizes. "Where's Meg?" I asked. "You live five blocks from here and you didn't ride together?"

Handing me the sweet potato casserole, Ethan answered, "Meg can't decide what to wear to meet your boyfriend. She was still standing in front of the mirror when I left the house. You know how put out Mama gets when we're late, so I came on without her. Don't tell my wife I told you that—she'll be annoyed with me for the rest of the day. Nick," Ethan said, holding out a loop of his khakis, "I hope you like my outfit. I will admit that I gave you no thought whatsoever when picking out my clothes."

"You look very nice," Nick answered. "I didn't think about you either when I got dressed. Your sister did tell me you always wore khaki pants, but don't we all?" With that, the three of us made our way into the house.

Meg arrived shortly thereafter, smartly dressed as always. She was very petite and generally looked like she had just stepped out of a Talbot's catalog. Carrying the stuffing, she apologized for running a bit behind while giving me a sideways hug. My mother told me several times how handsome and nice Nick was.

Grammy sat for a long time bending his ear about my childhood. And with more surprise than I could ever explain, I watched as my brother, the usually quiet ophthalmologist, engaged Nick in numerous self-initiated conversations. Aunt Tess was very artistic and owned a flower shop in Newport News. She, and cousin Alex were next through the door, carrying the center-piece, yeast rolls, and four bottles of wine. Alex and I disappeared to chat, as we had done for a lifetime, to the study. I brought her up to speed about my sapling romance, paid her the promised dollar, and shared a few giggles.

With everything hot and ready to go, my mother made the announcement that it was time to say grace. She always gave a sidebar of sorts, telling all in attendance to eat after they served their plates. Standing in a very large circle, we all held hands, bowed our heads, and listened as Sibby began to pray. Nick squeezed my hand several times during the lengthy blessing that left out no one, living or dead. Mama always became emotional when she spoke about my father's absence from the circle. Theirs was a love nothing could touch, and holidays without him were always the hardest. She included Nick, referring to him as "Sarah's new friend." That prompted several rapid squeezes to my hand.

The rattle of silver, china, and chatter brought a smile to Nick's face. "I love this day," Nick whispered in my ear. "Your family is wonderful."

Sibby leaned forward. "Nick is something the matter?"

"No—not at all," he replied. "Quite the contrary. I was just telling Sarah how wonderful this experience is for me. It's been forever since I had a real Thanksgiving. I appreciate your allowing me to attend."

Jane W. Rankin

"We wouldn't have it any other way," my mother said with a smile. "You and Sarah are still planning to stay the night, aren't you?"

"Oh, yes," Nick answered. "It'll be nice to not have to drive home after this delicious but enormous meal."

Working on her third glass of wine, Aunt Tess blurted, "So Nick, do you have any family?"

"Yes, I have an older brother, Jack, several cousins scattered around Pennsylvania, and my cousin George, who lives just outside of Hadley Falls and teaches with Sarah. My parents passed away years ago," he replied.

"Oh, I'm sorry to hear about your parents," she said taking another sip of wine, "but like Sibby said, we're very happy to have you celebrate with us."

"So Nick," Alex said, trying to lighten the conversation, "how did you end up in Greenway?"

"Now, Alex, we both know you found the answer to that and many other questions the day I met Sarah," Nick answered. "I can see by the look on everyone's face that Sarah hasn't shared that she paid her cousin to dig into my past."

"Well, you did the same thing," I said, a blush rising to my face. "George is the chemistry teacher at my school, and he had the goods on me from the beginning."

"My cousin has no idea how much he doesn't know about the real Sarah Sams," Nick said looking in my direction. "No one has the goods on you, my love."

"My love," Meg teased, tucking her short blond hair behind her ears. "What's that?"

"Yes, I'm sure it's what everyone wants to know, so here it is,"

246

Nick said, clearing his throat. "I'm crazy about this woman, and I do love her very much."

"Now, Nick," Sibby said, sitting timber straight in her chair. "You've not even known my daughter for two weeks; how could you possibly know that you love her?"

Before Nick could say a word, Ethan chimed in. "Now Mother, I remember hearing a story or two about dad saying early on that he intended on marrying you."

"That was different," Sibby answered emphatically. "We grew up together—I think I was ten years old the first time your father said that. In fact, if I remember correctly, it was summertime and during Sunday school. But forget that—this is not at all the same thing."

"My son always talked about how much he loved you and never wanted anyone else. I suggested that he didn't really know since he'd never been with another girl," Grammy said. "Russell said he didn't need another girl to know he wanted you."

Taking a breath and looking in my direction, Grammy said, "So Sarah, what do you have to say to all of this?"

I could feel the heat rising in my body "Nick makes me very happy. I love being with him, and I'm sad when we're apart. He's the balance I need, without choking my independence. I think it's more a measure of your heart than the days on a calendar. Plus he loves dogs and horses, and lets me eat in his car." I said smiling in Nick's direction.

Everyone was now realizing that this relationship was obviously headed in a serious direction. Grammy smiled. "Well, like I said before, I thought Russell was crazy when he told me he wanted to marry Sibby Thornton, but that marriage lasted for over forty years. So there must be such a thing as love at first sight even at ten years old. My David and I were so young when we got married that we hardly knew each other, much less anything else at the age of nineteen, and we celebrated sixty-two wedding anniversaries before he passed away. But Nick, make no mistake," she said, wagging her finger, "if you two do actually make it down the aisle, and you ever do her wrong, I will kill you."

Ethan took the floor, and I nearly passed out when he began to speak. "Nick," Ethan said, "my grandmother will not actually kill you—well, I don't think she would, but we are a very tight-knit family. Like every member, my sister is very important, and her happiness is paramount to us all. She has been through the wringer, so to speak, and we don't want to see that happen to her again."

Nick interrupted. "Neither do I. I would never hurt her in any way. I love your sister with all my heart, and that is why I had planned to announce my intentions over dessert, but since we're discussing it now, let me assure you that somewhere down the road, I do intend to marry her. There are a great many things to work out, but our mission is to be together. At our age, we don't have the luxury of youthful thoughts of forever, so we are working on setting goals that are attainable."

"How old are you?" asked my Aunt Tess out of left field and with glass number four working it's way down the hatch.

Nick said, "I'll be fifty-three next October."

"October the what?" asked my mother.

"October the thirty-first," he said.

Sibby smiled. "Halloween! How fun—we don't have any October birthdays in our family."

"Excellent," Nick said. "I like being the only October birthday. We can all go trick-or-treating together, but I get all the Butterfingers since it's my birthday."

Everyone laughed, and the interrogation was over as quickly as it had begun. The remainder of the evening was spent telling one "remember when" story after the next. It was wonderful, and Nick, occasionally asked questions for clarification, and appeared to be fully immersed in the O'Neil Family Thanksgiving of 2009.

When he went to the car to collect our bags, Sibby turned to me and asked if I had lost my mind. "No one plans to marry someone after only a week or two!"

Returning to the family table conversation I said, "Mama secretly you must believe in the possibility, at least, of love at first sight."

"Why on earth would you say that?" she said.

"Because you still remember the first time and place daddy said he was going to marry you—you were only ten years old— and y'all exchanged vows thirteen years later. Anyway if we do get married, it's still another year away." I also added that there had been no formal proposal yet, and that nothing was written in stone; it had just been discussed, and that was all.

"He *is* very handsome," my mother said, looking out the door, "and he has beautiful manners. I think he must have money, so he's not after yours. Has he ever been married, and does he have any children?"

"Yes, he was married years ago, and no, he doesn't have any children," I said smiling at my mother. "I haven't actually seen a bank statement, but I feel safe in saying that he does have a great deal of money. And Mama, please calm down. I know my own mind, and I'm not stupid. He makes me very happy. Maybe we should take the advice of my neighbor, Miss Madge, and just live together."

"You absolutely will not!" she said. "But I do think I like him. He seems to have a handle on you, and that's saying something for sure."

"Mother, you are something else, you know that?" I laughed. "Now here he comes. Please let's this drop for now."

"All right, you two," Sibby said, "Sarah, you know where everything is, so will you show Nick to his room? I'm going to bed. This has been quite a day."

"Okay, but first I need to take Annie for a short walk. Nick, want to join me, or would you rather sit down in the den and relax?" I said.

"I think I would like to stretch my legs and walk with you. You two can show me the sights of Iron Springs," Nick answered, helping me with my coat. "Sibby, I would like to thank you for the best Thanksgiving I've ever had, and I mean that. My family was a loving one, but in a very business-like way. It was always just the four of us, and usually at the country club. Today was wonderful—great food and family—nothing better."

"You're welcome, and your presence gave an old family a new twist. I hope you weren't too embarrassed by us. I'll see you both in the morning," my mother said, reaching up and giving me a kiss on the cheek.

"I love you, Mama," I said.

Nick talked nonstop during our walk about my family and how much he'd enjoyed the whole day. I was relieved—no, euphoric—that my family had passed with flying colors and my intense level of anxiety had been lifted.

"Well," I said closing the front door, "I feel better. After eating entirely too much, it really does feel good to exercise."

"I agree on all counts," Nick said, taking my coat.

Nick was collecting our luggage, and when reaching for my quilted duffel bag, he said, "What in the hell do you have in here? We *are* only staying for one night, correct? This thing must weigh twenty pounds!"

"Oh, it does not," I answered quickly. "I need all that stuff. Margaret says you always need a plan-B outfit, and usually she's right. Then there's the weather, and well, just give it to me, and don't worry about how I pack. When we go on trips, if you take very little, then I can take a lot, and it will all even out."

"I'm sure you understand that sort of convoluted logic, and I only worry that someday I may as well. But for now, bed awaits. Come on, Annie, you can lead the way," Nick said, and the three of us climbed the extra-wide creaky stairs.

At the top, I motioned using my elbow that Nick's room was on the right. "I'm over here," I said. "I hope Ethan's room doesn't freak you out. My mother never changed a thing after we moved out. Ethan was a serious Boy Scout, and a few of his mementos are still hanging right where they were in nineteen something or other. I know you think I'm exaggerating, but I swear to you that my high school graduation announcement is still pinned to my bulletin board, and the only doll I ever owned is on the shelf where I put her that ill-fated Christmas morning I decided Santa had made a dreadful mistake."

"I think it's comforting to know that some things never

change," Nick answered.

"I guess," I replied, "but it is somewhat like watching your life die of dry rot right before your eyes."

"God, I love you," Nick said giving me a kiss.

"Thanks. I love you too. Oh, and we have to share a bathroom. It's the next door on your side of the hall. My towels are on the bottom rack and yours are on the top. Let me know if you need anything," I said.

"Ladies first," Nick replied. "Just knock on my door when you're finished."

Annie had already found her spot in the middle of the large area hooked rug at the foot of my bed. I rummaged through my duffel bag to find my toiletries and giggled thinking about my twenty-pound suitcase.

Wrapped in my fetching periwinkle terry-cloth bathrobe with socks on my feet, I knocked on Nick's door, and a very handsome gentleman looked right into my eyes and said, "Your towels are on the bottom because you were too small to reach the top—yes or no?"

"Correct," I replied. "See, I told you things in the house have never changed."

"I beg to differ, my love," Nick said with a smile. "I'm here. Now sweet dreams, and I'll see you in the morning. Oh, what time should I get up?"

"Breakfast is at eight-thirty when we have company. You won't need to set an alarm. My mother makes enough noise to wake you and the dead, and she does it on purpose. Sibby thinks sleeping late is the devil's work. Sweet dreams. I'll see you in the morning."

Sliding between the sheets, I thought about the first night I'd slept in this funny old house. The leafless oak tree outside my bedroom window was making the same eerie shadows on the far wall tonight as it had done so many years ago. As the unwelcome limb puppets performed their stark ballet, I thought about Nick, our day, and our potential, and drifted off to sleep.

CHAPTER 40

The unmistakable aroma of bacon and warm maple syrup wafted gently under my bedroom door. Wiggling to the side of my bed, I dangled my left arm over to tickle Annie's head. "Good morning, sweet girl. Did you sleep well at Sibby's?" Annie stood up and let it be known that she needed to go out. "Good grief, look at the time. Okay, give me a minute to put on my clothes, and I'll let you out."

Pulling on my jeans, I laughed as my dog circled with excitement. "Now listen to me," I said, "don't drive Sibby nuts. You can wait two seconds for me to go to the bathroom and get downstairs." Annie sat and watched as I finished dressing, first with the powder-blue bulky sweater and then my shoes.

I took a left out of my bedroom door and she chose a hard right. I could hear her sliding across the foyer floor as she reached the bottom of the runner-covered steps. Her body made a soft but distinct thump against the front door and the dangling prisms clattering against the crystal lamp on the side table added the accompaniment. That happened every time we spent the night in Iron Springs; Annie could never put on the brakes as she descended the staircase.

I continued down the hallway, careful to tiptoe past Nick's room. The door was still shut and I didn't want to wake him. From the backyard I could hear what sounded like my dog barking and I needed to tell her to hush. Trying to be very careful not to make any noise, I worked to gently open the somewhat immobile window in the bathroom. Without warning, the bottom section of the window went flying to the top. "Yikes!" I said poking my head outside.

"Good morning, sleepyhead!" Nick said, looking up from the backyard while throwing a tennis ball for Annie to fetch. "We were wondering if you were ever going to wake up. Come on down, and I'll meet you in the kitchen."

As I made my way downstairs, I could hear Nick and my mother deep in conversation. "Good morning, all," I said. "Boy that smells good."

"Sibby and I have already eaten," Nick said, offering me a chair.

"Thanks," I said moving the place mats.

Nick smiled and said, "Why did you do that?"

"Oh." I laughed. "Habit, I guess. The girl pilgrim mat was always mine, and you should have the boy."

"Now, you two," Sibby said, "there's no fussing allowed at the table."

"We're not fussing," I replied. "I was simply explaining."

"Didn't you and Mr. O'Neil ever argue?" Nick asked.

"Not very often," my mother answered. "In fact, the first time we ever really locked horns was when Sarah wanted a horse. Between the influence of her aunt Lucy, her grandmother, and her own love for any animal, she never stopped asking. Finally Russell gave in and said yes."

Jane W. Rankin

"She is hard to say no to," Nick said.

"Sarah and her dad went horse shopping every Saturday afternoon for about a month before finding just the right mount. He was a great big bay named Lucky, and I guess he was lucky to belong to Sarah. She took him to college with her too. Sarah and that horse won everything there was to win, but he was getting too old for much riding after they graduated, so Sarah decided to give him to the equestrian center just outside of town. He died about a month after she gave him away—colic, I think it was—is that right, Sarah?"

"Yes," I said, looking down, "and you know I don't talk about Lucky, so let's change the subject. Did you two save me any breakfast? Oh, I trust you made Annie her pancake? Where is Grammy?"

"As ridiculous as it is, yes, I fed your dog a pancake"—Sibby made a pained face—"and yes, I saved you some breakfast. Your grandmother is over at Lydia's playing bridge. She's coming home around lunchtime. She told Nick that you two were not allowed to leave until she returned. Are you coming home for Christmas?"

"Of course! Why would you think otherwise?"

"Well . . ." My mother hesitated. "I didn't know if you, Nick, and the girls had other plans."

"No. Emma, Scott, Sidney, and I will be here for sure, and I hope Nick can come, too, but we haven't had an opportunity to discuss any plans."

"Count me in," Nick said. "In fact, Ethan and I were talking about going quail hunting for a few days after Christmas, if we can get things worked out."

"Really?" I said, astounded.

"Yes," Nick said. "Your brother asked if I liked to hunt—I believe he mentioned a special tract of land he hunts in Virginia—and asked if I would like to go." I nodded. "I love to hunt, but haven't had the opportunity in years, so I jumped at the chance. I'll need to speak with Coy about taking care of the farm first, and then we'll make definite plans."

"Well, that sounds wonderful," my mother said. "Ethan has loved to bird hunt since he was a little boy. He and Russell and a few others always went hunting after Christmas. Sarah asked to go when she was about thirteen, but I put my foot down on that one. Russell didn't give me any trouble about that decision; I think he really wanted there to be some time that belonged to just the boys. Sarah was very much a tomboy, and I wanted her to behave more like a young lady—well, you see where that got me. Has she ever told you the story about punching a boy in the nose and being suspended from school when she was in the eighth grade?"

"No, she hasn't," Nick said. "You punched someone in the nose?"

"Yes, but in my defense, he said I looked like a boy. Now, Mother, please—no more stories!" I said. I swallowed my last bite of pancakes. "I know—why don't we get out some of the Christmas decorations while we're waiting for Grammy to get home?"

"Marvelous idea," my mother said, clapping her hands together. "Nick, would you mind helping?"

"Not at all," Nick said. "Where should we start?"

"Let's see . . . Sarah, take Nick to the attic and bring down the three red containers, and there's one green one we'll need as well."

"Before we get the Christmas decorations, I want to show you something," I said, leading Nick into my bedroom and pointing to a wall of pictures. "That horse was my dream come true, but needed to be semi-retired. I thought he'd be happy teaching beginning riders, and the people at the equestrian center were happy to have him." I said, gently stroking the eight-by-ten picture of Lucky and me. "I had gone to the barn for a visit just the day before he died and I've always been thankful for that, but it still haunts me just a bit. You know—all of the 'if only' or 'what if' questions."

The tears were streaming down my face, and Nick took me in his arms. Holding me tight, he said, "Why don't you consider taking all these things and putting them up alongside all the pictures you have of Rascal and Sidney's mounts? I'm sure Lucky would be happier with you than being left behind in this room. Maybe it would be easier to think of him if he became more a part of your every day."

"I don't know why I never thought of that before," I replied, removing the riding crop made from the hair of his tail and inhaling the essence of years gone by.

"What's taking so long?" asked my mother, as she appeared in my bedroom doorway. "Oh, Sarah was just showing me the pictures of Lucky, and she's decided to take them to her house. We'll get right to work on the decorations as soon as we get the last few pictures," Nick said.

"Okay, I'll wait for you two in the living room," Sibby said. "But hurry up. I haven't had help decorating for Christmas in years, and now you've got me all excited."

"We'll get right on it as soon as we get these pictures sorted out," Nick replied as he reached for the highest picture on the wall.

With the pictures piled at the foot of my bed, I led Nick to the attic. "Good Lord," he bellowed, standing in front of fifty-plus years of living. "Look at all this stuff."

"No kidding," I replied. "I bet there are things up here from before they were married and some of Grammy's keepsakes too. Ethan and I have thought of suggesting that Mama do something about all this, but there never seemed to be a good time for that conversation. How do you weave getting rid of decades of memories into table talk without her thinking the end is possibly close at hand? But we really do need to do something." We moved in and out of piles of boxes and hanging clothes, looking for the required decorations.

"It will be Valentine's before you two get the decorations downstairs," Sibby yelled from the stairwell.

"Mother," I said with a chuckle, "there is so much stuff up here that it's taking a minute to find what you wanted. You know, you might think about donating these old hats and clothes to the Iron Springs Playhouse—they'd love to increase their wardrobe department, a bunch to Goodwill, and all these boxes of books to the public library. You could maybe even get a tax break."

"Oh, for goodness' sake," she replied, "who would want all of this junk?'

Nick took the lead. "This isn't junk, far from it. Is this your wedding dress?" Nick asked holding up a clear zippered garment bag.

"Yes it is," Sibby smiled with reflective delight. "Back then I still lived at home. I was a college student and worked part-time in the office at Dixon's Department Store. Every week I put back fifteen dollars from my paycheck until I had enough to buy it." Inhaling deeply she continued, "Well, Sarah, if the men go hunting after Christmas, then you and I can go through all this then. But for right now, I would like to decorate the house," she said, pointing to the far corner.

Sometimes the window of opportunity opens itself! I thought with a smile.

Nick and I were hanging the Moravian star in the center of the front porch ceiling when Grammy came strolling up the sidewalk. "So, I see she put you two to work."

"Actually," Nick said, "Sarah offered our help and we've been hard at work for hours. How was bridge?"

"Great," Grammy replied, "Millicent and I beat the pants off of Lydia and Ruth. I even won the kitty."

"What's the kitty?" asked Nick, "And do you have to clean up after it?"

"Clever," Grammy answered. "The kitty is a jar of money. Each time we play, we all put in a quarter, and if you get a hand with absolutely no points, you win the money."

"I see," Nick said, "so it's one of the few times losing pays off. Well, how much did you win?"

"I have no idea." My grandmother laughed. "Sarah has always counted my money for me in the past, and she can do it again today while I cook lunch."

"I'll be happy to tabulate your winnings," I said, "especially if you'll make broccoli and cheese soup and turkey sandwiches."

"It's a deal," Grammy said, moving into the foyer. "Sibby," she yelled, "your elves are freezing out on the porch hanging the star. What are you going to make them do next?"

I shook my head and softly chuckled as we finished hanging the light and collapsed the ladder. "Those two," I said, "I worry what will happen when one or the other goes to the home or their reward. They've been together forever. Seriously, when my grandfather died, Grammy sold the farm and moved in with us. I think I was maybe in the ninth grade."

"That would be a year after you punched that unsuspecting boy in the nose?" Nick smiled.

"Yes, and I bet I still remember how to land one good solid blow—so watch it," I said giving him a kiss.

Perhaps it was the family atmosphere of Thanksgiving, hanging Christmas decorations, or rummaging through all of that attic yester-year that prompted me to ask, "I know you told me that your parents had passed away, but if you don't mind telling me, how did that happen? How many years apart?"

"They died in a plane crash when Jack and I were in our twenties," Nick said. "My mother loved the city; she and my dad were on their way home from a trip to New York in their twin-engine plane. It was never really determined what happened, but the plane went way off course and they crashed into the side of a mountain in West Virginia. My dad was flying, and it was just the two of them on board. It took two days to find the plane and several more days to get them and the wreckage out."

"Oh my God," I said, horror-stricken. "I'm so sorry!"

"You know, it's always really bothered me that I never had the opportunity to say goodbye," Nick said, his voice soft. "They were just gone. But enough of that, we need to get back inside and thaw out before lunch."

Nick took the ladder around to the backyard and returned it to the overcrowded storage building. I scooted in the front door and stood on the oriental rug and shook for a minute before walking into the kitchen. Annie was happy to see me and had obviously been helping Grammy work on lunch. "You know, Sarah," my grandmother said, tossing Annie another piece of turkey skin, "I really like Nick. He seems like a good sort for sure, but I want you to take the slow approach."

"He is very nice," I said, snagging the last piece of turkey skin for my dog. "It's interesting how he gets me. I know that I'm not the easiest person to understand, but he does. Well, most of the time. We've never had any trouble asking each other questions or listening to explanations of things from the past. As for taking it slow, I'll remind you of the same thing I told Mama: if we really do decide to get married, it wouldn't be until next fall at the earliest. But my forever is a bit shorter than it once was."

"True, true," my grandmother said, "just take the time, to be sure."

"I will," I said. "Now could we please drop this subject and enjoy our lunch? I really am old enough to make this sort of decision for myself. But I love you, and thank you for loving me so deeply."

"Okay, ladies," Nick said as he came in the back door. "The ladder is stored away, the decorations are in their place, and I am starving."

Sibby said, "Nick, now that we've decorated for Christmas, the snowman mat on the table is Sarah's, and has been for forty years, so I don't want you to get into trouble by sitting there.

Ethan is the nutcracker, and company uses the reindeer ones."

"Then a reindeer I shall be," Nick answered kissing the top of my head. "Thank you for saving me from a nearly fatal seating error."

"Oh, you two are just hysterical," I said.

"Lunch is ready," Grammy announced. We all took our places and enjoyed a wonderful meal and conversation.

Backing out of my mother's driveway, we waved goodbye and through the open window, repeating what a wonderful Thanksgiving it had been. Sibby smiled and returned the wave and sentiment.

Halfway back to Greenway, Nick asked, "What do you want for Christmas?"

"Oh, gosh," I said. "I've never known what I wanted for Christmas, or for my birthday. I know it sounds weird, but I'm serious: I've never wanted anything but a horse. Now I have two of those, so I would be happy with anything. What would you like?" I asked.

"I have all I want as well," Nick said, reaching over to squeeze my hand. "Maybe instead of a gift, we could go somewhere or do something special? Perhaps the first of the New Year?"

"Hmm, I can't do much in January, I'm afraid. I have three book signings next month, and they're always on the weekends."

"Really? Where are they?"

"The first one is at the Biltmore Estate in Asheville. This is the first time I've been invited to that one. It's a big honor, so I'm really excited. It's in conjunction with a workshop on horsemanship, so sales should be good."

"I've always wanted to go to Biltmore."

"Oh, it's gorgeous. Anyway, the second is at an old friend's tack store in Prescott. I do the winter customer-appreciation day every year for her. I don't make a lot of money, but it's so much fun to see everyone that I don't really care. Lacey and I are old college friends and it's just a good excuse to get together. And I go to a Winter Writer's Festival the last weekend in January. It's a lot of fun. Occasionally there are other equine authors involved, and it's nice to talk shop."

"Wow," Nick said, "can I come to see you in action?"

"Sure, but I have to tell you, it's not really very interesting. It may sound a bit glamorous, but in reality, it's mostly a lot of standing around or sitting in very uncomfortable chairs."

"I still think I would like to see Sarah the writer in action. We can talk about it later. Are you still thinking about riding Buddy today?" We turned into Long Leaf Farm.

"Yes, but it will need to be a short ride, just enough to stretch his legs," I answered. "I have tons of stuff to do at home. The Rowdy Girls are going to Virginia early tomorrow for a ride at Moss Creek Farm, and then to Susan's annual dinner-dance fundraiser. We'll ride again early Sunday before coming home. I think this is the fifth year we've done this? It's great fun. Since she has an indoor ring, we can really have a nice ride regardless of the weather."

"Do you girls go to the dinner-dance alone, you know, like your summer camp?" Nick asked.

"Well, yes and no. All the husbands show up just in time for the dinner-dance part and stay the night. There's usually a round of golf—weather permitting—the next day for them while we ride." Turning absolutely ghost white, I looked straight at Nick and said, "Oh my God! I got that invitation in the mail the first week of October and haven't thought about it since. We sent a group RSVP the next day. I've been so wrapped up in Thanksgiving and your meeting my family that it just didn't occur to me. I went alone last year and . . . well, I just don't know what to say, but would you like a very-last-minute invitation to go?"

Before Nick could respond, it occurred to me: "Oh wait, I'm sure you got an invitation too. Y'all are such old friends."

"Yes, I did," Nick said with a thoughtful tone. "I sent my RSVP too. Funny, if we hadn't met at the hunter pace, maybe we would have met at this ball."

"Gosh, we've been so busy getting to know each other and running back and forth, I wonder what else we might have forgotten?"

Getting out of the car, Nick opened the back door and pulled out his duffel and hanging bags and said, "I really did forget all about that party. Not mentioning it to you was truly unintentional—I'm sorry. I'm sure I would have thought about it when I got inside. I think my invitation is still on the kitchen counter."

"Seriously, Nick," I said, "I'm sorry too—I only remembered what I was doing for the rest of this weekend as we were pulling into your driveway. So—what should we do?"

"Well, I'm sure you're going with or without me, and I know I plan to attend as well, so I absolutely think we should show up for the dinner-dance together. I'll join in with the Rowdy Husbands from Hadley Falls, if that's okay with you. I do think we need to talk about trying to remember each other in a more timely fashion from now on."

"I agree," I said, leaning against the side of my car. "I can't believe I forgot about the party. That Thanksgiving overnight was apparently more overwhelming than I thought. It's getting late, and I don't really have time to ride Buddy. I need to be heading home. I have to pack Rascal's things as well as mine."

"Well," Nick continued, "I guess the next time I see you it will be in Virginia. I can't wait to see you in formal attire."

"Yes, me too," I said. "I've never seen you in a tux—this should be lots of fun. Ooh, I'm so excited. I'll call Betsy on my way home and ask if Frank would mind picking you up. That is, unless you don't want to ride with them."

"Oh, no," Nick answered. "I would really like to get to know the men, especially Frank and Bill. I'll need to dust off my golf clubs too. Man, I haven't played in a long time. I'll call Susan and Roger and let them know we're coming and to put us at the same table. Interesting, I've never gone to this ball. I've been invited every year, but something always got in the way, or I just didn't make the effort. Now I'm going with the prettiest Rowdy Girl. I'm a lucky man."

"Thanks, and you're ridiculous," I said. "I doubt there's a vacant hotel room within fifty miles of their farm. The guest list is usually around three hundred people, and everyone who's still breathing attends this event. Susan always gives us dibs on the guest house, so please stay there too–there's plenty of room."

"I'll take care of that when I give Susan a call," Nick said, pulling me into him and kissing me deeply. His hands were halfway down the back of my jeans as he held me even closer for another kiss. "And be careful!"

"I am always careful," I said, my breath ragged, and then

calling for Annie to get in the car. She and Caesar flew around the corner of the barn, Annie filthy once again. With a huge sigh, I opened the car door, and in jumped my dripping-wet, muddy, no-longer light-blond golden retriever. "Good grief!"

"She sure does love the farm!" Nick said, taking one hand from the inside of my jeans to run the length of my spine. "I'll see you tomorrow."

"Okay," I answered, trying to catch my breath.

CHAPTER 41

*A*fter dropping Annie off at Paws & Claws for the weekend, I rounded the corner to the barn and saw Margaret backing her truck up to the trailer. Within fifteen minutes, we had everything hooked up and loaded.

All the way to Moss Creek Farm, we talked about our Thanksgiving holidays. She and Bill had no children, and except for Margaret's brother, who lived in Oregon, they had no family left and always went skiing in Aspen. They were exceptional downhillers and had all the latest gadgets, including a camera that mounted on her helmet. Those videos were breathtaking and horrifying at the same time.

I rattled on about Nick's reaction to my family and the upcoming overnight. I broached the topic of the sleeping arrangements, and how I was not sure just how to approach it with him. Margaret and I decided that I should just say, "you have the sofa," and then see what transpired. I said that I knew our physical relationship would happen eventually, but not this early, and certainly not with everyone else around!

"Honestly, Sarah, you can work yourself into a stew over the silliest things! Drink your diet soda and eat a cookie," said

Margaret. "Everything is going to be fine. Even if Nick refuses to sleep on the sofa, you are staying in the bedroom with twin beds and that will take care of the situation."

I began to howl with laughter. "Can you imagine trying to have sex in those tiny twin beds?"

"Of course, you could end up having sex on the sofa, or the floor, for that matter," Margaret suggested. "Ooh, or in the shower . . ."

"I am no longer your friend and I am not talking to you ever again," I said, folding my arms across my body.

Margaret shrugged. "That's okay, I'll always love you and be your friend. Even if you don't love me back."

Turning into the farm, I mentioned to Margaret that she didn't need to share our conversation with the others. Margaret smiled as she put her truck in park and we got out to join the others.

"What's the matter with you?" asked Betsy, looking in Margaret's direction.

"I can't help it, Sarah, sorry," Margaret said.

Nearly falling down with laughter, Margaret recapped our conversation almost verbatim. Everyone, including me, was in absolute stitches by the time Susan came into view. "Well, I see you girls have gotten into something on your way to Virginia," she said. "Let me guess: it's either about old Mrs. Pritchett's dress, Evelyn's boobs, or sex." Our laughter would have raised the roof, had there been one. "I guess sex is the correct answer. I'll venture a guess that it is in regard to the possibility of Nick Heart's getting lucky tonight?"

"Oh my God," I said, looking straight at Susan. "Don't you dare tell him *anything* about this!"

"What you and Nick do when the lights are turned off is your concern, not mine."

"Y'all think you're so funny—well, you're not. Now I have to get my horse off this trailer, and we need to ride. For the last time," I continued, "Nick I are not going to have sex tonight, and that is that!"

"You know"—Susan giggled—"those are famous last words if I ever heard them. I can't wait until tomorrow morning's ride to find out what happened. Now if the sex—I mean *six* of you can regain your composure, it's time to ride."

"I hate all of you," I mumbled, backing Rascal down the ramp of the trailer. "Good boy," I said rubbing his face. "These people think they are so damn funny. I'm having a heart attack, and they're in stitches."

"We love you, Sarah," they sang in unison.

"I know you do, but I still hate you all," I said with a smile.

Our ride was perfect as always. The flat lesson in the indoor ring was actually fun, and quite challenging. Susan had been to an equine clinic and was using us as guinea pigs testing out new things. At the end, she set up a very interesting jump course that involved weaving back and forth, jumping everything on the diagonal. Rascal thought it was fun once we figured it out.

"It's a beautiful day," Susan said, "so let's not waste it. Be in the cross-country field in fifteen minutes."

"I am not going to jump anything big," Elizabeth declared. "We haven't done anything since summer camp, and I'm not prepared for that."

I laughed and said, "I've given up pretending to have any control over anything to do with riding at Moss Creek Farm."

"What are you going to say?" Betsy asked. "You'll have to wait and see," I said, raising my eyebrows.

We walked six abreast, as we had done so many times before, to the center of the field. Susan asked if any of us had anything to say before we began. I raised my hand and said, "Considering the overwhelming importance of tonight, I would prefer to have an easy ride. If the opportunity for amazing sex does present itself, I would hate to have to ask Nick for a rain check."

Without missing beat Susan said, "You've got it." And with that we began an hour and a half of the most intense, difficult, and torturous riding I had ever experienced. When Susan told us it was time to go back to the barn, she said, "Sarah, there's ibuprofen in the bathroom cabinet. If you start now, you should be in good shape by tonight."

We had only two hours to be ready for the Moss Creek Farm Charity Soirée. We wasted the first fifteen minutes trying to decide who would go first in the bathroom. As it turned out, I was last in line.

While drying my hair, I was sure I heard male voices, and I became instantly nervous. With a wiggle or two I managed to finish zipping up my dress. I smiled in the mirror, applied one last layer of hair spray, and swallowed three more ibuprofen for good measure. Mentally I reviewed my outfit and softly said, "Showtime."

Standing at the top of the stairs, I could see everyone gathered around the seating area of the den. Nick was the first to look up, and the others followed. "Wow," Nick said as I descended. Taking my hand at the bottom step and giving me a kiss on the cheek he said, "You're beautiful; you look good enough to eat."

"Thank you," I said feeling myself blush. "You look very handsome as well. I love your tux. Where in the world did you find an equestrian cummerbund?"

"I've had this thing forever," Nick said. "Jack's children gave it to me one year for Christmas. I have never seen another one like it. I love your hair. I think I like it this way even better than the other night."

Just then Frank came out from the kitchen carrying a plastic cup and asked if everyone was ready to go. In different octaves, we answered yes in chorus. I looked in Betsy's direction and raised an eyebrow at the travel cup. I knew it was full of bourbon and branch, and that she didn't want him to drink at all, but she would settle for just not too much. Alcohol made Frank loud and slightly obnoxious.

"Don't say anything," I said, standing beside Betsy. "It's always so loud at this party, no one will notice. Plus if he drinks too much, he'll feel like crap tomorrow playing golf. When we get to the country club, we can tell the bartender to watch him and really water down his drinks. It will be fine. I promise."

"Thanks for being such a good friend, especially after all the grief we gave you today," Betsy said.

"You're welcome," I replied. "The limousine is waiting. Let's go have fun. Do you think old Mrs. Pritchett will have on that same bright green dress she's worn for the past five years?"

Piling into the stretch limo, Betsy laughed. "I don't think she has another dress. She owns half of Virginia, but only one party frock? What do you think, will Evelyn be nearly naked again this year?"

"Yes," said Margaret. "You know her ta-tas are taking

272

a serious journey southward, and her scantily clad look is becoming a bit scary."

"You girls should be ashamed of yourselves," Frank said. "You never hear men talking about other men the way women do. Perhaps old Mrs. Pritchett thinks she looks her best in that green dress. And who knows, maybe Evelyn has had some work done on her ta-tas, as you call them, and they are back in their original place. What do you think, guys, will Bud wear his plaid cummerbund again, two years in a row?"

"I for one pray he makes a different selection," Bill said. "Last year there must have been at least a dozen other men wearing the same outfit, and I know they could have just died."

"Oh, you two are just so funny," Betsy said. "There are six women in this car, and we all have on different dresses. And they are different from what we wore last year—that's all."

"I have always found it interesting and somewhat amazing," Nick said, "that women have the ability to remember what they, and other women, wore three hundred and sixty-five days ago. Most men can't tell you what they had on yesterday and couldn't care less."

"I've worn this dress before, but not to this function," I said. "Mrs. Pritchett, though, she just doesn't care that she wears the same dress year after year. Men, on the other hand, don't have to worry about such things, as a tux never really goes out of style. Except for Mr. Suggs—his tux is so old that the moths have eaten half of it. Plus it's so faded that it's no longer black. He's the only man in the world who owns a polka-dot charcoal-gray wool tux."

"Polka-dotted?" Nick asked.

"The black satin lining shines through the moth holes. I'll

introduce you to him and you can see for yourself."

Our driver pulled the car up to the front door of the club. Offering to help all the ladies out of the car, the valets commented on how lovely each of us looked. As Nick and I walked into the lobby, he said, "I think I am offended that he didn't compliment *me* on my attire."

"Stop it." I giggled. "Come on, let's go have some fun."

I loved that centuries-old structure. It was first a manor house of some founding father of Virginia, then the property was bought up by a group who'd turned it into a country club, mostly for the purpose of fox hunting, business deals, and telling lies over a glass of good Scotch. *If these walls could talk*, I thought. The club was beautifully decorated with horse paintings, rich tapestries, and so on, but tonight, with the addition of lights in the trees and candles everywhere inside, it was especially glamorous.

The party was a success: the food was delicious, dancing to the oldies was awesome, and the silent auction raised tons of money for the cause. It was great that some things never changed. Old Mrs. Pritchett appeared in the doorway, looking as ever like the world's largest shamrock. Evelyn made her annual appearance wearing as little as possible, and Lyle Bayshore, as he did every year, followed her around all night.

Nick agreed that Mr. Suggs's tux did take on the appearance of polka dots. Frank was very careful not to have too much to drink, and what he did have was slightly watered down, so Betsy was happy. Margaret and Bill were gifted dancers and shagged barefooted like it was summer time at the Pad in Ocean Drive— North Myrtle Beach to be politically correct. Elizabeth and

Jennifer, along with their husbands, Ian and Mickey, spent most of the night in deep philosophical conversation. Rose and the head chef spent a good bit of time discussing the ingredients for several of the food items, and in passing, I did hear the word "Paris" more than once. I was kept busy answering the question *So, Sarah . . . who is this handsome fellow?* Nick was such a good sport about it all and took me to the dance floor when he and I had had enough small talk for a while.

Roger walked onto the parquet dance floor, tapped on the side of his wineglass, and asked for quiet. After a few minutes their guests settled down, and a hush fell over the crowd. "Susan and I would like to thank all of you for coming out tonight. We appreciate your generosity and your commitment to helping feed the hounds. Be careful going home; it has turned very cold and there might be a slick spot here and there on the roads. Happy Holidays to all, and we wish each and every one of you a very happy and profitable New Year."

It was at least another hour before we were back at the guest house. Everyone was exhausted; it was most definitely bedtime. I began to worry about the next step. There had been no talk of where Nick would sleep, and I truly didn't know how to start that conversation.

"Good night, beautiful," Nick said, giving me a kiss. "I had a wonderful time. I hope you had fun too."

"I did, but I'm very tired," I said. "Susan tried to kill us on the cross-country field for hours before we came to the party. It's been quite a day."

"Well then, it is off to bed for you. I'll take the couch." Nick said removing the throw pillows. "Do you know where they keep the extra sheets and blankets?"

I walked over to the cabinet. "It's all in here. Just help yourself to what you need. I'll see you in the morning." I shivered. "It really is cold in here, isn't it? I think I'll turn up the heat." I went to the thermostat. "Huh."

"What?" Nick walked over.

"It's set to seventy-six, but it's only sixty-two in here. What do you think about that?"

"I think there might just be a problem with the furnace. Maybe it'll catch up the next time it clicks on. Here, take an extra blanket, just in case."

"Thanks," I said. "I'll see you in the morning." Walking up the steps, I waved good night. It was as cold as ice downstairs, but a bit warmer in my room. *Hot air rises,* I thought. *I hope Nick doesn't freeze to death.*

CHAPTER 42

$\mathcal{I}$ was startled when I awoke to Nick's hand pressing gently on my shoulder. "Sarah," Nick said. "It's just me." He removed his hand. "I hope I didn't scare you. I'm freezing to death downstairs, so I thought I could sleep in the other twin bed."

"Okay," I said, sitting up on my elbows, swiping the sleep from my eyes. "I guess the furnace is broken after all."

"I don't know, but I do know that I might have the beginnings of hypothermia sleeping downstairs." He slid under the covers of the other bed. "This is not how I'd envisioned our first night together!"

"I need to tell you a bedtime story," I said. I told him the conversation between my friends and me from earlier that day. Nick laughed here and there, and when I got to the fetching sleepwear part, I laughed and said how unsexy I must look now in my socks, sweat pants, and two shirts for warmth.

"Sarah, you would be fetching in anything. I'm not young, either, and I haven't been with a woman in a good many years. I've worried about this maybe even more than you have. Men might not care about what they wear to a charity function, but I'm sure we think more about being successful in bed than women do. When you and I do share a bed for the first time, I want everything to be perfect. Sarah, are you listening?"

"Yes," I said, finding myself suddenly very warm. "I'm just afraid that you might be disappointed in me."

The moonlight etched Nick's silhouette against the beadboard wall as he rose up on his side. "Are you crazy? You could never disappoint me."

"I hope not," I said. "What are we going to say tomorrow when you obviously didn't sleep on the sofa?"

"Sometimes," Nick said, "saying nothing is best. It won't matter what we say; they'll all think we slept together, though I don't know how any two people over the age of five could share one of these beds. So let them think what they want. You know, we could have some fun with this . . . then the topic of sex would be over as far as your friends are concerned."

"I think that's perfect!" I laughed. "We need to come out of this room and walk down the stairs together. I can't wait to see their faces tomorrow morning. I really do love you, Mr. Heart."

"I love you too, Ms. Sams," Nick said, reaching out for me to take his hand, and then he gave it a squeeze. "Now go to sleep, and I'll see you in the morning."

Nick and I woke up to the smell of breakfast cooking and the sound of hammering. "Hi," I said looking across the space between the twin beds. "Did you sleep well?" I asked.

"You know, I really did," Nick answered. "I'm usually a fairly light sleeper, but last night I was gone. It must have been because you were here."

"I'd like to take credit, but I imagine it was the hours

of dancing and several glasses of wine," I said, bringing my sock-clad feet to the floor. "Oh, we need to get ready for our grand entrance. I just hope I can contain myself."

"They're going to see anything you do as an admission of our having had sex last night, so it really doesn't matter," Nick said with a smile. "I can't wait to see the look on Betsy's face—she seems like the most open with her feelings. The men will just give me the manly nod of approval."

Nick and I took turns in the bathroom and then walked hand-in-hand, descending the staircase and stopping at the kitchen bar. Betsy never took her eyes off me, and Frank gave Nick a thumbs-up. Nick squeezed my hand, and I giggled just a bit. Taking a seat on one of the stools I asked, "What is that noise?"

"It's the furnace repair guy," Bill said. "I don't know if you two realized it or not, but we didn't have any heat all night."

"Really?" Nick said, with a smile. "I was as warm as toast."

"Me too," I said. "But you're right, it's as cold as ice down here. How on earth did you get him here on a Sunday morning? Betsy, are you making pancakes? I'm starving!"

"You know Roger knows everyone and most owe him a favor. I guess that list includes the furnace repair man," Betsy said, a smirk on her face. "And yes to the pancakes. I imagine you worked up an appetite during the night."

"I guess we both did," Nick said. He stretched out his arms and put one around me. "Frank, are we still on for golf?"

Frank smiled over his coffee cup and said, "If we can all muster the strength and the greens thaw, then we are off to the links while the girls ride."

As we each took our place around the huge dining room

table, I smiled at the richness of true friendship. The six women in the group had shared many meals, secrets, and good times around that table. We always held hands while Jennifer said the blessing. Betsy reminded her that the food would get cold if she took too long. Jennifer had a tendency to thank everyone on the planet for whatever part they had played in our enjoying this meal. With the final amen in place, everyone reached for the closest dish on the oversized lazy Susan.

"So Sarah," Margaret asked, "how did you manage to stay warm when the rest of us were freezing?"

"She had me," answered Nick. "I was probably the first person to realize the heating system had serious issues. I grabbed my things and all the blankets I could find and made my way up the steps. Sarah was kind enough to share her room with me, and well, we were just as snug as a bug in a rug. Would you please pass the syrup? I've got to tell you," Nick continued, "those have to be the smallest beds I have ever slept in." Not one person said a word while Nick poured syrup over his pancakes and asked if I would like some more.

"No, thank you," I replied. "Would you care for some sausage?"

"Frank, how about you—more sausage?" Nick asked, holding the platter.

"Uh—yes," Frank stammered. "I think I would. So what are you girls going to do today?"

"Die," Elizabeth answered. "I think Susan secretly hates us, and that's why she works us so hard. Between our ride yesterday and the party, I'm exhausted."

"We've planned endless strategies at this very table to

persuade Susan to let us off the hook, and not even one has ever worked." Jennifer said. "I think we should take a different approach, girls. You know, reverse psychology? If she says 'meet you in fifteen minutes,' we say fine."

"It won't work," Rose said, shaking her head. "She doesn't care what we say about any of her commands, and we all know that. I've found it best to simply do as I am told and pray that I live to see another sunrise. Thankfully nobody's died yet, so let's just enjoy the ride—if we're all up to it, that is."

"I for one can't wait," I said. "I love riding here more than anywhere. Seeing the next sunrise, as you said, is always of monumental concern, but you're right: we always have. I do worry about Rascal, though. He's getting older and I'm not sure he is truly up to the rigorous workouts here."

"Rascal is fine," Betsy soothed. "But you're right that he is getting older; so is Charlie. I guess we should start taking that into consideration from now on."

"I've given next summer some serious thought, and I'm not sure Rascal can keep up the pace," I said, and sighed. "I can't imagine my life without that horse, but it is getting closer. I can feel it."

"Well," Nick said, wrapping a warm arm around me, "it's not going to happen today, so don't worry about things over which you have no control. Enjoy your ride! If Rascal's not up for camp next summer, you can take Buddy."

"I guess I could," I said, trying to picture Buddy up here with the other horses. "That would be weird to ride a different horse. I've had Rascal for ten years."

"Wow, it's getting late," Nick said. "If we're going to play eighteen, we'd better get a move on. What time are you ladies supposed to be at the barn?"

"We were told to be on at nine o'clock," Margaret said.

"Well, it's eight fifteen," Nick replied.

"Sweet Christ," Betsy said. "We'll never make it."

"No, we won't be there on the strike of nine," Rose said, "but we do have a trump card this time."

"We do?" asked Margaret.

"Yes, we do," Rose said, standing up from the table and picking up her plate with a little smile on her face. "All we have to do is suggest that Sarah was not alone last night, and Susan will forgive us all for being late."

I nearly hurt myself as I whipped my head around. "You will *not* tell Susan that," I said.

Nick gave my arm a squeeze and said, "It's okay, baby, especially if it keeps you from getting in trouble with Susan. I'm off to the links—have fun, but be careful! I'll see you back here later."

"Okay," I said with a wink. "Remember—golf is a gentleman's game: there's to be no cussing, throwing of clubs, peeing on trees, or telling of falsehoods."

"Well then"—Frank shrugged and sat back down—"I guess we should just stay here."

"So," Susan said, "It's nice of you girls to finally show up."

"We had to talk to Sarah about her sexual escapades last night," Rose yelled. "Add that the fact that we had no heat, the furnace guy was banging about the house this morning, and, well, there you have it. We'll be ready in fifteen minutes."

"Sarah had sex?" Susan asked. "Impossible! No one could

manage that in those tiny beds. Sarah, how did you pull that off?"

"I'm getting ready to ride my horse," I answered. "And I don't kiss and tell—never have. But I will say that small beds make for a large floor area." You could have heard a pin drop as I walked by my friends. "So are we going to ride or not?" I asked with a Cheshire-cat smile I hadn't realized I owned.

After a fabulous three-hour ride, during which nobody died, we cleaned our horses, packed the trailers, and went back to the guest house to organize our personal things. I was folding my clothes when Betsy entered my room. "Sarah," she said, "I have to know the truth. Did you and Nick sleep together? I wanted everything to be perfect for you, and rolling around on this or any floor does not sound perfect to me."

"Betsy," I said giving her a hug, "Nick and I shared the best night, but it was without sex. He really was freezing, and he did sleep in the other Tiny Tim bed. We talked for a long time and it was absolutely perfect. He and I have never had much time to be together, and especially alone. I told him about my concerns. As it turns out, he has worried about some of the same things."

"But you said . . ." Betsy stammered.

"We didn't say anything," I chimed in. "The rest of you assumed, and you know what they say about assumptions . . ."

"Yeah, yeah," Betsy said. "Are you going to tell the others?"

"Yes," I said, "but it'll be sad to ruin their fun, especially Rose. She'll be so disappointed in me."

"I'll be disappointed in what?" Rose said as she passed by.

"Sarah and Nick didn't have sex," Betsy blurted out.

Rose collapsed dramatically against the door frame. "How completely devastating. But now you've at least shared the same room after lights out, so that breaks some of the ice. Oh, but good job, Sarah—you and Nick really had us going."

"You guys should have seen your faces when we walked down the stairs," I said.

"Honey, I'm home!" rattled the silence of the guest house as our noble warriors of the links returned.

"My husband is an absolute freak," Betsy said, laughing as she walked to the upstairs railing. "We're up here, dear. Did you have fun?"

"We had a wonderful time," Frank answered. "But our new friend Nick is a liar. He said he was a bit rusty, but he took us all to the cleaners."

"I just got lucky," Nick said.

"Luck had nothing to do with it. Well done! Are you boys ready to head home?"

"We are," Bill answered.

Nick came upstairs to collect his things, and I told him that I had come clean about last night. Nick smiled and said he was not surprised that I couldn't continue the deception, but was proud that we had given them all a run for their money during breakfast.

"Frank would not let it go. He razzed me for the entire front nine holes. I finally told him that my sex life was none of his business, but I did appreciate how much he obviously cares about you. He let it go after that, and then Bill started in on me. Around the fourteenth hole I stopped the game and told them the truth. I added that they were not to say another word about last night or ask another question. After a minute of silence, Ian said that he was very sorry to hear that news and wished me well in the future. We all had a good laugh—and I won fifty dollars."

From the bottom of the steps Bill yelled, "Nick, give her a kiss and let's go, man. I don't want to miss the game."

After a kiss that reduced my knees to butter, Nick said, "Next fall is not going to work out. I can tell you that right now. I hate saying goodbye, and I hate even more going days without seeing you. Call me when you're home. I love you."

"I love you too," I said. Nick walked down the stairs.

"I'd better be invited," Betsy said.

"Invited to what?" I asked.

"The wedding! And please," my best friend continued, "pick a date that is after camp."

"I'll do my best," I said.

CHAPTER 43

The next few weeks flew by with unconscious speed. I was completely immersed in school, the holidays, my family, and riding, plus Nick and I were still going back and forth between our houses.

The day before Christmas Eve, Nick phoned early in the morning and announced that he was taking me somewhere special that evening. "I know you're going to ask what you should wear, so wear something better than you would to school, but not good enough to go to the ballet."

I pursed my lips. "Well, if you will just tell me where we're going, I would know what to put on."

"Nope. It's a surprise," Nick answered. "You always look great. Just dress up a little bit and you'll be fine. I'll pick you up at six thirty tonight."

"I can't wait!" *What a fun twist to my day*, I thought.

I called Betsy to tell her about the mysterious date. She said, "You know it probably has something to do with your Christmas gift. What did you ask for?"

"Nothing," I said. "I did say once that there was not much I hadn't done, and very little that I needed. We discussed at one point taking a trip in January, but I put the kibosh on that with three book signings on the calendar for my free weekends. I think it's wonderful that he's gone to so much trouble to think of something different for me, but you know it's driving me crazy."

"Honestly. Stop it. Just go have fun."

"Thanks," I said, "He didn't say anything about exchanging gifts tonight, so I'm leaving mine at home. I think I'll go to the barn—hey—why don't you come over and ride in the indoor with me?"

"I'd love to, but I have to work at my barn. I have let things slide since Thanksgiving, and Frank said he would help me. You know that doesn't happen very often, so I have to take advantage. Call me tomorrow as soon as you wake up," Betsy said, "Frank and I are going to his office party tonight."

"Have fun!"

I had a wonderful but short ride. I needed to get home and give myself enough time to mentally quiet down. My phone rang as I was leaving the barn, and I fumbled around trying to answer.

"Hello?" Margaret repeated twice. "Are you there?"

"Yes, I almost dropped my phone. Listen to this," I said filling her in on my invitation.

"I hope you have a wonderful time," Margaret said. "I can't wait to hear about whatever it is, and I'd love to get a call tonight, but don't even think about that. Have fun where ever you're going!"

"Thanks," I said. "I still think it's something for just the two of us, though, but I could be wrong. I'll call you tomorrow."

I fed Annie and took her for an early walk. Making the final turn home, I noticed a green SUV parked in my driveway. "Damn," I said out loud, "what's *he* doing here?"

"Hi, Sarah," Parker said as we came up the sidewalk. "Hello, Annie, how are you?" Parker reached out to pet our once-shared wriggling dog. They were clearly very happy to see each other, and I was briefly sad that Annie had lost that part of her life. I had never thought about how she might have missed him.

"Parker," I said, not feeling at all delighted to see him. "What are you doing here?"

That wiped the smile from his face. "Well, it's good to see you too, Sarah," Parker snapped. "I came to drop off the girls' Christmas presents."

"I was just asking you a question," I said. "New Bern is two hours away. You could have mailed their presents. Plus, I can't imagine you'd think I would be overjoyed to see the man who left me after twenty-seven years and two children, but what do I know?"

"Since you put it that way, I guess not," Parker said, somewhat deflated. "Well, anyway, I just finished playing eighteen holes at Turtle Creek with Owen and Ed, so I was close and I thought I'd drop them off. Oh, and while we were having lunch, Ed mentioned that you have a boyfriend? Nick somebody . . . ?"

"Yes, that's right, and while we're on the subject, let me modify what I said earlier about your being here. I'm actually glad to see you, because I want to thank you for leaving me," I said, watching as the color drained from Parker's face. "If you hadn't left, I would have never found my true inner self. I love my new life, and Nick Heart. He appreciates me and applauds my individuality. We share so many of the same interests but still have enough differences to keep it interesting. I once wished you only the worst life had to offer, but I have grown beyond that point. I have come to realize that true healing can only happen when forgiveness is in place. It has taken a very long time, but Merry Christmas, Parker, and I honestly, and sincerely, forgive you."

Parker nodded and said, "Merry Christmas, Sarah. I wish you the best. I hope you and Nick are very happy."

"I'll make sure the girls get their gifts," I said, walking up my front steps.

I could feel a flood of emotions swallowing me alive. I needed to write. I sat down in my computer chair and Annie rested her chin on my knee. I stroked her head as the tears streamed down my cheeks.

December 23, 2009
Dear Debby,

Parker came to see me late this afternoon, and it was unsettling and wonderful at the same time. He really did want to bring the girls their gifts, but he also wanted me to know that he knew about Nick.

I sincerely thanked him for leaving me, and that I now know who I am, I love my life, and I love Nick Heart. I told Parker that I forgave him, and wished him Merry Christmas . . . and I meant it. I cannot tell you how good it feels to be free of those dark thoughts, especially the anger.

I have a much lighter heart now that I have had a chance to calm down. We need to talk about this. I was proud that I stood right there and said my piece without batting an eye.

The hot-pink folder has another new twist! I can't wait to see you next Tuesday!!

With all good wishes,
Sarah

CHAPTER 44

$\mathcal{I}$ decided on an outfit: my favorite pair of better-than-workday black pants, a black turtleneck, a lime-green quilted vest, and a scarf of both colors with a dash of turquoise. It was one of my standard-upgrade but not over-the-top outfits, and one Nick had never seen.

I was showered, dressed, and playing with Annie when the doorbell rang. "Hi," I said, opening the door and giving Nick a kiss. "Come in. Man, it's cold outside."

"You look wonderful!" Nick said giving me a passionate kiss. "Wait a minute," he continued looking more closely at my eyes. "Are you okay? It looks like you've been crying."

"Well, I was, but I'm okay now."

Nick rested on the arm of the living room sofa and said, "Please tell me what's wrong."

I launched into a quick review concerning Parker's visit and how good it felt to say out loud what I had been unable to verbalize before now. I said it was a good cry, and that there really was such a thing. Inhaling deeply, I added, "My eyes will be okay in a bit, and I really don't want to ruin our evening with this conversation. Now will you tell me where we are going?"

"No. You have to wear a blindfold," Nick responded.

"A blindfold? Are you kidding?"

"Yes! Well, actually I was going to do that, but didn't think you'd agree to it."

"I'm not sure I like it, but I trust you. If it's that important to you, a blindfold it is," I said. "Let's go before I change my mind."

At the car, Nick reached into the back seat and pulled out one of those sleep masks they offer you on long flights in first class. "This is all I could think of to use. It's your choice," he reminded me.

"I think it's fabulous," I replied, putting the elastic strap over my head. "I only hope it doesn't mess up my hair." I giggled. "This is fun. I bet I can figure out where we're going without even seeing anything."

I sat very still and quiet as it felt like we worked our way through the heart of downtown. "Well," I said. "That's the last light on Front Street and we're headed east."

"How on earth can you possibly know that?" Nick asked.

"It's a gift. I also think I know where we're going, but I need a little more time," I said smiling. "I really like this so far. I love a challenge. When do you want to exchange gifts?" I asked from behind my mask.

"Anytime," Nick answered. "Just let me know."

"I'd rather do it when it's just the two of us," I said.

When we turned from the highway, I knew we'd gone onto the drive of Long Leaf Farm. "We're at your house. May I take off the blindfold?"

"Not just yet," Nick answered. "I'm going to take you inside first. No peeking—you've done great so far."

Nick helped me out of the car and led me to the front door. I had never entered his house through the front entrance. "Hmm," I said, "why the front door?"

"Because this is special." He removed my blindfold.

I blinked a few quick times, and there before me were all my friends, Nick's friends, and a beautifully decorated house. I felt a rush of happiness, and my smile traveled from ear to ear. Nick knew he had topped the charts on the surprise list.

"Well," Nick said, "aren't you going to say something?"

"I-I'm speechless," I stuttered. "I don't know what to say."

"This is the first of our annual Christmas parties," Nick said. "Next year you can make all the arrangements, but this year it's my gift to you. No one loves to have a do more than you do."

The front hall was packed deep with faces, with Betsy and Margaret in the front row of what resembled a school-picture grouping. Pointing in their direction, I said, "You two are in big trouble!" A group hug followed, and I told Betsy the only way she was able to keep the secret was talking on the telephone and not in person.

"You're so right," my best friend answered.

"And then there's you," I said, turning my head toward Margaret.

"I have no idea what you're talking about." She smiled as she tucked her curls behind her ears.

"You're so full of prunes," I laughed.

The food was exceptional, catered by River's Bend, of course. I told Jennifer how delicious everything was and how much I appreciated the surprise. She was delighted, and she told me Nick had called her the Monday after Thanksgiving and given her full rein on what to prepare.

It took me a minute to find Elizabeth's petite frame, but after a few twists and turns through the crowd, there she stood. Beaming from ear to ear, she giggled as I walked closer. I knew without asking that her two favorite decorators had been hired for this job. They were amazing craftsmen with a few earmark touches that defined their jobs. The chandeliers were packed with greenery and ornaments so that only the light bulbs showed. A garland traveled the length of the banister and disappeared out of sight at the top of the stairs. Lights were intertwined as well as holly berries sprinkled with glitter. Amazing arrangements of various sizes sat atop every key piece of furniture in the downstairs. The pièce de résistance was the living room mantel with brass candlesticks of various heights growing up from an evergreen hedge full of sugared fruits.

"Kenny and Mark?" I asked.

Elizabeth laughed. "How did you know?"

"Are you kidding? No one else could have done this. I bet they had a good time with this wonderful old house."

I felt a tap on my shoulder. "Hi, Mom."

Turning around, I was delighted to see my Sidney all dressed up and smiling. "Well, hello to you too!" I reached out to hug and kiss her. "What a wonderful surprise."

"There's more," Sidney said, lifting one eyebrow.

"More?" I asked. "How could there be any more?"

"Mother, you look wonderful!" Emma said. Scott was standing just behind his wife and offered me a hug, a serious sacrifice for him. Scott really didn't enjoy being close to others, and my hugging him had become a game with us.

"Oh my gosh," I said. "I am just floored. I really don't know what to say about all of this."

"Well, there's a first," chirped another familiar voice.

In the doorway of the dining room, my entire family was waving. I felt the tears of joy welling in my eyes. "Don't cry," Nick said. "This is supposed to make you happy."

"I don't think anything in my life has made me this happy! That's why I'm crying. Give me a minute to get myself together," I said, walking into the kitchen. Lying on the floor was Caesar, and he too had company: my Annie. "How did you get here?"

Nick explained. "Sidney went by your house before coming here, traded her car for yours, got Annie, and packed your bag. I took the long way home and drove slowly so she'd get here before us. Both of your children, Scott, and you, are staying the night at my house and then going back to Brook Street tomorrow for Christmas Eve. I thought it would be easier for all of us to meet one another this way first, especially Emma and Scott."

"I love you so much," I said, wrapping my arms around him. "This is the perfect Christmas gift. I cannot thank you enough."

"Sarah," my mother's voice cried, "it's rude to leave all your guests to themselves, and you know it. Nick has done a wonderful thing for you and here you stand blubbering in the kitchen, with your dog and another enormous creature. For goodness' sake! Get it together and join the party. And by the way, I love your outfit, and your hair is very cute like that," Sibby said, patting the back of my head.

"Thanks Mama, and yes," I answered surprised at the flow of compliments to my clothes and especially my hair, which had been a topic of conversation for a lifetime, "you are so right. I am being rude. You look very nice too."

The remainder of the evening was beyond perfect. Annie and Caesar did escape their kitchen lock-down several times when the servers replenished the trays of food, but everyone seemed happy to see them. Their matching Christmas collars were quite a topic of discussion, and when asked, Nick said he found them online. There was one missing box of cheese puffs, and Caesar was presumed guilty of the theft.

Our guests began to thin out around ten thirty, and my closest friends were the last to leave.

Nick, my children, and I crashed on the sofa and chairs in the den as we listened to the catering crew collecting their things. "I can't believe this night," I said, looking around the room. "I don't think I have ever been so surprised."

"Now, Mother," Emma said, a mischievous smile covering her face, "you were fairly blown away when Sidney finally learned how to drive a car without hitting something."

"Shut up," Sidney replied, poking her in the ribs. "At least I never dated a boy with a criminal record."

"He stole a dirty magazine from the corner store. I hardly consider that to be a major offense," Emma volleyed.

"Okay, you two," I said, fearing a battle royal would spoil the golden evening.

Scott laughed and said, "Nick, you seem like a straight-up kind of guy. I need to warn you: it is always like this when they're together. One minute they're laughing, and the next it's a catfight. But they do really love each other. The best thing to do is not get them together too often."

"Thanks for the advice," Nick said, shaking Scott's hand.

"I've never had a family of my own and—"

Emma interrupted before Nick could finish his sentence. "And you picked ours? Mama said you went with her to Sibby's for Thanksgiving. Brave man."

"Like I said earlier," Scott said, "it's not too late to get out and run while you can."

"Scott, you just don't realize how lucky you are," Nick replied.

"Well, I for one am exhausted," I announced.

"It is getting late," Nick said. "Let's see, Sidney, you have the bedroom at the top of the stairs and Emma, you and Scott are across the hall, and my love, you have the back bedroom on the right. I think Adel put towels out for everyone, but if you need anything, just give me a holler. Remember that this is a very old house and it takes longer for the hot water to make its way to you. The electrical switches are in funny places and the floor creaks even when no one is walking on it. But don't be scared; there are no ghosts. I don't think so, anyway."

"I have to take Annie out before I can go to bed," I said, standing up and stretching.

"I'll go with you and let Caesar have a romp," Nick replied.

I could hear my children talking a mile a minute as we made our way to the kitchen. I was fairly certain that they liked Nick and me together.

Standing in the backyard, I took Nick's hand and squeezed gently. "You have given me the best Christmas gift ever," I said. "The party was wonderful, and you do know how I love to entertain. I'm not surprised you invited my friends, but to have included my family was simply wonderful."

"I'm glad it made you happy," Nick said. "This old house has never been so alive as it was tonight. It was pulsing with energy. I loved it, and I love you."

"I love you too," I said taking the initiative to give Nick a kiss. "I would love to have a nightcap with you."

"You don't drink," Nick furrowed his eyebrows.

"A nightcap doesn't have to be alcohol," I said. "What I really want isn't possible, because once again we're not alone, but I didn't really have the opportunity to eat much of anything, so I'll settle for food. I know the caterers put the leftovers in the refrigerator."

"Sarah Sams, you wicked girl," Nick said, nibbling my neck and running his hands under my turtleneck. "I'll put your suggestion at the top of the promise column and hold you to it. But for now, I'm hungry, too, and that will have to do." Giving the dogs a whistle, Nick opened the back screen door and guided me inside the warm house with his hand in the small of my back. I smiled, remembering the first time he had touched me, and the way it made me feel. It was no longer the same—it was better. We were on our way to a future, a home, and a family.

CHAPTER 45

Cooking breakfast the next morning, I smiled as my girls and Scott filtered down from upstairs and Nick came in from the barn. "Boy that smells good," Nick said giving me a kiss. "What can I do to help?"

"Nothing, but thanks for the offer," I said returning the kiss. "Are you sure you don't mind sleeping on the pull-out couch tonight at my house? I love it that you're going to stay the night, but I can't offer you the same Cadillac accommodations as you have here."

"I'm sure, and I can't wait, so you'll need to worry about something else," he replied with a smile and a pat on my behind.

The drive home gave me the opportunity to run a mental list of pros and cons on the subject of moving to the farm. My friends topped the column of cons. How could I possibly live more than two blocks away from Margaret or five miles from Betsy? I was in the single-digit years from retirement, if I chose to, and my school and the farm were on east side of Hadley Falls—so that was a closer commute. My roots of the last thirty years were in Hadley Falls, and I was comfortable there. I had always wanted to live on a farm, but LLF was thirty miles out of town, and pitch dark at night, which freaked me out a little bit.

Moving to the pro side, I had always wanted my own farm. Nick's house was twice as large as mine and would accommodate more people, and I loved everything about the property. To walk out my back door and get on my horse seemed more wonderful than I could imagine.

Pulling into my driveway, I couldn't help but smile as I saw my adult children lugging their things up the front steps. Was it possible that this cottage, not unlike my inherited house on Washington Street, had done her job? Could it be that my healing was nearly complete? Was I actually ready to move on, literally and emotionally?

Once inside with our things in place, I said, "Emma I know this is the first time you've met Nick, so what do you think about him? And I guess I should say, of us?"

"I really do like Nick, but I want you to be patient," Emma said. "You have survived a huge breakup and found a life you love and have earned. I don't want you to be too quick to give that up. But he is really nice, he's kind, and I think he really does love you. And apparently he doesn't care that you're a serious weirdo."

"Trust me, I'm being very careful to make the right choice."

Scott said that Nick seemed to be a stand-up kind of guy. Sidney said she thought he had a good heart, no pun intended, and that he appreciated my individuality. Emma laughed, saying that if Nick actually understands and accepts the real Sarah and still loves her, then that was all they really needed to know.

"I'm not *that* weird," I said, "I'm interestingly different. Going forward, I expect to be heard, and Nick is fully aware of that fact, and I know he is because I have told him so on several occasions. I don't *need* Nick in my life—I *want* him in my life, and I've finally learned that there is a huge difference between the two."

"Speak of the devil, I think your Prince Charming is here," Emma said.

The rest of the afternoon was spent enjoying each other and the spirit of the season. After dinner, the three younger adults grabbed their coats and said they would be home by ten o'clock, ten thirty at the latest. Nick handed them the promised tickets to the fireworks display and Nick and I were reminded of their concession that we could open only one gift each while they were away. All the rest would be saved for tomorrow morning with all of us. Sidney said she had counted the presents under the tree and would do a recheck when they got home.

A hush fell over my house and it was a welcome quiet. Nick was sitting on the sofa. "Come sit with me," he said patting the cushion. "The dishes can wait."

"I worry that once I sit down, I may never be able to get back up."

"I'll help you clean up later. It's going to kill you to have a mess everywhere isn't it?"

"Well . . . oh, who am I kidding? Yes, I would be much happier if things were cleaned up and then we had the rest of the evening free."

"Is it always going to be like this?" Nick asked, getting to his feet and leading me toward the kitchen.

"No," I said. "When I am dead or in Sleepy Pines rest home, I won't care if you never clean up, but until then, it's work first, play later."

After we were done, I said, "Now let's go in the living room and open one present each."

"Why don't you go first?"

"Okay," I said, reaching for my gift for him, a painting I'd done of his farm. I hadn't told anyone, not even Betsy, about the painting. Artists are funny about that sort of thing—that's why we have unveilings—no one sees your work until it's finished and you, the artist, are satisfied. "Remember, you never asked for anything, so you're getting what I decided I wanted you to have. I hope you like it."

"I'm sure I will love whatever it is." Sliding the bow from around the package, Nick tore off the paper and opened the box. "Oh my God, Sarah!" His face lit up with delight and surprise. "Did you paint this? When did you find the time?"

"Don't tell the NC Department of Public Instruction, but I used my planning time at school to work on it. It's from memory, and I'm not sure it's completely accurate. I can do another one sometime and get everything in just the right place."

"It's perfect," Nick said holding the frame with both hands. "Look," he continued, "you even have Caesar sitting in his spot in the yard. This is wonderful. I think it should go over the mantel in the den. What do you think?"

"I thought about that spot too—I thought the olivewood frame would look nice in there. But you can hang it anywhere you want, or not at all. Don't feel obligated to display it in your house; I want you to understand that you don't have to."

"Are you kidding?" Nick said, giving me as hearty a hug as he could manage while still holding the painting. "I'm trying to decide where it would look the best. It might show up better in the front hall over the antique chest of drawers that belonged to my grandmother. I'll have to carry it around and try it everywhere. Thank you so much—no. Thank you isn't quite good enough, but it will have to do for now." Nick rested the painting against the legs of the chair.

"Now it's your turn," Nick said, taking a small box out of his pocket. "You didn't ask for anything either, so I did the same thing."

I took the small box wrapped in rich glossy red paper with a huge white satin bow. "It's almost too pretty to open," I said, wiggling the ribbon from around the box. With one tear the paper was free, and I carefully opened the top. "Oh, how beautiful," I exclaimed as my eyes grew large. The earrings were round—a little smaller than a dime—dome-shaped gold circles with diamond and emerald chips scattered about the surface. "They are exquisite! I've never seen anything like this around here. Where did you find them?"

"There's a jewelry store in Pittsburgh that caters to the unusual," Nick answered. "I gave them a call, told the owner what I was looking for and a bit about you, and this is what they suggested. Put them on, and let's see how they look."

My hands were shaking, but I managed to free the earrings. "Oh, Nick," I said, putting them on and looking into the mirror, "they are simply gorgeous, and just my style—simple elegance. Thank you so much—wow—they're just beautiful. Sidney will try and steal them, so we'll have to watch her like a hawk," I said, giving Nick a kiss. "But most of all, thank you for knowing who I am. That's the best gift of all."

Later that night, while Nick settled himself in the sofa bed and the children went to their rooms, I smiled as I slid under the covers, thinking how much fun this day had been. *Hmm*, I thought, *I feel a bit like the Little Old Lady Who lived in the Shoe in my little house. When everyone is home, there really is more space at the farm.*

CHAPTER 46

Thankfully, Sidney no longer woke up hours before dawn on Christmas morning, but she was still the first to stir. She made just enough noise in the bathroom to wake me up, and then cracked my bedroom door. "Mom, are you awake?"

"I am now," I said, with one eye open and looking at the clock. "Sidney, it's not even daylight outside."

"Sorry," she said, sliding under the covers with me. "Mom, can we wake everyone else up now? Emma will sleep for hours if you let her, and I know Nick wants to open presents."

"How old are you?" I asked. "We all went to bed so late last night. Close your eyes and go back to sleep. We can get up at eight thirty."

"Okay," Sidney agreed, "but if we hear Nick moving around, then it would be impolite to leave him out there all alone."

"Yes, it would," I replied, "and it's also not very thoughtful to wake up your mother. Now hush and go back to sleep." Sidney always had to have the last word, and I was waiting to hear the final peep, but not this time. She was actually trying to fall back to sleep.

"Mom," a voice whispered as the broken light of sunrise

crept through the shutters and into my room, "Sidney's gone. She's not in her bed."

"What?" I asked, looking at Emma in my doorway. "No, she's right where she has been for the past twenty years on Christmas morning: in the bed with me."

"Oh, hi," Emma said, leaving the door open and acknowledging her sister's presence. "Move over." And with that, Emma climbed into bed, and I had both my children sharing the now-cramped space of my queen-sized bed, with me clutching the far side of the mattress. The girls were giggling about the night before, and asking me questions about Nick.

"I am not about to tell either one of you the most personal aspects of my life," I insisted.

"Well, Mom," Sidney said, "even old people enjoy sex. You do love him, don't you?"

"I might just throw up," Emma said. "The thought of our mother having sex is enough to make me ill."

"Why?" asked Sidney. "It's a very natural thing."

"Oh my God, Sid!" Emma squealed. "Sex is fine for you and me, but not our mother. One: she's our mother; two: she's old; and three: she's our mother."

"You said she's our mother twice. Why don't you think Mama should sleep with Nick? Maybe she already has." She turned to look at me. "Well? Have you?"

"Okay," I said getting out of bed. "This conversation has gone far enough. One, I am your mother and therefore I had sex with your father at least twice. Two, I do love Nick and eventually we will share that level of intimacy. And three—"

"Good morning, ladies," Nick said, leaning against the door

frame. "What is number three?"

"Oh, for heaven's sake," I said. "How long have you been standing there?"

"Long enough," Nick answered. "Girls: the subject of sex hangs your mother on a loose hinge, so let's don't talk about that today. I've started the coffee and poured you a diet soda. It's Christmas morning: who wants presents?"

Emma and Sidney piled out of my bed and hurried off to put on some clothes. Nick looked at me and said, "What is three?"

"I am not discussing this today," I said, my cheeks still on fire.

"I don't know why not," Nick replied. "How about this: We can talk about it on the way to your mother's?"

"It's Christmas," I said. "We are not talking about sex. You know I want it as much as you do, but not now."

"Okay, but you must agree that Christmas is the season of giving and sex is the gift that keeps on giving. But I won't forget your promise."

"Oh, good Lord," I said turning his body around and gently pushing him into the hall. "I'll be out in just a minute," I said, shutting my bedroom door.

Everyone got exactly what they had asked for and then some. Nick loved the weather vane I'd found him at a flea market and was pleasantly surprised with the horse motif cummerbund and matching bow tie. We laughed discussing his having a new outfit for next year's party in Virginia.

It had always been Sidney's job to hand out the gifts on Christmas morning. Sitting still for more than two seconds was not what she did best, and playing delivery girl gave purpose to her overabundance of energy. "Mom, there's one more gift under the tree, and it's for you," Sidney said. "The tag says, 'To Sarah, from Nick.' It makes an interesting sound too."

I took the package and gave it a gentle shake.

"Just open it!" Emma exclaimed.

Inside the box was the most handsome leather bridle and a D-ring snaffle bit. I had always wanted an Antares bridle, but they were a bit out of my price range. Lifting it from the nest of tissue, I admired the craftsmanship and the distinct aroma of new leather. "Wow," I said, "Thank you! This is lovely. I'm assuming this is for Buddy?"

"I had him in mind, but you can fit it to Rascal's head if you'd rather," Nick said with a smile. "But Buddy didn't come with any tack, and we've been using odds and ends to make the one you're using now. I just thought it might be nice for your new horse to have a new bridle, and it's a match to your Antares saddle."

"It's wonderful," I said. "I can't remember the last time I had new tack. This has been quite a Christmas. Thanks again," I said. I leaned over to give Nick a kiss.

The remainder of our morning was spent sharing a delicious breakfast, if I do say so myself, and getting ready to go to Iron Springs. Sidney, Emma, and Scott were staying overnight there, and then it was back to their respective homes. Nick and Ethan were going on a three-day quail hunt in Virginia, while I was being sent up to my mother's attic to help her sort through the last gazillion years of her life, and hopefully purging a lot of items.

I was putting the finishing touches on my part of the Christmas Day meal: the Cornish hens needed another dash of parsley, the wild rice was safely locked in an airtight container, and the twice-baked potatoes were lined in two tight rows on my largest jellyroll pan. Looking over my shoulder, Nick said, "It always smells so good in this house. Every time I come through the front door I feel as if I should announce 'Honey I'm home!' or something."

"A home is so much more than a house," I said stirring the gravy. "It's not just the smells that make you feel that way, it's the energy within. I'm as old fashioned as they come, I suppose, because I sincerely love to be at home. The summer months are my favorite nine weeks of the year, and not just because school is out, but because I can be at home."

"I have to ask you something: if we do get married, and you do move to the farm, do you think you can you make that house a home?"

"In a skinny minute," I said. "But would you allow me full rein?"

"Probably," Nick smiled, "but would you discuss ideas with me first?"

"Certainly," I said, putting my hand on his cheek, "but you do realize that regardless of your thoughts, I will most probably go ahead with my original plan."

"Oh . . . yes," Nick laughed, "that's a given, but it would make me feel better if I thought I had *some* say in the matter."

"I'm ready," Sidney announced, walking into the kitchen. "The hens look beautiful—for innocent birds that didn't ask to die."

Ah, my darling vegan daughter.

"Sidney, you look lovely," Nick said. "That turquoise sweater is so pretty with your eyes."

"Thanks," she said. "Sibby loves it when we dress up a little. I know my grandmother is happier when we all look nice sitting around her dining room table. Mom, did you make the rice I like?"

"You know I did," I answered. "Where's your sister?"

"They were packing the last time I checked," Sidney answered. "Scott was giving Emma a hard time about her carry-on being so heavy it would take two people to put it in the overhead storage bin. Let the record show that Sidney Sams has all her stuff packed and in the car."

"That's funny," Nick said, "all of you say 'let the record show' when you're trying to make a point."

"We've spent entirely too much time in court with my little sister," Emma offered walking into the kitchen. "As I mentioned last night, Sidney had a difficult time learning how to drive and, oh-I don't know, maybe every two months or so, we listened as some court-appointed official would say 'let the record show.' It became a catchphrase for our family—I think it was the only thing that got our parents through her teenage years. Scott and I are ready. Let's go!"

Our early-afternoon Christmas feast was exceptional, partly because the food was very good, but also because I was with Nick, my children, and my family. Annie was in heaven, going from one person to the next asking for a scrap of food or a pat on the head, and she was never denied either. Spent wrapping paper, conversation, and laughter fought for airspace in the living room of my mother's house. We each had several gifts to open, and it was so kind of everyone to remember Nick with packages as well.

Later, Nick went with me to take Annie for her nightly walk. "I absolutely love being with you," he announced. "I've had a very boring life compared to yours. My family didn't communicate like you guys, there was rarely disorder of any kind, and there was never this level of joy and excitement."

"Well, my family is a fun bunch, that's for sure. It gets loud and there're at least three conversations going on at any given time."

Opening the front door, Nick asked if he could have a cup of coffee and perhaps another piece of my coconut pie. I smiled and said that I was real close to the lady who ran the kitchen and I would see what I could do. Putting on the coffee and taking down two dessert plates was apparently a signal of sorts to the three younger adults in residence. Like moths to the flame, Emma, Scott, and Sidney (whose vegan ideals were conveniently pushed aside when it came to coconut pie) appeared in the kitchen. Nick decided to join them and was just before taking a seat when Emma said, "Nick, um, not to be rude, but—"

And before she could finish her sentence, Nick said, "I forgot! I am a reindeer. That was close; you know your mother is very protective of her place at the table, not to mention her snowman placemat."

"You are not funny," I said, flipping the dishtowel in his direction. "You may sit at my seat if you would like."

"What's going on in here?" my mother asked, walking into the kitchen and rubbing her eyes.

"They're making fun of me," I answered, "and we're having a little bedtime snack. Would you like a cup of tea?"

"I believe I would." She pulled a tea bag out of the canister. "How could any of you be hungry after all the food we've eaten today? Sarah, I would like a tiny *sliver* of pie with my tea, please. Why are you girls making fun of your mother?"

"Nick almost sat down at the Mrs. Claus mat," Emma

explained, "but apparently the etched-in-stone seating chart has already been explained to this very patient man."

"Yes, your mother took care of that over Thanksgiving," Sibby replied, handing pie to each person. "Sarah, this pie is wonderful. Is it my recipe?"

"It is, and it never disappoints," I answered, running the pie server between my fingers and devouring the crumbs. "Now, is everyone happy?"

The clatter of forks was all the answer I needed.

"This is one for the history books," I said, "the dishwasher is working on the second load, and Sarah Sams is going to bed with the third load of dirty dishes in the sink."

"Well, they're already rinsed and stacked," Nick said, poking me in the ribs. "That's just so horrible! How will you be able to sleep?"

"Come on, Annie," I said, patting my leg. "We're going to bed. They'll eat your pie and make fun of you all in the same breath. Good grief! Now, good night," I said, running my fingers through Nick's hair and giving him a kiss. "Thank you for the best Christmas in recent memory."

"Good night, darlin'." Nick held me tight and kissed my lips and then my neck. "I love you and thank you for the best Christmas I have ever had."

CHAPTER 47

Sidney, Emma, and Scott were up around eight o'clock the next morning. There were flights to catch and traffic snarls to avoid. But they spent some quality time with their grandmother and great grandmother before leaving.

Ethan was right on time to collect Nick and their cooler full of food from my mother, along with a complete list of cooking instructions. Standing side by side on the front steps, two generations of O'Neil women waved goodbye to their hunter-gatherers. I was somewhere between happy and sad.

My mother and I spent hours in the attic. We found ourselves off task a few times when we came across things we wanted to show each other, but tried to keep up with our job of making three piles: things to keep, things to donate, and others to simply be thrown away.

Sibby and I drifted into a conversation about my possibly moving to Nick's farm. I reviewed my pro and con list with her.

"Well Sarah," she said, "I think it's simply a matter of what, and who, do you love the most? Is it more important to you that you live near Margaret, or with Nick?"

"Mama, be serious."

"I am! If your riding buddies are truly your closest friends, then distance shouldn't be an issue. Is the mileage to your school really that critical? As for your house, you could keep it and rent it out, or simply sell it and put all the money in an investment of some sort to use after you retire. But I would encourage you to keep your finances separate from Nick's. I think you will be able to find your way without much difficulty."

"Thanks Mama," I said. "I do love him. I know you're concerned that Nick and I haven't known each other for very long, but when you know, you just know!"

"Who are you trying to convince?" my mother asked. "Your whole family likes Nick and finds him delightful, but we're not considering marrying the man—you are."

"I'm not trying to convince anyone," I said. "I've already decided what I'm going to do. I just needed to verbalize my thoughts with you for some assurance that I was headed down the right path."

"How is he in bed?" a voice asked from the attic doorway.

"Grammy!" I buried my face in my hands. "What kind of a question is that?'

"A very direct one, I would say," my grandmother replied. "Oh, don't make that face, either one of you. Sex is a big part of marriage. He's so handsome, I'll be very disappointed if the answer is 'mediocre'"

"I don't know." I felt myself turning red. "We haven't gotten to that point yet."

"Why the hell not?" Grammy demanded, throwing her hands in the air.

"Grammy, that is a very personal thing," I said. "It hasn't

been the right time yet."

"Oh, for heaven's sake." My grandmother laughed. "You don't plan sex; it just happens."

"Well, it hasn't happened yet."

Grammy made a disgusted look and huge sigh but before turning around said, "If any of that stuff is mine—I don't want it."

"Are you sure?" I asked.

"Positive," she said.

"I think it's time for a lunch break," Sibby said, cutting off that conversation.

Two days later, with the attic nearly emptied and five entire carloads of stuff donated, Nick and Ethan pulled in right on time, and I beamed as I came out on the front porch. Annie bounced down the steps and went straight to the dog trailer hooked to the back of Ethan's SUV. All the hunting dogs were barking and growling as she went from door to door. "Your man is quite a shot," Ethan said, trying to be heard over the canine commotion. "We bagged our limit every day, and some of his birds filled the back pouch of my vest."

"Good job," I said, hugging Nick and taking in the distinct odor of hunting clothes. It was not at all offensive; rather, it brought back oceans of pleasant memories.

"I'm dirty," Nick said.

"You're not dirty." I laughed. "You're woodsy."

"Ethan," Nick said, offering his hand, "I had a wonderful time, and I can't thank you enough for inviting me. I'm up for a hunting trip most any time—just give me a few days' notice."

"You've got it, buddy," Ethan said, shaking his hand enthusiastically and clapping his hand on his back. "Sarah, it was great to see you, and don't be a stranger. I've got to get home, or Meg will have my head."

"Bye, Ethan," I said, hugging my brother's neck. "I love you. I'm glad you guys had fun."

"Don't let this man get away," Ethan whispered in my ear. "He's really a good guy."

"I know," I whispered back with one last squeeze.

"Boy I'm glad to see you," Nick said with a hug that lifted me off the ground. "We had the best time; your brother is a lot of fun. I'll tell you all about it, but I'd like to take a quick shower first if you think that would be okay."

"Hi, Sibby," Nick said walking in the front door and giving my mother a peck on the cheek. "It's good to see you. Grammy, did you play bridge today?"

"Yes, I did," my grandmother said, "and Sarah was my partner."

"Did you two win?"

"Yes, we did." Grammy beamed.

"They cheated," my mother said, shaking her head.

"Sibby!" Nick said. "Why do you say that?"

"Because they always do," my mother answered, "and they have for years. Now what do you think of a grandmother who teaches her grandchild how to cheat at cards?"

"I'll need to think about that one," Nick said. "I hope Sarah told you about our going out to dinner tonight, and I'm hoping you'll join us. Are you girls up for a night on the town? I've got reservations for four at the Cutting Board at seven thirty. I need to take a quick shower, and we can be on our way."

"Yes, she did, and how fun," my grandmother said with a smile. "We haven't been out to eat in a long time. I'll need to change my clothes." Grammy scooted off to her room.

"This is very nice of you," my mother added. "What a treat."

"You are the sweetest man," I said at the top of the stairs, giving Nick a more passionate kiss now that we were alone. "Off you go to the showers."

"Glory day, I've missed you," he groaned, reluctant to let me go.

The conversation at dinner was nonstop, and everyone tried to speak at once.

After dinner, it was time for Nick and me to go home. Sibby and Grammy thanked Nick for the treat of dinner out. My mother hugged me and told me one last time how much the past three days had meant to her. Grammy gave me a big hug and told me to call her when I had the answer to her question. I had to think for a minute, but when I blushed a deep red, she knew I had remembered.

"Now," Nick said later, as we approached his farm, "what are your thoughts about New Year's Eve? We can do anything you want to do, or nothing."

"Hmm, I don't know," I paused. "Well, I know you'll think I'm a stick-in-the-mud, but it might be nice to do something close by since we've been so busy. What if we had a very late dinner somewhere on the river, and watch the fireworks? I guess that isn't very exciting. Oh, look at your house!" I exclaimed, interrupting myself. Each window had a wreath and a candle. The front-porch columns were wrapped in white lights. The fence line down the driveway was also aglow from miles of tiny lights.

"I called Coy and asked him to turn everything on," Nick said. "You didn't get to see that part the night of our Christmas party, did you? Oh, I talked to Sidney today. She was out riding Remember When, and Coy had a horse emergency. He called me and gave the phone to your daughter. She really does know what she's doing. She took care of the whole thing, setting up an IV and all."

"That's my girl," I said. "Part of Sidney's horse sense is that she doesn't get hysterical or even rattled."

Once inside, Nick suggested I just make a pile in the hall and he would take care of it later. I made a funny face, and he repeated his instructions. "I am trying to say goodbye; I don't want to be cleaning up." Nick laughed. "I promise I'll put it all away before the New Year."

Raising my eyebrows, I said, "You just said that to make me crazy. It's your stuff and your house, so you do as you please. If we have New Year's Eve here, Annie and I can spend the night, if you'll have us, and we can ride both days. I'll stay at my house until then, because the Rowdy Girls always go out for dinner and a movie on December thirtieth. What do you think about that for a plan?"

"If I'll have you? Are you kidding? I've wanted you here since—well, always. The rest sounds fine, but I'll miss not seeing you. Just promise to come to the farm early on New Year's Eve and stay late on New Year's Day—or can I talk you into the whole weekend since you don't go back to school until Monday?"

"Twist my arm."

He smiled and grabbed my wrist, pulling me close as he gently twisted.

"All right, the weekend."

Nick walked us to my car, and we said our goodbyes. During my drive home, I called Betsy and Margaret to catch up. It had been a whirlwind vacation, and I was more exhausted than I realized. I found my house extremely quiet. I had once enjoyed that very much, but now it felt empty.

CHAPTER 48

The annual Rowdy Girls dinner-and-a-movie night was perfect, as always. The dinner conversation was filled with everyone telling about their holiday, and naturally, Nick and me. The movie was a chick flick and enjoyed by all. On the ride home, I mentioned the possibility of moving if Nick and I did get married. Rose spoke up. "I think that would be the smartest thing to do," she said. "Considering Nick owns a farm, he really can't live here. We're a stone's throw away, and I think it should work out just fine."

"What are your plans for Rascal?" Margaret wondered.

"Well, I've given that issue a great deal of thought, and I'm just not sure what to do. I want to leave him right where he is for two reasons: first I worry that he's too old to be moved to new surrounds and secondly, I can't stand the thought of not being able to ride with you. But, because he is aging, it might be better if he's at Nicks—I'll talk to the vet and see what he thinks. Anyway, I just don't know right now. This is a biggie!"

"I understand, but I really don't want you to leave," Margaret answered.

"Me neither," said Betsy. "What about our Saturday

mornings, and the farmers market? We have done that for years."

"And we still can," I said. "The distance is just about the same as it is for Rose, and she did the same stuff after she moved."

"That's different," Betsy volleyed. "She doesn't have a husband and can do as she pleases. Once you're married, Nick will want you to do things with him."

"You're married, and Frank always lets you go play with me." I answered. "Nick is not the smothering kind; he'll be fine with this idea. I'm sure."

"What are you two doing for New Year's?" Elizabeth asked, changing the subject.

"We're going out to dinner somewhere on the river and then watching the fireworks," I said. "Annie and I are staying over at the farm."

"For the night or the weekend?" Betsy asked with raised eyebrows.

"The weekend," I blushed.

"Pack something fetching to sleep in," Rose chuckled. "The last time you spent the night, your children were there. This time it will be just the two of you. Girls"—she looked around at our group and held up both hands, fingers crossed—"I think there's going to be an unscheduled horse ladies dinner on our calendar— the title will be FINALLY!"

I could feel the heat rise in my cheeks. "Rose, you forget, I don't own anything fetching to sleep in."

"Oh, I'd bet Nick will be happy with nothing," Jennifer said. "Fetching is overrated, but *naked* is hot. Rose, I'll bet you ten dollars that their first time is without fetching anything."

"You're on," answered Rose, extending her hand.

"Well," Betsy said, giggling, "we all hope you and Nick have fun tomorrow and the weekend. Call me when you come up for air."

"I'll see you at the barn after school on Monday," Margaret said. "Don't call me: I want to hear this story in person."

"Maybe we can all trailer over to Falling Creek and ride together that afternoon," Elizabeth said. "I want to hear it in person too!"

"What a great idea," Rose offered. "Margaret, will you speak with Inez and get it organized for that afternoon? I couldn't manage being left out of that discussion."

"Rose, make sure to bring my ten bucks," Jennifer said with a smile.

"I am out of here," I said as Betsy pulled into my driveway. "You should all be ashamed of yourselves, but I know you're not. I do love you all, and good night."

$\mathcal{A}$nnie stood on all fours as we drove down the lane to Nick's farm. I could feel myself getting warm the closer we got to the barn. "Oh, look," I said to Annie. "Sidney's here!"

"Hi, Mom!"

"Hi there," I said, giving my girl a hug.

"I'm going to put my things in the kitchen and get ready to ride. I'll be back in twenty minutes. Please watch after Annie. Between your crazy dog and Caesar, I worry."

"What's new?" Sidney laughed. "You worry about everything: real or imagined."

Sidney went back into the barn, and I carried my bag into the hall. It took several trips for me to empty my car of food and dog stuff. Once all was in the kitchen, I got to work putting things away and getting organized. Staring at me from the hall was my black-and-white Vera Bradley quilted duffel bag. After a moment, I decided to leave it right where it was, unsure of where I would be sleeping. I was fairly certain but didn't want to jinx it, if that was the right word.

Dressed in my new riding breeches and jacket my grandmother had given me for Christmas, I walked toward the kitchen with a heavier footstep than on my way into the bathroom. "Good grief," I said out loud, "these boots are loud."

"Yes, they are." Nick's deep voice said giving me quiet a start. "Hi darlin'." He smiled from the kitchen doorway.

"Hello, yourself," I replied, offering an equally wide grin. "Are you going to ride with Sidney and me?"

"Of course." He lifted me off the floor and squeezed me hello. "I like your new outfit. I read somewhere that French Blue is the new color in equestrian fashion. Your

grandmother is quite the trend shopper."

"My grandmother called the tack shop and asked the clerk what she thought I'd like, then paid for it and had them wrap it up," I said with a giggle. "But I do love the new look. Come on. Let's ride." We went off hand-in-hand to the barn.

"Aren't you two cute?" Sidney sassed.

"Doesn't your mother look hot in her new French blue breeches?"

"For fifty, and in the eyes of an older man, I guess?" Sidney laughed.

"Do you want to continue riding at this farm?" Nick asked, trying to look stern.

Buddy was already in his stall. "I guess Coy is responsible for bringing in my horse?"

"No," Nick answered, "I actually did that. I was already dirty, and they were both at the gate. Hey, I made a reservation for dinner at the Boat Dock for nine o'clock. Linda and Nancy said the food was good, and we'd have a great view of the fireworks from any table in the restaurant. I hope that's okay?"

"Absolutely! I brought the makings for a big lunch, since

we'll eat so late tonight. I also thought it would be fun if Sidney and Coy ate lunch with us. What do you think?"

"Coy," Nick yelled down the aisle, "lunch is at the house today. Sarah is feeding us all."

The rest of the morning was spent in the bliss of riding and being with Nick and Sidney. Nick, Sidney, and Coy remained in the barn after we rode, working on the injured but healing horse. I excused myself to get started on lunch.

Within ten minutes I had figured out Adel's kitchen storage system and found everything I needed. I snuck down the hall to nudge the thermostat above "iceberg," and it was much easier to cook minus my chattering teeth. I thought Nick and I might need to have a bit of discussion concerning the heat, or lack thereof, in this old house. I'd freeze to death if he kept things the way they were.

"Boy, something smells good," Coy said as he walked in the kitchen. "Boss and Sidney will be here in just a minute. I'm sure glad she was here the other day when Billy Boy got hurt. That girl knows her stuff. The vet thinks she's something too, and I don't mean just 'cause she can fix a hurt horse." He raised his eyebrows pointedly, fighting a smirk. "Has she told you about him?"

"No, she hasn't, but I'll ask her about him at lunch."

Coy put his hands up. "You didn't hear it from me."

"What's for lunch that smells so good?" Nick said, giving me a kiss.

"Brunswick stew and hamburgers," I said. "Everyone can just serve themselves."

"I knew you could do it."

"Do what?" I asked.

"Make this house a home," Nick said. "I'll be back in a minute. I'm too dirty to sit down at the table." Walking down the hall, he called back, "Did you turn up the heat?"

"Not if I'm in trouble," I replied.

As he came back in, I reached into the refrigerator and put a bowl of fresh fruit at Sidney's place, and Nick said with a smile, "Oh, I'm sorry, but I always sit there."

"You do not," I said. "The first time I had dinner in this kitchen you sat at that seat. Now, if you had a Santa or snowman mat, I would respect your claim to that chair . . . but you don't." I giggled.

"Oh, is that so?" Nick said, opening a long drawer. "Well, what's this?" Nick asked, flopping down a very old and worn Santa Claus place mat.

"Oh my gosh, how perfect. Well, then, that is your spot forever," I said with a smile.

"Is there anything for me to eat besides fruit?" Sidney asked.

I reminded her that ungrateful and impatient children didn't deserve anything else as I took her plate of eggplant, sweet potatoes, and greens out of the warmer.

After dessert, everyone took their dirty dishes to the sink and thanked me for their lunch. Coy said how much he appreciated being included, but he had to get back to work. Sidney gave me a peck on the cheek and said she had to ride one more horse and then get back to Raleigh. As she pushed in her chair, I remembered. "I understand there's a good-looking vet who has his eye on you?"

"Who—how—? Excuse me, I have to get back to the barn and have a word with Coy," Sidney said.

"Careful, Sid. Be sweet to Coy. Remember, he runs the barn where you love to ride. I think he thought I already knew," I said as she flew out the door. I chuckled long after she was gone, the color in her cheeks telling me all I needed to know.

Our New Year's Eve dinner was very special. Nick seemed genuinely interested in hearing all about the upcoming book event in Asheville. Around quarter to midnight, the maître d' tapped a wineglass and announced that the band would play one last song, and everyone should dance before ringing in the new year.

Nick took my hand and we made our way to the dance floor and slow danced to "My Girl." The drummer gave a long drum roll and started the traditional countdown. The crowd joined in, yelling in unison, "Happy New Year!"

"Happy New Year, darlin'," Nick said after a very tender kiss that sent chills down my spine. "I love you."

"Happy New Year. I love you too," I replied, looking into his eyes.

After about thirty minutes of impressive fireworks and their reflections across the river's surface, we were back on the road to Greenway. As we pulled into the driveway, I became slightly unglued. I was fairly certain I knew what was going to happen next, and I knew I wanted it very much. The dogs bounded out the back door and went straight to tending to their business. Nick gave Caesar a quick, sharp whistle and the gigantic ebony canine returned with Annie in tow. Walking up the steps, I thought: *Just let things happen, and for once in your life, Sarah, don't talk.*

I stood at the kitchen sink pretending to need a glass of

water while Nick turned out the porch light and locked the door. I swear the sound of that dead bolt hitting the interior of the opposing frame was deafening.

"What a wonderful evening," Nick said leaning near me against the kitchen countertop.

"It was," I said. "Thanks for making such a perfect choice."

"You've said on numerous occasions how much you love the river," Nick said bending down to give me a peck. "I enjoy making you happy."

"Well, that you most certainly do," I said.

The kiss that followed was different from our previous ones. It was one of consent without the need for words. Nick took me by the hand and led me to the hall. "You don't have to do this," he said.

"Neither do you," I said. "But don't you want to?"

"Follow me and I'll show you." Nick devilish grin spread as he took my hand.

The midnight fireworks on the river paled in comparison to the electricity of Nick's bedroom. Nervous excitement darted back and forth between our bodies, creating a gravitational pull. Without rushing, he gently took my face in his hands. The first kiss was a soft and searching one, but the next was deeply passionate as his hands found their way to the buttons of my blouse.

I ran my hands along the top of his belt, freeing the tail of his shirt from the constraints of his trousers. Running my hands under his shirt and across his back, I felt the rise and fall of his toned muscle line, rippling gently beneath his soft skin. Nick carefully removed my blouse, turning it inside out on its way to the floor. Standing in slacks and my fancy black bra, I began to free his shirt buttons one at a time, alternating each release with a kiss to his chest. The smell of his skin was intoxicating, and triggered a much more hurried effort half the way down the button line.

Gently Nick reached his hands into the front of my slacks and released the top closure and lifted the tab of my zipper. I lowered my hands from his final shirt button and began the same process with his trousers. With the final snap of my bra released we pressed our bodies together and began what I will always remember as a kiss that had no equal. I had no thoughts of anything but how much I wanted this man. My body was absolutely his, and every part of me was on fire. I wanted this first time to last for a very long time. My passion screamed for instant gratification, but my heart was winning out in its insistence to make this a cherished memory.

Nick let go of me for a brief moment and moved to fold down the bed covers, then took my hand, leading me to the edge of the bed. With the most gentle of motions he sat me down and placed my body along the length of the bed. I no longer had the ability to hear over my rushing pulse as Nick carefully and sensually removed the last thing I had on, the infamous matching underpants.

Dropping his boxers to the floor, Nick moved across me and rested his body next to mine. As we melted into each other, the passion grew and my heart took flight.

Nick moved his hand along the length my torso, and when he placed his body on top of mine, we sank into a deep engulfing kiss. With the passion that followed, we became one.

After a time too intense to be measured, with heavy breath, Nick rolled over on his side and pulled me close. With his lips softly resting on the side of my face, he said, "I've never experienced anything like that. I know you don't believe me, but it's true. Sarah, I adore you. I cannot live the rest of my life without you."

"Yes," I said trying to catch my breath. "I have waited a lifetime for you, and I'm not going anywhere."

We fell asleep still tangled in each other's arms.

The quiet light of daybreak softly filtered in between the slats of the interior shutters. "Good morning, sunshine," Nick said, snuggling up against my back.

"Um," I moaned squinting my eyes against the light, "Good morning to you too. What time is it?"

"Let me see," Nick said rolling over and, minus his readers, tried to focus on his watch. "It's six forty-five. Happy New Year, darlin."

"Happy New Year," I said. "If last night is any indication, it's off to an amazing start. I'm absolutely starving—are you?"

"How can anyone stay as thin as you are and eat all the damn time?"

"Well," I said, stretching, "I have always been able to eat whatever I wanted and never seemed to gain weight. It probably has something to do with the fact that I'm never physically still—I burn it off as quickly as I take it in. I do think my metabolism is slowing down a bit, though. It's not as easy as it once was. Anyway, are you—hungry?"

"Yes, ma'am, I am," Nick said with a devil's smile I now recognized.

The second time was just as good as the first. In a way, it was better. The frightfulness of "first sex" was over, and the joy of familiarity took its place.

Later, dressed and in the kitchen, I was starting the coffee and sipping a diet soda when Nick said he would take the dogs out for a romp. "Before you go, what would you like for breakfast?" I asked. "Eggs, pancakes, French toast? You name it."

Nick lifted his eyebrows. "French toast is my favorite. But I need about thirty minutes to feed the horses," Nick said, giving my backside a pat and a rub.

"You got it. Bacon or sausage or both?"

"Surprise me," Nick said, and he and the dogs were out the door.

I smiled, thinking how perfect last night and this morning had been. Could it be possible that Nick really was as wonderful as I thought him to be?

"Dammit to hell," Nick said, storming into the kitchen ten minutes later.

"What's wrong?" I asked, somewhat startled.

"Sorry. The automatic waters have gone crazy in two of the stalls and no plumber is working today. If I can find one, I'm sure it will add up to a five-hundred-dollar day."

"Let me see if I can fix it," I said, taking the frying pan off the burner. "Come on, puppies, let's go to the barn and see what's going on."

"What do you know about plumbing?" Nick asked, walking closely behind.

"Not much—but Betsy has this watering system at her barn, and she's had the same thing go wrong. I've been there twice when the plumber came. Now let's see," I said, cutting the water on in the first stall. "Hmm, do you have a tool box?"

"Sure," Nick said. "Do you know what's wrong?"

"I think it's just a split washer," I said. "It probably froze, and the horse pushed it before it had a chance to thaw and it snapped. I bet they're plastic, and hopefully you have some metal ones." I rummaged through the toolbox. Within five minutes, both the water bowls were, for the moment anyway, up and running.

"You really fixed it!" Nick said, holding up his hand to give me a high five.

"What can I say?" I laughed, surprised they actually worked, "I'm gifted? Seriously, though, you should consider getting a real plumber out here on Monday. To say I know what I'm doing is a huge stretch, but they work for now. If it doesn't hold, we can hang buckets. Now let's get breakfast."

Walking back to the house, Nick took my hand and gave it a gentle peck. "I am a lucky man: my girl is a hell of a cook, she can ride like the wind, is an amateur Miss Fix-It, and in bed . . . well, wow! "

I smiled, grabbing his arm and leaning into him. "She is also as crazy as a bat, very insecure, afraid of the dark, cries over road-kill, and is ornery when not fed. But I'm a lucky girl to have found you. Now what are your bad qualities or sensitive areas that have yet to surface?"

Nick opened the screen door and we walked inside. "Well, let me think, you know how I am about a messy car and my clothes. I also hate housework of any kind, I have a very strong opinion on how things should be, I'm afraid of getting old, I really wish I had children of my own, I will not tolerate being lied to, I would be unhappy if you messed with anything to do with my office, and no decision can ever be made about the farm without my knowing it ahead of time. Have I scared you off yet?"

"Not at all," I said returning the frying pan to the stovetop, "I think these conversations are very important. It's extremely difficult for people who've been living alone to adjust to sharing their space. You and I have become set in our ways, and compromise might be difficult at times. But if our love and commitment to each other is strong and genuine, and we keep talking to each other, we can survive anything."

We had a traditional New Year's Day meal of roasted pork, turnip greens, black-eyed peas, and corn bread. The next two days were wonderful and unfolded much the same as the first—truthfully even better!

At the end of Sunday's lunch, I scooted my chair back a bit and crossed my legs. Nick dropped his head and said, "I know: you have to go."

"I do," I answered. "I've got to get my house back in order and get ready to go back to school."

"Call in sick," Nick urged, putting his hand on mine.

"You have clearly stated that you hate lying," I replied, "and that is a lie. But if I could, I would stay. Remember that next weekend I'll be out of town."

"That's right," Nick said. "Asheville. When are you leaving?"

"I'm taking Friday off from school," I said, "and after I drop Annie at Paws & Claws, I hope to be on the road no later than ten. It's about a five-hour drive."

With my car packed and Annie resting in the back seat, Nick said, "While you're away next weekend, I'm going to visit Jack.

But I don't intend to spend too many more weekends apart from you. We're just going to have to figure something out."

"I know," I said sadly, "this is becoming painful. We can talk about it some more on Tuesday, but for right now I've got to go."

"Not tomorrow?" Nick asked.

"No, the Rowdy Girls have laid claim to tomorrow afternoon, and I'm sure you know why." I smiled, blushing furiously.

Nick laughed. "Don't leave anything out."

CHAPTER 50

It was a long drive back to 528 Brook Street, and I knew why. I didn't want to leave Nick either. "This is miserable," I said to Annie. "What are we to do?"

After unpacking, I knew I needed to write a letter. So with Annie happily roaming the backyard, I sat down at my computer. My next session with Dr. Baxter was on Thursday, and selfishly I hoped the appointment after mine would be available. I didn't think I'd really need a reminder of the past few days, but I thought my initial reaction to it all was important to record.

January 3, 2010
Dear Debby,

WOW . . . that is all I can think to say . . . WOW! It, meaning sex, did finally happen, and it was the most wonderful experience of my life. I think it was the first time I truly appreciated that experience. I'm not saying I just went through the motions with my ex-husband, but this was just . . . different. I truly think it was so much better than any other time because I'm older and appreciate that level of closeness more than I did when I was younger.

Hopefully I will never again realize what paint color I want to use for the ceiling in the middle of sex: I did that once with Parker, and consoled myself by thinking the rush of endorphins brought me to think green. We both know that was not the reason.

I also hated leaving the farm—I love it there.

See you in a few days!

With all good wishes,

Sarah

Dr. Baxter laughed out loud as I walked into her office. "Your face is telling me that you have a great deal to share," she said, offering me a seat.

"Holy cow, yes!" I needed two hands to safely remove the folder from my bag and handed her the top page. "I'll give you a minute to read the first letter, and then we can talk. I also hope you might possibly have some extra time today? I have more to say than can fit in an hour."

"Actually, I do. Let me call the front office and tell them we're taking extra time."

The next two hours ran the gamut from December 23 to New Year's Day with letters to match the events. The final letter required the most conversation and reflection.

"Sarah, let's start with a bit of discussion about your decision to paint the ceiling green," she said with a hint of a serious smile.

"I've thought about that too. The truth is that the ceiling color was more beautiful than the sex with Parker. What does that mean?" I said.

"Exactly. What *does* that mean?" she replied, pushing back

in her chair and still holding the letter. "Let's start there."

On balance, the remaining time was the best session I think we had ever had. I realized that I had become complacent in my marriage to Parker and was just going through the motions. I also became painfully aware that subconsciously I had known this to be true for a long time. It's not always easy to take ownership of what is honestly and truly yours. Saying out loud that the breakup of my marriage was in some ways as much my fault as Parker's was a knife to the heart.

"Hi darlin'," Nick said as I walked through his back door that evening. "How was your session?"

"Eye opening," I replied. "I'm still trying to digest it all. I have to get home early tonight because of my trip tomorrow, so I stopped and got us BBQ. I hope that's ok?"

"Absolutely," Nick said.

"I'll be right back," I said walking down the hall, "I just need a minute."

"Take all the time you need. I'll be right here," Nick said, understanding and asking no questions.

CHAPTER 51

My early morning was the same as always: breakfast, a good walk with Annie, and a chat with Miss Madge. I asked that she keep an eye on my house and told her where I was going. After dropping Annie off, I was on the road and on schedule. The drive was long but pleasant, especially the last leg, from Hickory to Asheville. I loved the rolling hills and the towering mountains just beyond. I had always felt at home in the mountains, and suddenly wished Nick could have come with me. I opened my cell phone and gave him a call.

"Hi darlin' . . . where are you now?" Nick asked.

"Just passed though Morganton. I really wish you could have come with me. But it's good you're going to see Jack—give him my best, and Rea too."

"I will. I wish I could have come too," Nick replied. "Remind me what you're doing tonight after you get there?"

"There's a meet-and-greet at seven, and dinner is at eight o'clock. But I'm going to the barn before I do anything. If I have my trip timed out correctly, I should have, at minimum, two hours of free time before the cocktail party. I want to speak with the barn manager before tomorrow. The signing is at the barn in the morning and the main house during lunch. I always want to see where I'm supposed to be before it actually happens."

"It sounds interesting and very busy," Nick said. "What'll you do Saturday night, and Sunday?"

"Saturday is packed, ending with a black-tie dinner dance. The authors get in free, but it's two hundred dollars a plate to everyone else. Everyone who is anyone shows up, and the money raised goes to help feed the hounds of the Buncombe County Hunt. Not much happens on Sunday: a thank-you breakfast, more signing, and then at noon we're free to go. I'm still blown away that I was invited."

"Don't be nervous—you're as good as anyone there."

"Thanks," I said. "I love your clouded judgment."

Making the final turn onto the Estate and up Approach Road, I rummaged through my information packet and offered the security guard my participants pass for the weekend. He smiled and placed a special sticker on the inside of my windshield. I was now officially a part of the Equestrian Authors & Horsemanship Clinic, and I did truly think I was the stuff—at least for one fleeting moment.

I found my way to the parking area and the attendant helped me with my things, including several boxes of books, and showed me to my room. I asked for directions to the stables.

Carefully descending some very narrow granite steps that spilled onto a beautiful slate patio, I was greeted by a parking attendant who offered me a map of the Estate, and the keys to a complimentary golf cart. I had no idea that luxury came with my stay but was thrilled.

At the office area of the equestrian center, a short, thin

woman offered me her hand. "My name is Phyllis. How may I help you?"

"Hi," I said. "I'm Sarah Sams, and I'm participating in this weekend's events. I just wanted to take a look around and see where I'll be signing books tomorrow."

Phyllis smiled, but before she could say anything, I heard a familiar sound and turned abruptly. "Are you okay?" Phyllis asked.

"Yes, but I think I know that horse," I said, looking out the door.

"What horse?"

"That horse—the one you hear," I said. "That's my horse. I know this sounds insane, but I would know his nicker anywhere. But he couldn't be here." I walked around the corner and stopped dead in my tracks. At the other end of the barn I recognized the silhouette of the tall man leaning against the stall door. "It's you!" I said in total disbelief and walking quickly to where he stood. Wrapping my arm around the head of my treasured horse. "And Rascal! I'm speechless," I said, looking into Nick's eyes.

"Well, I hope you're happy to see us. I brought Chance along too," Nick said softly.

"Yes, of course I'm happy to see you," I answered with a huge smile and a hug. "How did you pull this off? I thought you were going to visit Jack."

"I have a few friends here and there, you know. The Jack trip was just a diversionary tactic." Nick smiled. "But listen before we do anything else, I need to know something."

"What's that?" I asked, still not believing they were there.

"Will you marry me?" he asked, holding out a box containing the most beautiful diamond-and-emerald ring I had ever seen.

I stood glued to the aisle floor.

"I hope you're not disappointed that I didn't get down on one knee, but at my age, I wasn't sure I could stand back up and that would have killed the moment for sure. But, will you—please?" Nick asked again.

"Yes," I said, tears streaming down my face.

"Why are you crying?" Nick asked, sliding the ring on my finger. "You're supposed to be happy."

"I am happy," I said, "This is very overwhelming." After a minute I stood back on my feet and looked at my finger. "I have never seen anything quite this beautiful. I'm going to guess it's the work of the jeweler in Pittsburgh."

"It is," Nick replied, "and I'm supposed to call him and tell him if you liked his selection. By the look on your face I'm guessing you do?"

"Yes," I said, "I love it! Hey, wait a minute, how long have you had this ring?"

"I got it at the same time as the earrings. I've been working on this proposal for over two weeks. I knew I wanted to marry you the first time I ate dinner at your house. I hope you'll let me stay with you this weekend."

"No," I said wiping my face. "I'm keeping the ring, and my horse, but you and Chance have to go home," I joked. "You've pulled another fast one on me. You're as sly as the fox you chase, Nicholas Heart. Margaret and Betsy know, don't they? Is this why Margaret insisted that I clean my tack the other day? She babbled on and on about some mold and mildew nonsense, but I guess it was all a ploy to have my things ready for you to pick up. Oh, and Betsy came over to help me pack, pretending she knew nothing. Does Annie know too?"

"No," Nick smiled, "but your children do. I asked their permission. Emma cried. It must be genetic. Sidney saw the ring and almost fainted. They, along with Betsy and Margaret, are waiting for a call by seven thirty tonight. Oh, and your brother knows too. I talked to him about it while we were in Virginia, and I called your mother last night. I wasn't convinced that she could keep this news a secret, so it was the eleventh hour for her. Sibby was so kind and very happy, as was your grandmother."

Before I could kiss my fiancé, Rascal put his head between us and pushed me gently in his direction. "Good boy," I said rubbing the distance of his blaze. "Were you a good little man for Nick?"

"He is the easiest horse to trailer that I've ever seen," Nick said. "I didn't even have to lead him on, he just walked up the ramp and stood in his spot. He and Chance sniffed each other and made quick friends. I thought we could have some fun riding together maybe tomorrow afternoon, if there's time, and before going home on Sunday. I also signed up for the morning clinic tomorrow."

Nick leaned in for a kiss, and Rascal put his head in the way once again. "Now listen," Nick said, pointing his finger at Rascal, "I am going to do this whether you like it or not. Get used to it!"

"He doesn't like it," I laughed. "Move over here, out of his reach."

My toes curled once again as Nick gently held my face in both hands and kissed me. "I'll love you forever Sarah, and you will never have reason to question my devotion. I promise to take care of you and to be your best friend. I will accept your children as my own and their children as well."

"I trust you with my heart," I said, "and that is the biggest gift

I have to give. I will never leave you, and I will always try my best to make you happy. I hope you never regret this day, Mr. Heart," I said, still sniffling. "Look, we have to be getting ready for dinner. Let me take care of Rascal real quick, and I'll be ready to go."

"What do you need to do for Rascal?" Nick asked. "I brought his grain and hay, and Phyllis knows the rest."

"Yes, I'm sure she does, but now he knows I'm here," I said. "It'll only take a minute."

After I gave him a nice brushing and some carrots, I said with a kiss on his nose, "Okay, I'll see you in the morning, little man. Be good."

As Nick and I left the barn, Phyllis asked to see the ring, and I was still shaking a bit when I held out my hand. She said she would take special care of Chance and Rascal and would look forward to seeing us in the morning.

"I'm guessing that you came prepared for everything to do with this weekend?" I asked sliding into the driver's side of the golf cart.

"Yes," Nick answered tossing his duffel and suit bags in the back and taking the passenger's seat. "When I called to reserve the stalls, I asked Phyllis if she would find out what I needed and also put my name beside yours on the guest list."

"You sneak! Oh, Mr. Heart, you are quite the romantic aren't you?" I said with a smile. "I absolutely love it. Most men would have put the ring on top of a plate of spaghetti in the absolute center of a meatball or something."

Nick laughed and reminded me that I was supposed to call everyone. "I don't think we have the time," I said, "but I'll try. Not one of them will accept any excuse if I don't."

Nick took his turn first in the shower, and I sat and called my children and then my friends. Emma asked for a picture of the ring. Sidney said she wanted the ring when I died. Betsy cried and said it was the hardest secret she had ever kept, and she wanted a certificate or something stating that she had in fact kept silent. Margaret was a bit choked up at first, but laughed when I called her out on the tack-cleaning issue. Sibby was very happy and said she was honored that Nick spoke to her last night. Grammy yelled in the background asking if I had the answer to her question. I told Sibby to tell Grammy she wouldn't be disappointed.

Nick came out of the bathroom. "Did you get everyone?"

"Yes—my mother thought it was wonderful that you had talked to Ethan and asked my girls' permission. I have to hurry—this is going to be one of those crazy hair nights."

"You'll look better than any other woman there, even if you go in what you have on," Nick said. "I don't think you know how pretty you actually are."

"People just look twice at me because I'm tall," I said. "But you have no objectivity, and I am grateful for that."

All during dinner, I kept staring at my ring. It really was incredible, and I couldn't help wondering how much it had cost. I would never ask, though. It needed to be insured, and I would be scared to death to wear it at the barn and riding, for fear I would lose it.

The book signing was more profitable than I had expected. Maybe my name did belong on the authors' list after all. Nick and Chance had a great time at the horsemanship clinic. After lunch, my betrothed mingled with the participants, vendors, and visitors. Rascal was happy to see me in the afternoon and even happier to be saddled up and taken for a ride. He absolutely hated to be left in a stall. There was enough time before dinner for Nick and me to have a wonderful ride along the east bank of the French Broad River and through the fields of winter rye.

Saturday evening's gala included horse people from all walks of life, big-money contributors, and "friends" of every organization that had friends. Not only did Nick come prepared for the evening, but he also wore the cummerbund and matching bow tie I had given him for Christmas.

I had dug into the archives of my closet for a dress that I'd had long enough for it to be back in style. It was the simplicity of the dress, along with the luscious midnight blue color, that made it pretty. My strawberry-blond hair hung down around my shoulders with a rhinestone clip pulling it up on either side.

"Wow," Nick said with wide eyes as I walked out of the bathroom.

"I don't think I'll ever get tired of hearing you say that," I replied with a smile while he finished pulling up the zipper. "You look mighty nice yourself, Mr. Heart."

"Do we have to stay until the end?"

"I don't guess so, but why would you want to leave early?" I asked, realizing my answer as we walked down the hall. "Nicholas F. Heart, you should be ashamed of yourself."

"Why?" he asked pressing the down button at the elevators. "You show up looking like that and I'm supposed to not notice? I can't wait to help you out of that dress."

Weaving our way in and out of tables, people, and chairs propped over to save someone's seat. Nick and I arrived at table three. Several couples were already seated, and I recognized one. His booth was next to mine, and his message was equine nutrition.

"Hi there," he said shaking Nick's hand and then mine. "I'm Milton Evans, and this is my wife May."

"It's very nice to meet you. This is my fiancée, Sarah Sams— she's one of the authors—and I'm Nick Heart," Nick said, holding out the chair for me.

"Yes, Sarah and I met earlier today. Fiancée, you say?" Milton replied entirely too loud. "When are you getting married?"

"We haven't had a chance to pick a date," Nick smiled. "She just said yes yesterday."

"Well, long engagements are overrated," Milton advised. "My bride and I have been married for forty-two years, and I still love her as much as I did the first time I saw her."

The dinner part of the evening was spent listening to Milton discuss the evils of treats for horses, his gallbladder surgery, their seven children and sixteen grandchildren. Naturally the narrative of his family tree came with pictures that resembled a full deck of well-worn playing cards.

The master of ceremonies announced that the band was getting ready for their first song and asked for some willing dancers to take the floor. Nick took my hand and quickly helped me out of my chair. "I love you," Nick said as we walked quickly onto the parquet dance floor, "and we have to dance so I don't kill Milton."

"Poor May—she hasn't said one word."

"When did she have the chance?" Nick asked, spinning me around to a big-band tune.

"Maybe that's how they've stayed together so long."

When we returned to our table, Milton and May had left for the evening, as had several of the other couples. I told Nick I was exhausted, and hoped we too could head back to our room.

After I got undressed, hung up my dress, and put on my nightgown, I flopped on the bed and said, "According to my children, I snore when I am very tired."

"Your children are correct," Nick said. "It's really more of a putter than an all-out snore. Do you always hang up your clothes before you go to bed?" Nick raised one eyebrow.

"I'm surprised you had to ask," I said. "I don't know if you snore and probably never will. When I go to sleep, I think I am one step away from dead."

"You know, Milton was right," Nick said. "We do need to pick a date. What are your thoughts?"

"Summer would be best for me, when school is out."

Nick pulled out his checkbook, and put on his glasses. "Let me see," he said, opening to the backside of the register. "What do you think about June?"

"June is nice," I answered. "I guess we should also take into consideration where we want to go for a honeymoon. Oh, this is hugely selfish, but Susan's horse camp is the third week of June. I hope you won't mind if I go this year?"

"I would never consider asking you to give that up," Nick said, moving me over toward the middle of the bed. "Now, about the honeymoon. I have actually given this some thought. How would you like to go to Scotland? I know several places where we can stay in a castle, ride horses, and tour around the countryside."

"Oh wow, that would be fabulous," I answered. "Sibby and I

took a trip to Scotland after my sophomore year in college; it's beautiful, but let the record show, under no circumstances will I eat haggis."

"Sissy. Now, moving on to the next question: *where* do you want to get married?' Nick asked.

"Well," I said piling pillows behind my back. "Don't laugh— but I would love to get married in the court-yard garden at Long Leaf Farm. Simple but elegant would suit me 'to a t', with all our friends and family. Jennifer could do the reception inside like the Christmas party. It would be great; even the horses and dogs could come. What were you thinking?"

"That I love you and the farm is perfect," Nick said, giving me a kiss. "So when do you get out of school?"

"June the tenth, I think," I answered. "So what is the last weekend?"

Nick scanned the calendar and said, "June the twenty-sixth is the last Saturday. What do you think?"

"The twenty-sixth it is!" I replied with delight.

He got ready for bed and turned out the light. "Are you asleep?" he asked.

"Yes," I answered. "Why?"

Nick didn't say a word . . . he didn't have to.

January 10,2010
Dear Debby,

I got back from the mountains earlier today, and I had to jot down some of my thoughts before coming to your office tomorrow after school. I miss Nick more than I can explain . . . . but the end of that is in sight.

I need to finish up about the green ceiling and then move on to the biggest news.
The hot-pink folder is growing in size!
With all good wishes,
Sarah

"Good afternoon, Sarah," Dr. Baxter said. "We have some catching up to do. There is an open hour after this one, and it's yours if you want."

"Yes, please, and do we ever have a great deal of catching up to do," I said, sitting down and pulling the folder out of my tote bag. "I honestly don't know where to start, but I think I want to go back to the green ceiling for a minute."

"Take your time."

"Huge thanks." I handed her the page about the book signing at Biltmore and the engagement.

Dr. Baxter read silently and said, "Wow! We'll get to all that, but let's start with your comment about the green ceiling. What have you been thinking?"

"Well, I've realized that I think I was more mad than sad that Parker left. I'm not saying I didn't love him—I did—but we were children when we got married. We didn't have two nickels to rub together and had no clue as to who we were or what we wanted. I really do love my new life and Nick Heart. Since being with Nick, I've never once opened my eyes and considered a new ceiling color. This is crazy to say, but I think I'm truly a grown-up now, and I know what I want and need."

The next two hours were worth the double fee and more.

CHAPTER 52

$\mathcal{S}$ettling into the cold short days of February, Nick and I were now almost always together and always at the farm. What had historically been a gloomy, depressing time of the year for me had taken on a radically different complexion with the addition of this wonderful man and our shared days and nights. My loneliness had been replaced with laughter, and the companionship of an incredibly passionate and thoughtful man.

Each night while I prepared dinner, Nick poured himself a glass of wine and took a seat on the stool. He often helped by peeling, stirring, or taste testing something on the menu. But always we talked to each other. The conversation was a smoothly homogenized blend of serious topics and lighthearted retellings of the events of our day.

Nick shuddered over some of my school stories and offered that he would last perhaps half a day as a high school teacher if that. He agreed with my analysis that teaching was not a job but a ministry to children.

I recognized the business side of the farm initially as foreign territory, and had to ask for clarification on many points, including the tax laws of farmland, the fluctuating cost of hay and grain, and having employees and a payroll. The working aspect of the property, however, was heavenly, and I took great delight in the discussion of those topics. All in all, we began to work together as a team, maintaining our individuality and always keeping things interesting.

I set aside Tuesdays and Thursdays as my Rascal weekdays, and dinner was in the Crock-Pot on those days. I would stop by my house on Brook Street to collect some of my things on my way to the barn. It was weird to walk in the front door of my little cottage and feel the emptiness. The warmth was somehow gone, and it made me sad for the house and for myself.

My computer was at the farm, but I had left my laptop at my house just in case I needed it. On Thursday, I booted up and began to write:

February 11, 2010
Dear Debby,

I'll see you next Wednesday, and I really need to talk to you about this. I am looking for a pair of shoes, crying, and talking out loud to my house. Hmm—where to begin:

In an effort to make the transition from Hadley Falls to Greenway easier, Nick offered to hire a moving crew and get it all done in one motion. But naturally I had to do it my way. My deepest feelings tell me that as long as some of my things are here on Brook Street, then I will always have a place to go. What happened to Parker and me could never happen again, so long as I have a place to call my own.

Abandonment is a horrifying thing to happen to anyone, and I can't allow that circumstance to revisit my life. I have absolutely no thoughts that Nick would do anything like that to me, but then let's face it, I never thought Parker would either. Being disposed of like yesterday's garbage is something one never forgets.

I just have to trust my gut feelings and let go of the past, the abandonment issues, and worries about and yet another broken heart, and not confuse my past with my future.

I did share the story about the green ceiling with Nick, and we made a pact that we would always talk out our feelings and tell each other the truth. We are too old to play games or keep things bottled up, and there have been a few times that one or the other of us has stepped on toes, so to speak. Sometimes it takes several days to regroup, but we always apologize for being thoughtless, jumping to conclusions, or whatever the problem was, and that's the end of it.

Nick's house is gorgeous, but it is not mine. Not one thing in that house, except for my clothes and my dog, belongs to me, or even whispers "Sarah Sams lives here." I still don't feel like I belong there; I feel like a very welcomed guest. I can't make myself talk to him about that feeling, either, because there are lots of layers to saying, "Your house is great—do you mind if we redecorate together, just here and there?" I feel like I will always have to ask permission to paint something or change things in any way. I know you would say that the two of us need to discuss this, and we do, but where do I start?

I really do want to live at Long Leaf Farm but I desperately need for it to have some reflection of Sarah Sams.

With all good wishes,
Sarah

I could smell the chicken and rice from the back door. Nick was stirring the Crock-Pot concoction as I walked into the kitchen. Annie wiggled all around my legs, and Cesar let out his usual deep bark of hello.

"Hi there, beautiful," Nick said with a smile and a kiss. "Why have you been crying?" he asked, laying the spoon down on the counter.

"What makes you think I've been crying?"

"Well, your eyes are red, and your mascara is messed up. What's wrong—has something happened with Rascal?"

"No, he's just fine," I answered, feeling the emotion well within me. "Uh, I am not sure how to say this or where to start. I also don't want to sound ungrateful or stupid."

Before I was able to construct the next sentence, Nick said, "Come here," and pulled me closer. "Let's go have a seat in the den and get to the bottom of whatever it is. Better yet, go change out of your riding clothes, I'll fix us a drink, and then we'll talk."

I chose my most comfortable leggings and sweater. Nick was already sitting on the brown leather sofa and patted the cushion next to him. Handing me a mimosa made mostly of orange juice, he said, "Now what is going on?"

I took a sip of my drink, cleared my throat, and said, "This may sound crazy but—I feel like I'm abandoning my house, and that took me back to Parker's leaving me. Also, I'll be leaving everything that's mine on Brook Street or in a packing carton in a storage building somewhere. I don't know just how to say this. Your house is amazing, but . . . well, it's just that it's your house, and not mine. There is nothing that says 'Sarah lives here,'" I finished with tears rolling down alternate cheeks. "Do

352

you understand any of my babbling?"

Nick pulled me closer and tucked me under his arm. "Truly, it never occurred to me that you might feel this way. I understand. Can you tell me what you want to do?"

"I don't know really. It isn't that I want to redo so much as it is I want to add—for example, where could I hang my pictures? Could we add a touch of femininity? Would you agree to my replacing your pots and pans with mine? Stuff like that. Does that make any sense at all?"

"Of course it does. There are some things in this house I can't part with, but we can find a middle ground. I don't believe this house will accommodate all our things together, though, so we'll need to combine our favorite things to create our home. What do you think about each of us making a list of our favorite pieces of furniture, and trying to figure out how it all might fit?"

"I think you're wonderful, and that you've come up with a workable plan," I answered with a smile. "We can talk about the rest over dinner."

"Rest—what rest?" Nick said, standing up quickly. "Why am I having flashbacks to the conversation we had over the travel drink and snack? I got sucked into the snack part without even realizing what had transpired."

"Oh, it's nothing so ominous," I said, looking over my shoulder. "Surely you agree that there is a great deal of brown in this house? It might be fun to introduce a touch of green for starters, just here and there. We could go a step further with a whisper of blue. I understand," I continued, clearing my throat and recognizing Nick's attempt to hide a growing smile, "that could be construed by some as huge sideways leap from the monochromatic color scheme we now enjoy, but it never hurts to take a look. Wouldn't you agree?"

"I would," Nick replied with a chuckle. "I like green and blue, but I hate lots of pillows. If you have to have fringe and ruffles on everything, you will need to pull out all the stops and use your feminine wiles to come at this from a different angle, if you catch my drift. I can be bought, but it will be very expensive."

"I have absolutely no idea what you're talking about!" I blushed.

"Really?" Nick said moving just a little bit closer. "Are you actually trying to suggest, oh, let's start with Adam and Eve for example, that women haven't resorted to a bit of calculated trickery—and yes, I'm including sex—to get what they wanted, or soften the blow that they wrecked the car, for example? It may start with a seemingly innocent offering of fruit, but you know where it ends," Nick smiled, giving me a peck on the cheek and a pat on my bottom.

CHAPTER **53**

*N*ick and I invested a good deal of time searching for solutions to the problem of making his house ours. Working from his suggestion, we each generated a list of our most treasured possessions in order of importance. My side of the tablet was considerably longer than his; I came with children. My girls would not require or expect their furniture to occupy either bedroom, but I needed for them to feel at home, and having some of their things sitting around or hanging on the walls would go a long way toward ensuring a feeling of acceptance and belonging. Nick agreed, and I went about placing a few of their most treasured photos and nick-knacks around the two rooms we decided would be best for them—the same rooms they had occupied that December night after the Christmas party.

I offered each daughter the opportunity to take her furniture from Brook Street and use it in her own home. Both were delighted at the suggestion and made plans for transporting the things they wanted. It turned out they were also interested in taking some of the things I wasn't planning to move to the farm, which brought happiness for all.

I began to feel more at home, and life was good. On my way

home from Hadley Falls one Thursday night in late February, my cell phone rang. Reading Nick's name on the illuminated face I answered, "Hey, babe—I know I'm running a little late, but I should be home in about thirty minutes."

"No problem. I just wanted you to know something came for you today by way of FedEx."

"Hmm, I wonder what that could be—I haven't ordered anything. Are you sure it's for me?"

"Yes," Nick answered, "Your name is on the very large package."

"It's not from Stuart Branch again, is it?"

"No, I don't believe so. I'll see you in a bit."

Nick offered me a mimosa as we stared down at the package. I smiled, thanked him for the drink, and mentioned that he had been very clever introducing alcohol to my system. They were still 98 percent orange juice, with a thimble of white wine, but I really did enjoy them. It was ridiculous at best, but I loved the glasses, and it became a thing we did without my actually drinking.

"It looks like a rug, don't you think?" I said. "But I swear to you I didn't order one. I would never do that without discussing it with you."

"I think it does too. There's only one way to find out," Nick said, handing me the knife. "It's addressed to you, so you need to do the honors,"

Placing my glass on the kitchen counter, I went about the task of carefully slicing through yards and miles of packing tape. "It is a rug," I said, "and it is beautiful! Oh my gosh—look," I exclaimed, continuing to free the remaining length of the floor tapestry, "it is absolutely gorgeous. You bought this rug, didn't you?"

"Yes," Nick answered, removing the knife from my hand. "Consider this to be my admission of your *too much brown* observation. I had the kitchen in mind when I ordered it, but we can find another spot if you like. I also thought about having the kitchen painted a lighter shade of green to bring that color out in the rug, but that too is just a suggestion."

"Oh my gosh, it's beautiful!" I said having a seat in the middle of the rug.

"Does that mean you like it?" Nick asked, watching as I stroked the center medallion.

"I love it, but I love the thought even more," I answered. "I have said it before—you, Mr. Heart, are an amazing man, and I am a very lucky girl!"

Within two weeks the kitchen walls had been bathed in two coats of the most luscious shade of sage green. The painters added a fresh coat of white to the ceiling and all the woodwork. Nick made the decision that the kitchen re-do was falling short of the mark and suggested replacing the countertops with whatever I wanted. My third-generation solid-walnut parson's table took center stage on the rug that had started it all, and Nick's hand-painted tole chairs finished the arrangement. The best part of the makeover was that we had made all the decisions together and without the help of a decorator. It was truly ours.

Like the thick beds of crocuses lining the front sidewalk, snips of color began to pop up around the house. Nick would smile when he noticed a new touch here and there. We were making serious progress, but it was not quite finished, in my estimation.

One afternoon I stopped by my cottage to look for some place mats and ended up in my attic. From the corner of my eye I spied a forgotten pillow wrapped in clear plastic and begging to be freed from the confines of the zipper bag.

"Yikes!" I said out loud. This would cost me big, as it had ruffles, but it was perfect for the stiff-as-a-board director's chair in our bedroom. The chair had been a thank you gift to Nick from his fraternity brothers, acknowledging a sizable gift of money to their scholarship fund. It proudly displayed their Greek letters in very soft rubbed gold, but it was not at all comfortable.

I giggled as I made my way down the narrow set of stairs and out the front door. I wondered if Nick had been serious about his earlier comment about ruffles and fringe, but I figured I was about to find out.

Three hours later, I was back at the farm and had placed the pillow in the chair. Nick came in from the barn, kissed me hello, and said he was going to go change his clothes. He had been there long enough to notice the addition, but there was nothing—not one sound except for the creaking of the old wooden floorboards.

I got to work on dinner and quickly forgot about the pillow. From my comfortable state of relaxation, I nearly jumped out of my skin when Nick appeared, holding the pillow and nibbling the back of my neck. "Whatever you are cooking, try and make it fast. I have to get up early in the morning for a grain delivery and I don't want to miss a minute of my ruffle compensation," he said with a satisfied smile. "A deal is a deal."

"You weren't serious about that—were you?" I asked, feeling my blood pressure rise.

"Oh yes—I was dead serious," Nick answered, "and like I said, we need to get an early start on dinner. The remainder of our evening could take a while; I am sure you have noticed that this is a very big pillow!"

"Shameful, you're absolutely shameful," I said running my fingers through his hair, then handing him an apple. "Most men, which includes you, are Neanderthals, and I feel a bit like Wilma Flintstone. I did love her dress, though. Do I need to put a chicken bone in my hair?"

"Not necessary," Nick replied while tasting the Bearnaise sauce simmering on the stove.

We had a late dinner that night. It was absolutely delicious!

I was so happy at Long Leaf Farm that I finally made my peace with the move and decided to put 528 Brook Street up for sale. She had done her job in my healing process, and I would be eternally grateful to the funny little cottage with the squeaky front porch, but as with so many things, it was time to move on. The house sold a week after it went on the market. A young newly married couple bought it, and my move was now permanent.

CHAPTER 54

$\mathcal{N}$ick hired a landscape architect to shape up, as he called it, the backyard area. Three months later, the gardens at Long Leaf Farm could have been featured in any gentle living magazine in the country. Late one afternoon, Caesar took off in full chase after a deer, flying across the pea stone walks, and separating the boxwood hedge. Within four weeks the backyard was completely surrounded with a historically correct handsome brick and white picket fence including gates and arbors.

Thursday night three weeks before our wedding, we were sitting in a restaurant having dinner, celebrating my last day of school, and I began to twitch.

"What's the matter with you?"

"I don't know," I answered. "I itch all over, and it hurts to scratch."

"Is it like a rash?" Nick asked. "Maybe it's poison ivy."

"I don't think so," I replied. "This morning when I got out of the shower, I noticed a funny place here and there on my torso. Whatever it is, it needs to go away."

"I think you should go to the doctor," Nick insisted. "I don't remember seeing anything on your back last night."

"I know," I said. "It came on very quickly, and I hate it!"

"I need to take a look at this when we get home," Nick said with authority.

"Okay," I agreed, "but please don't touch them; they hurt!"

By the time we left the restaurant, I was about to jump out of my skin. Nick pulled out of the parking lot and turned toward the highway. "I am taking you to the hospital," he announced.

He dropped me off at the emergency department door and went to park. I walked up to the desk, and in between switching her gum from side to side, the lady behind the counter said, "Do you have an emergency?"

"Yes. Why else would I be here?" I snapped.

"I need for you to fill out all four pages," she said, handing me a clipboard with an attached pen.

When it was my turn to go in, Nick followed me to the triage area and stood in the doorway while the nurse took my vital signs and asked one too many stupid questions.

"You're a terrible patient," Nick said. "They're trying to do their job and you're giving them a fit."

"This is ridiculous," I volleyed. "How could my tonsillectomy at age six possibly factor into this? I could be half dead and they wouldn't help me until I answered their questions."

Before Nick could reply, the curtain opened and a very young doctor, who could not possibly have finished medical school, stood there reading my chart. "So, it says here that you have something that's making you itch," he said, flipping through the chart.

"Yes," I said, "and I would appreciate it if you could help me out."

"Let's have a look," he said, lifting my fetching hospital gown.

I was looking at Nick's face when he caught a glimpse of the red, raised welts and horror would have been a close analogy. "What's that?" he asked.

"I think it's a simple case of the hives," the doctor replied. "Ms. Sams, are you under an unusual amount of stress?"

"Well, yes," I replied, "I am."

"Hives are strange in that they may resolve in one place and pop up in another, but an over-the-counter antihistamine should do the trick. Try also to reduce some of the stress in your life, and take a more calm approach to things," he said. "You should notice a reduction to the hives in a day or two, three at the very most. The itching should be resolved in several hours with the Benedryl."

"I'm getting married in a few weeks!" I said hysterically. "I have the most beautiful dress you've ever seen, and I cannot have this crud all over me."

"Well," he said calmly, "Ms. Sams, this just has to run its course, and that usually takes a day or so at the most. However, the sooner you can relax, the better. You have hives because you are overly stressed. You need to calm down."

On the ride home Nick talked to me about things I could do to lessen the stress. And then he asked, "What is really bothering you? Have you changed your mind?"

"Absolutely not," I said. "Why would you think that? I just want everything to be perfect. I've done this to myself."

As the days passed the hives began to fade. Here and there, I could still see the shadow of where they had been, but it was improving. My saving grace was horse camp. It was every bit as much fun as in years past and maybe even more—at least for me. My friends gave me a surprise bridal shower out by Susan's pool, and we had a wonderful time. Some of the women who boarded at Moss Creek were included, and I knew most of them. The riding was amazing, and Rascal was at his best, showing no signs of slowing down. Nick called me several times, admitting that he missed me and asked repeatedly that I be careful. We laughed about our first night together at that very place. Margaret and I talked all the way home about the wedding and the honeymoon. She was on Rascal duty while I was away.

I tried on my dress a week before the wedding and thankfully, no sign of hives. The closer we got to the twenty-sixth of June, the calmer I became. Perhaps it was just that I wanted the clock to tick a bit faster. I was also excited about my last visit to Dr. Baxter's office as Sarah Sams. What had begun as a nightmare of necessity had evolved into a delightful friendship, and as Sarah Sams or Sarah Heart, I hoped it would continue.

"Good morning, Sarah," Dr. Baxter said giving me a hug.

"Hello to you too," I replied with a curious smile.

"I'm happy and surprised to see you today," she said offering me to take a seat and pulling her desk chair around. "I know the hug is a first, but I am so happy for you that I couldn't contain myself. I guess it wasn't overly professional either, but we can make an exception this once. Now, where do we begin today?"

Dragging the hot-pink folder from my bag, I rested back in the corner of that beige sofa, handed her the top letter, and while she read, I said, "I bet you were surprised to see my name on your agenda, but I wanted some time to thank you for all you've done for me and how you've help me find the real Sarah. I remember like it was yesterday the first time I came here, Lord have mercy, was I ever a mess, but that's all gone now. Thanks to you, Nick, and my friends, I've found a peace and joy I never thought possible. I'm just so grateful, and I plan to continue my visits, at least for a while. But tomorrow is my wedding day, and I'm about as happy as the law will allow."

"I'm excited about tomorrow too," she replied. "Your invitation was lovely, and I truly appreciate having been invited."

"Absolutely," I said. "You are a huge part of my life, and Nick's, too, really."

With that we dug into the issue of the hives and all the latest renovations to Nick's house. The good doctor continued to coach me on the fine points of saying "our house," and using the word *we* more often in regard to that piece of property. We talked about my making sure not to forget about my friends, and I assured her that could never happen, telling her I'd be spending the night at Betsy's, and the Rowdy Girls would be having a big night out on the town.

"No rehearsal tonight?" she asked.

"There're are no attendants," I said, "It's just Nick and me and we've each had a wedding, been in a few, guests of a lot—so walking down a path needs no practice. You'll see: this is all about having a great party with the people we love."

CHAPTER 55

$\mathcal{I}$ spent the night before our wedding at Betsy's farm in Hadley Falls, and the Rowdy Girls had their night out on the town. It was such fun, and I was given a great deal of advice, most of which need not be repeated. Following our dessert, the next piece of our evening had clearly been planned in advance, with each friend handing me a gift, one at a time. Not new pots and pans, as you might expect, but rather a blast from the past in the form of lingerie. Each item was lovely, and also quite fetching!

Betsy and I shared an early-morning walk around her property, and Annie was delighted to have the company of Olive, Betsy's tricolor corgi. After a scrumptious breakfast of farm-fresh eggs and all the trimmings, I put my vanilla-white lace wedding dress in the car and asked my dog to please not shed. Waving goodbye to my best friend, I told her I would see her later and thanked her for her friendship. Somewhere along the drive to Greenway I couldn't contain my euphoria. I called Nick and said I was on my way, and I could hear the excitement in his voice as well.

With about two hours before the guests were scheduled to arrive, my five best friends in the world appeared at the bedroom door. "Hi! You're here early," I said, glancing in Betsy's direction. "I just saw you this morning, you didn't say anything about coming early."

"We're not early," Betsy said. "We know you didn't want a big fuss, but we love you, and we have decided that you should have attendants and they should be us. Don't worry about our not having rehearsed—we know how to do this." And with that, my friends pulled out five phenomenal dresses. My colors were the softest blue and a dusty brown and they had five different dresses of those two plus a touch of white. Months ago, Nick said he like the combination but asked why blue and brown? I told him that the brown represented his sofa and the blue my pillow—he laughed.

"How wonderful," I said. "But Nick doesn't have anyone."

"Yes, he does," Margaret said. "Our husbands are his groomsmen. We left them all in the den when we came up here. Nick's known about this for a long time, but we knew it would send you around the organizational bend, so . . . yes, we kept it from you. End of discussion."

"I hope the uneven number won't drive you crazy—five women, four men—that art-and-balance issue?" Rose said with a smile.

"Well, on that topic," Betsy smiled. "I knew it would, so I spoke with Nick, and we agreed. So after hanging up, he phoned Jack, made sure he felt well enough, the answer was yes, and he's number five. Actually, Nick asked him to be his best man. How sweet is that?"

"Look out," Elizabeth said, "Daisy Mae is going to cry."

"I can't help it," I said. "This is the sweetest thing, and you guys are the best friends in the world. I love you all so much."

"We love you too," Betsy said, "but if you don't calm down, the hives will come back. Shouldn't you be getting dressed?"

The day was perfect and even more so with my friends standing by my side. As the music began to play, I got a lump in my throat as I tried to tell each one how much she meant to me, but I was unable to speak. One by one as they walked ahead of me, I thought about our collective journey though life over the past seventeen years.

Ethan was giving me away and realized I was becoming emotional. He took my arm, pulled it gently through the crook of his, and patted my hand. When it was our turn to walk down the aisle, I visually raced across the line of my friends and their smiles of joy.

Turning my attention to Nick, his face said it all—it was an expression of caring, pride, and love, with a touch of that boyish grin I'd come to adorer. He never took his eyes away from mine and I swear I could see to his heart and the love it held inside.

We recited our vows, exchanged rings, said *I do*, and shared that first married kiss. The minister pronounced that we were husband and wife. Turning to face our family and friends, I had a sense of peace I had never before experienced. Nick held my hand in his and squeezed it gently. The horses ran the fence line when the trumpets sounded the recessional. Emma and Sidney each gave me a kiss as I walked by, and Scott offered a heartfelt hug.

The reception was even more fun than the Christmas party. Jennifer outdid herself, and the food was amazing. Our wedding cake had powder-blue icing, a string of edible white pearls wrapping around each layer where they joined one another, and a soft brown-and-white striped marzipan bow sat atop with its ribbons cascading to the bottom.

Kenny and Mike were once again in charge of the decorations, and their efforts were magnificent. I shuddered to think of the cost, but on strict orders from my husband, was not allowed to ask.

Nick and I had decided to spend our first night of married life at the farm. Our flight to Edinburgh was not until the next evening. With our last guest out the door, and the caterers packed up and their chorus line of vans headed toward the highway, Nick looked at me and said, "I love you, Mrs. Heart."

"I love you too, Mr. Heart," I replied, standing in the middle of the foyer. "I'm starving. Would you like a snack before we go to bed?"

"Not really," Nick said, taking my hand and moving me down the side hall.

"The kitchen is that way," I replied.

Nick stopped and said, "Yes, it is, but I don't really want a snack. I would prefer a full-course meal, and not in the kitchen. But if you're really that hungry, well . . ."

Blushing like the new bride I was, I burst out with, "Dear Debby!"

"Dear Debby indeed," Nick replied with a wink, switching off the lights.

ACKNOWLEDGMENTS

$\mathcal{A}$ heartfelt thank-you to all my family and friends for their love and support—family and friendships are the essence of this book. Thank you to everyone who had a hand in helping *Sour Grapes & Sweet Tea* become a reality. Special appreciation to my editor Betsy Thorpe and my copy editor Maya Myers both of whom adore the delete key on their computers, and to graphic designer Diana Wade for her cover design and book layout. I could never have done this without the three of you. And finally to my readers: I sincerely hope you have enjoyed the read and continue to treasure the ride through life with dear friends!

RECIPES

Sibby's Coconut Pie
The best coconut pie you have ever eaten!

3 eggs
1 ½ cups flaked coconut (I add a bit more)
1 ⅓ cups sugar
7 tablespoons melted butter
½ cup evaporated milk
1 teaspoon vanilla
Pinch of salt

Preheat oven to 350 degrees.

Beat eggs, then whisk in remaining ingredients. Pour into two unbaked regular pie shells.

Bake for 25 minutes or until filling does not adhere to a toothpick.

Sibby's Georgia Pecan Pie
Look out hips! But man, oh, man is it good!

1 cup dark Karo corn syrup
3 whole eggs
¾ cup brown sugar
¼ cup butter (4 tablespoons)
1 teaspoon vanilla
⅓ teaspoon salt

1 ⅓ cup pecan halves-per pie shell
2 unbaked regular pie shells

Preheat oven to 350 degrees.

Mix all filling ingredients except pecans. Line the bottom of each pie shell with nuts—don't be stingy. Pour filling over pecans.

Bake for 35–40 minutes or until pie filling does not adhere to a toothpick.

Yum Yum!

Southern Sweet Iced Tea

Makes one gallon

3 family-sized tea bags (black or orange pekoe)
2 cups granulated sugar
Ice
Water
Mint leaves or lemon wedges for garnish (optional)

1-gallon pitcher, or 2 half-gallon ones
Long-handled wooden spoon

Bring 4 cups of water to a boil. Remove from heat.

Dunk the tea bags a few times to make sure the tea is completely wet. Allow bags to steep for 5 minutes, then remove.

Pour sugar in a gallon pitcher (or 1 cup in each if you're using two pitchers)

Reheat tea and pour over sugar. Stir until sugar is completely dissolved.

Add ice to the halfway mark of the pitcher. Top off with cold water.

Refrigerate until very cold, at least 4 hours.

Sweet tea will keep in the refrigerator for about a week.

ABOUT THE AUTHOR

Jane W. Rankin is the author of *The Woman Equestrian*, published in 2003 by Wish Publishing. She has been published in "The Chronicle of the Horse" periodical, and more recently in the "Amateurs Like Us" weekly blog. Jane is a retired public school art educator and mother of two. She and her soul-mate, Bruce, live in Denver, North Carolina.

CPSIA information can be obtained
at www.ICGtesting.com
Printed in the USA
JSHW021156030623
42668JS00001B/5